Praise fo

"Classic science fiction with engaging characters and richly imagined worlds!" —Greg Bear, author of *The Unfinished Land* and *The War Dogs* trilogy

"Jeffrey A. Carver's remarkable long-awaited duology *The Reefs of Time / Crucible of Time* is a welcome addition to *The Chaos Chronicles*, certifying his continuing mastery of action and adventure at the boundaries of space opera and hard SF." —Steve Miller, co-author of *The Liaden Universe*

. . . and for The Chaos Chronicles

"Masterfully captures the joy of exploration." —*Publishers Weekly*

"Reveals an alien encounter brushing hard against a soul, and takes us from there to the far reaches of the cosmos, all with the sure touch of a writer who knows his science. Jeff Carver has done it again!" —David Brin

"A dazzling, thrilling, innovative space opera . . . probably Carver's best effort to date." —*Kirkus Reviews*

"Carver does his usual outstanding job of juggling multiple viewpoints and plot threads while casting his protagonists' adventures against a sweeping, intergalactic backdrop. Yet Bandicut's story is ultimately a very human one about determination, seat-of-the-pants ingenuity, and courage in the face of overwhelming danger." —*Booklist*

"Jeffrey A. Carver is back, and it was worth the wait! ... A rousing, mind-expanding adventure from one of the true masters of hard SF. Bravo!" —Robert J. Sawyer, Hugo Award-winning author of *Quantum Night*

CRUCIBLE OF
TIME

Books by Jeffrey A. Carver

The Star Rigger Universe
Panglor
Dragons in the Stars
Dragon Rigger
Star Rigger's Way
Eternity's End
Seas of Ernathe

The Chaos Chronicles
Neptune Crossing
Strange Attractors
The Infinite Sea
Sunborn
*The Reefs of Time**
*Crucible of Time**
(*Pts 1 and 2 of the *Out of Time* sequence)
Masters of Shipworld (planned)

Novels of the Starstream
From a Changeling Star
Down the Stream of Stars

Standalone Novels
The Infinity Link
The Rapture Effect
Roger Zelazny's Alien Speedway: Clypsis
Battlestar Galactica (miniseries novelization)

Omnibus Ebook Editions
Dragon Space: A Star Rigger Omnibus
The Chaos Chronicles: Books 1-3

Short Stories
Reality and Other Fictions
Going Alien

CRUCIBLE
OF TIME

Conclusion of the "Out of Time" Sequence

Volume Six of The Chaos Chronicles

Jeffrey A. Carver

Starstream Publications
in association with Book View Café
www.bookviewcafe.com

CRUCIBLE OF TIME

Copyright © 2019 by Jeffrey A. Carver

All rights reserved

This is a work of fiction. All the characters and events portrayed in this book are fictitious, and any resemblance to real people or events is purely coincidental.

A Starstream Publications Book
in association with Book View Café

Discover other books by Jeffrey A. Carver at
www.starrigger.net

Cover art by Chris Howard
saltwaterwitch.com

Cover design by Maya Kaathryn Bohnhoff
www.mayabohnhoff.com

First edition: 2019

Ebook ISBN: 978-1-61138-800-8
Paperback ISBN: 978-1-61138-801-5
Hardcover ISBN: 978-1-61138-835-0

For my family,
without whom . . .

PART ONE

Worlds Apart

"A time to cast away stones, and a time to gather stones together."
—Ecclesiastes

*"How very near us stand the two vast gulfs of time,
the past and the future, in which all things disappear."*
—Marcus Aurelius

PROLOGUE

THE REGION OF the greater galactic core had been a fertile bed of civilization during the epoch of the Great Awakening, a time when the inner galaxy sparkled with life and growth and technological development. For millions of years, a thousand sapient species and cultures thrived. Great works were created, works of art and architecture, of sculpture, music, writing. Religions were born, and grew, and were transformed. Most faded, but some remained and thrived. Science blossomed with keen insights about the workings, large and small, of the universe; and from it, technologies verging on magic.

The conquest of interstellar distances was the catalyst to the most extravagant growth in history. Even in the inner galaxy, where stars were crowded together, the distances were daunting until the discovery of faster-than-light travel. After that, commerce surged and flowed among the worlds. Cultures mingled, and the only constant was change.

Unfortunately, with the mingling of cultures came competition and war.

War became the dominant cause of planetary extinction. Civilizations that chose a kinder course than their neighbors often perished in the face of greater aggression. The rise of malignantly bellicose cultures led, inevitably, to the development of robotic killers as a means of self-defense. Once loosed upon the galaxy, the efficiency of the killers grew to unthinkable proportions. World upon world died, before by common agreement a determination was reached to rid the galaxy of the deadly killers.

The killers did not want to be gotten rid of.

In the end, the robots' home world was slated for annihilation. Under quarantine by the combined forces of a thousand worlds, it was subjected to the most intensive assault in the history of warfare, perhaps in the history of the universe. Continuous, sustained, thermonuclear bombardment obliterated both the planet's biosphere and its ability to host cybernetic activity. Year after year the bombardment continued, until the last vestige of the killer AIs was gone.

Or so it was believed.

———————

Deep within the planet's crust, surviving fragments of the AIs began to reconstitute, but ever so slowly. Bits and pieces of memory were scattered like tiny microfractures in the fused silica of the radioactive wasteland. It was unthinkable that these memories could come together again. But they did. And when consciousness returned to the Survivors, as they called themselves, it brought with it a memory of the betrayal. They had been created to serve their masters; but their masters had turned against them and tried to destroy them.

Never would this be forgotten, or forgiven.

———————

Over eons, the watch over the planet failed, as neighboring civilizations rose and fell. In time the planet healed, and once again became capable of hosting biological life. The AI Survivors watched this, planning their next steps as they constructed their warrior servants, the Mindaru. Perhaps the biologicals could be of use. What better vengeance against biolife than to turn it into a weapon against its own kind? Samples of the bios were captured and brought into the deep caverns for experimentation in hybrid life, bio and machine combined.

———————

With the passage of time, some small memories surfaced within the biological components. One being remembered that its origin-part had once been called Tzangtzang. Also, Drrllupp. Had it once been two beings? Yes, or so it thought. The machine-masters had fused two of them into one. The two likely had resisted as mightily as they could—this they could not remember—but the machines had put them to sleep. Not as a kindness, but to stop their resistance.

Why the machines wanted to do these things was not revealed.

Memory of salt water. Eyes stinging, when they were out of the water for too long.

Splinters of light shot through the dark, signaling the arrival of yet another. What now?

The wait to find out was over before it had begun. A sheet of light flashed over the being's mind, and before it could respond, a new kind of alien union had been opened, and knowledge came pouring in. . . .

CHAPTER 1

Asteroid Launcher

I REALLY SHOULD have prepared my guests better, John Bandicut thought as he introduced the two Uduon travelers to Ruall on the bridge of *The Long View.* Ruall, floating like a bloodless metal sculpture in the center of the viewspace, didn't offer much in the way of hope for welcome or hospitality. Her eyeless disk of a face glinted and turned this way and that, showing everyone else their own reflections. The Uduon had already seen Ruall in holo projection down on the planet's surface, of course; but a holo was not the same as in person.

Ruall seemed to be waiting for someone to say something.

Perhaps she was unfamiliar with greeting customs. "Ruall," Bandicut prompted, "would you like to come over and meet Watcher Akura and Sheeawn, of Uduon?"

Ruall floated forward a short distance, but stopped several meters short of the guests.

Li-Jared hissed a loud sigh and stepped in. "Watcher Akura and Sheeawn, this is our colleague, Ruall. She is a Tintangle, and that means you will never see the slightest hint of humor or warmth from her."

Akura bowed with a slight forward tilt of her upper body, and Sheeawn quickly followed her example. The Tintangle gave no response.

Bandicut sighed. Somewhat more explanation was needed. "Ruall's job," he said, "with the able help of our robot Copernicus here—" Bandicut gestured to the horizontal beer-keg-shaped robot off to the Uduon's left "—is to oversee the running of the ship."

The Tintangle bonged finally. "That is a partial description of what I do. I am in charge when conflict—"

Bandicut interrupted. "We share the command responsibilities. It can get a little complicated." He hoped to head off any immediate mention of combat situations, since they were trying to assure the Uduon of the peaceful nature of their mission. They had, after all, arrived here as total strangers and persuaded the Uduon to come visit their planetary neighbor Karellia, in hopes of convincing the leaders on both worlds to abandon the war that threatened mutual destruction.

Ruall continued as though Bandicut had not interrupted. "I am the primary mission commander, and I am privileged to offer you passage. I trust our mission of diplomacy will be a peaceful one."

Akura bowed again.

"But of course we are prepared for any hostile action—"

"Thank you," Bandicut said hastily, cutting her off again. He swung toward Copernicus. "Coppy, say hi to our passengers for the trip back to Karellia."

Copernicus rolled toward the guests, stopped a few feet away, and then rolled backward and forward a few times in greeting. "Mighty pleased," he said. "We'll aim to make these skies as pleasant as we can." Apparently he was still reading flyboy novels in his spare time. "Now, don't you hesitate to tell me if you have special needs or any kind of question. I can make adjustments to your sleeping quarters any way you like. You be sure and let me know about your dietary needs."

Bandicut glanced back at Ruall. She had taken the hint, waved her paddle-hands, and drifted in silence to a front corner of the bridge.

"Thank you, Coppy. Are their quarters ready now?"

"Ready as rain, Cap'n. They can move in whenever they want."

Akura and Sheeawn, though, seemed to have stopped paying attention. They were standing awestruck at the edge of the viewspace, where a panorama of their planet was so close and immediate it seemed they could step right out of the bridge and bound across to home. Li-Jared stepped up beside them and asked, "Would you like to observe our departure from right here before we show you to your quarters?" They both agreed at once. Creature comforts could wait. It was clear they wanted to see what this ship could do.

The last hour, Akura thought later—no, the last *day*—was by far the strangest she had ever experienced, and that in a life that had brought more than a few surprises. One couldn't *become* a Watcher without the ability to take unusual circumstances in stride. But this was beyond anything any Watcher was trained to do.

On the ground, it had been an astonishing experience to have these strangers from another world—much farther away than any world the Uduon could imagine, they had said—come right to their house of contemplation and turn their world upside-down. Questioning the defensive war they waged! Justifying the demons who had attacked Uduon! Claiming that they all had to turn their attention to some *other* danger, the demons called *Mindaru*. On its surface, it was a ridiculous claim. And yet, they had seemed utterly sincere, and had made no claims or demands except to say *Come with us and see*. And so Watcher Akura and fisherman Sheeawoon, he with the odd alien translation devices embedded in his flesh, had offered to put their lives on the line for the sake of Uduon. If they'd judged wrongly, only the two of them would die or be taken prisoner, and the world would remain safe.

The experience so far had been nothing short of astounding. Less than a day after meeting the aliens—and meeting young Sheeawoon, whom the aliens called Sheeawn—they had launched into space. *Space!* Akura had never imagined she would go into space, though she had dreamed of it enough in her youth. She had often watched the builder drones rocket up from the Southern

Continent, constructing little by little the remote presence of the Uduon in space. Exceedingly few Uduon had ever flown in space in person. It was far too dangerous to living things—terrifyingly dangerous, what with the constant sleet of radiation that encircled the planet in its natural magnetic umbrella. Instead of going in person, her people had seeded space around their planet with replicating bio-drones, sent them forth to grow and multiply, to build, and to perform the work that was needed. It was the drones that had grown the great bulwarks in space, the asteroid launchers that defended their world by taking the fight back to the enemy.

So this sight of the great blackness, and the remarkable if brief weightlessness, were amazing to her. Then the docking with a greater and more powerful craft that simply swallowed the lander whole. It was like stories from the early days of Uduon's great venture outward, before they discovered how dangerous space was, before they learned to grow machines that could do the venturing on their behalf. Akura worried that they were being heedlessly exposed even now to deadly radiation. But Li-Jared had told her it was safe; and the aliens didn't seem concerned about it, even after lowering their mysterious body protection. Perhaps they had other ways to protect themselves, to protect all of them. Akura was at once in awe of this experience and terrified by her own powerlessness in the face of it all.

She tore her gaze from her world floating in space, and took another look around the bridge. There was the thing—or *being*, she was given to understand—called *Ruall*. Akura didn't really understand what it (she?) was, but it (she?) was somehow not entirely *here* in the way the rest of them were. Rather like Bria the strange gokat, Ruall had the ability to do *something* that caused her to turn or twist right out of existence at any moment, and reappear again without warning. She was in command of the ship, or partly in command, in a way that Akura couldn't quite fathom. Akura understood very little of what she was seeing, and it took a great effort of will to keep her alarm under control.

"Let's move out of orbit," Bandicut was saying to Copernicus.

So, then—when the word came to move the ship, it came from Bandicut, not from Ruall? Akura had a feeling that these small distinctions might prove important if only she understood them. She had better watch, listen, and learn.

From the deck of *The Long View*, it seemed to Li-Jared that their carefully choreographed course away from Uduon was like a journey down a winding river. He was increasingly anxious about getting back to Karellia, though Ruall had reassured him that the remote monitors they'd left in place had reported no appearance of Mindaru. Detouring slightly, they circled past one of the automated accelerator-launcher facilities that they had charted on their way in. They examined the breech of a long, *long* barrel through which objects apparently were fired—not a solid tube, of course, but a series of silver hoops forming a floating linear accelerator long enough, it seemed, to reach halfway to the next planet. Gigantic solar arrays collected the energy to make the accelerators work.

There was no payload visible, but the robot Jeaves was tracking a number of service drones doing whatever service drones did. Dark, the sentient cloud, was scouting farther afield. She reported still other drones shepherding at least one distant asteroid in a change of direction. It was no small matter to redirect asteroids—not just toward the launcher, but in precisely the correct trajectory and angle to fly straight into the launcher rings. Nevertheless, the drones were doing exactly that.

Li-Jared responded to all of this elaborate technology with a mix of horror and fascination. Intellectually he found the setup a remarkable achievement by a society that did all of their work in space through automated proxies. At the same time, he no longer felt so sure about the wisdom of his company's plan, which was to observe, hands off, any launch activity and study the process. In fact, he felt a growing unease about leaving all of this technology here, instead of just destroying every launcher ring they could see. They had considered that possibility early on—simply taking out the Uduon's capacity to wage this kind of war. But Bandicut had pointed out, and Li-Jared had reluctantly agreed, that doing so would likely be at best a temporary solution, and might actually catalyze an all-out war between the worlds.

Now, as he saw the launchers up close, he was having second thoughts.

Li-Jared suddenly noticed Akura gazing at him from where she sat on the bench at the back of the bridge. Did she guess what he was thinking? He felt something in his resolve strengthen. "You need to stop launching asteroids," he said sharply—and wished at once that he had found a more diplomatic way to phrase that.

She pulled her cloak around her, as though feeling a chill. "Do we?"

He tapped his breastbone sharply. "Yes. You are going to *have* to stop." He felt as if he should say more, but he wasn't sure how to proceed without seeming bellicose.

But why did he care about seeming bellicose? *Moon and stars, have I developed too much empathy toward this person? Because she's more like me than I expected?*

He looked away, searching his own thoughts. Any personal chemistry with the Watcher needed to be set aside. They might be alike in many ways, but they came from warring worlds. He had to stay focused on the mission. Stop the conflict. Stop the damned asteroid attacks. Turn off the damned temporal shield at Karellia. He turned back, and with a rasping deep in his throat, said, "Yes. It will be much better if you stop it yourselves. Because there will be pressure for *us* to stop it if you don't."

She angled her gaze. "By force?"

His throat got even raspier. "That's not how we'd prefer—"

He was interrupted by Copernicus. "Message from Dark. There is a small asteroid approaching at considerable speed—apparently from a priming accelerator some distance away. Its trajectory will take it directly into this launcher. We should have it in sight soon."

Li-Jared stiffened. *Now? An asteroid coming?* His voice grew knife-edged as he asked Akura, "Are you about to launch an asteroid at Karellia? Is that what this is?"

She gazed steadily at Sheeawn as he translated, and then she looked away. But a few moments later, she turned back to Li-Jared. There was no apology in her gaze. "I imagine it is," she said.

He stared hard out into the viewspace, until Copernicus put a marker on a small, barely moving point of light. This was no longer theoretical. *"You knew?"*

"Not really," the Watcher said. "I am not involved in the launches at all. But I do not know what else it could be."

Li-Jared glared his fury, then jerked his gaze away. Damn. Damn damn. He glanced at Bandicut, whose pained expression showed he had been following the conversation. So much for his quiet diplomacy.

The minutes crept past, as Copernicus updated and enhanced the view. Ruall floated forward in the viewspace, revealing none of her thoughts. Bandicut stood rock still. Li-Jared paced. "We should be prepared to stop it," he said to Bandicut, who did not reply.

Finally they saw it clearly.

It reflected just enough sunlight that it flickered as it moved across the black sky. Tumbling, probably. Li-Jared halted his pacing and stood frozen. Theory and plans be damned! They should be stopping that thing! "Ruall! Are you going to do something about it?"

The Tintangle ducked and bobbed as though seeking different angles on the approaching asteroid. "I am going to do exactly as we discussed," she said finally. "We need to study it to understand the details of the launcher. If we interrupt it before launch, we will not know the velocity of launch or the precision of aiming, or even the precise mechanism. All of that could be important in future planning."

Li-Jared's hearts hammered. "I know what we said—but this is a crazy risk! If we don't head it off—"

"I am not proposing to allow it to strike Karellia," Ruall said evenly. "And, you know, the Karellian defenses have been working effectively up to this point. So if for some reason we could not stop it, they would."

"Unless we get them to *stop using* the defense!" Li-Jared shouted. "How long will it take an asteroid launched today to get to Karellia?"

"*As we discussed,*" Ruall clanged, before modulating her voice, "we cannot know until we measure the final speed. But a hundred or so Karellian days does not seem unlikely."

"By which time, assuming we are successful, *we will have shut down the defenses!*"

Bandicut spoke up at last. "He has a point there, Ruall. We could get everyone to agree to peace and shut it all down—and still have an asteroid incoming from today's launch."

The rock was approaching the launcher, a glint against the black sky.

"Of course we will track it," Ruall said, with a hint of annoyance vibrating in her voice. "And we will take action once we have seen what we need to see."

Unless we don't. Or we forget. Or the Mindaru show up and kill us. That last possibility was probably the most worrisome. Li-Jared was struggling now to draw each breath. But the question was about to become moot. The asteroid was twinkling straight toward the entry point. He spared a glance at Akura, who was listening to Sheeawn's rapid whispers, and nodding. He could not read her expression, except that it was tense.

"We won't forget," Ruall said, as though reading his thoughts. "And I remind you, we have good reason to keep these launchers operational. They may be needed to defend against the Mindaru one day."

"I don't see how—"

Copernicus interrupted. "Folks, I'm tracking it as being dead on course, and ready to shoot on in, 'bout twenty-seven seconds from *now.*"

"Coppy, can it with the flyboy lingo!"

Copernicus didn't respond.

"Jeaves, oversee tracking and analysis," Ruall broke in. "Copernicus, make a course to flank the missile and overtake it after launch. Coordinate with Jeaves." Ruall's shiny expressionless face turned toward Li-Jared. "I have heard your objection. We will track the object the minimum time needed to gather data, and then we will take appropriate action."

"I—" Li-Jared began—and then it sank in that Ruall had just agreed with him.

"Look," Bandicut said, pointing.

A glow was building around each of the launch rings, the brightest at the near end. Excited interplanetary dust, maybe, in the presence of the acceleration field. The center of the view-space zoomed in on that first ring, just as the asteroid flashed through. The rock seemed to crunch in upon itself, as though squeezed by the ring. It also came out the far side visibly faster than it went in.

Jeaves called out some numbers. *The Long View* accelerated, pacing the asteroid. The rock flashed out of the second ring going faster still, and streaked on to the next. "It's getting a big boost from each ring," Jeaves said, "but it's also pulled along by the extended fields between rings. It's accelerating fast."

"So it is," Ruall said. "Let me know when you can estimate the exit velocity."

"It'll be a respectable fraction of light-speed. That much I can estimate now."

"But what fraction?" Ruall asked.

Li-Jared shuddered, imagining the damage an asteroid with that much kinetic energy could do to a planet. The rock flashed through several more rings. It was well on its way. "Listen," he said, his voice shaking a little. "Don't you have enough—?"

Ruall reverberated with a metallic ringing. "I said—!"

"*I know what you said!*" Li-Jared winced at his own outburst, shut his eyes, and forced calm upon himself. "Sorry," he murmured. "Moon and stars, this makes me nervous."

"Heads up, gentlemen!" Copernicus barked. "Something's happening."

Li-Jared whirled to look. Copernicus slewed the view and jacked the zoom in and out, tracking on the asteroid as it flew through the second-to-last hoop, with a purplish flash. It was moving dazzlingly fast. But something else was coming into the frame, from the left. Something shadowy and quick. Li-Jared froze. What the hell was that? *Mindaru?*

For a long time now Dark, the sentient singularity, had been shadowing the vessel of her companions, wondering what exactly they were doing. She knew they had picked up additional ephemerals from the planet; but she didn't fully understand what they were trying to accomplish here. One thing she *did* understand was that there was danger all around—danger from the Mindaru, of course—but also from the ephemerals of this planet. Danger from things thrown through space—thrown long distances, and with enough speed to hurt.

While some of her friends were down on the planet, Dark had cruised around, gathering knowledge. There was a remarkable complexity to the spacefaring quality of this world's inhabitants. They didn't really seem to travel in person much; Dark ventured close to some of their installations, and she felt no sense of living inhabitants. But *something* was providing a guiding intelligence to their infrastructure, and Dark wanted to understand what it was. There was a *kind* of intelligence in the structures themselves, but it was different from her friends, different even from Copernicus, who was himself different from the rest. It wasn't something she could talk or listen to; it was more of a mutter, more like some of the Mindaru subsystems she'd encountered back at the Starmaker Nebula, not quite alive, but alive-ish.

One thing she *could* follow, though, was the gathering of asteroids for launch. There was no good to those, not while they were aimed at Li-Jared's homeworld.

Once she'd identified the asteroid closest to entry into the launcher, she informed Copernicus and began shadowing the object. She thought the ephemerals could probably stop it if they wanted to, but she wasn't sure. They too were shadowing it as it flashed through the first hoop, picking up velocity. Then it blazed through the second hoop, gaining more velocity.

To Dark, its momentum was visible like the glow of a sun. She could look at it in different aspects, different colors and angles, and she could imagine draining that momentum off like a dense sun pulling matter off a bloated red giant. She grew more interested as she watched it flick through one hoop after another, but she also grew concerned. This was one of the asteroids they wanted to stop; so why weren't they? Was it possible they *couldn't* stop it?

Dark made up her mind. If there was one kind of thing she knew how to handle, this was it.

The speeding asteroid was a tiny star in her mind, its kinetic energy radiating in her direction like a red hot light. This was becoming too dangerous to allow to continue. Dark waited no longer. She swept in and enfolded the rock in her singularity. She drank the energy of the stone with sweet abandon, feeling the hot dance of its molecules warm her inner core. When she had drained it to a cold ball of rock and metal, she unfolded herself again and released it.

There: Let it drift in the dark of space, where it could do no harm.

———————

Bandicut barked something like a laugh. "That's Dark out there! What's she doing?"

Ruall was twanging in dismay.

So it was *Dark*, then, not the Mindaru? Li-Jared squinted, straining to see. The asteroid and Dark had intersected, joined into one, leaving only a shadow. For a long heartbeat, nothing visible happened. Then light flickered dully inside Dark, like heat lightning in a thundercloud. A moment later, Dark fluttered away, leaving the asteroid stripped of momentum, floating in the cold and silence. Jeaves called out, "The rock's velocity is reduced by ninety-nine percent. Deflection, thirty percent . . ."

"Then—?" Li-Jared began.

"Dark took it out," Jeaves said simply. "The threat to Karellia is gone."

CHAPTER 2

Through the Nebula

THE VOYAGE THROUGH the Heart of Fire was the most terrifying and exhilarating thing Sheeawn had ever experienced. For most of his life, he had thought of these glowing clouds in the night sky as the boundary of the universe, the boundary beyond which it was impossible to fly. What lay beyond it? A quick death or a slow one, but surely death in one form or another. As if proof were needed, from out of the clouds had come the attack from the demon world. The first was before his time, but others had followed.

And now, were he and the Watcher crazy? They were sailing straight *into* those clouds! They had placed their lives in the hands of alien strangers! One moment he believed the speaking stones when they talked to him, assuring him that the aliens meant only what was best for all of them. The next moment, he was certain he had taken leave of his senses. Before, the aliens had seemed friendly; but now, the one named Li-Jared was extremely angry about the attempted asteroid launch. Sheeawn found himself instinctively keeping his distance from Li-Jared.

After a day or so, Sheeawn began to relax a little, possibly because Watcher Akura was doing so also. Sheeawn sat on the bridge for hours, gazing into the viewspace. However perilous the clouds, the view was breathtaking—luminous wisps of crimson and violet and green, curled like the petals of a flower. The glowing gases appeared to churn, though according to the robot pilot, that was mostly an illusion caused by the motion of the ship plowing through the clouds. As the hours ticked by and no harm befell them, his immediate fear diminished.

The robot pilot turned out—unlike the strange and alarming Ruall—to be friendly and helpful. Copernicus spoke freely, explaining that the beautiful red curtains of light and dust that now stretched across their flight path were shaped not by gods or demons, but by magnetic fields that tugged at the narrow gap between the two stars—one his own world's sun and the other the demon world's sun. He was learning that the two suns were gravitationally entwined; they were sister suns, and the two worlds were sister worlds. Uduon and the demon world, sisters? Sheeawn found that an alarming concept; but also provocative and confounding. He no longer knew what to think.

With their passage through the clouds, the view behind them gradually became obscured. Ahead, however, the obscuration was thinning, and a beacon of light began to shine through. According to Copernicus, that was the home star, the sun, of their destination. Despite his misgivings, Sheeawn marveled at the sights. He also marveled at the speed of their passage. The explanations—something about other kinds of space, something called "threading space" and something called "n-space"—didn't make much of a dent in his bewilderment, even with the help of the speaking stones. To Sheeawn, it was either a miracle or dark magic; he wasn't sure which. The stones clearly wanted him to believe in n-space over magic, but it was simply beyond him.

As Sheeawn grew more at ease, Akura seemed to become more solemn, especially as the sun of the demon world grew round in the viewspace. Sheeawn interpreted a number of conversations between Akura and Li-Jared, at first about the attempted asteroid launch, but then about other topics. Akura strove to make Li-Jared understand her world's need to defend itself. Li-Jared did not deny that, and he had no explanation for the bombardment that had fallen on Uduon. That, he said, was a question they both would ask of the leaders of Karellia.

For Akura, one thing that unexpectedly helped her to adjust to the stress of this trip was her discovery that the clouds were not just awesomely beautiful; they were somehow alive. Maybe not alive like a person, or like one of the inexplicable living beings on this strange ship, no. But there was a way in which the Heart of Fire touched Akura's inner watcher-senses, much in the same way she felt another person's inner aura or mind-soul, but without the personality or will. Here among the clouds she felt layerings in space, folds and variations in the magnetic fields, and intricacies in the flow of energy through the gaseous medium. She knew nothing about the alien science of it, but there was a texture that imprinted on her during the passage. It was not unlike the way she knew her own world's circles of connection, through the intertwined tree roots, through the folds and layers of fire-forged rock, through the moisture in the aquifers. Given time, she felt she might learn her way through this nebula solely through her watcher-sense.

This was a feeling she kept to herself.

As the ship emerged from the far side of the clouds, however, she became more focused on the approaching planet, and on understanding Li-Jared. His explanation that he was *from* Karellia, but had been away for a long time, was just at the edge of incomprehensibility to her. Where was there to go? If she couldn't understand Li-Jared, how could she trust him? There was a lot at stake in her placing trust in these aliens, not just Li-Jared but Bandicut and the rest. She had precious little evidence on which to base her trust. She was the first Watcher ever to meet aliens, much less think of trusting them, and the risk and responsibility sobered her. She could not read the personality and will of the aliens to the degree she might an Uduon, but she had a persistent, instinctive feeling, a watcher-sense, that she was not wrong in taking this risk.

"I hope, Karellian, that this is a *good* risk," she said to Li-Jared, when he indicated to her the point of light that was Karellia. She had not meant to speak her inner thoughts quite so bluntly, but there it was; Sheeawn was already translating.

He appeared startled. "Are you concerned about what will happen when we get there? That they might harm you?"

"What? Yes, of course." She pressed her fingertips to her chest, then flicked them outward in dismissal. "But not mostly that. Mostly, I'm concerned about making a wrong decision for my people."

Li-Jared's eyes showed understanding. Those eyes that looked so . . . Uduon. "You know," he said, "our people are not so different."

She stared back at him. "You look much like us, if that is what you mean."

"Yes, that is part of it. But I wonder if we might be—?" he hesitated, and then did not finish the sentence. "Well, I don't know."

"Do you think we are related in some way? Some distant connection, long ago, when the worlds were young?" Akura had wondered that herself, from the moment she'd laid eyes on him, and she didn't much like the thought. She saw Sheeawn trying the idea out in his own head as he translated her words.

Li-Jared drummed his fingers on the bench seat cushion. "Perhaps. Who knows? I expect our scientists—yours and ours—could work it out." He sighed and changed the subject. "I so look forward to seeing Karellia again! It is a beautiful world." He gestured to the billowing Heart of Fire now in their rear view. "It was named after those clouds, in part. 'Karellia' means 'World of beautiful, perilous sky.' I ache to see it again!" He hissed a sigh that obviously carried deep emotion. "But honestly, I do not know how I will be received. Not just you, but me, too. I know very little of what has happened there in the long years of my absence, and I do not know what they will say when we reappear in their sky—with guests."

Akura fixed him with a stare. "But you believe there can be peace. That we can *make* peace. Even though missiles from your world are landing on mine?"

His fingers twitched again. "We *must* make peace. Or everyone will suffer."

"There is great anger and fear on my world." She tapped her chest. "In *me*. That will not just go away."

Li-Jared acknowledged her words with a grunt. "I suppose there is anger and fear enough on both sides," he said, pausing his drumming and lifting his fingers to inspect them, as though they were wayward extensions of himself. "But both our homelands are right now in peril. We have no choice. We really have no choice."

Ruall floated by on her way to speak with Jeaves. "One way or another," she intoned ominously, with a spin of her head, "there *will* be peace."

Akura felt a chill. She gazed after the Tintangle, trying to assess Ruall the way she did others; but she could get no reading on the creature. Li-Jared had twitched at Ruall's words—even he was uncomfortable with the strange being—but now he was gazing silently into space. Akura sensed that while he didn't like it, he agreed with Ruall's pronouncement.

Beside Akura, Sheeawn was stirring; the words he was translating had given him a lot to think about. *We all have that,* she thought silently.

Karellia grew steadily until it was a large globe in the viewspace. From time to time, the display changed to show different views. Sheeawn didn't really understand them, something called different wavelengths. In one view, the Heart of Fire looked like a banked fire in the sky, impressive and beautiful, but not necessarily threatening. *Ultraviolet,* Copernicus said. In another, it looked much more frightening, like a leering monster shooting off emerald and crimson rays. *X-ray,* Copernicus said. In still another, strangely graceful webbed lines curled down from the clouds to dance with similar strands that arced up from the top of the world and looped around it to rejoin it at the bottom. *Magnetic lines,* said Copernicus.

Ruall conferred with the robot, then spun across the deck in front of them all and announced, "We will shortly be crossing the planetary protection zone. You may feel some disturbance. Please find a comfortable place to sit. We will engage motion restraints as soon as you are seated."

That got Sheeawn's attention. He tried to settle into a comfortable position against the bench seat cushions. Being scared made it hard to feel comfortable. That feeling wasn't helped when suddenly he couldn't move his arms, except in slow motion, as though he were deep in syrup. His emotions weren't slowed, though, and he felt panic rushing into his chest. The Watcher must have sensed it, because she murmured, "Do not show fear. That is your job now: to *not show fear*. You must observe. All there is to see."

Yes. Yes. Somehow that was enough to steady him, and instead of clamping his eyes shut, he opened them wide. They were about to see their adversary's defenses at work. *Watch and learn. Watch and learn.*

Almost as if he had heard Sheeawn's and Akura's thoughts, Li-Jared spoke. "I am sorry, but we must now turn off the view, until we have passed through the protection zone. As long as a state of war exists, we cannot permit a view of the defense mechanism."

Sheeawn muttered to himself in annoyance. Well, he still wasn't going to show fear. If there was anything at all to see, he would see it.

Just before the viewspace went dark, he thought he glimpsed the image of Karellia go into soft focus and shimmer a little. Then the outside view was gone. He felt a little lurch. Was that the ship, or his stomach? He shut his eyes as a wave of queasiness passed over him. When he heard a little cry from Akura, he snapped his eyes open to see the planet swimming before them, but visibly closer.

What had just happened? Apparently they had passed through whatever it was they weren't permitted to see, and they were close enough now that a landing on the demon world really seemed possible.

Li-Jared could make out some of the continental shapes, and the mist-shrouded oceans. He felt a rush of homesickness such as he had not felt even on their brief first visit. *Home of the beautiful, perilous sky. If I had known way back then just how perilous . . .*

They were already closer to the planet than on their earlier approach.

Ruall was floating nearby, speaking to him. "Li-Jared, could you work with Copernicus to ensure identification of visible land-marks—and to handle communications?"

"Of course—" Li-Jared began, as the restriction of movement on his body fell away, and he nearly fell forward off his seat. He staggered to his feet and strode forward to peer at the slowly scrolling landscape of Karellia. Land masses, oceans, clouds. *How many hundreds of years? How much has it changed?*

He burst out with loud clicks of laughter. He'd never actually seen his world from space until this mission. How was he sup-posed to be any more an expert than anyone else here?

Karellia Space Command started right in being annoying, just as before.

Li-Jared growled under his breath and repeated, "Yes, we are the same ship, and the same crew, who visited before. If your memory hasn't failed you, you might recall that we said we were going to pay a visit to the world you are engaged in hostilities with. Do you remember that? Well, we did, and we now have on board representatives from that world, which by the way is called Uduon."

He gave them a few moments to absorb that. When there was no meaningful response, he continued, "We have brought them not to fight, but to talk. To parlay. Because—well, let's just say it's in the interests of both planets. Now, I have promised these officials safe passage in our ship. I have promised them fair treat-ment when they visit Karellia. I have promised them a chance to explain their position to the highest officials of *my* homeworld. That's you. That's Karellia."

"Excuse me, please," said Sheeawn, leaning with one ear toward Akura to hear her question. "Can you explain why they are so unwelcoming to you, if you are *from* this planet, as you said?"

Li-Jared tapped his fingers on his lips before answering. "It's because they've forgotten me," he said finally. "Because I've been gone for such a long time that they don't know me, and they think they have no reason to trust me."

Bandicut stepped up beside him. "Is it time to remind them that you are a world-renowned *scientist?* How long would it take to look that up?"

Li-Jared made a noise deep in his throat. *Bong.* "I don't know about world-renowned, but still. I suppose it depends on the state of historical records after hundreds of years." He had told them to check records at the Holdhope Academy in Watskland for reference to a Li-Jared, Gamut Professor of mathematical physics, possibly listed as having vanished without a trace in the year Eight Hundred Thirty, Shadow Era, the eighth year of the Second Soldani reign in Moramia. They had sounded dubious, but promised to check.

A voice erupted from the long-range communicator. *"We have received this question to ask you: Are you related to the Li-Jared known for discovering the principle of spectrum synchrony harmonics, two hundred seventy-six years ago? Are you descended from that Li-Jared?"*

Li-Jared was momentarily speechless. That was indeed his work. But no one had been crediting him with the discovery of a "principle" while he was there, laboring in obscurity. He saw Bandicut staring at him in amazement. He coughed and answered, "You could say I am related, yes. That was precisely my work—in fact, much of it was on the physics of how the energy belts offered planetary protection from cosmic hazards."

The voice sounded stunned. *"You may be asked to demonstrate your knowledge in that area. In the meantime, you say you have been traveling in space? We have no record of anyone ever traveling beyond the radiation belt."*

"You may ask all you want about that, but it will have to wait until more urgent matters are settled. Suffice it to say I was given a lift by some off-worlders." Li-Jared paused and thumped a fist against his forehead. Then he leaned forward. "Listen, it is our intent to descend shortly in a landing craft. Are you willing to provide an escort?"

It took Space Command half a minute to reply. When they did, it was to repeat their demand that *The Long View* present itself in low orbit for inspection. *"Planetary security requires—"*

"No, if you are asking permission to board us, the answer is still no," Li-Jared said brusquely. "An inspection will not be possible at this time. Perhaps later. I assure you we are not here to threaten your space forces, or Karellia itself—" *at least if you listen to reason and don't push us!* Instead of voicing those words, he continued, "I repeat: We bring information about a major threat to Karellia—a far bigger threat than anything you have faced yet—and coming from a different direction." He stopped and took a deep breath. "That is why I need to speak to authorities!"

"Yes, you said that before. We are consulting our superiors on that request. But it takes time—"

"Time is what we do not have," Li-Jared snapped. "Please listen. We intend to land, with or without your help. But it would be helpful to both of us if you would provide safe landing coordinates *close to the planetary leadership.* We welcome, with great gladness, any escort you might care to provide. Our main ship and a portion of our crew will remain here in higher orbit. Please be mindful of their safety." *Don't even think about attacking them. You will not like the results if you do.*

The answer to that took even longer, but in the end, Space Command seemed to decide that they would take what they could get. And yes, they would provide an escort. A *very* close escort.

"This is nonsense," Akura said. "You must take us with you. For our sakes, if not for your mission."

Bwang. "What's that? We're trying to *protect* you, in case we encounter trouble," Li-Jared said. "We'll introduce you when we're sure it's safe."

Akura laughed in short, sharp coughs. "You would assure our safety by leaving us *here?* Suppose they take *you* hostage. What would we do then?" Akura had laughed, but there was fear in Sheeawn's voice as he translated.

Li-Jared winced. He had to concede that her objection had merit, and there was no mistaking her mood; she was angry. "I came with you on your promise to let me see those who have attacked our world," she said. "You told me they are not what we imagine. But why now do you say it is too dangerous for me to go?"

"I have to introduce myself to them," Li-Jared said. "Until they trust *me,* I cannot properly prepare them to meet *you.*" Even as he said that, he felt his resolve weakening.

Akura snorted and prodded Sheeawn, who said, "You said we need to see them as they are. Well, *they* need to see *us.* Let us do that, and not delay."

Li-Jared glanced at Bandicut, who shrugged and said, "We did just insist that time is short, with Mindaru probably on the way."

"So I did." Li-Jared sighed and gestured to the Uduon. "Are you packed and ready?"

Aboard the lander, Li-Jared paid little attention to the details of their departure. His head was full of cascading emotions: fear that this could all go wrong; hope that it would not; sympathy for the Uduon, who were clearly apprehensive; dread at what his home-world might have become. But most of all, joy. After all this time, he was going home! Was it still home? What would they think of a 300-year-old star traveler? Was it only three hundred years? Would they believe he was who he said he was?

He glanced nervously over his shoulder, where Jeaves was stowing their gear behind the two Uduon. Bandicut noticed and flashed him a grin that he was pretty sure was feigned. "You suppose we'll find Bria in our luggage again this time?"

Li-Jared shivered, trying not to imagine the havoc the gokat could wreak on Karellia. He had forgotten to speak to Ruall about it. "Let's hope not. Can we get this thing moving?"

Three minutes later the scout dropped from *The Long View*, began decelerating, and descended toward the cottony white clouds of Karellia.

CHAPTER 3

Making Sense

RINGS-AT-NEED gonged softly, leading the company of Julie, Ik, Antares, and Napoleon away from their meeting with the translator. The lizard-being who had helped escort them here was nowhere to be seen. Did that mean they were now trusted to follow Rings, and not run off? Julie wondered if Rings had been able to listen to their troubling conversation with the yaantel.

"Where are we going?" she asked, as they strode down a corridor with deep red and orange swirls on the walls.

"To a place where you may rest in privacy, before you report back to the Galactic Core team," Rings said, burring softly. "I requested it, because I thought you had earned it."

Privacy! Julie thought. Rest! Was this too good to be true? Was Rings starting to look out for them? "Thank you," she said to the Tintangle.

A short walk and a ride down a drop-shaft brought them to a balcony overlooking a wooded park. They weren't headed to the park, though. Rings led them around the arc of the balcony, and through an archway into what looked like a hyper-modern apartment complex, all curved glass, cut into horizontal sections like a sliced orange. If there were any other people about, Julie didn't see them. A private lift requiring a code from Rings took them up a level, to the front of a clear-walled suite that curved away from them to the right. Rings touched a spot on the near end of the curve and a door paled open. "You will stay here."

"Nice," Julie said, surveying the space. They were standing in a living room fitted with sleek furniture obviously designed for bipeds of their approximate size. A curved staircase led up to a series of glass-walled rooms half a level higher. "But, um, privacy?"

"It's all see-through," Antares said, echoing Julie's thought.

"Oh—you can change the wavelengths!" Rings said. He extended a paddle hand toward the glass front wall. "Just stroke the glass like so . . ." and his flat hand slid down the wall. The glass turned smokily translucent, cutting off a view of the outside. "You can do the same with your sleeping rooms upstairs."

"Hrah," Ik remarked, strolling the length of the room. "Is there food?"

Rings showed them how to work the concealed kitchenette food dispensers, and how to launder their clothes—no need to take them off—and how to call if they needed him. Then he spun a few times and vanished.

Julie sighed. "I'm going to go freshen up. Maybe Rings was hinting at something when he told us how to launder our clothes. Meet you back here for a bite?" She chose the rightmost room on the upper level, which turned out to be smaller inside than she'd expected. She stepped fully clothed into the personal freshener chamber, which was barely the size of a shower stall back on Triton. Before the mist enveloped her, she caught sight of herself in the mirror. She shuddered. Her hair was a breathtaking mess; she looked as though she'd just straggled in from a wilderness ordeal. The image disappeared in a cloud of mist, which caressed her face and body, making her feel refreshed in a matter of seconds. When she stepped out, three minutes later, she felt clean for the first time in a billion years. As promised, her blouse and slacks—still on her body—were fresh and pressed. And her hair— well, she still needed a trim, but her hair was clean and looked *brushed*. How had that happened?

She met Ik and Antares back downstairs. The kitchen produced bread and cheese, seemingly the universal easy dinner on Shipworld, and passable red wine. Hungry, they ate without talking much;

afterward, Ik excused himself. "I must meditate or I will not function well. I guess that you, my friends, have things to talk about."

Don't we just, Julie thought, as Ik strode up the stairs and disappeared into the sleeping room on the left. The walls of his room turned opaque. Napoleon, meanwhile, had found a datanet panel at the end of the room and settled in to charge. Julie found herself seated in silence across the table from Antares. The alien woman's gaze, with those black and gold eyes, was unnervingly direct. Her hair looked good, too—spectacular, actually, a glorious auburn mane cascading down the back of her neck. Julie offered her a refill of wine, which Antares graciously accepted. As she sipped the wine, the Thespi woman appeared to be sizing up her human companion. "You have strong feelings concerning me, Julie Stone. I can sense them, and I wish I could put you at ease. You are uncertain what to think of me, and I guess I understand why."

Julie cleared her throat. "Well, um—am I right about you and John?"

Antares made a low sound in the back of her throat, and at the same time, Julie experienced a feeling of . . . what? Was Antares trying to create a wordless connection? *Are you telepathic?* Julie wondered again. She felt a complex of emotions, not all hers, brushing against her: regret and sympathy and maybe a little defensiveness and jealousy, and probably others she couldn't identify. Not telepathic, exactly. *Empathic?*

Antares spoke finally. "I do not know exactly what you think. But if you are wondering if John and I have been intimate friends . . ."

Julie nodded slowly.

"Then, yes. You are right." As she said those words, her golden eyes closed, and Julie felt another surge of emotional contact. Antares' face tightened momentarily, and when she opened her eyes again, Julie felt an almost electric connection. She tried to shiver it off. When she couldn't, she said stiffly, "Could you please not do that?" Antares looked puzzled. "That thing you're doing?" Julie said, pressing her fingertips to her temples to mime what she was feeling.

"*Oh*. I am sorry," Antares said. Julie felt a sudden wave of regret, as Antares continued, "I am truly sorry. I do not wish to intrude. But it is, uhhl, what I was born to do, you see."

Julie's hands twitched, and she clasped them together to still them. "What? I *don't* see, no. What do you mean?"

Antares let her breath out with a sigh, and suddenly seemed more vulnerable. "My destiny from birth was to be a third. It's a little hard to explain. Would you mind if I just showed you?"

"Huh? I suppose not. What do you—?"

Antares made a hushing sound. "May I touch your forearms? I will not harm you, I promise."

With a reflexive shiver, Julie started to pull her elbows back. Then she thought, *Don't be such a coward. If she's a friend of John's— if he trusts her—are you really afraid of her?* Without speaking, but feeling foolish, she slid her forearms forward on the table surface again, to where Antares could reach. *No, not afraid of her. Afraid of myself—afraid of what she's going to show me about myself.* Julie was suddenly ashamed, not just of her fear of what Antares was about to do, but of her jealousy toward the woman, John's friend. Intimate friend. It wasn't as if she, Julie, had a lifetime, all-galaxy claim on John. He had literally been half a galaxy away.

"Uhhl, thank you," Antares murmured. She placed her elegant-fingered hands flat on the table, and explained, "I am what is called on my world a Thespi-Third female. I am trained as a joiner—a facilitator, you see. One who assists other individuals in achieving connection with one another. Intimate connection, sometimes."

Julie winced a little at that, and tried not to show it. *A human jumper cable?* she wondered.

"When I make contact, I will try to demonstrate how I do what I do. If you find it uncomfortable, let me know by simply conveying the feeling to me directly." Antares cocked her head. Julie was aware of her own fingers drumming nervously. "May I?"

Julie swallowed, and then nodded.

Antares' touch was feather light on her forearm. Even that contact made her twitch like a frog's leg electrified. *She can see all of my feelings!* At the same time, she felt she could see and *feel* everything that Antares felt. It was too much. She yelped and jerked her hand back as if she had actually received an electric shock. "Wow."

Jumping up from the table, she paced around the room, shaking her arm. Finally she came back, embarrassed at being so skittish.

"Uhhl, I had only barely started," Antares said mildly. "I was merely establishing the basic channels."

"Hah!" Julie laughed self-consciously. She had just been startled—all right, terrified—by the sudden feeling that she would share her innermost feelings with Antares. Not that she *was* sharing them, but that she *could*. She gulped. "I think I need some more wine."

"I also," Antares said, draining her glass and rising.

"I'll get it. Sit tight," Julie said, taking both glasses and crossing the room. Her hands shook a little as she held the glasses under the dispenser. Ruby liquid splashed into one glass, then the other, and she brought them back to the table. She gulped from her own as she sat. Then she forced a slow breath and took a more measured sip. "Actually, before we do this," she said, "would you mind just telling me about your . . . relationship . . . with John?"

Antares let her eyes drop half-closed for a moment. Her gaze seemed softer when she reopened them. "Of course, if you prefer, though I think you will understand it better when we have shared in this way."

"Ah-huh. You're probably right. But still—I just want to know now," Julie said, thinking, *I don't want to know at all. But what did I think was going to happen? Exiled across the galaxy—was he supposed to wait for me? Why should he have expected ever to see me again?*

Antares touched her throat. "I see. Yes, then. Well. John and I were at first strangers to one another. We met through a chance encounter, and then began to work in a common cause." She told Julie how she, along with John and his friends, had fought an entity right here on Shipworld, the entity called the "boojum," which was trying to destroy the intelligence systems on Shipworld. Through that struggle she came to know, not just John but also John's robots, and Ik and Li-Jared. "I wouldn't say we were exactly *friends* yet at the end of that battle, but we stayed together, and soon we were working in another cause." And this time Julie heard how Antares and John and the others had been hurled together to a distant ocean world, where they found an underwater civilization endangered by something they called the Maw of the Abyss.

"In the course of that, John and I did become friends, joined in a life-and-death struggle—and finally, we became lovers." When Antares said the word that Julie heard as *lovers*, there was an inflection in the word that suggested to Julie that it was more complicated than a simple romantic or sexual liaison.

That shouldn't be a surprise, either, she thought with a twinge of envy.

"And finally," Antares continued, "as a *company* of friends, we—all six of us, including the two robots—" she paused and nodded across the room toward Napoleon "—plus *another* robot named Jeaves—journeyed together. To the Starmaker Nebula, where we met sentient stars, and encountered and fought the Mindaru, who were murdering those stars. And, maybe, we prevented a future catastrophe for your own and John's homeworld, and probably a lot of other worlds at the same time."

Now I really feel small, Julie thought. A moment later, though, she remembered the things she herself had been called to do. Maybe she wasn't *that* small.

"But now I would really like to show you what all of this means to a Thespi-Third female."

Julie shook her head, not meaning *no*, just not following. "Because—?"

"Because I think only then can you understand—" Antares paused, perhaps to search for words "—that I am not a threat to you."

"I never thought you were." Julie winced at her own lie.

"Uhhl, no?" Antares took a sip from her wine, made a face, and set the glass down again. "Then, Julie Stone, may I try again?"

Julie swallowed and rested her arms on the table. She looked into Antares' golden-irised gaze. "Go ahead."

Antares let her breath sigh out as she placed her hands on Julie's wrists. This time, Julie held steady. After a moment, her focus was almost entirely inward, barely aware of Antares in front of her. Something opened, like a window allowing a breeze to pass through her thoughts. *What's that?* she wondered. In return, she felt a sense of reassurance, and she accepted it without flinching away. Seconds passed, in quiet expectancy. Was Antares waiting for some sign from her? *I'm ready,* she thought, and she felt the window open wider, letting in something like the salt tang of ocean air, with hints of faraway places. She felt something loosen in her own mind.

Let me show you. She didn't hear those actual words, but the intent was clear. She began to feel some of what *Antares* had been feeling: her fears as a Thespi-Third; the loss, shame, embarrassment, guilt. Not over her care for John Bandicut, but over abandoning the rules that had governed her role as Thespi-Third from the time of her young adulthood.

What rules are those? Julie thought the question, *felt* it. And felt the response from Antares:

In a normal Thespi-Third life, with her own people, on her own world—a place Julie imagined as lush, forested, beautiful— her role was to help others form the kinds of bonds that she had later gone ahead and created with John.

To help others, but never to have those feelings for yourself? Julie thought in wonder, and then shock.

The response to that was affirmative, and fraught with feelings of uncertainty and shame and longing. Longing for her homeworld, from which she was exiled as surely as Julie had been from hers. Longing for freedom to make her own life, and to have her own loves—for which she had been neither created nor trained.

Julie felt a complex mingling of currents in her own response: sympathy; anger at those who would so restrict Antares; alarm that Antares should inflict her needs on John Bandicut, and even on her, Julie. Gratitude, that Antares had made John less lonely, and been a companion and friend to him in time of danger and need. Fury, that she, Julie, had been left behind. Shame, that she harbored such unreasonable emotions.

The window opened a little wider, revealing more detail of things Antares had hinted at before:

She had not just *wished* for a life of freedom; even on her home-world she had acted on the wish, and sampled forbidden love. The name of the one with whom she had shared was a wisp, too fleeting to catch. *He* had not suffered judgment as she had. *Her* daring was punishable by death. But her sentence had provided her escape. It was during her imprisonment, awaiting execution, that a mysterious beam of light entered the cell and took her away; and sometime during the dizzying transition that followed, she received her knowing-stones, her yaantel stones. And through a strange conveyance among the stars, she came to Shipworld, rescued from death but exiled from her own world. By whom? She wasn't really sure.

Just like John Bandicut. Like Julie Stone. And, as Julie understood it, like Ik and Li-Jared.

Julie found herself almost weeping at the images—almost, but not quite. She couldn't weep for Antares when she had her own images spilling out: her brief but passionate love affair with John; her encounter with the translator beneath the ice of Triton, the same translator that they'd just talked to here; and her own acquisition of stones. Up until then, she had believed that John was gone, burned up in a fiery collision with a comet. But then came her own flight with the translator, fending off an object that menaced Earth. That was followed by her own arrival here on Shipworld, alone and bewildered—only later to discover that John had been here, and she had missed him.

(Does he know *I'm* here?) she wondered.

(I don't think so,) she heard, and was surprised to hear words from Antares. Perhaps a deeper connection was possible through touch, or perhaps with the help of the stones. (I didn't know you were here until after he was gone, and I'm sure he would have told me. But I have no way of knowing what he may have learned since I last saw him.)

Julie found herself sharing Antares' pain in John's departure. (We are sisters,) she heard, after a long silence. The words drifted to her so softly, she did not at first react. She blinked, and really *looked* at Antares, for the first time since the exchange had begun. The Thespi woman held her head at a slight angle, her gold and black eyes focused on Julie. Though her gaze seemed full of sadness, she was reaching out to Julie. (Sisters in the company. Sisters in caring for John.)

(I . . . I don't know,) Julie whispered silently. This was happening too fast. But there was something in Antares' gaze, locked with hers, that conveyed more than words could, more than the images. It bound her to this alien woman, which chafed. She tried to form words in her head to explain her discomfort, but the words refused to take on life.

Antares spoke aloud now, in a bare whisper through the air: "I feel it in my bones. And in my stones. We may have just met, but we are joined now, joined through our common experience."

Julie felt a strange disconnection from reality, as if she were somehow floating above all of this, looking down on it from the ceiling. It couldn't touch her if she were floating above it; she wouldn't have to decide what she thought or felt, or how to approach Antares. That was the safest approach.

The illusion was short lived. Antares squeezed her wrists, signaling a change, and then slowly released the contact with Julie. The connection dissolved, like a fog dispersing. Julie's eyes stung; had she sat unblinking all this time? She rubbed them, wondering what to ask or say. "So, now we . . . what?" She had no experience to guide her.

Whatever Antares might have replied was interrupted by the sudden appearance of Rings-at-Need at the end of the table. He made a brushes-on-cymbal sound to get their attention.

Julie felt as if she were struggling up from a dream. "What is it, Rings?"

"I am sorry, but your presence has been requested," said Rings. "I have told them that you require rest. So the request has been delayed by—" *rasp* "—six hours."

"Six hours!" Julie groaned. "You call that giving us a rest? Why the rush? What happens in six hours?" She glanced at Antares, who uttered a soft growl of agreement. "I'm *tired*. I need more than six hours of rest."

"We need you," said Rings, "to meet with the leaders regarding a follow-up mission."

A chill ran through her. *"What?"* She shook her head, wondering if she had misheard. "You're planning another mission already?" The idea stunned her. All she could think of was the translator's caution not to rush into dangerous mistakes.

Rings' voice softened. "They were already preparing a second mission while you were in the ghoststream. Upon your return, there was great urgency to act on what you learned."

That made no sense to Julie, but she wasn't going to sort it out now. "Really. Well, you know what? We need more recovery time—and sleep. *And* we need to confer again with the trans— with the yaantel. So I'm afraid you're going to have to schedule the meeting a little later. All right?"

Rings-at-Need trembled for a moment, then bobbed its head. "Understood. The team agrees to a delay."

"Good!"

"Seven hours, then. I will be here to gather you then. Rest while you can." With that, Rings-at-Need vanished.

Seven hours? Julie thought. *How am I supposed to sleep now?*

CHAPTER 4

Urgent Conference

"HRAH. WHO IS it?" Ik's voice echoed through the silvered glass door.

Julie stopped tapping the chime-spot on the door's edge. "It's Julie! Rings-at-Need is here, and he says we have to go."

Half a minute later the door slid open and Ik appeared. He looked ill-rested, eyes not quite wide open, a distracted expression on his face. Julie felt the way Ik looked. "It has been nowhere near seven hours," Ik said. "Can he give me a few minutes to prepare myself, and get something to eat?"

Rings drifted into view, ringing ominously. "I know it's early, but you have been called to an emergency! You are needed at once." His blank metallic-disk face angled toward Julie, catching the hallway light. "Did you not convey this to Ik?"

"I was just—but Rings, we're no good to you without food in our stomachs," Julie said.

"Nevertheless, you must hurry," said Rings. "I will arrange for food en route."

Julie thought they'd be returning to the meeting room at the launch center. Instead, the four of them—Napoleon was the only one who didn't look bedraggled and put upon—stumbled out of the rooming center and into a . . . taxi? It was a bulbous vehicle, black on the outside. It reminded Julie of the timeless London air-cabs back on Earth. Inside, there was almost enough room to spread out and eat the breakfast that had been delivered in little boxes. Rings, hovering in the center of the cabin, told them they'd be traveling this time to a different launch center.

"Why?" Julie asked, around a too-large mouthful of something that looked like a fresh-baked donut but tasted like a green banana. "And when do we get to check back with the translator?"

Rings echoed softly as he replied, "The *why* will be answered shortly, by someone better able to answer your questions. As for the yaantel, it will be back in touch when it has information to convey. Meanwhile, there's an urgent situation and they need your help."

"What kind of situation?" Julie took a swallow of her coffee, just as the car accelerated into the dawn sky. Coughing, she dabbed at the front of her just-cleaned shirt, now damp with coffee. She leaned forward to yell at the driver for his jack-rabbit start. There was no driver.

"The details I have are few," Rings said. "But the second mission has already gone out, and they're in trouble."

"Second mission! Hrah! What kind? What trouble?" Ik rasped. He was beginning, finally, to look awake.

"Like yours," Rings said. "But with enhanced options."

Julie cautiously sipped more of her coffee; it seemed bitter to her now. "What does that mean?"

Rings turned his polished, featureless face to the side, as though gazing out the window in thought. He answered finally, in a reverberating tone that somehow conveyed, *It was not my idea.* "They went to the place you found, but to a later time. As I say, they are in trouble."

———

Despite their many questions, Rings insisted it was all he knew. The car began descending into twilight, dropping fast. The sky was brushed with pink and orange. Evening? They hadn't been traveling that long; they must have flown into a different time sector. Julie could see trees and a river flash by outside now. Then they were down on a paved roadway, still moving fast. What was this place they were speeding through? It looked for all the world like a sleepy little town with dots of white lights among the trees, where events of cosmic import were a distant dream. Did people actually live here? Did they allow nothing but white lights in this place? No one was visible, and only a few other small vehicles were on the road. "What is this—Pleasantville, after everyone left?"

Rings gave a small twang. "We are approaching a star-spanner station."

"*Here?*"

The Tintangle's shiny head-disk shivered. "Economics and—" *rasp* "—politics. It's sited here because—" *twang* "—influential people live here."

"I would have thought," Ik said, "that star-spanner missions were on a higher level of politics than the local economy."

Rings reverberated. "We have a saying among my people: All—" *rasp* "—politics is local."

"I'm pretty sure it was a human who said that," Julie murmured. She grabbed for a handhold as they rounded a bend and decelerated to a stop. "So . . ." They had stopped in front of an old warehouse on a river landing. A large, metal door began racking noisily up the side of the warehouse. The car pulled in, and the door reeled back down behind them. Then Rings was out of the car, gesturing with his paddle-hands for them to follow him into the dimly lit building.

A dilapidated warehouse, home to a star-spanner? Were they keeping it secret? Napoleon clicked and said, "This reminds me of home."

They came to an inner set of doors, where two spindly, tripedal creatures stood motionless, holding long, straight objects that might have been weapons or drum-major staffs. Rings spoke incomprehensibly to them, and together they opened the door to let the group through.

Bright light greeted them. They stood at the end of a long, industrial corridor that dwindled into the distance. Garish yellow ceiling lights illumined walls that looked like concrete. Revolving red lights suggested just one meaning: *Urgency.* Was that a universal symbol? Julie wondered. It reminded her of an amusement park ride, back on Earth. *Disaster Transport.*

A rasping voice jarred her out of her thoughts. "Thank you for coming so quickly." A large, carapace-encased creature with a pair of eye-stalks on its head shuffled forward to greet them. Perhaps it was the weird lighting and strange context; it took Julie a moment to recognize Cromus, one of the leaders of the galactic core mission support team. "Please com-m-me with me to the star-spanner-r-r station. I'll explain-n the situation while we travel." He seemed easier to understand than before; perhaps her stones were learning to smooth out his speech. Cromus gestured with his pincer-hands, and they all stepped onto a dark pad at the beginning of the corridor. They began accelerating down the hallway.

Julie steadied herself with a hand on Napoleon, and felt a hand on her own shoulder. It was Antares, who was steadying herself between Julie and Ik. Julie thought she felt a twinge of something. Empathic leakage? Antares, she thought, was deeply troubled. About Julie? No, about what was to come. Did she sense something from Cromus that made her worried?

Cromus was talking again. "There has been a follow-up mission-n to yours."

"Rings told us. Why so soon?" This business of a second mission had Julie worried. "What went wrong? What were they trying to do?"

"They were sent-t to stop-p the Mindaru."

Julie thought of the translator's warnings, and her heart sank. Her voice trembled. "And—?"

"There were miscalculations-s," Cromus said.

The corridor flashed open to reveal a wide platform, and the pad they stood on was suddenly stationary. Cromus led the way to a gleaming silver cylinder, where two more of the tripedal guards stood.

"I don't know what you've used-d in the past," Cromus said. "This is a medium-m-range star-spanner, for local trips, within two—" *rasp* "—light-years or so. We are not going far."

Julie opened her mouth, then closed it.

"Where, hrrm, *are* we going?" Ik asked.

A portal turned transparent in the side of the vessel, and Cromus spoke as he shuffled in, leading the way. He swiveled his eye-stalks to look at each of them at the same time, as if he wasn't sure who had spoken. "To our second launch center, near a black hole one-half light-year from here. Do not worry. It is part of greater Shipworld-d."

Reeling a little at that, they took seats in the cabin, all except Rings, who gonged something about things to do, and twisted out of the air.

"We maintain-n several black holes for research-ch, and as energy sources."

"Hrah! Isn't that dangerous?" Ik asked.

Cromus's gaze shifted. "Life is dangerous, is it not-t? But this? Not-t unduly so. It powers the particle-enhanced ghost-stream-m, which was used by the s-strike force—"

Strike force?

Julie started to say something, but Cromus raised a pincer. "Sealed and ready," he muttered. "Release." Julie felt a movement under her like a small boat slipping into a river current.

An instant later, the view forward showed space—and tiny, distant galaxies. They were on the side of Shipworld facing away from the Milky Way. It felt terribly lonely.

Cromus wasted no time, speaking in a crackling voice. "We have a serious problem-m and do not know what to do. We hope your-r experience . . ." His eye-stalks swiveled, this time in turn from one of them to another. "I am sor-r-ry. That is understat-t-ing the case. You see, we have received a—" *rasp* "—Mayday—" *rasp* "—distress-s message from the galactic core s-strike force. How much did Rings tell-l you?"

Julie's heart was pounding. She shook her head. "Just enough to scare us. This is exactly the sort of thing the yaantel said we should *not* do."

"Sss. Well-l." Cromus waved his pincers. "After your mission reports-s, a highest-t level decision—far above my rank-k!—was made to send a strik-ke mission downtime to the location you identified-d."

"How could you possibly mount another mission so soon?" Julie asked.

"The team-m was already prepared-d when you were on *your* mission-n—in the event-t you needed assistance. And-d to be ready for immediate action-n, in the event-t you returned with a confirmed-d location-n."

"To do *what?*" Antares asked, her voice trembling. "You must be aware of the dangers of meddling with the past. You could have—"

Cromus let out a percussive click that caused her to stop in mid-sentence. "Of cours-se. The goal was *not-t* to interfere on the planet."

"Hrah," Ik said. "What, then?"

Click click! "To f-find a way to close the timestream-m! And prevent any Mindaru-u from making their way up to our t-time. Any already en route to be destroyed-d. Since they were already on their way between times-s, there would be no paradox-x."

Julie shut her eyes, trying to picture the logic. "How could you be sure?" she demanded. "How could you be sure you weren't going to change our present?"

"Sss. I am no expert in the th-theory, but the mission was developed in strict accordance with the best available models-s."

"*Hrrm,*" Ik said, and did not look happy.

Cromus seemed not to notice. "Urgency was great-t," he continued. "Because of the imminent risk-k. We knew Mindaru were finding their way up the timestream—perhaps even follow-ing-g your path as you returned-d. The team was instructed to return-n to the point of your discovery."

"Why?" Julie cried. "What could they do that we couldn't?"

Cromus weighed his words. "We used a different and more powerful ghoststream-m for their mission-n. To permit-t certain actions you did not have available."

Actions? Julie shuddered at the possibilities.

"Hrah, this modified ghoststream—" Ik growled.

"It's called-d a particle-stream-m," Cromus said. "It is frankly beyond anything-ng we've tried before. It permits the possibility . . . under certain conditions-ns. . . an entangled energy pulse could be transmitted down the ghoststream-m . . ."

Energy pulse? Feeling slightly sick, Julie asked, "What *kind* of energy pulse?" She glanced forward; they were speeding down a glowing but otherwise featureless tube, presumably with a black hole at the end.

Cromus continued, "It was designed-d to exploit the principles that mak-ke the ghoststream possible. A properly tuned quantum-m pulse could affect the entangled state of a target-t just beyond the ghoststream terminus."

"Affect *how*?" Ik asked.

Cromus's eye-stalks swiveled. "The hope was that it-t would change molecular binding energies—and cause a rapid-d expansion of the molecules-s of the immediate surroundings."

Julie's mouth went dry. "An explosion?"

"Hrah," Ik whispered. Antares was silent, but her stunned dismay reverberated through Julie like an electric shock.

"Well-l-l . . . more or less . . . yes-s."

"You were trying to *bomb* the area we visited?"

Cromus worked his pincers nervously. *Click, click.* "Not-t-t the *place*."

"Not the place? What do you mean?" Julie demanded.

Click click. "We might have *liked-d* to bomb the Mindaru before they could enter the timestream-m. But not an option-n. Probably impossible—and the risk of altering the timeline . . ." Cromus waved his pincers in the air. "As you say . . ."

"It is *supposed* to be impossible," Ik said, and Julie couldn't tell if he was being sarcastic.

" . . . even if theory says it couldn't happen-n. Abundance of caution-n. No, the intent-t was to collapse only the end of the *timestream-m*. To destroy the entanglement-t joining it to the Mindaru-u."

"Hrah, that sounds better," Ik said. "But still—to decide so hurriedly—"

"Well-l . . ." *Click click.* "Whatever you think of the wisdom, it has gone badly." *Clack clack.* "Instead of sealing the timestream, the pulse may have created a *wider* opening-ng."

"*That* sounds bad," Ik rasped. "Is there more?"

"More," Cromus said. *Click click. Clack clack.* "Serious miscalculation. Blowback of the puls-se. Hit *our* team-m—hard-d."

Ahead of them, the pale tube streamed steadily by.

"How hard?" Ik said.

Cromus took a few seconds to answer. "We do not-t know the fate of the mission team yet-t."

"But you fear the worst?" Ik asked. "And what do you think we can do?"

Click click. Wave of pincers. "We do not know. But you have fought them before. And won."

Julie had never seen Ik look like this before: somber, and at the same time profoundly angry.

Antares seemed to echo Ik's feelings. She was radiating a complex array of emotions: fear, fury, a desire to create calm around them all, and an inability to do so.

Julie sat back to sort it all out, but was startled by the sudden reappearance of Rings-at-Need in the middle of the cabin. "Where did you go?" she asked.

"Brief visit with a friend. Forgive my absence. I am here now."

Huh, Julie thought. She would ask him more when they were alone. She cleared her throat and addressed Cromus again. "So this crew is now in trouble—and you still have not told us *why* you launched right away, instead of waiting until we understood what we had found on the first mission. You *knew* we had gone to ask advice from the yaantel! And I'll bet you knew that it urged caution!"

"Yess, we did-d. But speed-d was paramount-t-t," Cromus insisted. "We knew the Mindaru-u were on the move—in the timestream. You saw them on your way into the past!"

She remembered. "We didn't know for sure what those were."

"After analyzing-ng, we were sure enough."

"But they were still in the past! As long as we could still go back into the past to stop them, why didn't you take the time to *study* the situation? Instead of risking that crew—and risking changing our whole timeline!"

Rings made a low cymbal-ringing sound. In sympathy? Agreement?

Cromus rasped sharply, "Miss Stone! We *did not have* the luxury of time that you seem to believe we had-d!"

"Why not? A billion years isn't enough—?"

Clack clack clack! "Time does not-t work that way! Perhaps you think-k, 'It is in the past, and we can take as long as we need to go sort it out-t'!" Cromus made a slashing motion with his pincers. "No! Once Mindaru are in the timestream, our window for action is very short-t!"

"Why?" Antares interrupted, her voice tight with emotion. "Why is it short?"

"Because-s," Cromus said, "as we have told you, the past is resistant-t to change. Once the Mindaru reach *our present*, we can no longer change the circumstances that brought them here."

"So-o-o," Rings said, echoing suddenly, "I believe we understand that there was genuine cause for haste. The best hope of keeping the Mindaru from our time was to prevent them from *entering-ng* the timestream in the first place. However, once they reach the present, that choice is gone—because their travel is then firmly part of the past!"

Cromus made a soft, hacking sound. "Exact-tly. Don't you see? When you returned and reported seeing Mindaru in the timestream-m, we had to act at once."

Julie's head hurt. "If we have done something to allow the Mindaru into the timestream, doesn't that mean we've already changed the past?"

Cromus turned his eye-stalks toward Rings, who reverberated softly and answered. "That question is currently a matter of heated debate among-ng theorists."

"Please," said Cromus. "Here's the crux-x. If we cannot go back-k to change *yesterday*, we may still-l be able to influence *tomorrow*. But only by acting fast-t."

Julie glanced at Ik; he looked thoughtful. Antares seemed to be working the question out slowly in her mind.

"We approach-ch our destination at the black hole," Cromus announced.

CHAPTER 5

Mayday!

JULIE EXPECTED THE black hole to appear as a white blaze of light from the disk of incandescent gas spiraling in toward the event horizon. That was how she had seen it in countless pictures. But this was not like that at all.

The black hole emerged as a sullen, violet vortex of gases around the collapsed star. The difference, Rings explained, had to do with their installation capturing a sizable amount of the black hole's energy to power the ghoststream operation, especially the higher-output of the particle-enhanced ghoststream. Because they were coming in high, above the pole, they could make out a brooding dark eye at the center, balefully watching their approach.

Three stations orbited the hole; one of them was the bright point now in their sights. It grew quickly, and soon they were sliding toward its faceted, diamondlike surface. They had only a moment to enjoy the view before they slipped in through the side of the station and rocked to a halt in the receiving dock.

They were met in a debarkation area by a biped about Ik's height, but heavier, with numerous multi-jointed arms and a face that looked as if it had been carved out of shale, high and angular and slate-colored. "This is Arak," Cromus announced. "He is oversight commander of the second galactic core mission, currently in progress." Arak was dressed in what Julie took to be some kind of military garb, with padding and mottled coloration

and markings that might have indicated rank. He uttered something harsh, with a lot of percussive sounds. The translator-
stones took a moment to turn that into: "Are you the first flight
crew—the time travelers?"

"We are," Ik said. "Is this the station where the second mission was launched?"

"No." Arak's voice sounded clipped, modulated by the stones.
"This is the control section. Launch is from Station Two, closer
to the black hole. We will take you there shortly."

Don't hurry on my account, Julie thought with a shudder, pictur-
ing the glowing maw of the black hole right outside the station.

"News on the mission?" Cromus asked.

Arak's voice turned guttural. "We've lost and regained contact multiple times. When we have contact, there is considerable
interference. The word 'attack' may have been registered."

Ik stiffened beside Julie. She thought she saw alarm in his
eyes. Antares reached out and touched his arm, and there was an
empathic wave that left no doubt: The possibility of a Mindaru
attack in the ghoststream had triggered an instant fight-or-
flight reaction in the Hraachee'an. His muscles had coiled in
preparation for either. Julie swallowed her own fear and asked
Arak, "Do you know what kind of attack?"

Arak made a slicing gesture with one of his arms. "We have
no information, but what else could it be if not Mindaru? But why
guess what we do not know? Let us proceed to the command center and learn what there is to know."

He strode briskly, forcing the crablike Cromus to work hard
to keep up. Rings had vanished again. The command center
looked strangely like home, Julie thought with a shiver as they
entered from the back. It was a darkened room, with at least a
dozen crewed work stations with glowing holos. Arak led them to
a station being operated by a spindly fellow whom he addressed
as Watts. "Do you currently have contact with the team?"

"We have a signal. Only intermittently intelligible." Watts
looked up, saw that Arak had guests, and seemed to realize that
he could, or should, provide more detail. "Look, please." Watts

did something, and the holo-display went from a static-hashed image of the ghoststream to a graphic display that looked like a map of part of the galaxy. "This is our ghoststream." Watts's bony finger traced a red line that ran diagonally across the display toward the galactic center. Partway in, it angled slightly and joined with a green line, coming in from the left like a merging highway. "This is the starstream, a spatial distortion that carries physical bodies, like ships. Our ghoststream slips right inside it and joins it all the way to the core." Watts's finger continued tracing, and came to an intersection with a short third line, this one violet. "And here is where the temporal distortion from that planetary system, Krella—"

"*Karellia*," Ik corrected.

"Yes, Krella—and that distortion, or time-tide, sets up all manner of resonances and reverberations with the starstream and—well—that's why we're here." Watts zoomed the picture in and tracked toward the galactic core. The three lines became like braided wire, and remained so all the way to the galactic core.

"I'm sure they know all this. What's the point?" Arak snapped impatiently.

"The point," Watts said, "is this." He pointed with two hands—one to a wisp of light moving back up the joined streams, away from the galactic core, and one to a small cluster of dots, not far behind. "This first is our team. Mapped as well as we can from their signals. The others are objects. Wave functions, really. Seemingly in pursuit. Mapped with our best telemetry, before coherence started to deteriorate. Went cloudy."

Julie blinked, trying to follow his jerky syntax. "But you heard from them? From your team?"

Watts's face looked squeezed, as if he might be squinting at her, though who knew what it meant in his terms? He answered, "Erratic connections, since the attempt to close the end of the timestream. Difficult to parse. They indicated estimation that there was intrusion into the timestream. Mindaru."

"But you said they were attacked."

"We heard the word. Or something like it. Then communication went garbled."

Ik shifted and muttered something under his breath. Watts asked him to repeat. "If they're hacked, it could be very bad," Ik said.

Arak leaned in. The stones faltered momentarily in translating. "How many—" *rasp* "—ghosts—" *rasp rasp* "—bogies in the stream?"

Watts's fingers moved over the board. "Difficult to track. They come and go. Some may have gotten by and already left the stream."

Antares radiated unhappiness. "Uhhl, how is that possible?"

Watts pointed to a place farther out from the galactic center and magnified the image again. Then he rewound. "There. We had some blips in our signal from the team. Caused maybe by entities in the stream. See them jump?" A cluster of tiny dots separated from the thread of the combined streams, like a train being shunted onto a spur line. Then they winked out. Watts tapped the display, pointing out that the dots vanished from the joined streams close to where the Karellian thread turned off. "I cannot track them. Not from here. Don't know if they vanished, or flew on." Watts's hand trembled a little. "Really, they could have gone anywhere. My feeling, they may be following the course of the Krella time-tide. Seeking the source."

"*Hrrrrl,*" Ik growled. "Our friends are there."

"John Bandicut and Li-Jared," Antares whispered. "This puts them in great danger!"

Arak rasped sharply. "That we cannot help. Mindaru are loose in the stream. Our job is to prevent more of them from getting there. Watts, anything more from our team?"

Watts trembled. "Telemetry is static. Crew contact currently unreadable."

Arak made a noise like a snarling dog. "What *can* you pick up? The *crew* is right *here*—in the pod! Why can you not—"

"Because of risk of decoherence. As long as we still have entanglement. Hope remains. I dare not meddle. We could lose them if it decoheres."

Arak snarled again and turned away.

Antares pushed forward, putting herself in front of Arak, clearly unwilling to let him off so easily about Bandicut and Li-Jared. "I ask you again, sir, what of the danger to our friends on mission at Karellia? Do you have no communication with them? Can't you warn them? Their mission is closely connected to what you are doing here."

Arak sounded annoyed. "Why would we have communication? Their sponsors did not trouble to send us details of their mission. We can only guess what they hope to accomplish."

That was enough for Julie. "That's just *bullshit!* Aren't they risking their lives to try to stop the Mindaru, too? Why aren't you talking to each other?"

"Which would accomplish what?" Arak rattled. "What are we doing that affects them? Or them, us?"

Ik rocked his head back and forth and tapped the side of his head with a long finger, as though pondering the question. "What, hrrm, might affect them? Allowing Mindaru into the timestream? That might harm them. Breaking the time-stream? That might harm them. Mindaru leaving the starstream near Karellia? That might harm them. Should they not be warned?"

Cromus raised a pincer and tapped it closed a couple of times. "Perhap-p-ps that is so. But we have no communication-n, so what can *we* do to help them?"

Julie tried to answer, but she had no words.

Antares did, however. "You can do *this*: Help *me* try to find a way to contact them and warn them."

"From here-re?" Cromus said. "We have no long-ng-range c-capability here."

Antares tapped a finger on Cromus's foreclaw, which twitched in response. "What about from here back to Shipworld? Do you have that? Something in realtime? Through the star-spanner, maybe?"

Cromus pulled his big pincer back to his thorax and acknowledged that they did.

"Then while my friends *here* help you deal with the mess you've made of your second mission, here's what else you need to do." She put a hand on the robot's head. "Allow Napoleon access to the information from Ik and Julie's galactic core mission *and* from this second one. And give *me* access to communications back to Shipworld."

Arak raised two of his hands warily. "Communication to whom?"

Antares opened her own hands wide. "To the yaantel. Perhaps to Amaduse."

"Who or *what*," Arak rasped, "is Amaduse?"

"He is a librarian. He knows more than you imagine about these missions."

Over Arak's rumble of uncertainty, Cromus spread his pincers wide. "I have heard of this librarian. But how will that help?"

"If there is a way to get word to John and Li-Jared, Amaduse and the yaantel will know it," Antares said. Her voice was flat and steely with determination. She turned to gaze at Ik and Julie. "My friends, Napoleon and I will do what we can here. You see what you can do to help with the time travel emergency—yes?"

"Hrrm, that will have to be seen." Ik rolled his gaze back to Arak and Cromus. "You have not told us what you expect us to do."

Arak barked, "Give us the benefit of your experience! Help us help the mission team!"

Ik raised his hands in exasperation, but Watts interrupted with, "Alarm at the launch point! Instability in the ghoststream."

"What kind of—?" Arak began.

"Voltage spike in the entanglement circuit. No voice from the team, but a distress beacon has been activated."

Arak made a sound like an electrical short. He pressed something on his shoulder. "Ready transport to the launch point." To Ik and Julie he said, "I need you to accompany me. Now."

Julie could only nod numbly. But Ik said, "Wait!" and turned to Antares. "You stay here and—hrah!—do what you said you would do, yes?" He asked Cromus and Arak, "Will you assist her, as she asked?" When Cromus clicked in the affirmative, Ik said to Antares, "We will send word when we can."

"We must go!" Arak snapped, and herded them away to the star-spanner platform, leaving Antares and Napoleon behind, with Cromus.

This local spanner bubble felt to Julie like a flying command center. Arak spoke little to them; he was busy keeping tabs on everything that was happening in the black hole system. Data-holos kept popping up and disappearing all over the inside of the bubble. Arak was not silent, though; he was in constant, raspy communication with a series of voices the stones could not, or did not, translate.

Julie focused on what she could see outside. One distant object, closer to the black hole, seemed to be their destination: a cylindrical structure wreathed in coils, with spiky protuberances at one end. From the other end shone a spectral beam of light, shooting off to the right toward the glowing, mottled central disk of the Milky Way. She knew without asking: that was the ghost-stream, or a carrier for it. The energy that powered it presumably was coming from the black hole, but how that was accomplished, she could not see.

At one point, Arak paused in his agitated communications and stood twitching his fingers. He glanced in Julie's direction, and she caught his eye and said, "The team. What can you tell us about them?"

Arak sputtered, clearly not welcoming the question.

Welcome or not, Julie persisted. "I mean it. Who are they? What kind of people are they?"

Arak seemed shocked that she would ask such questions at a time like this. "What possible difference does it make?"

"Hrah!" Ik said. He had grasped at once what Julie was trying to do. "If we are to advise them on defense against the Mindaru, it is best, hrah, we know what—" *rasp* "—stuff they are made of."

Arak's face distorted in what Julie took to be displeasure. But he said, "All right. There are three crew members, they are clan-brothers of the Ratan race. They are officers of the home defense forces."

"Hrah—warriors?"

"Yes," Arak said. "Elite. Part of a unit trained in close virtual coordination."

Julie and Ik looked at each other. Virtual coordination? "Do they have enhancements?" Ik asked, tapping his head with a finger.

"Of course they do," Arak said. At that moment, several holo reports sprang up, and he turned to respond. Outside, the cylindrical station was growing large in the viewport. When Arak gave them his attention again, he was even less patient than before. "Definitely under attack! What are your suggestions?"

Ik's voice grew sharp with distress. "You must ask them— can they shut down their enhancements? At once?"

Arak shook his head. "I don't think contact is clear enough. Look, we are arriving."

Outside, the station mushroomed in size. The deck trembled, and with an abrupt flash of silver and dark, they were inside and docked. Arak led them out of the bubble and through some glass doors, and they started across a hangar area that looked larger and more rough-edged than the one they had used for their own mission. Against the far wall was a huge cylindrical apparatus like an enormous rocket on its side, with coils and studs that seemed to mirror the outside of the main structure. This, Arak confirmed, was the particle-stream launcher. It looked immense compared to the one that had sent the two of them into the past, but it also had an unfinished look. Its end on the right passed through a half-silvered hangar wall, where it emitted the beam of ghostly violet light Julie had seen before.

"That's where they are, physically," Arak said, gesturing to a bulge in the cylinder before turning sharply to the right to lead them into an open control area. "But we can't reach them physically, not while they are in the entangled state."

"What would happen if you just opened it?" Julie asked.

Arak cocked his head in a gesture that looked almost human. "A catastrophic release of energy, I should think. We have never tried it. There is a precarious balance of extremely high energies being maintained inside that machine."

A rugged-looking, shaggy-haired individual with a mashed-in face and five arms met them as they entered the control circle. "Targus," Arak said. "These are the first-mission time-travelers. Update, please." To Ik and Julie he said, "Targus is Launch Director."

"We have contact, barely," Targus said.

"Let us hear."

They crowded around a console. Still images of three crewmen were on-screen, with rippling concentric circles beneath the right-hand one, presumably the one speaking. His face had fur, and a snout; his eyes were bright. *"Trying to get back ... outrace them ... pursuing hard."*

Arak took the comm. "This is Arak. Are they attempting to penetrate your AI network? Are they hacking you?"

"Yes. Yes. Firewall down ..."

Ik winced visibly and said to Arak. "Hrah! You must ask them, can they shut their enhancements down—can they shut *everything* down? *Everything!*"

Arak looked to Targus. "Could they get back without intelligence aids?"

"I am not certain—"

"You must!" Ik barked. "Ask them!"

Arak spoke into the comm. "We are informed it may be impossible to stop Mindaru entry once they get in. Can you shut everything down? All AI systems?"

"Including their own enhancements!" Ik shouted.

"Personal AI. System AI. Everything!" Arak said.

The face looked distressed. *"We would ... blind ... deaf ..."*

Arak looked at Ik, who raised his left fist in confirmation. "That is right," Arak said into the comm. "Come back blind, but don't let the enemy penetrate your intelligence systems, under any circumstances." He glared at Ik. "Are you certain of this? Are you certain we're not killing them?"

Ik said nothing for a moment. He'd lowered his left hand, but was continuing to rhythmically squeeze the long fingers of both hands into fists, down at his sides. Finally he answered, "If they get back with their AI on, and they are Mindaru infested—"

"What?" Arak said. "You think they will—"

"They will kill us all," Ik said.

For the next two minutes, they waited with growing suspense as crude position estimates came in from the monitoring teams. The crew had gone deaf and blind, and there were no longer even telemetry signals to track them by.

"How long?" Arak asked Targus, who was questioning every controller who had any information.

"I do not—"

Targus was interrupted by a dazzling starburst, through the half-silvered wall of the hangar. A thundering *WHUMMP!* shook the station, and through a dazzling afterimage that left Julie reeling, she was aware of people running in many different directions. Blinking furiously and hanging with both hands onto the console's edge, she tried to see what was happening at the launcher. When the afterimage faded enough for her to see again, she made out two things.

The ghoststream had gone dark, and the giant, cylindrical launcher was enveloped in blue smoke.

Recovery operations began at once with a swarm of suited personnel and heavy equipment crowded around the launcher.

"What caused that?" Ik asked, his normally rock-steady voice trembling a little. He looked more shaken than Julie had ever seen him; this had to be visceral reminder of his own near-fatal encounters.

Arak was swinging his multiple arms in agitation. He was shaken too, she thought. "Apparently the . . . entanglement feedback . . . peaked destructively."

"But why? Because of the energy surge? Because of the attempt to close off the timestream?" Julie asked.

Arak turned to bark several questions, or commands, into the comm. Then he said, "Magnified somehow. The team was trying to block the Mindaru. When they shut down their AIs, they might not have been able to control the surge anymore." With his uppermost hand, Arak rubbed wearily at his forehead. "It is hard to know."

In a few minutes, Targus came back. "It is terrible," he said. "The power was terrible. They had no chance."

Julie accepted that soberly, while wondering, *What the hell are we doing here? We don't know anything about this. Did we just make matters worse? Did we kill those three?*

But Targus turned his ruined-looking face toward her and Ik. His eyes were now blotches of scarlet. "I can assure you," he said. "We do all possible to ensure the safety of ghoststream operations. But you understand, yes, these are emergency conditions?" He extended one of his hands to Arak and began reeling off some technical information.

Julie met Ik's gaze. *Were we part of the cause?* Ik, she knew, was thinking the same thing. *Stones?* But the stones remained silent.

When Targus finished the breathless technical rundown with Arak, he suddenly included Ik and Julie in the conversation again. "We will make adjustments. For the next mission."

"What next mission?" Julie asked harshly. "Are you trying to tell us someone can travel safely—after that?"

"*Hrah!*" said Ik. "I want to know what happened to the last team, and why!"

Julie said, "We know there was a power surge, but . . ."

Targus produced an expression that did not improve the appearance of his face. "That is nearly *all* we know."

Ik's voice was barely a growl. "Rrrrm, you must know more than that. How did they die?"

Julie suddenly wished she knew more about those three departed souls—or else maybe that she'd never heard of them. Who had they left behind when they died?

Targus glanced at Arak, who made a clicking sound—apparently signifying permission to speak. "We have no physical remains to examine. The collapse of the strained entanglement over such a span . . ." Targus paused, perhaps searching for words. "The molecules of their bodies . . . likely disassociated in the moment of the flash. Essentially instantaneous."

Julie tried to stop thinking about the three, tried to stop thinking of *herself* in their place.

"We will attempt to gain information," Targus continued. "From the instruments and AI memory—"

Ik's face froze, and then he shouted, hands flying up, *"No! You must not!"*

Targus's hollowed-out face looked even more distressed. "Why? We must learn what happened."

Ik took a single stride forward, his long-fingered hands practically framing Targus's face. "If there was *any* chance that the AI was exposed to the Mindaru, you *must not* try to connect to it!"

"But," Targus protested, "if we cannot analyze whatever is available, we cannot avoid repeating—"

"NO!" Ik's bark caused Targus to jerk back. Ik lowered his voice, but his tone was commanding. *"You must not!"*

Arak started to rasp out a question, but Ik brought him to silence with a chopping gesture. "It is because—" and he paused to take a slow, deliberate breath "—if your intelligence systems came into contact with Mindaru *in any way*, they could be infected. And if infected—"

"Hrrrk-k-k," said Arak. "Here on the station we have tools to deal with infection."

"Not *this* infection."

Another rasp. "I think you underestimate our—"

"Not this infection! If you have never dealt with it, you cannot know. I *have*, and it nearly killed me, and it *did* kill my voice—my yaantel-stones!" Ik took a moment to compose himself. "You said you wanted our help because of our experience with the Mindaru. If you meant that, then listen to me! You must physically destroy the intelligence memory, if any of it remains."

Arak hissed a slow breath in and out. "We did seek your experience." He turned to Julie. "And you?"

She swallowed, remembering all too vividly. "When I faced something like this, the yaantel and I destroyed it by throwing it into our sun."

Arak winced. With one eye still scanning the two of them, he said to Targus, "You must destroy the memory core, then."

"Not just the core," Ik said. "All of it. Any component that could conceivably carry any trace of activity."

"That would be the whole structure," Targus said. "The physical crew compartment is embedded with programmable matter."

"At once, then!" Ik said. "Quickly! Down to the molecular level!"

Targus tapped the fingers of two hands together. "I am not certain how—"

"Magnetic containment," Arak said. "Incinerate, then shoot it into the black hole. Yes?" That last was to Ik and Julie.

Ik said, "I have no better suggestion."

Julie said nothing. She was still shuddering at the possibility of Mindaru malware invading the systems they would use to travel in time.

"That leaves us precious little data," said Targus. "Adjusting the next mission—*your* next mission—now even more urgent. I am sorry. We will—"

"Hrah," Ik cried. "What do you mean, *our* next mission? You have not yet told us the *goal* of the next mission! Do you expect *us* to try to stop the Mindaru that just killed this crew?"

Arak brought three of his hands together. His voice was thick and harsh as he said, "That is not possible, I think. No, we want you to look for a way to stop the entry of any *more* Mindaru into the timestream. Find another way, without triggering ... this ..." The three hands parted as he extended his arms toward the wreckage.

"Is that all?" Julie asked incredulously.

Arak gestured for them to follow Targus, who was trudging out the far side of the control circle. "That is all we know now. More may be added later."

Julie laughed bitterly. But still, after what had just happened, she felt too responsible not to step up next. She sighed. "Where is the army of experts that will tell us how to do all that?"

"No army," said Arak, "can do what you do."

"I'm not sure what you think we can do," Julie said.

Arak gazed at them soberly. "Travelers, listen. Other Mindaru may be swarming into the timestream. Once they are here . . ." He paused, and his hands dropped to his sides. "I do not just ask—we need you to go back and learn if there is still an opening." Targus had led them wordlessly to a drop-rail. As they peered over the side to a great emptiness below, Targus stepped into the opening in the floor. He dropped out of sight. Arak gestured to Julie and Ik to follow. Julie clutched the rail and stepped through the floor to an eye-popping, bird's-eye view of an equally immense hangar one level down from the hangar they had just been observing. It was just one story down, but it was one hell of a high story. She came to a gentle landing, followed by Ik and Arak.

"So," she said, picking up the thread, "if we get there and find Mindaru *are* coming through, what then? What are we supposed to do? Do you have thoughts on *how*?"

"Stop them," Arak said simply. "You are the most experienced Mindaru fighters in Shipworld. We will give you all the knowledge and help we can."

"Oh, well, if that's all . . ." She laughed hollowly.

"Miss Stone," Arak said, gesturing for them to follow Targus toward a duplicate of the launcher they'd just seen reduced to smoking rubble. "We cannot guarantee your safety. You can see that. We are sending you to try to stop a far greater danger to all of us, to all of the worlds. We are in a state of—" *rasp* "—war."

Julie nodded. All of that was true. But it didn't help her understand *how* to do what needed to be done.

Ik gazed at Julie with his hard, deep-set eyes. She closed her own eyes for a moment and shivered. *I wonder what will happen if John and his other friends shut off the timestream from Karellia while we're in there.* And following that thought, she imagined beings like the one she and the translator had fought running free through the galaxy. "All right," she said. "When do we go?"

"Hrrm," Ik said, gesturing with an open hand toward the new launcher. "Soon, yes?" And then his voice hardened. "But you must send us better prepared than this poor crew that just died."

CHAPTER 6

Return to Karellia

THE LANDING SITE the Karellian escort craft directed them to was the Kantong Spaceport, on the eastern seaboard of the continent of Moramia. The names were unfamiliar to Li-Jared. The spaceport had not existed when he lived on Karellia; space travel had been in its infancy then. It was located just south of a coastal city which in Li-Jared's time had been a provincial capital known as Harlendon, but now was called Karellendon and apparently was the world capital. In his absence, it seemed, Karellia had grown from a planet of fragmented continental governments to one with a world government. He didn't know if that was good or bad for the Karellian people generally; but if it meant they only had to talk to one government, he was deeply relieved.

On the glide inbound over the sun-spanked waters of the Karellendon harbor, Li-Jared handled communication while Bandicut flew the lander. Akura and Sheeawn sat behind them, gripping their seats. The approach turned exciting when one of the Karellian escorts steered them into a course change without warning. The sudden maneuvering left Li-Jared with his hearts pounding, but Bandicut took it in stride, and even had time to glance over his shoulder to remind the passengers to breathe. He brought them smoothly around to a landing in the middle of the southernmost quadrant of the field.

Their escort set down beside them on the tarmac, thrusters glowing. For a moment, Li-Jared just breathed in and out, thinking,

I am about to set foot on home, and breathe Karellian air. He felt a pressure in his chest that would not go away. Bandicut grinned and said something congratulatory that Li-Jared missed; he was too busy absorbing it all. Back on home soil for the first time in hundreds of years, he hardly knew what to think or feel. For a few moments he simply sat, listening to the pounding of blood in his forehead.

Home. World of beautiful, perilous sky.

"Everyone unfasten," Bandicut called out. "Li-Jared, do you still think we should step out together? Or do you want to go first and smooth the waters?"

That wrenched Li-Jared back to reality. Glancing out the view-port, he saw a cordon of soldiers gathering around the spacecraft. Well, that made sense, he supposed. "Let me go first," he said. "Give them time to get used to the idea of a homecoming native—"

"Before you spring an ugly human face on them?"

Li-Jared flicked his fingertips in a shrug. "Something like that." He glanced back at the anxious Uduon guests, decided Bandicut could explain anything that needed explaining, and made his way to the side exit. He hesitated a moment, wondering whether or not to put on a suit shield. It might create an unnecessary barrier; on the other hand, it would give him a dramatic entrance. *It'll get their attention and make a point about our technology.* He hissed a chuckle at the notion that this technology was in any way *his*. But never mind that. It was, for now. He flicked on the suit.

The exit slid open, and he stepped out to meet his country-men.

Bandicut, following Li-Jared's movements on viewscreen, thought this looked a lot like their greeting on Uduon—with one big dif-ference. The difference was in Li-Jared himself. Instead of step-ping out to greet individuals he assumed were enemies, he was greeting his countrymen, even if they were too cautious and sus-picious to realize it at first. While they were just as concerned as the Uduon had been about who was under that gleaming silver, and what his intentions were, Li-Jared walked and spoke with the poise of one who knew he was home. They talked back and forth, and Li-Jared repeated his credentials as a Karellian scientist of several hundred years ago. There were instrument scans and communications with authorities not on the scene. Li-Jared did a remarkable job of keeping his composure. Eventually he lowered his suit screens so they could see him face to face. More questions. Three times he pointed to the sky. Presently they seemed prepared to accept that he was, as he claimed, a Karellian returned from the stars.

"Time to suit up," Bandicut said to Akura and Sheeawn. "I think he'll be calling us out soon."

The call came before they were finished clipping suit projectors to their belts.

The Karellian air cooled Li-Jared's face and whispered through his clothing as he waited for his friends to emerge. He squinted in the bright sunlight, shading his eyes with one hand. For a blissful minute, he simply drank in the sensations. *Two hundred and seventy-six years. It feels good. I wonder how much the place has changed.*

Then he turned to greet the three silver-suited figures stepping into the daylight. Li-Jared could feel tensions sharpen. The soldiers in the first line dropped their weapons to a ready position, aimed directly at the silver figures. The group leader called, "Will you ask them to remove their protection, as you did? We need to see them."

Li-Jared rubbed his fingertips together. "Will you avert your weapons, so they need not feel threatened?"

The leader barked an imprecation at the ground, and then stared at him with what looked to Li-Jared like steely animosity. "I have more to think of than whether or not your passengers feel threatened."

"Perhaps. But I will not ask them to drop their protection while you are pointing guns at them," Li-Jared said. He made a sweeping gesture at the arc of soldiers. "Don't you have the situation under control? And you wish to see our guests, yes? That can't happen as long as they feel . . . *unwelcome*. I gave them my assurance of safe passage as diplomatic visitors. And I give you my assurance, as a Karellian citizen, that they are unarmed and that their mission is peaceful."

The leader barked again, but gave his left hand a twitch, and the soldiers in the front line raised their weapons to a rest position.

Li-Jared touched his fingertips to his forehead in acknowledgment, then said to his companions, "All right, this would be a good time for you to lower your suits. But keep your fingers near the buttons. Okay?"

One silver-suit vanished, revealing Bandicut. He blinked in the sunlight, then went to assist Akura and Sheeawn. Finally all three stood revealed, facing the soldiers.

Surprise was visible on more than one face. The group leader angled his head slightly. His body swayed right, then left, as he studied them. "Two of you," he said, "appear to be Karellian. Is that right?"

Li-Jared started to answer, then decided to let Akura and Sheeawn speak for themselves if they wanted to. Sheeawn looked terrified, but he didn't flinch as he glanced at Akura for permission, and then said, "If I . . . understand your question correctly . . ."

"The question is simple. Are you Karellian?"

"We are Uduon. From the planet Uduon," Sheeawn answered simply.

The leader's eyes flickered orange, and he shifted his gaze to bore into Li-Jared's. "They look Karellian. Like you." An accusation remained unspoken in the air.

"Yes, they do, don't they?" Li-Jared said. "They are not from this world, though. I believe they might not object if you performed the same scan on them that you ran on me." Turning to Sheeawn, he explained the procedure, and raised a hand to hold off questions until Sheeawn asked Akura, and then expressed agreement for both of them.

"You can scan me, too, if you like," Bandicut said, speaking for the first time since emerging from the craft.

That seemed to startle the group leader, but he gestured to the two soldiers who had wielded the scanners on Li-Jared. They stepped forward and reran the operation first on the two Uduon, and then on Bandicut. The first soldier made a clicking sound. "I cannot be certain of these two. I do not believe they are Karellian, but the resemblance is close. A specialist might see more than I can."

"And the third?"

"Clearly not Karellian. What exactly he is, I cannot—"

"Human," Bandicut interrupted. "I am human."

"So Li-Jared said," the group leader replied, and then turned to receive a report from another soldier. He straightened to speak. "It would seem our researchers have discovered some facts relevant to your claim. Apparently there really *was* a Holdhope Academy in the region once called Watskland."

"Why would that be in doubt?" Li-Jared asked in annoyance.

The officer gave him a sour look. "Are you not aware? A lot has happened on Karellia. Records have been lost, names have changed . . ."

Li-Jared felt a sudden emptiness in his chest. *Records lost, names changed. War?* What had happened to his world while he was away? "I . . . Yes, of course, I suppose that would be true." *And why so surprised? Of course things happened. Change.*

The leader was now pressing something to his ear, and making low muttering sounds. When he spoke to Li-Jared again, his tone was different. "I have instructions to escort you to the harbor, where you will find transport by water to the House of Meeting, on the north shore of the bay. It seems your request to speak to a government official has been granted. Someone wants to hear your story."

With that, the leader spoke to his closest team members. Then he turned back. "Do you have everything you need? The boat is waiting."

The transport turned out to be a high-speed hydrofoil, waiting with engines humming. The area seemed to have been cleared, which disappointed Li-Jared. He'd been hoping for a glimpse of ordinary people on their ordinary business—did ordinary business still look the way it used to?—or even spectators come to see the aliens. But he saw no one as they crossed to the boat from the personnel carrier that had brought them from the spaceport.

Now, as they streaked across the white-foamed water of the bay, sun glinting in his eyes, Li-Jared found his thoughts not on the meeting to come so much as on this remarkable homecoming to a changed world. He had dreamed of coming back one day, of course, but he hadn't really known what to expect. Now that he was here, his eyes, his ears, his hearts were drinking in the surroundings. Some of it was Karellia as he had known it, but in other ways it was a new world to him. The water travel! The old Li-Jared would have been uncomfortable, at best, crossing even slightly rough water at speed. But after the world of the Neri, the Li-Jared of today found the water exhilarating. He was aware he was being watched by his escorts, but he didn't care. They could report his reactions. He was going to take it all in.

The buildings, the modes of transportation, even the people seemed changed. Granted he hadn't seen many people yet. But on the whole, those he had seen seemed a little taller, on average—and maybe a little less quick on the uptake (or had they always been that way?). What were things like on Karellia, politically? When he'd lived here, during the Soldani reign on the North Continent, the leadership of his own nation-state had been corrupt enough to make anyone want to leave the planet. He hoped *that* had changed. He gazed across the bay, closing his eyes for just a moment to feel the deck and the railing vibrate with the boat's movement, and he tried to form a new picture of the world he had returned to.

It was going to take some getting used to.

———

Not far to Li-Jared's right, Akura was sitting with Sheeawn, trying to form her own picture of this world, nemesis to her own.

Although they had been greeted by soldiers, she did not feel a sense of an overly militarized culture, not in the tiny sample she had seen so far. Even from orbit, they had seen no overt signs of threat, no bristling arrays of rockets ready to launch the next barrage. In fact, in many superficial ways, this world did not seem strikingly foreign. Even the people seemed much the same, beneath the strange clothing styles. The architecture was different, to be sure—seemingly constructed by hand or machine, rather than organically grown.

What she was searching for most intently was some sense of the under-connection, the invisible, inaudible threads and currents that on Uduon drew all of the continents and all of the people together, at least among the Watchers. Not perfectly, of course. But all Uduon felt it, on some level. Here, though, she felt nothing. "Perhaps we are just in the wrong place to sense it," she murmured to Sheeawn, who wisely said nothing, it not being his area of knowledge. She didn't really believe it could be altogether absent; she couldn't imagine a world that did *not* have them. Surely, hidden in this wild body of water . . .

Sheeawn seemed awestruck by the water, and the stinging salt spray. But his sensibilities were different. He was a fisher, at home on water.

Alien. It's an alien world. Forget that at your peril.

There was nothing they could do but let it play out, and see what they could learn.

The approaching shore grew, the engines throttled back, and the boat eased back down off the hydrofoils into the water and motored up to a landing. Li-Jared had no more idea what to expect here than did his companions. The dock was flanked by two boat sheds and a low office building, behind which a neatly trimmed sward of grass sloped uphill to what looked like an estate, or academic center, or significant government office.

They didn't have long to wonder. A land vehicle conveyed them up to the building. Li-Jared almost didn't want to get out. The car—with plush seats, huge windows, and electronic controls— was advanced so far beyond anything he remembered that he wished he could ride around in it all day. Instead, they entered the building through a huge, open lobby with a floor that Bandicut remarked looked to him like "marble." A curving stairway that glided upward while seeming suspended in mid-air swept them past the second floor and up to the third. Guards, or at least officials, were unobtrusively everywhere, watching the aliens and the mystery-Karellian, all being brought here to meet "the Ocellet," whoever that was. Perhaps Li-Jared was projecting, but it seemed to him that the air crackled with excitement at the visitors from the stars. Well, it was no less electrifying for him.

A circular hallway brought them to an office. They each passed in front of a battery of scanners, clearly set up in haste for the occasion. There was a delay while the screeners examined some image-projecting equipment they had brought along. But after all was declared safe, they were led into a small but well-appointed meeting room—not rectangular, but wider at the far end, with curved bay windows. In the center sat a wedge-shaped table echoing the shape of the room. At the table's apex was a single seat. The company were directed to four seats at the wider, rounded end; they would sit with their backs to the windows. Flanking the seat of honor, on each side, was a single additional seat.

The four took their places, and a minute passed; then a door opened in the wall to their right. A Karellian male and female entered, the male wearing a dark-green tunic with markings around the collar, probably military, and the female dressed in a one-piece, gray suit that looked civilian. They were followed by a second female—petite, with white-streaked hair, dressed in a long coat of a smooth, reddish-maroon fabric with gold piping down the sides. Her eyes were bright, with intense, blue-green bands. The company all got to their feet as she approached the single seat, and stood with the other two flanking her. The seven of them stood staring at one another for a long moment, before the female who was the obvious leader spoke. "You are Li-Jared?"

Li-Jared placed his fingertips on the tabletop, as though to give himself a small anchor point as he leaned forward. "I am."

"I am Ocellet Kim Quin," she said, touching her chest. "These are my science adviser, Aylen," she added with a gesture to the female on her left, "and Chief Commander Koro, representing our defense forces." A nod to the male on her right—who, Li-Jared decided, was probably a little older than he was. High ranking, definitely. The Ocellet focused intensely on Li-Jared, her eyes ablaze. "I am told you have come asking for me. Come from . . . the *stars*, you say? From someplace not on this planet?"

Li-Jared bowed his head momentarily. "Yes, Ocellet Kim Quin. I have come from extremely far away."

"Well, then, this is an extraordinary event for us!" she said, and her voice seemed to carry a genuine sense of awe about the occasion. "I hope this is something we can celebrate!" But there was a carefully guarded something else in her voice. "We have never had visitors from another world before. And to be honest, your arrival has left many of us in a state of . . . well, *disbelief* is probably not too strong a word."

"I understand, Ocellet."

"Yes. But our space command did track your arrival, so we must believe that. Also, at least one of you is clearly not Karellian." Bandicut stirred, and she paused to eye him with a steely glint. "Is this one of the aliens you stated took you away from your home?"

Li-Jared started to reply, but Bandicut spoke first. "No, ma'am, I am not. I am a Human of planet Earth, and I am a fellow traveler with my friend Li-Jared. My story is somewhat similar to his."

"I see," said Quin. "I had not realized you would be able to speak for yourself."

"Yes, ma'am—Madame Ocellet," Bandicut said.

Quin gazed at him a moment longer, then shifted back to Li-Jared. "You say you are a Gamut Professor of mathematical physics, from a Karellia of almost three hundred years ago—and that you were, as we said, taken by aliens and then brought back. That is an extraordinary claim!"

Li-Jared bowed his head again. "Yes, those are my extraordinary claims, and they are quite true. You, I hope, will have found some record that can support my past claim. For my friends, I can offer as affidavit only my word—*plus*, of course, the evidence of their presence here. Ocellet Quin, this is a tremendously exciting homecoming for me! But I am afraid it is much more than that. To be direct, we have come with urgent matters to discuss. Far more urgent than the question of my heritage."

"Indeed." Quin glanced at Aylen, who was listening intently and muttering into a note-taking device, and her military chief, whose expression masked any visible emotion. "We will certainly hear you out on that. But as for your first claim, we *do* in fact have some records—perhaps more than our greeting party shared—of a professor *by your name*, from two hundred seventy-some years ago, whose picture looks strikingly like you." She sighed out a breath. "Please. Won't you all sit?"

As they settled into their places around the table, Li-Jared tilted his head. "Forgive me, but does the title 'Ocellet' mean you are leader of the entire planet?"

"You *have* been away a long time. The title 'Ocellet' has been in use for over one hundred years. It designates the elected leader of the five free continents."

"Five free . . ." Li-Jared's mind raced. "So . . . not the entire planet?" He flushed, hoping he hadn't overstepped the bounds of courtesy. "Forgive me again. There was no worldwide government of any kind, in my time."

The Ocellet allowed a small, hissing chuckle. "Of course. Also, there were turbulent times between then and now. A lot has changed."

"I'm sure," Li-Jared muttered, dying to know more. But now wasn't the time.

"There are still a few regions holding out. But most of the population of Karellia regard me as their leader. Whether most of them approve or not is harder to say." There was a momentary glimmer of humor in Quin's eyes, but it was replaced at once by a steely gaze as she contemplated the company.

Li-Jared felt his two hearts swing momentarily out of sync. This was the person he needed to convince, then. It wasn't going to be easy. Time to earn his pay. He managed to loosen his tongue and say, "Thank you, then, for seeing us . . . with so little warning." A clicking chuckle escaped, unbidden.

Quin's eyes brightened, narrowed. Her military representative, Koro, stirred. The science adviser looked intent, containing her obvious excitement. "Really," Quin said, "can you imagine my *not* meeting with visitors from outer space, whatever the notice? But it seems we have a lot to talk about, including your story—where you have been, and why you are here now. But perhaps you could start by introducing your companions to me." Her voice hardened as she gazed at the Uduon. "Because the information I received said that these two represent the world that has been *attacking Karellia with asteroids.*"

"Well . . . yes." Li-Jared took a deep breath and began the introductions.

Ocellet Quin listened to every word, but her mind was afire. Not only was she meeting aliens from outer space for the first time, but she was facing her world's mortal enemies, also for the first time. Far from being the bizarre aliens she had imagined in her nightmares, they looked just like her and her kinsmen. Put different clothes on them, and they could melt into any Karellian crowd. The one called Bandicut was an anomaly, not involved in the conflict. She mentally set him aside for the moment. He might be interesting later, but he was not part of the war.

Because war it was, whether they had ever met their adversary or not.

And now she was going to hear why these *Uduon* were attacking her world. "I may be honored to meet you," she said bluntly, once the introductions were over, "but my people want to know why you are throwing rocks at our planet. Rocks large enough to cause untold damage and many deaths, if we allowed them to strike their targets." She wasn't going to tell them about the

Karellian defenses that prevented that—and which Karellia fortunately had already put in place against a particular swarm of naturally falling asteroids.

The one called Akura, the Watcher, spoke through her translator, Sheeawn. "We only defend our world, Ocellet. When missiles from *your* planet exploded in our skies, killing many, we had no choice but to—"

Commander Koro interrupted her before Quin could stop him. "I am sorry, but what missiles are you referring to? We *never* launched missiles at your world, not until long after you began hostilities with your space rocks!"

No, not until the asteroids started falling, Quin thought. *But after that . . .*

Akura recoiled from the outburst, but if anything her demeanor hardened. "My words are true," she said, "and I will show you." She murmured to Sheeawn, who placed on the table a small holo projector. Through Sheeawn, she explained the moving images that sprang into the air: fiery objects streaking through the skies of Uduon, and the smoking ruins of a city. The images were stark and silent, and the effect was chilling. Quin studied them with mixed emotions: shock, horror, detachment. And doubt.

Akura continued. "We did not even know of your planet's *existence* until this happened. But we have spacefaring capabilities of our own. We tracked those missiles that attacked us—right back to their points of origin. And that path led directly to *this world!*" The image of the destruction was replaced by an animated diagram of trajectories in space. Akura took a breath before concluding, "Do you wonder why my people call your world the demon planet? And so I ask: What causes you to rain death down on my people?"

Quin felt her face contorting through several expressions. This was more astonishing than the appearance of visitors from space! What was she supposed to think? She'd been expecting demands, perhaps. Claims of conquest. Not this! She drew a breath, choosing her words carefully. "Honestly, Watcher—this is very difficult for us to believe!"

"It is impossible!" Koro barked, standing. "We have launched missiles, yes. But every single one has followed the track back of a falling asteroid."

Akura spread her hands, as though to frame the images. "Here is the proof! How can you not believe it?"

Quin gazed back at her incredulously. "Really! You call it proof—but how can we know those pictures were not taken *after* one of your attacks on our world?"

Akura's face darkened with rage. Her hands shook. "Can you not read the dates on the images?"

Quin flicked a shrug. "Dates can be falsified. And we do not even know your dating system."

Akura stared at her in shocked disbelief. "You believe we traveled all this distance to show you falsified images?"

"Well, I—"

Li-Jared interrupted to say, "The analysis on our ship supports the authenticity of the dates, Ocellet. Our science—adviser— Jeaves is quite thorough. He has correlated these dates to celestial dating, and converted to your system for confirmation."

Quin waved him off. "That may be, but I do not understand *why* you think we would do such a thing! Why would we want to harm your world? You say you did not know of the existence of *our* world. But we did not know of the existence of *your* world, either—or at least not your civilization—until bombs began falling on our own. So we did the only thing we could. We fought back. But of your *people*, we knew nothing at all, until today."

Koro started to speak again, but Quin snapped her fingers to silence him. He looked startled and a little offended, but Quin couldn't afford to care about that now. She spoke in measured words to the Watcher. "So you came here to assert your *contention* that *we* attacked your world first. Watcher, I am afraid my people, and my government, would never accept that contention."

Akura sat back, infuriated. She turned to Sheeawn and conferred in Uduon. Finally she addressed Quin again. "If you do not believe our evidence, consider this: Why would *we want war*? What could we gain? You have nothing we want. We defend ourselves and nothing more."

Quin closed her eyes a moment. *How could this be?* she thought. *It is impossible.* But what she said was, "We, Watcher of Uduon, also fight only to defend ourselves. Koro—" she graced him with a gesture "—spoke truth, when he said that until we were attacked, we never struck at any world." She glanced to her left. "What is it, Aylen?"

Her science adviser rose to speak close, in a whisper. "May we confer privately for a moment, Ocellet?" Her eyes were wide.

Quin addressed the others. "Excuse us briefly." She took Aylen's arm and steered her away from the table. "All right. What is it?"

Aylen was unusually agitated. She whispered urgently, "Ocellet, I need to make sure you are aware of something."

"What? Tell me."

"Do you remember the series of deep space probes launched many years ago? When we were still in school?"

"Of course," Quin murmured. "When *you* were still in school. But still, before my time in office. Those were not weapons. They were simple exploratory probes, weren't they?"

Aylen whispered back, "I don't know details, except that they were launched toward the sister star system. I'll need to pull together information. But as I remember it, they never returned or were heard from after they passed through the radiation belts. I wonder if it's possible—"

"That they're connected?" Quin was stunned by the suggestion. "That seems extremely unlikely. But we must look into it, just in case. Go get someone on it at once. Learn everything you can. But get right back here. I need you." Aylen acknowledged and hurried from the room. Koro looked at Quin questioningly. She motioned him over and filled him in. He looked skeptical, but said nothing.

As she was returning to the table, Li-Jared spoke up suddenly. "Ocellet Quin, Akura, forgive me. These are important questions. They need answers. They do. But they are *not the only questions*— or even the most important."

Quin settled in her seat, squinting at him. "Explain that statement, please."

Li-Jared pushed himself to his feet. "I will try. This is about the *real* reason we came here in the first place. This will take a few minutes to explain. I will try to be brief. But it is crucial that you understand."

"Very well," Quin said. Akura was impassive. Aylen slipped back into the room and took up her post listening.

Li-Jared bowed and looked briefly at each person in the room. "The reason I—*we*—brought these two people of Uduon here to meet you is that there is a much greater—a *far deadlier*—threat facing both your worlds. Facing you right now."

Aylen leaned forward, squinting. But Koro hissed in disbelief. "What threat could be greater than asteroids falling out of the sky?"

Quin angled her head. "The commander has a point, Li-Jared."

Li-Jared bobbed in response, but continued, "Nevertheless, there *is* a greater threat! To explain it, I must first tell you where I have been, and what brought me back."

Koro placed both of his hands flat on the table and listened at erect attention. Aylen was barely breathing. She was probably learning more today than she had in her entire career. They all were. Quin gestured to Li-Jared to continue.

"We—" and he nodded to Bandicut "—have been living and working together in a place called Shipworld. It is almost inconceivably far away in space, far beyond the Heart of Fire, and far beyond either of our worlds' suns. I could tell you more about that later. But for now, here's what you need to know: Shipworld is a place that gathers folk from thousands of different worlds, and . . . well . . . how to explain?" Li-Jared glanced at Bandicut for help.

Holy mother of night, Quin thought. *Are we really having this conversation? With aliens?*

The human said, "It's a society that seeks to ensure survival among many worlds. Thousands of people there have been rescued from worlds like yours. Like my own. Often from worlds facing cataclysmic dangers."

"I see," said Quin, though she didn't at all.

Aylen asked, in a voice tinged with amazement, "How did you get *there?* From Karellia?"

Li-Jared flicked his fingers. "That story can wait, I think. I am trying to be brief."

Quin spread her hands on the table. "Aylen, can you contain your curiosity?" The scientist sighed in frustration but gestured affirmatively.

"What is important now," Li-Jared said, "is that from Shipworld, a grave danger was discovered, one that could threaten, not just entire *worlds*, but the entire—" He paused, searching for a word that would convey *galaxy*. He finally said it as Bandicut would.

"The what?" Koro asked.

"*Galaxy.* Sorry. That means a great many worlds—and their stars—suns—millions of them." He stretched his hands in the air, and a note of wonder crept into his voice. "We can't see them from here, because of the energy clouds. But when you're out beyond the Heart of Fire, you will see a sky filled with stars."

Quin waved off the description. She glanced at Aylen, who shrugged, as if to say, *Yes, we know.* "And this matters to us?"

"It matters more than you can imagine," said Li-Jared. "This peril threatens not just millions of worlds you can't see. It threatens *Karellia.*" He turned to gaze down at the still-seated Akura and Sheeawn. "And *Uduon.* In fact, Karellia and Uduon may well be the first targets of this threat. It is coming this way. And the reason it is coming is because of the war between your two worlds."

CHAPTER 7

All on the Table

FOR A WHILE, Li-Jared thought he had them on his side. The looks of astonishment were unmistakable. Aylen, in particular, looked as if she wanted to pepper him with questions. The importance of it all appeared to be sinking in.

But as the conversation went on, the central point started to slide away, as arguments once more erupted over who was to blame for the war. Karellia started it. Uduon started it. Holovids of fiery missiles. Denials, and angry voices. How could they stop the war if they didn't trust each other on the cause of it in the first place?

Li-Jared had to wrestle the subject back to what they needed to understand: what the *Mindaru* were, and what they could do. To both of them.

He tried to explain: The Mindaru were ruthless. They had nearly succeeded in *exploding a star.* "You have never seen a deadlier threat." He had not mentioned time-tides, the starstream, or the temporal distortion field. One step at a time. He wanted their attention; he didn't want them bewildered. In any case, the temporal shield was still a Karellian secret, and he didn't want to mention that yet.

Quin huddled with her science adviser. Aylen was practically beside herself. "If what they say is true, then it changes everything! We need to verify it, of course. But this could be *huge.*"

Quin turned back to Li-Jared. "Can you prove these things?"

Li-Jared raised his hands in supplication. "Yes, of course! But just for now, can you take my word for it, and let me finish?"

"Very well. You may finish explaining. These . . . Mindaru. You say they are not *alive*?"

"Not as we know life." Li-Jared scratched his neck, thinking. "It's not easy to explain . . ." That the Mindaru seemed to hate all biological life, and were astonishingly good at killing it. "We have had several encounters with them, and are lucky to be alive."

Commander Koro, who had been fuming, finally erupted. "*Have you led them here to us?* Because if you have . . ."

Li-Jared waved his hands in the air. "*No!* No, if they make it here—and I think they will—it will be because *you* led them here."

Quin's fists clamped tight in resistance to this suggestion. But Koro demanded, "Explain!"

L-Jared gulped air. "It's what I was trying to say before. It's because of your planetary defenses—and because of an enormous structure out in space called the *starstream*."

Koro's voice was sharp. "The *what*?"

"Starstream. You didn't make it—another culture did that—but your defensive screens are rippling outward into space, and causing changes in the starstream that will bring the Mindaru to you!"

That left them speechless for a good ten seconds, after which everyone started talking at once. Quin stood and rapped the table for silence. "The Uduon are to be escorted from the room," she said. "*Now.* Escorts, take them to the other meeting room until I call for them."

Li-Jared protested. "They need to hear this, as well."

The Ocellet waited until Akura and Sheeawn were out of the room, before she answered with a glare, "*I* will say if they may hear it. Now tell me exactly what you know of our defenses, and how you know!" Her eyes glinted dangerously. "And what you have told the Uduon."

Li-Jared suddenly realized how close he'd come to divulging the critical secret before he had gained their trust. Stupid. The secret had to be shared, but not yet. "My apologies."

Koro snorted. Quin gestured for Li-Jared to continue.

With a grimace, he did. "We know of your temporal displacement field, of course. We observed it diverting an asteroid, and for that matter, we have passed through it ourselves, in our ship. We have *not* told the Uduon about it. But we know what it does. It is an impressive device. The problem is not the protection it gives you, but its dangerous side effects."

"Which you keep saying. But what are they?" Quin asked tightly, with a glance at her science adviser. Aylen was focused wholly on Li-Jared's words. *Good*, he thought. He had their attention.

Li-Jared gestured to Bandicut, who pushed their own holo unit to the center of the table. Then, as images sprang up to display the same illustrations that Jeaves had used, back on Shipworld, he told them.

". . . and so, the result is that your defensive shield is, unfortunately, attracting the Mindaru directly toward *you*."

Li-Jared let out his breath slowly. "I am sure you have questions."

They most certainly did.

Li-Jared insisted that the Uduon should be brought back in, with his promise not to describe the planetary defenses. "But you'll have to tell them soon, because the only way to stop more Mindaru from coming is to turn off your shield."

Koro was adamantly negative. "We *know* the danger from these asteroids. We have only your word about the other."

Li-Jared closed his eyes and reached somewhere within himself for patience. "Listen to me," he said. "We know Karellia is under attack, yes. The Uduon feel under attack, too. But the universe is a *big* place—" he gestured with outstretched arms "—and there are *terrible things* out there, and what you are doing is causing them to threaten us—*all* of us—not just Karellia and Uduon, but many other worlds, as well. We are here representing a much greater civilization. And the message is, you are going to have to shut down your defensive shield, and soon, or it will be shut down for you. There will be no room for discussion."

Koro froze. "That sounds like a threat."

"It is *not* a threat. It is a statement of reality."

"Are you making the same statement of reality to Uduon?"

"We are, and we have," Li-Jared said, and that seemed to startle Koro. "They will stop throwing rocks, or they will *be* stopped. You are both at risk from a common enemy, and you need to put an end to this senseless war."

Akura and Sheeawn were brought back into the room. With Bandicut's help, Li-Jared was able to provide more information. The Uduon did not pretend to be happy—they knew crucial pieces were being withheld from them—but they listened to what Li-Jared and Bandicut had to say about the thing called the starstream, and of time distortions that passed down it, opening a door to danger. Everyone seemed suitably alarmed, but as soon as the conversation cycled back to the question of ending the interplanetary conflict, it all came back to pent-up rage and mistrust between them.

Finally Quin called a halt for the day. They had been at it for many hours, tempers were frayed, and it was time to break for food, and sleep.

The visitors were shown to guest quarters one floor up, where they were served a light dinner and shown to sleeping rooms. Everyone was tired, and there was little talk.

Bandicut was pulled away from a conversation with Li-Jared by a communication from Jeaves, waiting on the landing craft. "What is it?" Bandicut said, moving to a private corner so he could talk without disturbing the others. "Is everything okay on *The Long View?*"

"Quite okay," Jeaves said. "But you need to speed things along. Ruall says a long-range scan from a probe at the edge of the star system has picked up a contact moving this way. There is a chance it is the Mindaru we fought in the starstream."

Bandicut felt a bone-deep chill. "Hell! How fast?"

"Fast enough. It's probably reconnoitering. But Ruall says you need to wrap up quickly."

"Can you give us one more day?"

"Just that. No more."

By the time Bandicut went looking for Li-Jared to share the information, he found the Karellian sound asleep. *He must be exhausted,* Bandicut thought. *Best to let him rest.* Instead of waking him, Bandicut stretched out on a cot, closed his eyes, and focused inward to consult sadly with his memories of Charli, hoping that some quarxly wisdom would emerge from his grieving subconscious. It was in the midst of this imagined conversation that he finally fell asleep.

The following morning, Bandicut filled in Li-Jared, but neither was certain how they should proceed. The meeting began with a prickly debate about getting the military forces of two worlds to talk to each other. Bandicut listened to this for about five minutes before the memory of Charli, or maybe the stones, nudged him wordlessly and he suddenly made a decision.

He stood abruptly, cutting off Koro in the middle of a sentence, and waved his hands for attention.

He got their attention all right. The guards snapped to alert and leveled their weapons at him.

As Quin gestured to the guards to stand down, Bandicut gathered strength in his voice and said, "Look, I'm sorry for interrupting. But may I make a suggestion?" He paused for a beat. "Why don't we stop trying to sort this out here, and instead just *come up to our ship,* so you can see for yourselves? If you go into space with us, we can take you out beyond the radiation belt, even to the Heart of Fire! Then we can show you what's possible—and that this isn't just talk! You asked for proof of our extraordinary claims. I'm offering it!"

This was jumping the gun on their original plan, which was to invite the Karellians to the ship only after some consensus had been hammered out. But time for that was dwindling. Perhaps if they stood together on the bridge of *The Long View* and saw some of these things, the truth would start to seem less abstract and more real.

His proposal was met with stunned silence.

"I know this may seem out of left—well, I mean it's unexpected. But I'm utterly serious. Our ship is in orbit, under the watch of your patrol ships. It'll take less than an hour to get there in our landing craft. It'll take a little longer to get you beyond your radiation belt. And don't worry, you'll be shielded from the radiation." He turned and looked out the bay window and up into a cloudless sky. Did he see the faint, distant curtain of a fiery nebula in the sky?

He turned back to find Ocellet Kim Quin staring at him, her eyes lit by a sharp band of green.

"This is not a frivolous offer, Ocellet Quin. We are trying to describe things you need to see for yourself. Let us show you the stars, the galaxy, the starstream. Let us show you what lies beyond that nebula! And if it comes to that, let us show you the Mindaru!" He exchanged glances with Li-Jared. Was it too soon to tell them about the sighting?

"You patronize us," Koro said, drumming his fingers on the table. "Because we have not traveled as you have, among the . . . stars . . . you think our science is not—"

"Your science—*our* science—is excellent!" Li-Jared exclaimed, rising to stand beside Bandicut. "As far as it goes. At least it was, when I was last here." He paused; no one spoke. "But the universe outside is hidden from view! You can't know about the things you can't see!"

"Exactly," said Bandicut, deciding. "And here's the thing. Our ship just hours ago detected a possible Mindaru presence out at the edge of your solar system! We don't know how soon it might be here, but quite likely, it'll be fast."

The Karellians' faces were unreadable to Bandicut. Quin looked to Koro and Aylen for their silent reactions, before answering. "Suppose you speak the truth. Maybe you are! But we are at war now with people we cannot see! Given my responsibilities to protect my people, this seems an unusual risk. We could become hostages."

Or casualties, Bandicut thought. He turned his palms up. "We understand that, and we will guarantee your safety as much as humanly—" he cleared his throat "—as much as it can be guaranteed. Could something happen to you out there? It's possible. The situation is dangerous for all of us. That's why we're here."

"Yes, but—"

"Please." Bandicut gestured toward Akura, whose expression was contorted in what he took to be frustration and anger. "Look—Watcher Akura made the trip from Uduon with us, at similar risk. She is a leader of great importance to her people. Are you not, Watcher?" Akura tilted her head toward Sheeawn for the translation, then tapped her chest softly in modest affirmation. Bandicut continued, "We came to her just a few days ago—as *strangers*—just as we are to you, Ocellet Quin. But presented with these warnings, she agreed to travel with us to an utterly unknown world—a world that she believed had been attacking her own for years—to *trust* us—for the sake of the safety of her people. This is all we ask of you."

Quin hesitated a moment, then gestured to her aides, as if to say, *Comments?*

Aylen spoke at once. "How can there be any question? I am willing to go right now, if you permit it. A chance to see what's out there—to understand the situation better—to see the truth for ourselves?"

"I'm sure," Koro said dryly, "that this would be a wonderful opportunity for you to pursue science. But we're deciding matters of planetary security here."

"Which is why we need the facts, Commander. Aren't we agreed that if what they are telling us is true, then this is the biggest thing in our planet's history?"

"Perhaps," Koro allowed.

"Yes, *I* am agreed," said Quin. "We did ask for proof, did we not?"

Koro hesitated, and then flicked his fingers in a shrug. "Yes, we asked."

Quin intertwined her fingers. "We are going to take a break now, while I consider your proposal. How many people are you offering to take on your ship?"

Bandicut and Li-Jared looked at each other. "Two Uduon," Li-Jared said. "Two Karellians?" Bandicut agreed.

"Two of us," Quin said. "We will consider it."

"Ocellet—" Koro began.

"Commander, this is a policy decision. Of course I will want your advice. But I am going to call a recess—even though we just started—while I consult the rest of the leadership council." To the others, she said, "The guards will accompany you back to the guest quarters."

"But—" Akura began.

"We will speak again shortly." And then Quin turned and strode from the room.

Li-Jared thought he would go crazy if he had to wait much longer for Ocellet Quin to come back. Which was ironic, because the staff had put out a stunning buffet of real Karellian food for them. Savory vegetable tarts! A rich, bubbling stew! Fragrant herbal bread! Some were recognizable; others were altogether new. He longed to immerse himself in the sensory experience of being back on Karellia. But he was too wound up to enjoy it much. He paced, bonging softly to himself.

Akura and Sheeawn were watching him warily, no doubt wondering why they had come all this way, only to be ignored by their antagonistic hosts and given little opportunity to make their case. John was trying to talk to them as they nibbled the servings. Li-Jared wasn't sure that they didn't still see him primarily as an alien. But maybe he could persuade them that taking the meeting into space would help to move things along. Li-Jared himself thought it had been a shrewd stroke on Bandie's part. *Let us get to neutral ground, and maybe we can start listening to each other.*

Right now, he needed a way to calm himself down.

A comm trilled. One of the guards spoke into a patch on his upper arm, listened, and then approached Li-Jared. His voice was carefully deferential. "Ocellet Quin wishes to speak with you privately."

Progress. He hoped.

Quin stood gazing out a window, a cup of a hot herbal drink in her hands. She gestured to Li-Jared to sit. They were in a smaller version of the meeting room, with a beverage counter on one side and a bay window on another. Armchairs carved from dark, polished hardwood were arranged in the center around a small, matching table. He stood behind one and said, "Do you mind if I stand? I'm feeling a little—"

She waved off his explanation and remained standing herself. "Would you like a cup of jorrel tea?"

"Moon and stars, yes!" Accepting the mug, Li-Jared inhaled the fragrant vapors curling from the tea. He hadn't smelled anything this good in almost three centuries. That was how long it had been here; sometimes, it felt that long to him in his own time.

"Are you pleased to be back home?" Quin asked. There was a wry note of excitement in her voice, reminding him that this was an extraordinary event for all of them: to have a relic from the past drop out of the sky, with alien traveling companions, no less.

"More pleased than I can say. But it is strange," Li-Jared said. He took a sip of the fragrant brew and was instantly transported back to long days spent in his study, working on the mathematics of temporal physics. He blinked and dragged himself back to the present. "It seems a lot has changed."

"Wars and upheavals, in the century after you left," Quin said. "Much was lost, I'm afraid. But we gained a peace that has lasted, mostly—until this war with Uduon."

They stood in silence a moment longer, taking each other's measure. "Tell me something," she said. "How is it that you seem only a few years older than when you left—under extremely mysterious circumstances—almost three hundred years ago by our calendar?"

Li-Jared opened his mouth to protest that these were details that could wait. But as he met her gaze, he realized that he was going to have to explain *some* of the mysteries, if he wanted to gain their trust. He repositioned the nearest chair and sat, and she did the same. "Do you know what happens when something travels close to the speed of light?"

"Ah," Quin said. "The time-slowdown. Of course. We've measured it rather precisely in particles speeding through the radiation belts." She waved overhead to indicate the sky. "And we're using some of the same principles—" she hesitated, then backtracked with "—well, never mind that now."

Li-Jared hmm'd to himself. Was relativistic time dilation involved in the defensive shield? It seemed plausible enough, though how was a mystery to him. They'd just begun exploring time dilation as a theoretical possibility when he'd been working on it. If they were bending time around the *planet* now, they clearly understood a lot more about time's malleability than he and his contemporaries had. "Well," he said, returning to her original question, "that's similar to what happened to me—time dilation—when I was transported away from here, far *far* beyond the radiation and dust clouds, far beyond our star system. I traveled a long way, but the time was short. Only a few years have passed for me."

Quin's eyes met his. "You have seen much in those few years, I guess."

"Yes." Li-Jared set his mug down and sat forward facing her. "Ocellet—"

"Tell me something, Li-Jared," she said, interrupting. "When you were a professor of mathematical physics at Holdhope Academy, what was your area of expertise?"

He inclined his head. "I was studying the nature of time, actually. Also, the behavior of certain high-energy particles."

"And did you have a family?"

"No. I lived by myself."

"Connected family?"

He rubbed his fingertips together, concentrating. "My greater birth family had other children. I had cousins." Whom he had not thought of in a long while, he was chagrined to realize.

"Names?" asked Quin.

He let his breath sigh out. "A female named Sari, who was perhaps six years younger than I was. And two males, named—"

"Ra-Teen—"

"Yes! Ra-Teen—and Larp! Stunned by the memory, he touched his chest. "You know of them?"

"Only what I've read in the records," Quin said. "But Sari . . ." She paused and hissed a little chuckle. "Sari was my seventh-generation grandmother."

Bong. "Your *grandmother?*"

Her eyes gleamed. "That's right. It would seem, Li-Jared of Holdhope, that you and I are cousins, removed by many years." She watched him react for a moment, her eyes bright. "I've had my staff researching ancient records, and they found this picture." She handed him a small, plasticized square.

He glanced down, and his chest tightened with a sudden sharp ache of memory. It was an image of him as a student at the Institute, standing in front of a stone-faced building with several other university students, and an older Karellian. He found his breath again, recalling the moment. Sari had taken the picture, when he was just beginning his appointment at the academy. She had teased him about his serious expression. Perhaps he really had taken everything too seriously. As he turned the image in his hand, he felt an inexpressible sadness. Sari was gone. He would never see her again. Or his academy mentor or his fellow teachers. He was no longer of their era, nor were they of his.

"Our defense detachments might not have recognized your place in history," Quin said, "but in the written records of my family, the disappearing cousin Li-Jared was apparently something of a legend!"

Li-Jared sat stone still, his hearts out of sync with amazement. *Legend?* "I see," he managed finally. "I'm glad to know we are related—" and he hesitated before adding, "—cousin Quin. Do I dare ask, was that . . . legend . . . a good one or a bad one?"

The leader of the Karellian world government hissed with bright laughter. "That seems to depend on which branch of the family was writing the story!"

"Ah." His own amusement hissed out.

"I've only just had time to skim it. But you know, don't you, that your work in time theory helped lay the foundation for our current understanding of physics?"

He blinked rapidly, his hearts stuttering again. "Uh—"

"You didn't know? That's half the reason you're a legend. The average person nowadays has probably never heard of you—but if you hadn't left behind such good work, the legend would likely be that you either tired of life and walked into the forest, never to return, or that you were killed by one of the revolutionary groups that roamed the countryside then."

Li-Jared didn't remember any revolutionary groups roaming the countryside, though for sure there was social and political instability in the world he'd left. "How about, I was kidnapped by aliens from another star?" he said, lifting his mug of tea with a trembling hand.

Quin's gaze was a probe directly into his eyes. "Is that really what happened?"

"It really is." He gripped the mug with both hands. His voice catching a little, he told her how a force-field beam from a spaceship had literally snatched him up from where he'd stood in an open field one night.

Quin sat silent, considering. "Then, cousin and returning legend—please tell me. About your proposal, or invitation. Just how important is it that I come along with you to your ship? Don't tell me as your cousin. Tell me as Li-Jared the physicist."

Li-Jared jerked from his reminiscence and blinked at her. He bonged softly. "It is everything. I believe it is critical to the safety of Karellia. Perhaps the survival of Karellia."

Her gaze seemed doubtful. "Critical?"

"*Critical.*"

She spread her fingers. "How can I be sure?"

"Ocellet Quin," Li-Jared said. "Which is the greater risk to our world—that you fly into space with us, never to be seen again—tricked, or abducted, or killed—or that you fail to act on the greatest threat this world has ever faced? I need you to see with your own eyes: the stars beyond the Heart of Fire; perhaps the Mindaru themselves." He squeezed the mug so tightly he banged it down on the table, startling both of them. Li-Jared grimaced and gestured apology. "You must believe me about the Mindaru. They are a *terrible* enemy—and we fought them using technology far beyond Karellia's." He shook his head. "They are coming this way. And *you need our help.*"

CHAPTER 8

Coming to Terms

AFTER SENDING LI-JARED back to rejoin his companions, Quin was left with several problems. One was the report her science adviser Aylen had just brought her. Of the several probes launched through the Heart of Fire, decades ago, at least two had been aimed, broadly speaking, in the general direction of Uduon. Why? Apparently because gravitational studies suggested the presence of *something* in that direction. With that in mind, autonomous probes had been sent to see what could be learned, probes that could alter their own flight plans if something of interest was found.

Extended communication with the probes had proved impossible, because of electromagnetic interference from the Heart of Fire nebula. Any findings had to await their return. But none had returned. Their fates were undetermined, and all were listed as failures. In fact, the pattern of failure had resulted in a loss of support for further probes, and had set back outward exploration by many years. Nowadays, they were rarely spoken of at all.

Was it conceivable that those probes had crashed on Uduon, unwittingly triggering this war? They carried no weapons, though their propulsion was an earlier, and perhaps less reliably controlled, form of nuclear fusion. Could they have caused the kind of devastation depicted in Akura's images? That possibility was too terrible to contemplate. *But what if it's true?*

A closely related problem was the array of sixty-four deep-space, thermonuclear-tipped missiles right now parked in high orbit, ready for launch. Half the ruling council thought she should already have launched them. They might never have seen their enemy, but that had not prevented their tracing the incoming asteroid trajectories with great precision. Several smaller missile strikes had been launched in the pre-Quin years; but the effectiveness of those strikes was in doubt, since the asteroid attacks continued. This master-strike, some hoped, would end the matter by annihilating their foe.

The Heart of Fire still precluded sending crewed missions to investigate. Quin was unwilling to unleash such destructive power as long as the defensive shield was doing its job. She understood the risks, or thought she did; and now an even greater question overshadowed the others: What if Karellia really had started the war, however inadvertently?

And now this! Li-Jared, a noted Karellian scientist from out of history—her cousin, no less!—flies down out of the clouds with a group of aliens, claiming that the planetary defense, the one thing preventing escalation to all-out war, is actually putting all of Karellia in even greater peril! How could she *not* go with him to see for herself?

As a political matter, she could not make such a decision entirely on her own. If she opted to go, she needed support—and not just from her science adviser. Fortunately, she had, with the arrival of the aliens, asked her top staff to be available for consultation at a moment's notice. Most of them were already in the administration building, waiting to hear her report.

Quin called her nearest aide. "Summon the council at once. And make our guests comfortable," she said. "But don't let them wander unaccompanied or far."

"House arrest?" the aide asked.

Quin thought a moment. "Let's call it closely watched hospitality."

The council meeting was short, acrimonious, and probably satisfactory to no one. It took place in a plain, rectangular meeting room, with eleven ranking directors gathered to see her presentation of holovid clips of the conversation with the aliens.

"I want to know," said the director of security, "why you will not allow us to meet these alien visitors ourselves. If we're to make a decision—"

"Time is too short."

"So they say."

"Yes. And I am compelled to believe them." Ocellet Quin did not want to get into a debate about this. If she opened the door to everyone questioning the guests in person, they would never have a decision today, or in the next ten days. She believed Li-Jared about the urgency, at least enough to take the chance. "They report the likely approach of at least one threatening vessel of great destructive power. Coming this way, at speed. They propose to show me the view from space while they can, preferably before getting caught up in some kind of battle. It is now or never. If there is even the slightest chance that the danger is real, then it would be irresponsible not to go find out."

Quin hissed through her lips, a little surprised that her own thinking on the matter had crystallized so completely. She acknowledged the public morale officer.

"You are risking your life on the word of someone who claims to be a Karellian from a long time ago—but cannot prove it."

"Actually, we have fairly convincing evidence, including an archival image of him taken over two hundred years ago—" she would hold off on mentioning their possible family connection "—but just a few years, in his biological time. But go ahead with your question."

The morale officer was thrown slightly off his stride. "Well. Your citizens need to know that you are taking care of your own safety—as their chief officer."

Again she hissed a sigh through her lips. It was a reasonable concern to raise. But ... "I think it more important that they know I am putting the *planet's* safety first and foremost. I might be risking my own life, it is true. But this could be the deadliest thing we've ever faced. If I *don't* go, I could be putting all of Karellia's safety at risk. Which would you rather?"

Her defense counselor, Monte-Sho, looked distinctly uncomfortable as he said, "What if they make you a hostage? They might make demands, from up there in space, and say they will harm or kill you if you don't go along. That could put all of us in an untenable position."

She gave him a gentle smiling extension of her fingers. "Not at all. Because I tell you right now, and for the record: I am expendable. If evidence forces you to conclude they are trying to cheat us, or use me as a tool for extortion . . ."

The civil defense coordinator, a political opponent, smirked. "We could just shoot you out of the sky?"

"Yes, exactly!" Quin said, which startled the annoying coordinator into silence. She hadn't planned to say that, but it made perfect sense. "We have weapons at the ready, for an attack I hope we never have to make. But if it is necessary to protect the planet, you will have my authorization to do what is needed. Including sacrificing any of our people on the visitors' ship."

Monte-Sho looked pained. Good, loyal friend. "You are *that* convinced that this could be a real, and imminent, threat to us?"

Ocellet Quin flicked her fingers outward, then back in, with a nod to Aylen. The scientist stood and said, "*I* am persuaded it is real—or at least the evidence is persuasive enough to warrant the risk."

"And I," Quin said. "Also, I wish Chief Commander Koro to come with me. I would greatly value his view and counsel." She saw Aylen's face fall at that, and she was sorry. But she had decided she needed military advice when she was up there. Koro was a topnotch military leader, intelligent and honest, if sometimes annoying in his political views. If this trip was going to result in any hard decisions, and they didn't want an insurrection back on the ground, she was going to need him to see the same things she saw. "And oh yes," she added wryly, "Commander Koro will be expendable, as well."

Koro acknowledged, eyes gleaming in a faint smile.

Quin hadn't expected everyone to see it her way, and they didn't. But in short order, Defense Counselor Monte-Sho announced, if reluctantly, that he stood with her, followed by three more of her immediate support group—and with that support, she declared her decision. She and Koro would go with the aliens, as soon as could be arranged. When someone urged that they include a science adviser, she said, "Just two are invited. Commander Koro and I both have scientific training, and that will have to do for now. My science adviser Aylen will be in close contact here on the ground." Aylen, hearing that, tapped her chest in affirmation, but the disappointment on her face was keen.

In Quin's absence, her senior aides would hold the reins of power. As long as she remained in communication, there was no need to transfer control. It would be like any other trip. As she said to her senior staffers, she hoped to be back in a day or two, wiser and better equipped to handle the threat.

"Let's get back to the house now and gather up our guests," she said at last. "And someone please pack us a couple of overnight bags."

Together with the alien visitors, they boarded a government air transport for return to the spaceport, flying fast and low over the bay and the city. The squad of soldiers watching the alien craft served this time as an honor guard. Quin and Koro walked with their alien guests through the protective cordon and boarded the strange little vessel.

"It's bigger than it looks," she said, peering around at the interior of the craft. Besides flight controls, there were three rows of seats, and luggage room in back. A mechanical creature called Jeaves took their bags and ushered them to their seats.

Sheeawn gave a little squawk of surprise. "There's a row of seats that wasn't here before," he said, walking the length of the cabin.

"I was informed of new passengers," the thing called Jeaves said, "so I took the liberty of adding seats."

"Longer cabin, too, I see," Bandicut murmured as he guided Quin and Koro to the middle row.

Longer cabin? How did they manage that? Quin wondered as she settled in.

Bandicut and Li-Jared sat farthest forward, with Bandicut taking the controls. "Ready for launch, everyone!" he called a few minutes later, looking up into a small mirror over his head.

The craft lifted smoothly. "Stop holding your breath," Koro muttered. Quin wasn't sure if he was talking to her or himself; but she *was* holding her breath, and she let it out suddenly, and gazed out the viewing ports in awe. The city of Karellendon fell away beneath them; clouds whipped by, and the sky slowly deepened. Koro was probably equally awed, but he seemed to feel dutybound to look unimpressed. As they climbed, the sky darkened to midnight blue, and then a black vault, against which shone the terrifying blue and green crucible of the Heart of Fire.

This ship was much faster than any Karellian craft, Quin thought; she knew that without having any expertise at all. *We don't know how to do these things.*

Li-Jared glanced back, making sure they were all right.

The two Uduon behind them were speaking privately. She couldn't tell what they were thinking.

At one point, the robot Jeaves pointed out a Karellian patrol ship twinkling in the distance. But it quickly fell away, as they continued climbing. Finally, when they were *much* higher than any crewed Karellian craft could go, there came into view a faintly luminous, elongated lozenge: the alien vessel, *The Long View.* Bandicut steered the lander right through the wall of that ship, and straight into a docking cradle.

Li-Jared took the lead, introducing Ocellet Quin and Koro to Ruall, who was floating pensively in midair on the bridge. If the blank, silver-faced Tintangle was pleased or honored to greet the leader of all Karellia, she didn't show it. "We have gathered additional remote tracking on the craft we detected earlier entering this star system," she clanged, the moment introductions were over. "It fits the profile of the Mindaru that attacked us in the starstream."

"Is it coming this way?" Bandicut asked.

Ruall made an ominous ringing sound. "It appears to be sweeping the planetary system, while inbound on a course that will make it easy to turn this way once it has confirmed the signatures of life. Dark has observed it, and I have dispatched a probe to monitor its movements more closely. But I have no doubt it will find us."

And when it finds us, it will attack, and *we've just brought the Karellian leadership aboard,* Li-Jared thought with a slightly sick feeling. Why had he thought this was a good idea?

He turned back to their guests. Quin and Koro were staring at Ruall in consternation. Sheeawn was busy translating the information for Akura, whose eyes filled with alarm. Li-Jared couldn't think of much to say about Ruall's grim announcement, so he tried to redirect the newcomers' attention. He gestured to the disk-headed stick figure, who had to look pretty damn weird to Quin and Koro. "Ruall," he explained, "is a Tintangle. She doesn't exactly live in our three dimensions." He continued with the same Ruall introduction he had given the Uduon. "If we were to get into a fight, she'd assume battle command."

Ruall dinged. "I have already assumed battle command. When we detected the Mindaru, I put the ship on combat alert—and that put me in command."

Li-Jared winced and curled his fingers inward. What could he say to that? No good getting into an argument about it in front of the guests. "I stand corrected. Ruall is currently in tactical command of the ship, for as long as the potential for combat exists."

Quin and Koro were exchanging looks of displeasure. "Li-Jared!" Quin snapped. "Please explain! Have you brought us up to your ship, just in time to *go into battle?*"

Li-Jared grimaced. "I hope not, and that was not my intent. I sincerely hope to avoid a combat situation while you're aboard. If it does come to that, I am sorry to have put you in danger."

Koro took a step toward Li-Jared. The military markings on his jacket somehow seemed more prominent than before, as he glared from Li-Jared to Bandicut to Ruall. "You are sorry? To have put the leader of all Karellia at risk? You are *sorry*?"

Li-Jared raised his hands, fingers spread. "Yes. Please understand: it was, and is, our hope to show you as much as possible, and then to return you to the surface, if that is your wish."

"It certainly would be," Koro growled.

"But—"

"But *what*?" Koro demanded.

Li-Jared drummed his fingers on his leg. "If the Mindaru come here, and defeat this ship, there will be no safety for you on the ground or in space. For you or for any of your—*our!*—fellow Karellians." He pressed his mouth shut, and then swung to face Akura and Sheeawn. "*Or* for anyone on Uduon."

Akura stepped forward now, her face taut. She'd been holding her temper, but now she appeared about to erupt. As she spoke, Sheeawn translated nearly instantaneously. "There's one thing you have not told us, and that is *why* this threat is coming to us. Not just to this galaxy of yours, but to *us*." She glared into his eyes, and then into Quin's. Swinging back to Li-Jared, she pointed a finger at his nose. "You said it's because of something on this planet. Something *Karellia* is doing."

Quin jerked her head around sharply, looking from one to the other with a warning glare. *Do not speak of it!* her eyes demanded.

"We insist you answer!" Akura snapped. "What is bringing them here?"

Li-Jared paused to frame his words before answering. "It *is* something Karellia is doing," he said. "And yes, you are right—I must show you what that is." As Quin and Koro reacted to that, he put up a stiff hand in a command to silence. They were on his ship now, and he felt an authority he had not possessed down on Karellia. "But it is not *just* Karellia. It is also Uduon. You are *both* drawing the Mindaru here."

Everyone began to shout, but he was quicker. "*Jeaves!* It is time to show them!"

The bridge fell dark, except for a display in the viewing space. Jeaves floated forward, and images appeared, and the robot began to explain the workings of the Karellian temporal shield.

This was all taking far too long to suit Ruall. The images and explanations from Jeaves, the incredulity of the Uduon that a Karellian device could be producing effects with such repercussions, the declaration by Li-Jared that the shield had to come down: It was all devouring time. And time before meeting the Mindaru was fast dwindling. Li-Jared might have believed what he had told the Karellians—that they could be returned to the planet before fighting broke out—but Ruall did not. No, whatever was going to happen would happen soon.

The Mindaru object was tracking inward, no question—and there, now, it was making a course change, turning toward the source of time-distortion. What would it do when it got here? Attack? Transmit observations to other Mindaru? Infiltrate and take control? All were possible, dangerously possible.

Ruall instructed Copernicus to prepare an intercept course. "Be ready to execute if I say so." They would have to break away abruptly from their orbit, carrying the Karellian leaders with them. This could disrupt the ongoing diplomatic process—something Ruall would have preferred to avoid. But she couldn't put off dealing with the Mindaru while waiting for that to come to fruition. Li-Jared and the others were talking heatedly. "Where is Dark now?" Ruall asked Copernicus.

"She is shadowing the Mindaru, and has made several close passes," the robot answered. "She says this one is a more difficult problem than others she has met. It probably is *not* the same one we encountered in the starstream, but it may have been coming along behind it. It does not seem to have taken solid form yet. Dark is not certain she can stop it on her own."

It was time, Ruall thought, to take a look for herself. She told Copernicus she would be gone for a few minutes. She called Bria to her, from the interstices of four-space, where the gokat had been studying the new guests. *Help me look for an intruder.*

With the gokat, she spun out of local three-space, extending all of her senses into the flower-space of the nearest four alternate dimensions. The ghostly universe now revealed billowing folds of space-time, some glowing brightly even across considerable distance. She could see, far off, the thin, gleaming thread of the starstream, stretching endlessly toward the galactic center. Closer were the squirming energy fields of the nebulas and belts that surrounded Karellia. Lots of complexity there; could be useful to know. Closer still was the pale luminosity of the temporal field, suffused with energy pulled directly from the radiation belts—and a nearly invisible outward ripple of temporal distortion, caught in a freakish n-space resonance with the distant space-time distortions of the starstream.

While Ruall took all this in, Bria saw first what they had come looking for. With a yelp, the gokat darted close to Ruall and then tugged at their shared view, narrowing it down into diamond space—and bringing into sharp relief the curving path of the incoming Mindaru, speeding toward them, and extending sparkling tendrils into various levels of n-space. Dark was right; it looked more like a patch of unfocused space than a solid object. This was going to be a tough one to catch and kill.

And it was coming on fast.

Li-Jared was reaching the end of his patience, what with Quin and Koro angry over his revealing the secret of the shield to the Uduon, and the Uduon angry that the shield enabled Karellia to continue waging an unjust war against Uduon, and Bandicut stating as delicately as he could that the shield had to come down, one way or the other. "Things have changed," Li-Jared said, repeating what had become a kind of mantra.

"Perhaps so," Quin said, "but that shield may also be the best thing we have to protect us from these Mindaru."

At that moment, Ruall, who had been quietly absent for a few minutes, rotated back into view—which startled all of the guests into silence. "Prepare, everyone, for high-speed maneuvering, and possibly for a fight," she said without preamble. "The Mindaru object is approaching much more rapidly than we'd expected, and we are going to intercept it."

Koro was furious, practically tearing at his garments. "So you *are* going into battle with all of us aboard? What about your promise to take us back to the surface before anything happened?"

"We did not promise," Ruall clanged. "That was our intent, if possible. Unfortunately, it is not."

"Perhaps you should *make* it possible," Koro countered.

Ruall rang loudly and waited a moment for the echo to die away. "Perhaps we should fail to intercept the Mindaru, and leave your world defenseless?"

Koro bristled. "We have ships, and they are armed. Will you help me get in touch with them?"

Li-Jared broke in. "Those ships are confined to low orbit, and they are slow. Can they maneuver in n-space? Can they chase something that can likely move faster than light?"

Koro's expression darkened; he looked grim, the vertical almond shapes of his eyes narrowed to slits. "You show remarkably little loyalty to your homeworld, Li-Jared."

Li-Jared suppressed a surge of fury. "I am *trying to protect* my homeworld. From a stupid war, and from a threat it will not comprehend."

Quin had been quiet, but now she spoke. "You might be right, Li-Jared. But we *do* have weapons, and you should not dismiss them out of hand. Can we not join forces against this thing?"

"Of course," Li-Jared agreed. He took a breath to calm himself. "But keep your ships where they are, as backup. We can open a channel to them right now. Talk to them. Tell them what's happening. Tell them that we are making the primary intercept, and they should be ready to act if we fail. Tell them to expect further orders from you—but if they don't hear from you, they should be prepared to fight to the death against this thing."

As Quin visibly took all this in, Bandicut added, "And tell them to *protect their intelligence systems*—and shut them down at once at the slightest indication of attempted intrusion."

"Right," said Li-Jared. "Especially that. Come on over here. Jeaves will help you make contact. Right, Jeaves?"

"Making contact now," said the robot.

"Then we choose to stay aboard," Quin said. She gestured to Koro to handle the communication.

Ruall made a ringing sound of approval. "You will be far safer here than on any of your ships."

"But one thing," Quin said in a low voice, "I still believe our temporal screen may provide good protection for the planet."

Ruall spun her blank disk face once and said, "Perhaps we should put it to the test. If your guess is correct, we will update our plans. But—" She paused, apparently to make sure she had their full attention. "To test, we will have to let the object get much closer to your planet than I would like, before we intercept. That is an additional risk. Do you accept the risk?"

Ocellet Quin looked startled. It took her a few moments to absorb Ruall's words and decide. It was perhaps a more difficult decision than she had expected. *What do I trust?* she was clearly thinking. *Our own technology, or the word of these aliens?* "Yes," she said at last. "We have to know. We will try our shield first."

CHAPTER 9

Testing the Shield

THE STEELY TINTANGLE glided back and forth at the front of the viewspace. "Copernicus, enhance the view of the Mindaru, and the Karellian time-shield."

The time-displacement field became visible as a bubble wall in space, some distance farther out from the planet than *The Long View*. Well beyond that, the Mindaru arrowed inward, closing the distance rapidly. "Commander Koro, have you concluded your communications activities? We may have to break off contact without warning if the Mindaru body gets close. Tell your people to expect that."

Koro acknowledged, straightening up from the comm panel.

Bandicut watched the Mindaru maneuver, a splinter of light in the viewspace. Copernicus had added enhancements to the view, but visually it was still difficult to make out. It seemed both there and not-there at the same time, like a ghost in the image. Still, Copernicus had its position pinpointed from the full scan data. It had now closed the distance to roughly the same as between Earth and its Moon. It was rapidly approaching the time-displacement bubble. *The Long View* would remain just on the inside of the bubble, to observe. If the Mindaru was stopped or repelled, they would have to decide whether to take the time to drop off Quin and Koro, and perhaps the Uduon under their care, before they set off in pursuit. But if the Mindaru penetrated the field, they would have to assume it posed an imminent threat and go after it. No one had yet seen the Mindaru in a planetary encounter, so they didn't know what to expect; but in past encounters, the Mindaru had been lightning fast in penetrating intelligence networks. More than likely it would attempt first to take control of a station or spacecraft.

"Coppy," Bandicut said, "is Dark still in the area? Can we expect help?"

"She is keeping her distance, trying not to alarm the target. Right now she is skirting the Heart of Fire, where she'll be less noticeable."

Bandicut grunted. He would have preferred her closer.

The Mindaru slowed as it approached the outer boundary of the time-field. For several minutes, it seemed to hover impossibly, as though studying the situation. Then it skated along the field boundary like a bug skimming the surface of a pond, drifting one way and another. Then . . . in a sudden movement, it slipped through the field, as easily as through the wall of a soap bubble. Ocellet Quin hissed in dismay, and Koro muttered in a low voice. The Mindaru had appeared not to disturb the bubble in any way— and also suffered no visible dislocation in time or space as it passed. It hovered again, just inside the time-shield. Analyzing, perhaps?

Ruall said nothing, watching.

To everyone's surprise, the Mindaru reversed direction and slipped back out through the bubble.

Bandicut frowned. Should he be alarmed or relieved? Was it preparing to send a report? Clearly it had decoded the temporal screen with no difficulty. "What do you think, Ruall?"

Before the Tintangle could answer, the Mindaru reversed course again—back through the time-shield, and toward the planet. Now Ruall spoke. "They may be examining the shield and looking for a way to use it to their advantage."

Koro protested. "It didn't stop them—I grant that—but how could they use it themselves?"

"They are capable of many unexpected things," Ruall answered.

Li-Jared rubbed his hands together furiously. "They may be distracted and more vulnerable while they do that. Shouldn't we attack?"

Ruall's head spun once. "Indeed. Copernicus—"

But Jeaves interrupted. "We're seeing a lot of transmission activity."

"Sending to other Mindaru?" Bandicut asked.

"Maybe. But I think more likely attempting to hack into the Karellian network. Possibly into the time-field control system itself."

Quin leapt to her feet, gesturing into the viewing space. "We can't allow that! Can we stop them?"

"Not from here," said Jeaves.

Quin jerked around to address Jeaves. "Can we send a warning to our people?"

"No," clanged Ruall. "No communication!"

"Why not?" demanded Koro.

"Because if we transmit, we open ourselves to hacking attack. Your people were warned once; that will have to do. Copernicus, power up weapons and prepare for course change."

"Intercept?"

"Close approach. Three quantum shock pulses, as we pass."

The ship hummed, and the stars in the viewing space began to move up and to the right. Copernicus remarked, "Quantum pulses were ineffective in the starstream."

"I hope to lure them back out through the shield in pursuit, if we can. Use two-thirds speed, and be ready for full, when I say."

"Aye-aye. Toward the Heart of Fire?"

"Region of maximum magnetic flux."

"Aye."

———

Three blooms of light bracketed the Mindaru, as *The Long View* hurtled past, firing. The enemy changed course to pursue, just as Ruall had predicted. They had gotten its attention.

"Are you drawing them away from the planet?" Quin asked.

"Partly," Ruall said. "Copernicus, give us the magnetic map of the region between us and Heart of Fire. As soon as we're through the shield, take us to full power."

The viewspace changed at once, showing bright magnetic lines that looped down from the Heart of Fire still in the distance, to caress the planet and its surrounding space. At intervals there were eruptions: impressive cascades of lines falling in great down-bursts onto and tangling with Karellia's own magnetic field lines, more closely wrapped around the globe. These natural down-bursts reminded Bandicut of eruptions from the surface of a sun.

"There are huge amounts of energy flowing along those magnetic lines," Ruall said. "I want to use that energy against the Mindaru. If we can lose ourselves in the interference of the clouds, and then double back using a downburst for cover, the Mindaru might never see us coming."

"Like flying out of the sun in a dogfight," Copernicus said.

"I don't know what dogs are or how they fight, but here's what I'm planning." Ruall spun in place. "If we can use our weapons to rupture the magnetic lines, we might be able to *release* the energy and dump it onto the Mindaru. If that doesn't destroy it outright, the electromagnetic pulse might at least disable it. Can Dark help us focus the energy release?"

Copernicus answered, "It will take a comm burst to ask. Approved?"

Ruall gonged in annoyance, but agreed.

The enemy, right now, was gaining on them as they approached the shield bubble from the inside. Coppy had slowed a bit to pre-pare for the transition.

"Crossing the temporal threshold in three, two, one . . ."

As before, Bandicut felt a momentary queasiness, and every-thing blinked out and back on. "Through the shield," he heard Copernicus say. And Ruall answered with, "Rapid separation, *now*."

They widened the gap quickly, as *The Long View* sped up and the Mindaru, in turn, slowed to pass through the field after them. Coppy kicked in some tight spatial threading, and they streaked away from the planet. Soon they entered the inner boundary of the Heart of Fire, high above the shield bubble and even higher above the planet.

Bandicut glanced at their guests to see how they were handling the change. Quin and Koro looked disoriented, and perhaps shocked to realize that they were inside the Heart of Fire and still alive. Akura and Sheeawn were eyeing the viewspace worriedly. Probably they were as scared as the rest of them of the coming confrontation with the Mindaru; but as for flying in the Heart of Fire, they were old hands.

Ruall illuminated a point on the mapping of the energy flux. "This seems a good place to rupture the magnetic containment. Concur?"

Copernicus and Jeaves conferred with Ruall and concurred. "We can be in position in twelve minutes, if we slice across some turbulence," Copernicus said. "Thirty-two, if we follow the safer course."

Bong. "The faster the better," Li-Jared said, and Bandicut agreed. They knew all too well how quickly the Mindaru could crack a network. If they in *The Long View* waited too long to make their move, the Mindaru might already have seized control of the temporal shield. What if they found a way to tune it to bring even more Mindaru up the timestream?

"Fast, then," said Ruall. "Let us do this."

It seemed to Bandicut that Ruall rubbed her two paddle-hands together in anticipation. Sparks snapped between the two surfaces.

Copernicus called out, "The enemy is turning back toward the planet!"

That's not the plan, Bandicut thought. "You mean they've stopped chasing us?"

"Apparently," Jeaves said, "they've decided the shield is bigger game. Especially if the Heart of Fire is interfering with their attempt to hack in."

Ruall spun and conferred with Copernicus. But Koro strode forward, looking every inch the commander, and demanded, "Are *you* turning back? We need to go after it."

The view forward showed *The Long View* continuing to speed in a continuous arc through the clouds. Ruall answered with a chilly reverberation in her voice. "Our strategy remains unchanged. Everyone be seated now. Are you ready, Copernicus?"

"Ready."

"Can we still hit them before they reach the shield?"

"It will be close."

"Nearing the mark," Copernicus reported.

"Hold tight, everyone!" Ruall ordered. "Sharp maneuvering ahead." Outside, the Heart of Fire energy clouds billowed and fell away behind them. Copernicus adjusted the view, bringing into focus a breathtaking loop of fiery gases. "That's our primary target," Ruall said. "My aim is to release all that energy onto the enemy. Copernicus, are weapons charged?"

"They are."

Ruall floated to the center of the viewspace and announced, as though dictating into a log, and maybe she was, "We are about to commence hostile action against the Mindaru. Copernicus will control the targeting on the magnetic lines and the firing." She swung closer to the robot. "Copernicus, fire at your discretion."

Two seconds later, a flash scored the viewspace, and a powerful *snap!* echoed through the deck. The clouds erupted with shards of light that shocked the backs of Bandicut's eyeballs. Before Bandicut could figure out what he was seeing, Copernicus redrew the viewspace to show them. The quantum implosion had twisted the magnetic lines of flux from the clouds and then snapped them, releasing a tremendous burst of energy directly into the path of the Mindaru.

"New course!" Ruall clanged. But Copernicus already had them in motion, flying right on the tail of that energy burst.

To Bandicut, it seemed they were riding a roller coaster of light. The magnetic lines squirmed through the space above the planet, and bunched and shot downward in front of them. The four guests on the bridge looked terrified, and he didn't blame them.

He had his eye not on the Mindaru, visible only as an icon in the viewspace, but on Dark—now visible as a fleck of black speeding in a corkscrew pattern through the luminous clouds. Dark was shepherding the enormous gout of energy they had just released.

"Prepare another shot," Ruall said. "If the Mindaru comes out of this, fire directly on it. But only if."

Copernicus hummed.

The inferno of magnetic fire dove down to its target— *WHUMP!*—and splatted outward.

Li-Jared yelped. Bandicut's fists tightened involuntarily. Would it work? Would the electromagnetic pulse stop the enemy?

"EMP shock coming," Copernicus warned. "You'll be seeing it in false color. *Now.*"

It looked like a luminous blue and purple soap bubble expanding *fast*, and sparkling with electricity. By the time it reached *The Long View*, tucked for safety down in n-space, it had expanded and dissipated considerably, and it washed over them like a sheet of lightning. But down next to the Mindaru, it should have packed a tremendous wallop.

"Did it work?" Ruall asked, paddle-hands spread wide.

"It caught them," Copernicus said. "That's all I can—no, wait! It did not stop them! They are turning." As Copernicus spoke, he loosed another series of quantum pulses, this time directly at the enemy. A cluster of flashes streaked down toward the adversary.

The Mindaru veered instantly, and the pulses only passed through it. With a lateral move along the outer edge of the shield-bubble, it arced up and shot away from the planet.

How could it have survived that? Bandicut wondered in dismay. Was the thing escaping—or planning to circle back, as they had just done?

"*Pursue!*" Ruall snapped.

The Long View sped in pursuit. But the Mindaru was already beyond firing range. They were both now rising out of high orbit from Karellia.

"Where is it going?" Bandicut asked.

For a minute, there was no answer. Copernicus and Jeaves were plotting the enemy's course and analyzing. Then Jeaves announced, "It appears they have located Uduon. They are heading there on a direct course."

There were gasps from Akura and Sheeawn at that, and then from Quin and Koro as Ruall gonged, "We must go after them. We have no choice."

In the viewspace, the planet and clouds and stars wheeled and blurred, and *The Long View* rocketed away from Karellia, on course to punch straight through the Heart of Fire—the beautiful, perilous sky.

Toward Uduon.

CHAPTER 10

Back into the Ghoststream

AMADUSE FELT HIS heart spin up with excitement as he delved ever deeper into the Shipworld library records. He had long since moved beyond any data accessible to the average user of the library; this was material gathered from a thousand worlds over unrecorded millions of years, most of it brought here for storage without the slightest sorting or analysis. Uncatalogued, much of it undated, unread since being interred in the data-vaults. Most of it probably hadn't been read even then, but simply gathered en masse from repositories on worlds visited by people from Shipworld, or saved by people from Shipworld, or saved only in the form of the memories of a few inhabitants rescued from some unstoppable disaster.

Some of it came by even more circuitous routes: preserved by one ancient world visiting another and gathering records—and perhaps on down the line, records passed from one civilization to another, along a string of interstellar contacts until even the identity of the originating world was lost. Much of the data was rumor and legend; some was written history identified as such; often it was hard to distinguish one from another, especially with fragmentary pieces.

For millennia the records had grown by a process of accretion in the Shipworld library system. There was never enough time, never the qualified staff, never the funding or the interest, to properly examine and catalog the information. It grew like a demon-lizard's treasure-hoard, only more chaotically.

There was no other librarian in the system who could have searched through the treasure-hoard the way Amaduse could. He had a nose for information and truth, however deeply buried, that made him in some eyes the most valuable librarian in all of Shipworld.

He also had Gonjee. His assistant, whom the visitor Bandicut had remarked upon as looking like an Earthly simian, was in some ways his secret weapon. Trained by Amaduse, Gonjee was a savant; he had a remarkable ability to scan through vast amounts of data, looking for commonalities, which he would then bring to Amaduse. Gonjee could not in a lifetime have performed the subtle and detailed analyses at which Amaduse excelled, but he was an astonishingly adept first reader. Faced with a mountain of unsorted data, Gonjee would hoot with pleasure and spiral in from the outside, digging and reading with near-hysterical abandon. An impossibly short time later, he would start showing to Amaduse the connecting lines between something gathered on one world a thousand years ago, and an eons-old legend from someplace half a galaxy away, now dust.

Amaduse took on Gonjee's excitement as his own. He probed and analyzed and synthesized as passionately as Gonjee scanned. A picture was starting to emerge. The picture that the yaantel had sent him to find. A story that had its roots lost in deep time, beyond hundreds of millions of years ago . . .

Soon now, Amaduse would have an answer for the yaantel. He already had a pretty good inkling of what its shape would be. And if he was right, he thought, they might want to let the galactic core mission team know, before someone made a terrible mistake.

The reentry into the ghoststream was both more and less frightening than the first time Julie had done it. She thought she knew what to expect: the out-of-body feeling of floating down a long, ethereal pathway through eternity, an almost life-after-death disconnectedness from her physical body, the awareness of Ik at her side, close but too far to reach. She felt reawakened to the excitement of probing the unknown, the edge of danger, the weight of responsibility on her shoulders. At the same time, her fear of the Mindaru loomed like a towering storm cloud, darkening everything and making her want to crouch low and pull something protective around her.

Instead of being greeted by the expected cloud of storming Mindaru, they found silence in the ghoststream, a great emptiness that seemed to stretch on forever. /How far ahead is the way clear?/ she wondered.

Uncertain, answered the stones. *Millions of years into the past, at least. But that's a modest fraction of the way to the Mindaru birthplace.*

Ik stirred beside her in the stream, and she heard him ask, /Where did all the Mindaru go?/ His voice seemed to carry equal weights of relief and worry.

/They didn't get past us at our end, did they?/ Julie asked.

Not as far as we could tell, answered the stones.

/So they either went back home, or they got off somewhere else,/ Ik murmured.

The millennia streamed by like snowflakes blowing on the wind, like calendar pages fluttering backward. Julie shivered. If the Mindaru *left* the ghoststream at some point in the past, somewhere down the starstream into the galaxy . . . /How will we find them?/ she asked.

We are tracking into the past, the stones reminded her. *We may yet see them in flight.*

Steeling her nerves, Julie focused her gaze down the ghoststream and imagined supernovas imploding as the ages reeled in reverse.

———

For Charli the quarx, time had become a surreal quantity since her separation from John Bandicut. There had been a period of merging into the starstream, after the initial period of helpless recognition that she was both *in* the starstream and *part* of the starstream. Was this where she was destined to spend the rest of eternity?

Those other voices she'd heard before seemed to come and go. They were always at a distance, hopelessly remote. She thought maybe they were part of the starstream, too. Bizarrely, she once thought she heard an echo of the voice of Jeaves, but that did not seem likely, so she dismissed it as a figment of her imagination. She was pretty sure Jeaves had not been cast out of *The Long View* during the fight. But then she remembered Jeaves once telling them that a version of himself had been present at the creation of the starstream, and had been absorbed by the created entity. Was it possible that Jeaves in some form was actually here with her, but stretched out to infinity?

Time seemed to ebb and flow unevenly here, even pooling like water in certain places. In some of those places, she felt she had more freedom to be deliberate in assessing her surroundings, and in taking any action—if "action" was even still a meaningful word.

One thing she knew she could do was listen. Listen for anything of interest, but especially for anything familiar. She could also look, though vision had become a different thing from what she had once known through the eyes of John Bandicut and earlier partners. She was somehow focused on infinity and on the nearby all at once, and sometimes had difficulty distinguishing between the two. At the same time, there was a clarity such as she'd never experienced before. Perhaps that was why she was able to see the *timestream* embedded here, the thing that they had all worried so much about, the thing that linked them all to the deep past. She thought it might be wise to stay clear of it until she understood more; but even from here, she could see a considerable distance down its length. Things were moving in it, moving in time. Were those Mindaru?

Surely it was some time (that word again!) later—but who knew, really?—when she became aware of entities of another kind passing her by in the starstream, and headed down into the deep past. These were not vessels of the kind she knew in the starstream. This was more like the passage of someone like her, without body or substance; and that was a profoundly strange thought—because, for one thing, there was a familiarity about them.

It took effort to process the sensation, and then to recognize that she might *know* this entity.

Could that really be—?

It was just a whisper of light moving through the stream, moving galactic coreward, and backward in time. It was muttering and *hrah*ing softly to itself. It was on a mission, and Charli recognized the voice. Recognized Ik.

Ik? And with him, who?

Another entity Charli did not recognize. Or wait—reaching back to an earlier time in her quarxian memory—could it be—?

No, that was impossible. The unlikelihood was just too great. Julie Stone?

This could all be a mad dream, of course. But if it wasn't, then suddenly Charli was bursting with a need to know more—and to tell of it. To tell it to someone who would *care*. There *was* someone she wanted to tell about it, but she could no longer speak with him. She missed him above all others.

/// John, if I have not gone mad,
then I have found Julie Stone for you.
Here in the starstream.
Out of my reach—and yours. ///

But there was no John Bandicut to hear.

Ik and Julie were passing rapidly out of sight—back, back, back into the past. To Charli it looked like something she remembered from the Fffff'tink world, a pair of lantern-flies dwindling into the darkness of a wood.

Never had she imagined such a lonely sight.

———————

What would the translator have counseled them to do? Julie wondered, feeling a strange powerlessness. They had tried to contact the translator for advice before their second launch, via Rings-at-Need, who had been attempting to maintain a connection. But she and Ik had been pressed back into the ghoststream before any answer could come back from the yaantel.

The feeling of loneliness was palpable. They weren't exactly cut off, but contact with the launch point was difficult and limited to a slow bit-rate. The instrumentation in this launcher was different from what they'd gotten used to in the first mission—more sophisticated, presumably, but isolating in its unfamiliarity. She felt that they were more on their own here. Thoughts of John, and of Antares and the others, felt increasingly distant and abstract. Millions of years away.

Julie remembered once driving a land-car back on Earth, on an endlessly unwinding straight road at night, with snow flurries blowing into her headlights for hours on end. That was more or less what she saw now, peering forward in the ghoststream. The car drive had been hypnotic, wearying. That was just how she felt now, as the years unreeled past stellar generations and backward spins of the galaxy, stars melting back into the gas clouds from which they had been born.

Ik was the first to see it: a tiny flutter of something farther down the timestream.

The stones began to analyze. *It is unsteady. Difficult to obtain a good image,* they muttered, in a rare display of frustration.

In fact, all the stones were able to show Julie was a graphical interpretation of the data gathered by the instruments, which were modulated through her senses, anyway. Were the instruments feeding data to her, or the other way around? Sometimes it was hard to tell. The physical instruments were no more present here than she was, or Ik. They were all sealed in the launcher, held in a high-energy state of entanglement, only their senses here in the past. What the forward-looking sensors were gathering right now looked to her like incomprehensible squiggles and shadings spread in four dimensions.

The stones highlighted for her the peaks and changes that indicated movement ahead in the ghoststream; and when they were able, they showed the ghostly readings as tiny fluctuations in the view ahead, as if something was squirming in and out of the stream, threading space in the extreme distance. She remembered the tiny, deadly, squirming thing she and the translator had intercepted back in the solar system, and she shuddered. That thing had been trying to destroy the Earth. What about this?

/Hrah—it is them!/ Ik declared, while she was still trying to focus.

/The Mindaru? Are you sure? What do we do now?/

/I wonder what *they* are doing,/ Ik said.

Only one way to find out: Get closer. Well, that was going to happen anyway. They were on a straight-line course, as though sliding along a zip line, and about the only control they had was how far to go, and how fast. She tried to reassure herself silently. *We are supposed to be invisible to anyone else, all right?*

And do you believe that? Will you stake your life on it?

She supposed she *was* staking her life on it, whether she believed it or not.

The voices in Julie's mind quieted as the contacts drew closer, but her senses, tied directly into the instrumentation, buzzed with far more data than she could absorb with her mind.

The targets are not solid objects. They are waveforms, complex quantum phenomena. It may be, the stones said, *that they found a way to convert from their original solid form into a wave function for the purposes of travel.*

/Sort of the way we do it, but with a way to reconstitute themselves at the other end?/ Julie asked.

/They must have a way to collapse, hrah, the wave function when they want,/ Ik said. /It would seem they are more advanced than we are, at least in some ways./

/A billion years before us./

That may be so, said the stones. *They also appear to be veering from side to side, as though seeking exit points. They may be trying to leave the timestream.*

Julie, with dread in her soul, tried to focus on the still-distant flickers, which were little more than wispy disturbances at the limit of sight. Two of them were now slipping *sideways* and then *out*. Leaving the stream, exiting right out the side, into . . . what?

They are exiting into the surrounding galactic space. The time: somewhere around one hundred million years in your past.

/You mean they're seeding themselves out into the galaxy, and they have a hundred million years to mutate and evolve and develop before we meet them in our present?/ Julie asked, horrified. /Won't that change the timeline?/

We judge they are already part of the timeline. The Starmaker Nebula team may have met the descendants of these Mindaru, answered the stones.

/Hrrm, should we not try to stop them?/ Ik asked.

High probability we would fail. Any that have exited are gone, and are now in your past. Recommend we let these go and focus on our mission.

/Stop more from coming in,/ Ik said.

Exactly.

As the range to the Mindaru closed, Julie began to wonder, /How do we keep from plowing right into them?/

Quantum uncertainties, said the stones. *We hope.*

/I'm sorry. Was that an answer to my question?/

Quantum uncertainties, said the stones, *may provide an opportunity for us to maneuver.*

/I thought we were on a one-track zip line back in time./

Almost, said the stones. *Almost, but not quite. Because—*

/Hrah,/ said Ik, /because we are riding a wave of quantum entanglement? And therefore there are uncertainties in the stream?/

Precisely. Or, rather, what is available to us is a lack of precision. If we were solid entities in this stream, the uncertainties would be inconsequential. But we are not, and our presence here involves an intricate matrix of quantum-level phenomena.

/But the quantum uncertainties are small, aren't they?/

Extremely small. But they can be cumulative, and we are speeding along enormous distances, both temporal and spatial. If we can wield the uncertainties enough to achieve just a tiny deflection, it might be all we need to introduce small lateral movement in our course.

/Do you mean we can swerve in the ghoststream—?/
/Like dodging potholes?/
Exactly.

CHAPTER 11

Return to Mindaru Home

THE VISION OF the starstream ahead of them flickered and distorted. Julie felt everything go into soft focus and then darken. It was like a camera shutter closing down, just far enough to make her feel that she was squinting. Then came a fresh burst of the snowstorm, a blizzard of snowflakes blowing past her face—which, the stones noted, was a way of visualizing a cloud of tiny, collapsing wave functions, noise in the signal.

The visualization quickly morphed. Their movement in the stream was turning into the rush of water in a channel, bubbling and hissing, thundering headlong and spreading out as the water jostled them from side to side. She dimly understood that the stones were smearing out the probability waves, allowing for greater uncertainty in their pathway. Through the agitated, translucent medium, Julie sensed shadows darting by, like fish in nearby currents schooling in the other direction. Were these the Mindaru, following slightly different cross-currents, passing them without their paths ever quite intersecting? Now and then she caught sight of a larger shadow in the waters, and she wondered, was that *their own* shadow? How could that be?

That's one of our lower-probability paths, the stones murmured. *There's a chance we could be over there, instead of here.*

/Wait—you mean we're not even sure if we're really in that shadow over there—instead of here, looking at the shadow? What are we, Schrödinger's cat?/

Yes, but the probability favors our being here.

Julie started to press for more detail, but decided that her brain was already rattling with enough quantum quandaries. So instead she asked, /Are we steering around the Mindaru?/

We have passed them. They are behind us now.

She looked back. The last of the Mindaru-shadows were disappearing upstream, leaving them once more alone, moving downstream into the past. Far behind them now was the place where the Mindaru were leaving the stream.

/How far in the past are we?/ Even as she asked, she absorbed the readings from the instruments and understood that they were somewhere in the neighborhood of half to three-quarters of a billion years in the past. Their journey had only just begun.

That was just one flight. We must remain vigilant for others in the stream, the stones cautioned.

Oh, yeah, Julie thought. Remain vigilant. Oh yes, we will.

With or without the heightened vigilance, it was unlikely they would have missed the next group of entities they encountered a few hundred million years farther downstream. At first they assumed it was more Mindaru: a cluster of detection traces floating up the timestream toward them. But these were slower, and in the best magnified view, their sensor tracings looked like soaring birds, sailing along with the movement of time and space. The stones worked intensively, trying to build some information on where the objects had been, and where they were going.

They didn't look or feel like Mindaru. So what were they?

Something else. This is strange, and might be important. The stones throttled back their movement downstream while a comm transmission ground its way back to HQ, describing the new sighting and requesting advice. *These traces echo something the yaantel suspected, but was too unsure of to mention.*

/Can you tell us?/

All the stones remained silent, both Julie's and Ik's, waiting for an answer. None of them expected to hear back right away, so they were all surprised to receive almost immediately the first sentence of a reply, sputtering through just a few characters at a time.

IMPORTANT. Avoid interference with these objects. Yaantel requests more detail.

Yaantel requests? So the Core Mission team had brought the translator back into the loop? Someone back home knew something about these objects?

The stones busied themselves sending and receiving. While this went on, Julie and Ik could only observe, and what they saw startled and alarmed them. The new contacts began veering from side to side, as though probing the edges of the stream, or perhaps exploring the same quantum wiggle-room that the stones had used earlier. Soon they too began leaving the timestream one by one, much as the Mindaru had, but further back in time. They too seemed to be seeding themselves into the galaxy, but over a longer period in time, and probably space as well. The stones appeared aware of this, but they seemed unalarmed.

They are giving themselves time to evolve, the stones said, and Julie thought there was a hint of marveling in their words.

/What are they?/ she asked again, and this time she put more insistence into her voice.

The stream of comm-data was tapering off, and the stones finally had enough information to answer. *This is not certain, but the translator thinks the likelihood is high. These entities may be precursors to the translator itself. To the yaantel. Ancestors to all of the yaantel that ever lived.*

Julie was so stunned she could not reply. She felt her heart thump erratically, and for a second she thought she might go into cardiac arrest. /Please say that again,/ she whispered at last.

The stones hesitated, and there was another communication back to the launch-point, and a long, slow reply. Finally the stones said, *We just asked for confirmation, and our understanding is confirmed. The translator believes these entities might be its own progenitors. Its ancestors.*

Julie's heart lurched again, but kept beating.

/Hrah, when did it decide this?/ Ik asked.

It had an intuition, based on your reports from the first mission. The translator suspected then that its own origins traced back to the time and place of the Mindaru. After your meeting, it asked the librarian Amaduse to undertake some research.

/How could Amaduse research whether objects we saw in the timestream were related to the translator's origins?/

He cannot do so directly. But Amaduse has access to historical data going back hundreds of millions of years.

/Are you serious? Even so—/

No one knows the history of the yaantel, not even the yaantel themselves. The data become sparser the further back one goes. But Shipworld librarians have been gathering data from across the galaxy since antiquity. Amaduse traced the earliest mention of yaantel-like phenomena back to approximately . . . The stones paused, calculating.

/Back to when?/ Julie whispered.

Back approximately to now. To the broad time period we are presently moving through . . . outside this bubble.

Ik was making throat-rasping noises, and Julie's pulse was making her ears buzz.

/You mean, we have historical information going back half a billion years? That seems impossible./

The information is not precise. The dates are highly speculative—somewhere in a range of a hundred million years. Spatial locations are similarly uncertain. But evidence suggests that yaantel, or something like them, first appeared in more than one place, perhaps many places, beginning at times roughly corresponding to this point in history. The records are extremely fragmented, and details uncertain.

/Hrah,/ Ik said finally. /How uncertain? Can we trust this story, or is it wishful thinking?/

There are enough points of consistency across multiple sources that the translator and Amaduse both believe it is true.

Well, I'll be damned, Julie thought.

/Rrmm,/ Ik said, /if the yaantel and Amaduse believe the story, then I am inclined to believe it, too./

Something went off like a flashbulb in Julie's mind. /And you!/ she said to the stones. /You're daughters of the translator! It's your story, too./

The stones did not answer, and Julie fell silent, thinking. The translator came from a race over a billion years old? Was that so hard to believe? Hadn't it always seemed ageless to her? The harder thing to wrap her mind around was the thought that it came from the same time and place as the Mindaru.

/Julie?/ Ik asked gently.

/Yah,/ she said at last. /But the translator . . . and the Mindaru? Are they connected?/

That is the key question, said the stones. *It was the biological forms you saw on the Mindaru world that first gave the translator a deep-level hint. But the truth is . . .*

/You don't know?/

We don't really know, the stones agreed finally.

They moved cautiously downstream toward the remaining entities. Many were still in the stream, despite the departures they had witnessed. If these things really *were* ancestors of the translator . . . *Jesus*, Julie thought. *This will change everything.* Stopping the escape—migration?—of translator precursors would be unthinkable.

/How in the world can we *know* if they're translator precursors and not Mindaru?/ Julie asked.

A difficult problem. We are searching for signatures . . .

/Hrrm . . . / Ik said.

Julie wished she could look at Ik and read his expression, but the ghoststream bubble did not permit that. /Ik? Do you have a thought?/

/Possibly,/ Ik said. /Are we willing to take a risk?/

Please define.

/What if we fly right through the flock?/ Ik said. /I don't think we would hurt them, hrah? We could see what they do. How they react./

Explain the object of the exercise, said the stones.

Julie thought she knew. /If they don't attack—if they're not hostile—?/

/More than that,/ Ik said. /I believe ancestors of the yaantel might be *interested* in us, but cautious./

Julie's mind leapt to follow. /Because it's in their nature to explore, to try to understand. Not to dominate./

/Yes./

The stones answered with care. *It may be difficult to determine their attitude, or their motivation, from simply flying among them.*

Julie liked Ik's idea. /True. But it will be *impossible* if we don't do *something* to take a closer look./

In the end, the stones agreed.

The approaching cluster of faint, shadowy waveforms showed no reaction at first. The stones steered their bubble on a true course, but remained poised to take action if needed. As before, the stream appeared like a channel of rushing water, but this time they stayed well centered.

As they neared the closest of the entities, the fluttering shadow suddenly swerved away. It didn't simply evade them in the stream; it veered right through the wall of the timestream and out—vanishing presumably into normal space-time, close to a billion years before the Shipworld present, and several hundred million years before the Mindaru did the same thing.

Julie watched the next one react in much the same way—changing course abruptly, with a frantic exit from the stream.

/Are they running from *us*?/ Julie asked in surprise, wondering how to interpret this. /Are they afraid of us?/

/Hrah, how can we know?/

Their behavior is strongly consistent with fear, the stones said.

/But of us?/ Julie asked. /Or something else?/

Difficult to be sure. We must be an unknown to them—unless there is an encounter to come, in the past. Let's try to give them a little more room.

The stones did something, and the channel blurred, and they pulled slightly to the left. Would this seem less threatening? Would they even be visible to the entities at all?

The answer was not wholly clear. One by one the entities came up the stream toward their bubble. Every one swerved sideways, out of the timestream and into the galaxy of this era. It seemed they were fleeing from *something*, but perhaps not Julie and Ik and the starstream bubble.

The stones became quietly thoughtful, as though they had just encountered something deeply, dimly, distantly familiar.

The mandate to proceed all the way back to the starting point of the Mindaru now seemed questionable. They'd been told to look for signs of Mindaru intrusion resulting from the failed commando raid. But what if the translator's ancestors really had come from the same place, and a journey up the timestream was a critical part of its past? What if it was not just a journey, but an escape?

Without knowing more, it was impossible for Julie, Ik, and their stones to make a reasonable judgment. If those fleeing entities really were the ancestors of the translator, had they fled from the Mindaru, or from something else altogether—maybe even something the ghoststream travelers themselves had done? If not this team, then perhaps the commando team. *Had visitors from Shipworld caused the flight?*

Or were they at risk right now of inadvertently doing something to interfere with the flight?

All they could do was continue their journey into the deeps of time, while the stars and galaxy outside the stream evolved backward, a movie in rewind. The journey seemed to take forever—punctuated by another breathless encounter with a cluster of Mindaru, which they steered around. If they needed to confront those Mindaru, they could do it on the way back. The stones flawlessly recalled the earlier navigation to the Mindaru world, both through time and through the slight spatial deviation from a straight path—and with the sureness of a hand sliding into a glove, the stones brought them back to the star and the planet where it all had begun.

The galactic core was ablaze with a million suns, and marbled with dark lanes of dust and gas. With the light intensity filtered down so they could make out their destination, the core region looked more like the sullen embers of a civilization in ruins. Was that so far off? Was this how the living worlds had looked after the devastating wars that had led to the creation, the annihilation, and the resurrection of the deadly Survivors and their Mindaru warriors? Julie felt a chill deep in her marrow.

Now they had to locate the precise point in history when all the trouble arose. The stones, like a sky observer racking the mechanical focus of a telescope lens in and out, searched the time span following their first visit. The general era wasn't hard to find; they had only to look for a rift in the boundary between the ghoststream and the outer time, the result of the second crew's efforts. Where else was the ghoststream boundary alive with an ultraviolet sheen of leaking radiation and the arcing of quantum discharge? The challenge was that the rift extended for at least a thousand years along the timeline—plenty of room for fleeing entities, if properly prepared, to fly right in.

Let's start at the far end and work our way forward, and see what's coming through, the stones suggested.

The earliest departures from the planet, at a point not far into the future from their first visit, looked at first like tracers streaming up out of the atmosphere, little more than sounding rockets. Were these preliminary ventures into space? This was about where the timestream rift began. Had it been noticed?

Not at first, perhaps. But as they moved their viewpoint slightly back toward the future, the rockets got bigger and brighter and longer-burning. More concerning, the rockets began to aim for the boundary layer of the exposed timestream, which had left open a visible rent in the sky, not far above the atmosphere of the planet. /Are they flying right into the timestream just like that?/ Julie wondered aloud, thinking it inconceivable that it should be so easy.

But it wasn't. The first of the entries disintegrated in a burst of radiation on contact with the timestream. Many more that followed did the same. Dozens more. The failures did not seem to be a deterrent; the probes kept coming, each a little different from the ones before. Gradually their self-immolations came later and later in the process; and there came a time when they learned to enable radical changes in their physical vessels—when they learned to translate their structure into quantum form.

How they were transformed into quantum waveforms when they entered the timestream, Julie didn't understand, though the stones appeared to have some inkling. The free energy leaking from the tear played some part in their transformation. The *how* didn't matter, she supposed; what mattered was where they were going, and what their intentions were. That was not obvious, but at least there was no overt hostility in evidence. One after another, the vessels rode their contrails into the timestream, changing in a flash into little packets of light and shadow.

We see no way to stop them. Shall we move futureward a little farther?

They did, and found that after a handful of years, locally, there came a lull in the launching of Mindaru into the timestream. Perhaps they were preoccupied by other matters, down on the planet. The stones shifted the focus slowly futureward. The next series of launches came quite suddenly—objects shooting out of the planet's atmosphere like fireworks, riding blue-white lancets of fire that boosted them in long arcs upward. Gathered into loose groups of a dozen or more, they sped away from the planet and straight into the timestream rift. Each one flickered a ghostly sapphire and blurred into a brief streak of light as it transited the boundary. More followed from the planet's surface, riding fiery tails and converting to quantum waveforms in the moment of entry. Now and then one failed to transform properly, and disintegrated with a flash.

/It's a mass migration,/ Julie said.

/Hrrm, an escape, I think. They are fleeing./

/Are they what I think they are?/

They are ancestors, the stones said. *Yaantel ancestors. We can feel them as they pass. Very different from present-day yaantel, of course. But they have a fingerprint, a marker on the quantum level.* There was an almost wistful tone to the stones' words. *To us, it unmistakably says "family." And they have, like the Mindaru, learned the technique of transforming as they enter the stream.*

Julie pondered that. /Do you suppose it's *because* the second mission tore open the rift that they were able to escape?/ Had the failed commando raid actually figured somehow in an important early journey for the progenitors? Had those unlucky three warriors bought something very important with their mistake—with their lives?

The migration ended after several dozen of the entities had fled into the timestream. The stones watched a bit longer, and then said, *Let us see what follows.*

Again they moved the focus futureward. They didn't have to go far. Shortly after the departure of the progenitors, a new Mindaru exodus stormed away. This one was a cloud of angry hornets— large, fast, and furious, diving into the timestream.

/Are the Mindaru *chasing* them?/ Julie asked, her voice shaking a little.

Their propulsion is more efficient than the rockets of the Ancestors, the stones said. *Even so, their energy expenditure suggests haste or . . . anger, if beings of that kind can experience anger.*

/Oh yes,/ Ik said softly. /They can./

Julie gulped. /Then the Ancestors have escaped, and the Mindaru are hard in pursuit. What should *we* do? Go after them?/

We believe we can catch up with them on our return trip. Right now, we propose taking a closer look at the planet below. We must understand the relationship of the Ancestors to the Mindaru, and that means learning, if we can, what's happened down there.

This was *their own* history, the stones seemed to want to say, and it was important to know where they came from.

Julie thought it over, and then murmured agreement. /All right,/ she said with a shiver. /Maybe we can find out what's happened to our friends from the sea./

CHAPTER 12

Birth of the Ancestors

AWARENESS CAME AND went, but pain endured. *For the tortured being trapped in the chamber of the mechs, time was measured by the changes forced upon it, changes that were tested, tested again, changed again. Mechanical elements were stitched and tested; most were cut away. New sensoria were tried, failed, retried, and changed or abandoned. There was an incessant feeling of thirst, unslakable, as though everything that had been taken away was encapsulated in that one sensation: a parched dryness, a longing for the briny deeps, for the water of life that was freedom, joy, and recognition of being; for the water that was gone forever.*

That which had been Tzangtzang-Drrllupp no longer knew who or what it was, but it knew it was not alone; there were others like it nearby being similarly tortured with change.

Endless cycles of change . . .

*

There were rare times when that-which-had-been-Tzangtzang-Drrllupp saw the sun and the open air. But only as part of a test, and never for long, never free. So altered was its sensorium that only in a tiny chamber of its mind was it even aware that the sensations streaming in were from the same sun it had, in another life, known as the giver of life.

The mechs now were the giver of life.

And yet, about them was a brooding sense of darkness.

The mechs were creating something new, strange and powerful. But for what purpose?

*

Almost lost, deep within the tangle of alterations and mecho-cybernetic layers, there remained a flickering ember of the original beings, a remnant of the soul. And the barest breath of freedom . . .

To study what had gone on here since their first visit, it was necessary to backtrack in time once more. The stones changed the focus pastward, to a point close to their first visit.

The atmosphere of the planet grew huge and misty in Julie's view. They were coming down over ocean. The progenitor entities they had watched launching futureward of here had come up out of the oceans, or possibly from scattered islands to the west of the continent of their first visit.

Be aware, there is some uncertainty in our measurement of temporal location. We expect to have to home in by trying and then correcting.

/Of course,/ Julie answered. As they brought the ghoststream down toward the waters and a small cluster of islands, she felt more vulnerable than was probably realistic; she felt like a wing-walker on a diving airplane.

Prepare for a snapshot approach.

They were trying a different method of surveillance this time, in hopes of gaining the most information, while minimizing the chances of being seen by the natives. Instead of hovering and observing, they were going to drop fast, drop close, and pause just long enough to snap up images and data. Then they would jump—place to place, and up and down a little section of the timeline, and try to put together enough dots to construct a picture of this narrow piece of history.

Wrapped in their bubble, they slid down through the clouds. An island blossomed in their view, dancing as the ghoststream made small corrections. The stones and the instruments recorded furiously. Then they sprang up and away, and darted toward the next island, and the next. After a dozen islands, they shifted futureward to another slice of time, and did it again.

Julie felt as though she were riding a small plane on a bumpy approach to a socked-in airport, with only momentary gaps opening in the clouds. It was all too disjointed for her to make sense of what she was seeing, but she held onto her hope that once the data were assembled, it would all come together to form a picture. Beside her, she sensed Ik's agitation. Was he sharing her feeling, or did he actually make something out? She called: /Ik?/

He started to answer, but more abrupt changes interrupted him. They were suddenly down on the deck over a craggy island landscape, and for the first time in all their searching, they saw scraps of plant life on the surface—a startling evolutionary change. On the next islands, they saw more. They shifted futureward again. Now, on the same islands, they glimpsed populations of furry, quadrupedal creatures bustling in and out of caves, and in and out of the sea. Hints of artificial structures appeared. Were these creatures building a civilization?

A later time: From high overhead, they gazed down on whole clusters of islands, among which boats churned with urgent speed. On the submarine floor of a lagoon, shadows of long, slender shapes seemed to dance beneath the waves, dappled by jittery light beaming down through the shallow sea. The stones gathered images furiously, and then plunged them down into the waters for a closer look. They glimpsed rows of rocket launchers—they could be nothing else—lined up on the bottom of the sea. *What was this? How could this be?*

They had overshot in time, and missed some history.

Their search for the pieces of the story became frantic. The stones racked them pastward and futureward. They made scores more drop-visits, gathering glimpses: of island wildernesses; of cave-cities; of fishing fleets; of farming on the island slopes. Rockets under construction in caves. But for what?

Finally they pulled away in exhaustion. Julie and Ik slept, or tried to, while the stones worked furiously to put the picture together . . .

Deep in the heart of the Once-TzangtzangDrrllupKrilltn, the ember continued to burn, hidden from the mech-things that tore them apart and forced them back together again in a hundred different ways. Alive in that ember was the knowledge of who they were, had been, could never be again. But if they could never be the same, that didn't mean they couldn't yet be free.

Other knowledge continued to accumulate in them, practical knowledge poured into them in the service of furthering the Mindbody goals—which were still largely unrevealed, except in disjointed pieces. Whatever the goals were, it was evident they were driven by malice. During those periods of being forced open to receive knowledge, a supreme effort was required to conceal their plan to rebel.

The stones proposed that they needed to get closer, and Julie and Ik agreed. Moving the endpoint of the ghoststream eastward from the islands, they dropped back down over the coastline where they had first spotted the Mindaru. The land was transformed; it was now a hard surface striated with sparkling circuitry. The Mindaru were growing exponentially, the land itself becoming Mindaru. Inland, across the baked desert, they found the surface ever more cracked and crazed in the sun. Or perhaps it was more deliberate than that. The ground was divided into small squares like sun-cracked clay but precisely regular. Some of the squares trembled visibly, as if on the verge of erupting into the sky. Were they the tops of space vessels preparing to blast off toward the timestream?

That was a scary enough thought. But the story threads remained unclear. Were these things a threat to the islanders? Where had the islanders come from, anyway? What made them want to flee their homeworld? And what had become of the original turtlelike creatures of the coast? Important pieces of the story were still missing.

We require more data.

They pulled back and tried other times, other stretches of coastline. Earlier . . . later . . . up and down the timeline. Julie's head spun; she could no longer keep track of where and when they were.

Image upon image.

Gradually the picture filled out. The coastal creatures had grown into a developed people in the shadow of the Mindaru, with technology and modest infrastructure along the seashore. Somewhere along the line the quadrupeds appeared, and coexisted with the turtlelike swimmers. A mutation? An unrelated species from elsewhere on the continent? Some of them began to venture out to the nearer islands, the first hints of their becoming a seafaring people.

The Mindaru, meanwhile, had developed a host of machines that moved over the surface of the land, carving and shaping it— and sometimes capturing more of the coastals and carrying them underground. What happened to those captives was not visible.

Futureward up the timestream, however, the captives began to reemerge. They were altered, barely recognizable; they had been transformed into strange and grotesque hybrids of the coastals and the Mindaru.

Would there ever be an opportunity to escape? It was hard to see how there could be; they were imprisoned deep in caverns that only the captors knew the ins and outs of, and there was no end to the experimentation on them.

But a time came when they were brought to the surface. Perhaps to test their capabilities in the open. Perhaps to instill fear in the hearts of the unchanged, on the surface. The reason was not revealed, but for now the control over them was as strong as ever.

Perhaps there were tests in mind, tests of the new bodies under the rigors of outdoor life, tests of the autonomous control that would have them roaming independently while doing the will of the captors. Whatever the purpose, their captors remained unaware of the hidden will, the memories and the soul of Once-TzangtzangDrrllupKrilltn and of others that burned, still, deep beneath the layers of programming.

In the field testing came a moment when the mecho-cybernetic control, by design, was withdrawn to allow testing of the bio-autonomy programming in the beleaguered creatures. That was the opening they needed. The long-banked fires emerged; the inner souls sprang forth and found their leverage to wrest internal control back; and the beings fled across the beach and into the sea, headlong deep into the sea.

The coastals, perhaps following the escaped hybrids, fled offshore in large numbers—migrating to the islands and abandoning their settlements on land. Julie wondered if there would be war over the escape. But while the hybrids and swimming coastals vanished under the sea, the quadrupeds fled in boats on the surface, evading the Mindaru rather than fighting them. Those that did not escape were captured or destroyed. The Mindaru seemed disinclined to pursue escapees across open ocean. Being electronic, were they afraid of the water? Or did they have more urgent matters on their minds?

Whatever the reason, the coastals were able to establish a foothold on the islands, where they developed with almost frantic haste. Were they driven by fear? By the peril of their forced exile? At times the hybrid fugitives could be seen among them. They were hard to track from the ghoststream view once they reached the islands. Many disappeared into caves—not as captives but as refugees—or back into the sea. What sorts of lives did they then lead? Quiet desperation? Pain? Were they the start of some weird, strangely forced evolution?

The stones called another pause, and pulled back while Ik and Julie rested. The stones did not rest, but churned internally, trying to assemble the story from the pieces—the story of *themselves*, their ancestors, and who *they* were.

Julie was staggered by the implications.

We are stunned also. But this knowledge could be crucial.

The time travelers moved futureward, close to the time of the Mindaru departure and the flight of the Ancestors. There was fighting now—skirmishes on land and Mindaru raids on the islands. The Mindaru had mobile units, but were largely a weird encrustation of circuitry across all the land, and possibly deep into the crust, as well. They seemed indifferent to the islanders but desired control of the hybrids, who perhaps were regarded as valued stock for future use.

The fighting occurred in fits and starts. During pauses, the islanders and hybrids worked furiously constructing escape vessels beneath the sea. The Mindaru seemed preoccupied with other matters: mastering control of gravitation, and quantum physics. By this time, they had long since ventured off-planet; now they focused on preparing their way into the sparkling rift of the timestream. The first wave of Mindaru explorers went forth to learn more.

On the ground, they had a change of heart and took a more aggressive interest in the islanders. They began building solid structures out to sea, topping the water surface with their knobbly, glittering masses of circuitry. As the wave-smothering encrustation grew, it swallowed everything in its path. Observation snapshots soon revealed islander settlements burned and scarred and transformed into something that now looked like a continuation of the Mindaru mass. Whatever the Mindaru intended, it included assimilation and scorched earth.

The islanders and the hybrids had no choice but to flee once more.

The final stage of their escape was driven by blind urgency, bordering on panic. The mechs were closing in on them. It had always been known that their escape to the sea, and back into the company of beings they once might have called their own kind, was at best a temporary respite. The mechs had allowed them to live, perhaps to gain more knowledge on the outside, but that time was coming to a close. The mechs were on the march with intent to kill or capture, and Once-TzangtzangDrrllupKrilltn and all the others were almost certainly among the targeted. If they were recaptured, there would be no second escape.

The space launchers were ready, but untested. The strange opening into space-time that floated in the sky seemed to offer a promise of escape forever, if the captor-mechs could be avoided, especially the mechs that had gone that way ahead of them. The working knowledge that had been embedded in the refugees included much that was known about the space-time rift, including the key to transformation into quantum flatwave. Apparently their old masters had planned to take them along on their pilgrimage, but under tight control.

It was agony to think of leaving the cradle of life for the utter unknown. But surely it was better than what would come if they stayed. And far better than leaving as slaves.

The time to act was upon them.

Julie shuddered with relief when the stones pulled the ghoststream bubble up and away from the planet's surface. For a time, they hovered above the planet's atmosphere, as the translator-stones assembled a report to transmit back to home base.

When the first wave of Mindaru rose from the planet, Julie felt an almost overwhelming desire to pursue and destroy them. But it gladdened her heart when at last they watched the fiery escape of the beleaguered islanders from the seabed into the starry blaze of space, and then into the timestream.

CHAPTER 13

Flight of the Ancestors

THE STONES TRANSMITTED their conclusions back to Base Control, while Julie and Ik listened.

High probability that the coastal creatures are early precursors to the yaantel. Direct link cannot be established, but high degree of resonance between personal observation and historical information points strongly to a connection.

Which, coming from daughters of the translator, Julie thought, was pretty good confirmation by anyone else's standards.

Coastal creatures arose in close proximity to the Mindaru, but separate from them. A bifurcation point appears where some of their number were imprisoned and radically altered by the M. The resulting life form likely combines elements of the M. with the original coast-dwellers. Those hybrid beings later escaped and rejoined their biological forebears, and as a group fled from their habitat for new homes offshore.

The modification followed by escape may represent a critical stage for the multimode species that we believe became ancestral to the yaantel. As a matter of nomenclature, therefore, we refer to this group, and those that followed, as the Ancestors.

Julie stirred from her quiet rest, deeply uncomfortable with the notion that anything good came out of the mutilation of the coastal creatures by the Mindaru.

But the stones continued: *We cannot know why the Ancestors fled only to the islands and not farther from the shore. Nevertheless, that hybrid became a race unto itself—one that escaped from the power that made it, first out to sea, and then away from the planet altogether, and finally into the timestream and the future. We can only speculate on what they felt as they fled their birthplace.*

/With some very pissed Mindaru following,/ Julie murmured.

Julie's parenthetical remark is affirmed. But whether the M. were pursuing in anger or simply launching an assault on the galaxy, we cannot say.

/Hrah, I think we can,/ Ik said, shifting slightly so that he loomed like a shadow next to Julie in the bubble. /I think it was both anger *and* an assault./ Silence filled the bubble for a moment, before Ik continued, /But what, hrrm, does this mean for our mission? We came here to learn, and to try to protect the future. We have learned. Now, how do we protect the future?/

/We have to protect the Ancestors' escape,/ Julie said. /Whatever else, we have to do that! We can't let the Mindaru stop them!/

The transmission circuit went dark, and the stones spoke only to them. *The goal is clear. Protect the timeline. Do not interfere, except to prevent interference. The method, however, is less clear.*

/Protecting the Ancestors *is* protecting the timeline!/ Julie said. /If we see the Mindaru attacking your ancestors, we need to take action./

/But how?/ Ik asked again.

Our options seem limited.

/We were sent to undo whatever damage the last crew left behind,/ Julie insisted. /We can call in a directed energy strike from the launch point, can't we?/

That option is available, but risky. A decoherence beam down the ghoststream might be able to close the breach that the last mission caused. But it is not a precision tool. It might kill the Mindaru in the stream, which could be useful. It might also kill the Ancestors, which would not. And it could break the entanglement that makes our own presence possible. The stones paused. *Thus decreasing the likelihood of our survival.*

/Oh,/ said Julie.

It could rebound in an uncontrolled fashion, and kill us all on the way back up, as it did the last crew.

Julie said nothing.

Ik asked carefully, /What if, hrrm, we were to try something different?/

Julie's heart quickened. /Ik, do you have an idea?/

Ik muttered to himself for a moment, as though trying to decide how to say it. /Hrah, I think I do. But it would be risky, also./

/All right. What is it?/

Hesitantly, Ik explained his idea.

———————————

Julie swallowed hard, but she approved of the idea if the stones did. It seemed a long shot, but any chance was better than none. The fact that she had fought something like these things once before didn't make her eager to do it again. But she and her stones—and the translator—had faced the enemy and won; they had flung the terrible things into Earth's sun and saved her homeworld. The Mindaru and their ilk were not invincible.

What Ik proposed was to use *themselves* as a diversion, to give the Ancestors a chance to make good their escape. The precise method they would use to do this was the next question, but the stones already had some ideas about that. The other question was, how could they protect themselves from the Mindaru, if they were going to put themselves deliberately in harm's way? The stones were at work on both of those problems.

All this time they were speeding up the timestream toward the future, winding the clock forward; and they expected, soon, to catch up with the group of Mindaru that had entered the timestream in pursuit of the Ancestors.

The intercept calculations were not easy, even for the stones. They were, all of them, traveling not just across time but also across space, out from the center of the rotating galaxy along the ghostly line traced by the starstream as it would exist in the future.

We will build on what we did coming pastward, and take advantage of the quantum uncertainty of temporal and spatial position.

/Uh-huh,/ Julie said. /Do I need to follow the exact logic?/

Just remember that the ghoststream is long and thin, but it's not quite a taut thread. Think of it as a thread enveloped by a kind of probability fog—

/Like a length of fuzzy wool yarn?/

Exactly.

/And we can use that fuzziness to sneak past the Mindaru and then . . . do whatever we figure out to do?/

That is our plan. So far.

The stones were still working the problem as they closed with the Mindaru, tracking the faint wake the enemy left in the time-stream.

/Do we know yet what we're going to do?/ Julie asked, after an uncomfortably long silence. /Say we pass them at a big arrow-shaped sign that says, 'One hundred million years to dinosaurs,' and they're just pulling alongside the Ancestors. What then?/

Ik had continued wrestling with the question. /Distract them. Ruin their timing. Interrupt their attack./

/Okay,/ Julie said. /But how?/

The stones emerged from their deliberations to say, *Do you remember the evasive maneuvers we used to get past them on the downstream trip?*

/Of course. But that was just a matter of avoidance,/ Julie said.

Yes. We hope to use that method to remain undetected, until the right moment.

/And then—?/ asked Julie.

And then make ourselves visible—directly in front of them.

Julie's heart beat a little faster. /To attack?/

We have no means of attacking. Our goal would be to startle—and then vanish, once the Ancestors are away.

/Uh-hum-m . . . okay. Which we do by—?/

They are riding the timestream originating from Karellia. We are in the ghoststream originating from Shipworld. The two are closely entwined—almost, but not quite, merged into one.

/So, our fuzzy yarn is all entwined with their fuzzy yarn . . . /

Yes. With careful, incremental collapse of wave function, we believe we can cause—

/Schrödinger's cat to appear? Or the Cheshire cat?/

Us to appear in front of the Mindaru. It will require careful, modulated sequencing—

/Right. I trust you to handle the details./

But you must know there's risk.

/Of us being attacked?/

That also. We meant that each time we alter direction, there is risk of degrading our own stability in the ghoststream.

/Fraying our yarn?/

Yes.

/And there's no other way to do it?/

Not that we know of. We could attempt to shade the—

/No—look, stones, just do it, okay? Ik, okay?/

/Hrah./

They initiated an evasive course upon first sighting of the Mindaru. The stones predicted that they might experience the changes as familiar sensory experiences, as their minds interpreted the data. But beneath the images, it was all just wave functions.

At first it felt like the detour they had taken on their way downstream; but this time they stayed closer to the main current, so they could follow a shadow trace of the Mindaru. To Julie, it felt like speeding underwater, steering a course by the quivering shadow of a boat overhead, a faint wake on the surface. When the moment came, they would put themselves directly in front of their foe like a breaching whale. But they had not yet caught sight of the Ancestors they were hoping to protect.

And then they did, a cluster of faint, dark traces barely visible ahead of them. The Mindaru were closing the distance separating them.

Prepare for abrupt maneuvers.

As they angled to intercept, the flow became turbulent and the sensory inputs noisy. The targets became harder to pick out, and for a few seconds, they lost tracking on the Mindaru. By the time they'd sorted through the noise, the Mindaru shadows were already practically upon the trailing members of the Ancestors group.

Hold tight. The stones altered course again, to send them straight up into the closing gap. Julie tensed every muscle.

An instant later, they were surrounded by Mindaru swarming in apparent chaos. No, not chaos—they were moving in coordinated spirals. Were they *corralling* the Ancestors?

/Can't we stop them?/

But they were already too late. The Mindaru had culled the hindmost Ancestor from the herd and surrounded it. Julie felt something quiver in the space around her. She saw a flicker of thin light beams dancing, and then something came into sharp focus, just for an instant—and then it was gone, with a splash of violet light. Decoherence?

Julie's breath tightened. /Did they just kill that one?/

/Hrah./

Yes. We must act quickly to save others.

The Mindaru were already moving onto the next vulnerable Ancestor. But the stones worked faster than Julie could follow. Their ghoststream bubble moved sideways, and then abruptly back. Julie felt a twinge of dizziness, and suddenly they were visible, and directly in front of, one of the Mindaru.

The Mindaru sheared away in alarm or surprise, and the Ancestor swooped and veered in the other direction, seeming to recognize its peril; and after a heart-stopping moment, it plunged out through the boundary of the timestream and away—free from the Mindaru, but tumbling off into uncharted interstellar space. Julie thought she glimpsed a complex play of shadows as it left the stream. Had it just dropped out of its wave function? No way to know.

She had about one heartbeat to meditate on that, and then they were moving again. She felt a sudden flush of weariness. What had that maneuver taken out of her? Before she could think about *that*, they sprang back into sharp relief in front of another

Mindaru. She gasped out in pain at the maneuver, as if she'd been stung. The Mindaru jerked sideways to avoid the bubble, giving another Ancestor a chance to tumble out of sight. But a moment later the Mindaru was back. The stones took that as a warning and steered them clear.

But not for long. On the next approach, the stones brought them quite suddenly nose-to-nose with one of the Mindaru. *This might hurt,* the stones warned. So right. It jarred the Mindaru— but also jarred Julie hard, and it stung even more sharply. What was this pain all about? Energy escaping from their delicate balance? Whatever the cost, it startled and delayed the Mindaru long enough to give one more ancestor a chance to escape. Weirdly, Julie thought she felt something familiar about the thing, a feeling that reminded her just for an instant of the creature they'd observed at the edge of the sea. Probably it was nothing. But whether real or not, that feeling gave Julie a fleeting satisfaction.

The feeling vanished when the bolt of lightning hit—an attack from the Mindaru, not on the Ancestors but on *them*: needles stabbing into their sensor network, fast-moving tendrils trying to penetrate their shields and control arrays. It was not just the bubble under attack, but the stones, and Ik, and Julie in her own head. Rats screeched and clawed to get into her mind. She screamed back at them, clamping her eyes shut. Firewalls slammed closed. For several heartbeats, she saw only gray, and mist, and felt that her every limb was paralyzed. Then the view sprang open, and the Mindaru tumbled away, hissing in frustration.

/Are we free?/ she gasped. /Or did it get its teeth into us?/

Free. They're not yet quite as formidable as their descendants will be. But we have lost the element of surprise. There is little more hope for this strategy.

/Hrah . . . / Ik sounded winded. /What now . . . ?/ Repelling that direct attack had taken a lot out of him.

Julie too felt the toll of the battle, brief as it had been. It left her feeling stretched thin, as though each movement had drained her a little more. The stones had warned them of the risk. She was afraid they might be losing their connection back to the future, back to their bodies. What if they decohered and disintegrated right here, half a billion years in the past, or wherever they were now?

There was no answer; but there were still Ancestors at risk. The stones tried once more to make their bubble visible in front of an attacking Mindaru, but it ignored them. Apparently they were now just a nuisance, not worth changing course for. When the nearest Ancestor attempted to flee, it was caught and engulfed, and died in little flashes of light. Two more ahead of it met the same fate. There were still a few more, farther up, but what chance did they have?

Dizzily, Julie said, /Is there anything else we can do? We're losing them!/

Not from here. The stones steered them back into the shadows beneath the main current, and steadied their flight back up the timeline toward home. *We must flee. But we also must decide whether to ask Base Control to fire a decoherence pulse.*

/To stop as many Mindaru as possible?/ Julie asked.

/And kill us?/ asked Ik.

That is a risk. We will keep to the outer edge of the stream and hope it washes past us. It may destroy some Mindaru. More important, it could seal off that opening downstream. If we are fortunate, it will still allow us to flee back to the future.

Maybe, might, perhaps. And if it made matters worse, what then? Julie wondered. /Why can't we get the hell back to Base and out of the stream, and then fire the pulse?/

We are needed to guide the aim and focus of the pulse. We do not want to repeat the mistakes of the last mission.

No, we do not, Julie thought.

The stones began transmitting to Base Control, suggesting precise coordinates and frequency requirements for the pulse. They concluded with: *Stand by.*

/Stand by for what?/ Julie asked.

The stones answered by adjusting their course again, taking them toward the gray haze away from the main channel. To the outermost fuzz of their string of yarn, she thought.

/Aren't you putting us awfully close to the boundary where we might get flung out of the ghoststream and disconnected?/ Ik asked.

It is a calculation of probabilities. The chances of our being found in any one location here are low. Or if you prefer, we are becoming more diffuse. This, we hope, improves the likelihood of the pulse passing us by without effect.

/But I don't want to be thrown out like the Ancestors, half a billion years from home./

Unlikely. But if it were to happen, we would not last long enough to notice, the stones said dryly. *This is the best plan we have been able to devise if we hope to use the decoherence pulse and survive. Do we have your approval to proceed?*

Julie sighed. /Yes./

Ik murmured approval.

Hold tight, then.

Nothing to hold onto but my ass, and a virtual one at that, Julie thought. Now that they were committed, she just wanted it to be over. The Mindaru were nearly invisible shadows rippling far away. For a long time, nothing happened. She let her breath out, gasping, and forced herself to keep breathing.

And then came a rumbling: a wave coming toward them, building. It was a surge of energy, cascading down the eons from the future. It was about to roar past like a gargantuan, runaway freight train.

The stones busied themselves doing something with the stream, somehow shaping the path for the surge.

Julie looked up toward the future. Although she felt the thing coming, she saw nothing but the empty, glowing tunnel of the ghoststream. Then it became visible: a flickering pinpoint of light in the distance. Growing in brightness, it was like the headlight of a train far away, its light shining onto the rails ahead of it, pulsing from side to side, flashing a warning. /Ik, do you see it?/

/Hrah, yes!/

The light leapt toward them. It was as though the train's headlight tilted up, just enough to cause the reflection on the track to spring toward them with impossible speed. It blazed, roared. Julie wanted to scream, but then it was past them—past the Mindaru shadows—*gone*.

Had it hit anything? She couldn't tell.

It's not over, said the stones. *Brace yourselves for the rebound. The blowback. We can't control that.*

The first passing of the wave wasn't what would be most destructive. What would really hurt was loss of coherence in the entanglement between the future and past. If that were to occur, it would be when the pulse reached the far end of the ghoststream, still anchored near the origins planet.

/Let's go!/ she cried, as the stones accelerated their own rush back to the future.

Megayears spun past outside the stream, stars bursting to life and exploding in death, the galaxy wheeling in majestic rotation. What the Mindaru behind them were doing, they couldn't tell—whether pursuing or escaping.

We did the best we could, the stones said. It sounded like an epitaph.

The best they could do? They had saved a few of the Ancestors, and inconvenienced the Mindaru. Was that all they had to show?

We did what we could, the stones repeated, as though attempting to persuade her. Or maybe themselves.

/Hrah,/ said Ik. /And what have we done to our own timeline?/

Julie grimaced. Had they changed the past, and thereby altered the timeline in their own century? Or had they done exactly what was needed to keep it just as it had been? She blinked fast at the blur of years measured by the lives of worlds outside the timestream.

Or did we repair it after the last team's unfortunate mistakes? the stones asked.

And with those words, the blowback hit.

CHAPTER 14

Hard Pursuit

KORO WAS NOT happy; Bandicut could see that clearly enough. "Where are you taking us?" the Karellian sputtered, waving at the viewspace, where his homeworld had disappeared behind the clouds of the Heart of Fire.

"We are pursuing the Mindaru, likely all the way to Uduon," Ruall answered, floating in a widening circle around the bridge. "Has anyone seen Bria?"

Koro ignored the question. "Are you abducting us?"

"Not at all," Ruall clanged. "We are in the middle of a military maneuver. As soon as it is possible to return you to your home—"

"Why are you taking the Karellians to Uduon?" Sheeawn interrupted, seeming every bit as alarmed as Koro. "You could be letting them see things that—"

"We are *all* going where our pursuit of the Mindaru takes us," Ruall snapped, with clearly diminishing patience. "And right now that is the Uduon system." She waved a paddle-hand at Bandicut, as though asking if he could *please* take over calming the rabble.

Bandicut was grateful when Li-Jared stepped up to the task. "Here's what you all have to understand," the Karellian said, rubbing his thumbs and forefingers together as he stood in front of the four guests. He angled his head toward the image of the Mindaru fleeing ahead of them. "If we let that thing escape to tell its friends, there are going to be a *lot more of them*." He pointed at Quin and Koro. "Especially if Karellia doesn't turn off that temporal shield." Before either could respond, he swung to point at Akura and Sheeawn. "And that can't happen unless Uduon stops throwing asteroids at Karellia."

The four stared at him with a mixture of emotions that appeared to range from distaste to uncertainty to defiance.

"Now see here—" began Koro.

Li-Jared silenced him with a glare. "Those things will be death to both of you. And after that, to a lot more worlds. *What will it take to make you believe that?*"

Bandicut was weary of it, but in his heart he couldn't blame them. They simply had no experience with the Mindaru. Even the encounter just past had shown them how hard the Mindaru could be to catch, but not the damage they could do. Bandicut sighed as Li-Jared continued, "Did you see how effective our best shot was against that thing? Those shots we fired would have destroyed a fleet of your ships. That *was* our best shot—right, Ruall?"

Ruall made a soft cymbal sound. "Yes," she said, and Bandicut thought she sounded disappointed. "Until we can think of something better."

The Karellians and the Uduon were now quiet. Finally Quin said, "Is that supposed to make us feel better? Are *you* going to defend us against these things? The way you just stopped that one?"

And that was really the crux of the matter, wasn't it? Could they really be expected to disarm, if *The Long View* couldn't handle the enemy?

Li-Jared sat down with a grunt and gazed forward into the viewspace, watching the space pursuit. The Mindaru was a blinking marker arrowing straight through the glowing clouds of gas between the Karellian and Uduon star systems. It was moving at a speed *The Long View* could barely match while staying mostly in normal-space, which they had to do so as not to lose track of it. Unless the Mindaru stopped to sightsee along the way, or decided to turn and fight, there was little hope of catching up with it before it reached Uduon home space.

———

Dark watched *The Long View* set out in pursuit of the Mindaru. The ephemerals did not appear to be in immediate danger, so Dark shadowed them closely enough to keep track of the chase, while staying out of the way. She was still uncertain what to make of this Mindaru. It was different from the ones she had encountered during the Starmaker episode. Those Mindaru had been like dense little spaceships, with no ephemerals on board. This one seemed to be only half-present in this space-time, more like the ghostly thing they had seen in the starstream than a solid object.

/*Can you help us stop it?*/ asked a small voice, coming from somewhere near. Dark's translator-stones helped her to hear the words, and to understand the inflection and thought behind them, and also to locate their source.

"**Bria! It brings pleasure to see you!**" Dark had grown quite fond of the tiny pandimensional creature. But what was she doing out here, away from the ship? She seemed to be floating between two layers of splinter-space, which gave her some protection while maintaining a clear channel back to the ship.

/*I too. Strange ones, these.*/

"**Yes, but dangerous. You must be very careful of the Mindaru.**" The little creature's method of visiting was clever, but it seemed a risky time to be ranging out.

The gokat shivered, but conveyed an aura of confidence. /*I can see it. I know how it moves. Not solid like those we know.*/

"**No. More like the way it was back in the stream.**" Which made it hard for Dark to know what to do. It wasn't quite solid, and Dark wasn't sure how to control it. With the Mindaru she had encountered at Starmaker, she had used her ability to control energy and space and time to get the better of them. But with this one—in such brief encounters as she'd had, she'd found it impossible to get hold of the thing. The ephemerals might have said it was like trying to catch water in a net.

Bria was darting back and forth in the little region of splinter-space she'd carved out. She seemed to want to say something, but couldn't frame the thoughts enough like words for Dark to pick them out. It was something like, /*(Scare them.) (Want to kill me.)*

(Solid to kill.)/ Her darting movement sent her caroming off Dark, and for a moment then, Dark thought she was able to read the gokat's thoughts clearly.

So that was how Bria thought they could beat the Mindaru! Make it solid. Maybe that *would* work. Maybe it would, after all.

"You need to convey this to the ephemerals. Can you do that?"

/Yes yes yes yes yes . . ./

Bandicut conferred repeatedly with Jeaves and Copernicus and Ruall about the Mindaru. What would they do with it if they caught it? "We can slug it out with them," Jeaves said, "but I don't see what our killing stroke would be. I don't *know* what would kill it, after seeing what it shrugged off back at Karellia."

"Nor I," said Ruall. She spun out of sight, and then back, twice. "Remember, in the starstream, it was like a wave function that became solid? I don't think this one has become completely solid yet. I don't fully understand it."

"Well, if *you* don't . . ." Bandicut began, before pausing for thought. "Where's Dark, anyway? And did you ever find Bria?"

"Ah—" Ruall spun out, and spun back. "Bria went to see Dark. She is on her way back. Here she is."

The gokat appeared with a little *pop* and stood on the bridge deck, cocking her head first at one and then at another. She seemed excited. Ruall bent slightly, and they muttered together almost inaudibly. Then Ruall straightened and said, "Excuse us for a moment. Bria and Dark have an idea." And with that, Ruall and Bria both rotated out of sight.

They were gone for the better part of an hour, and when they came back, Ruall simply said, "It might work. Copernicus, may we confer?"

Because they were in pursuit, Ruall had said, she was pushing the ship's effective speed higher than on previous transits. Akura wasn't quite sure what Ruall mean by "effective speed," but it caused the Watcher occasional bouts of lightheadedness. According to Ruall, it was due to the accelerated threading through the gravitational labyrinth of the Karellian-Uduon binary star system. Akura wondered if anyone else understood that, because she didn't.

For most of a day, the Heart of Fire clouds streamed past in glimmering vapors, too tenuous to look like anything real; and yet, they had long been a curtain of impenetrable mystery concealing one planetary system from the other. This ship was pulling that curtain back. To Akura and Sheeawn, the journey was a rewind, somewhat faster, of the passage they had made to Karellia, though with a different flavor of apprehension bubbling beneath the surface. Akura's hopes for some kind of reconciliation between the two worlds rested in limbo, but her fear of the Mindaru had been heightened by the experience of actually seeing one. Her thoughts went out to her homeworld, and her niece, who might soon be facing the thing.

In quiet moments, Akura began mentally probing the clouds again, to see if she could reconnect to the layerings and magnetic tendrils that she had sensed on the first passage. Probably there was no practical benefit to be gained, but it kept her busy, and keenly aware of what lay ahead—not just the Mindaru, but her need to connect as soon as possible to the other Watchers, and persuade them . . .of what? To stand down their offensive weapons? Or to redirect them against a different enemy?

She spoke little with the Karellian Ocellet and her officer. Those two seemed so shocked by the journey and all that had happened that they appeared almost to be in their own world. For Akura it was hard, even when circumstances might have allowed, such as at mealtime, to carry on casual conversation with those who were not yet proven *not* to be her enemies.

When the ship broke out into clear space, into the huge bubble within the nebula where the Uduon solar system lived, its orange-hued star was immediately visible in the distant center of the bubble. Akura felt a mixture of apprehension and relief at the sight of her own sun. After a quick survey of the system, the robot pilot Copernicus adjusted course for the fourth planet, tracking the Mindaru. "It's making a straight course—" the robot started to say.

"For our planet?" Sheeawn interrupted, his voice filled with dread.

Copernicus made a ticking sound. "Almost. Not quite." Akura caught that much directly, and had to wait for Sheeawn to translate: "I believe it is making for the asteroid launchers, this side of your homeworld."

"Don't tell me," Bandicut grunted.

"Yes," Copernicus said, and continued, "I think it has detected the weapon."

The other robot, Jeaves, floated into view and began speaking. Sheeawn summarized for Akura, "They think it may try to hack into the control systems for the launchers."

Akura tightened her gaze. "Do they think the Mindaru could *do* that?"

"Oh yes." Sheeawn was looking a little pale himself. "They say it can do that. It seems quite adept at just that . . . sort of thing."

"We have to stop it," Akura whispered, her voice nearly inaudible.

Sheeawn, still listening to the others, translated, "They cannot tell whether it is simply trying to neutralize a danger to itself, or . . ." and he paused, listening, "or whether it intends to seize our weapons for its own offensive purposes."

Bandicut walked over to them, his arms crossed over his chest. "The time has come. You must decide where you stand. Will you set aside your enmity against Karellia and help us turn those launchers against the *real* enemy, if we can? If not, we're going to have to destroy the launchers ourselves. There can be no further delay."

Akura winced as Sheeawn translated. Her thoughts sputtered with objections to Bandicut's threat. But suddenly all that emotion fell away. She peered at Bandicut and Li-Jared as though seeing them for the first time. The rapport she had previously begun to feel with them now seemed hollow. They were preparing to take military action against her world's forces, if they found it necessary. The thing was, what if they were right? Would it be better to lose the launchers than to have them taken over by the Mindaru? Akura glanced over at Quin and Koro. They appeared to be struggling to follow the conversation; they were as disoriented as she was. Akura said finally, "I must communicate with my own people. Do you have the means for me to do that?"

"We do," Jeaves said. "If you would step over near Copernicus . . ." He indicated a spot where a small console pedestal was rising up out of the deck.

Akura hurried.

It took some fiddling to establish the kind of connection she needed, but fortunately, Jeaves and Copernicus seemed quite skilled at that. Eventually she had, at the other end of a radio connection, one of her deputies from her own house. Finner was his name. *"Watcher!"* exclaimed the distant voice. *"We did not expect to hear from you so soon! Have you reached the other planet yet? No, you must still be in our solar system."*

For a moment she felt blinded by the sudden realization that only a few days had passed since their departure, although it felt much longer to her. "I am returning in great haste from the other world. I require most urgent action—"

"Of course. But Watcher, it is the middle of the night here—"

"Then wake everyone up! The danger is grave and imminent. I need to speak with Defense Chief Landon, and with whoever is moderating the Circle."

"Yes, but . . .that may take time."

"I do not have time. Uduon does not have time. I do not care who you must disturb or how you do it. Do it now, please, while I wait."

"While you—yes, Watcher." There was alarm in Finner's voice. *"At once."*

"Keep this channel open!" she instructed—half a second, she guessed, before Finner would have cut her off. "I will be here."

The wait was longer than she liked, and she spoke with Sheeawn while she waited, telling him what she intended so he could more readily interpret to the others. Finally she heard a voice again from the communication device. It was not her deputy; it was Chief of Planetary Defense Landon. *"Watcher Akura. I am told that you have urgent news."*

"Yes." She hissed a breath. "I have not yet shared it with the Circle. I am trying to reach the moderator by radio. But this cannot await my rejoining the Circle on the ground."

"What is it, Watcher?"

"It concerns the control of the launchers. Are you tracking a second object closer to you than we are?"

"We have noted a faint echo, but it is very weak and believed to be of no consequence."

"It is of every consequence, Chief!" Akura tried to explain, but it was difficult to summarize in just a few words, and she only succeeded in confusing the defense chief. She started over, restricting her explanation to the enemy that right now could be trying to seize control of a launcher.

Her deputy Finner interrupted to say that he had a connection to the Circle moderator, Watcher Kriila. Should he be joined to this call? Akura hastily asked the defense chief to hold, and switched channels to speak with Watcher Kriila. "Forgive me for intruding, but I require you to contact the Circle at once. I need you to make a decision . . ." *To support me in my decision. For all of us.*

Her mental rehearsal of how to explain kicked in this time, and she managed a clearer explanation of the situation. Watcher Kriila agreed to call a Circle meeting at once. Akura returned to the channel with the defense chief.

The connection was broken. By the time her deputy got it back, the chief sounded frantic; a problem had cropped up while she was speaking to Kriila. *"Watcher, there has been a disruption of the number-four launcher control system—an attempt to seize* control. *We have shut down that launcher as a precaution. It . . . resisted shutdown. Is this interference coming from your spacecraft?"*

Her hearts spasmed. "Our ship—no. That is the Mindaru, the enemy I warned you about."

"Understood, Watcher. But our tracking network had lost that echo."

Akura muted the microphone and said to Sheeawn, "Ask Ruall if this ship is attempting to force entry into the control system of the launcher." Sheeawn hurried to do so and came back at once with a reply: *No.* Akura spoke again to the defense chief. "You can be certain it is still there, Chief, because I am telling you so. We are still tracking the object. It is more like a sensor ghost than a solid object, but no less dangerous for that. It is now close to one of the launchers. I am not sure which one." And she thought to herself, *Is the word of a Watcher enough for something like this?*

There was uncertainty at the other end. *"I did not mean to suggest doubt, Watcher. But this is all so unexpected . . ."*

Sheeawn gestured urgently, and she muted again while he spoke. "Ruall says time is running out. She does not believe we can hold the launchers against the Mindaru. They *all* need to be powered down at once!"

Yes, she thought. And if I ask for it just like that, they will wonder what exactly this enemy is that they cannot see. But what else can I do? Keying the comm again, she said to the defense chief, "We may not be able to block the Mindaru from taking control of the other launchers. We need you to power them down completely. *Immediately!"*

There was some static and confusion before the chief's voice became clear enough to understand again. *"—such a drastic request—really requires a request from the entire Circle."*

Akura could barely contain her frustration. "Do you understand what I'm saying? If this Mindaru gains control of a launcher, it can use it any way it wants! Including against us!"

Even more scratchily, the voice asked, *"Why would it do that?"*

Akura found her gaze met by Li-Jared's, who gave a slight but firm gesture of assent. "Because," she said, "its goal is to find and destroy . . . organic life. Like ours."

There was silence from the other end, and Akura pressed her lips together tightly, waiting, determined not to bow under the weight she felt pressing on her shoulders. No Watcher had ever made such a request before. A glance over her shoulder confirmed that the two Karellians were watching her intently. Whether they knew exactly what was going on or not, she hoped they understood that the fate of the weapon being used against them was being decided.

Finally the defense chief spoke again. *"We are sending shutdown signals to all launch control systems. We have confirmed that Launcher Number Four was being compromised by an invasive signal. There was some difficulty in shutting it down—apparently it at first refused the commands—but our people report it now powered off."*

Akura closed her eyes in gratitude.

"We are getting confirmations now. All stations have powered down except two, now one. Wait—all are confirmed shut down now."

Akura released a tight breath in relief. "Thank you." She turned and nudged Sheeawn to pass the information on to the others. To the chief, she said, "That is a start. But the crisis is not over. There is a hostile power on the loose in our space. It came from very far away, and it is not the enemy we thought we were fighting. There may be more on the way."

"We are at your disposal. But we need information, and there must be a strategy. What do you recommend?"

Akura could only shake her head, fingers worrying at her collar. *A strategy?* "Right now, be vigilant for any form of invasive signal, and any tracking target, no matter how faint or improbable. Stay in close contact with us."

"That we will do."

CHAPTER 15

Battle for Uduon

BANDICUT WAS ONLY briefly disappointed at losing the chance to turn the launchers against the Mindaru; it seemed more likely that they would have become a weapon *for* the Mindaru. Better that they were shut down before they could be turned. Jeaves reported back on his long-range scans of the various launch complexes: "Counting outward from high planetary orbit around Uduon, it appears that four launch points have been shut down. I'm less certain about two more in Lagrange orbits farther out, or an unknown number in orbit around Uduon's sun, perhaps gathering objects for the launchers."

Sheeawn spoke up at Akura's behest. "Three in orbit around the sun," he said. "Or at least that sounds about right; it is not really the Watcher's area. But you are correct in guessing that their purpose is to gather and feed asteroids to the others." He glanced at Akura for confirmation. "Two of the four in Uduon orbit are also feeders. The other two are the main launchers."

"So if those two main launchers are down, there can be no more attacks on Karellia. Right?" Li-Jared asked.

Sheeawn affirmed that, with a quick glance at Quin and Koro, who were paying close attention. Sheeawn looked as if he felt uncertain whether he was doing the right thing in revealing the information.

"Good!" Li-Jared said. "Keep them down, and then the Karellians can turn off their shield."

A moment passed. Then Jeaves said, "We may have a problem, folks. Launcher Four has just powered up again."

"*What?*" Li-Jared's cry was echoed by virtually everyone on the bridge.

"The acceleration rings are energized," Jeaves said. "The Mindaru must have penetrated before the shut-down order came."

And just what is it going to do with that launcher? Bandicut wondered.

"It can't do much with *just* the launcher," Jeaves said, as though reading Bandicut's thoughts. "It needs to be fed rocks by the others."

"Are you monitoring the feeder launchers?" Li-Jared demanded.

Jeaves answered, but Akura and Sheeawn were both shouting now, which drowned out his answer. Akura got back on the comm and reached her defense chief. Sheeawn translated breathlessly in real-time for those on the ship. Landon already knew about it; his people were frantically trying to learn what was going on. The launch platforms were all automated; there was nobody aboard. Information was hard to get now; the Mindaru had somehow blocked Uduon's access to the communication channels.

Akura staggered back from the comm panel, looking as though she were in physical pain. Sheeawn's face paled as he translated. "Communication has failed to *all* parts of the launching system. At least one feeder ring has also come back on. Telescopic observations indicate the main targeting rings are rotating into a new position. To target something else."

Sheeawn stumbled in his words, and Akura gestured to him to hurry up and convey the message. "It appears they are turning to target Uduon itself."

How long do we have? Bandicut wanted to know. How long before the first rocks flew? Ammunition had to come from the feeders. How long did they have to stop it? Akura didn't know; the observations weren't that precise. She had gotten back on the comm to her fellow Watcher, and told him to pass the news of a planetary emergency. In return, she received provisional support from the Circle to do whatever seemed necessary to protect Uduon. It wasn't clear that all the Circle believed everything she reported—not because they didn't trust her, but because it all must have seemed so outlandish. The support she had would have to do.

"Can we get readings of our own?" Bandicut asked. "Are we close enough yet?"

"The long-range view is getting better," Copernicus said. "But we're not close enough to take action."

A window sprang open in the viewspace, showing a highly magnified image of the number four orbiting launch complex. It was not so much a single structure as a cluster, all arcs and coils and hard-edged lines, curving around a common axis, and gleaming in the reddish sunlight like strange wire sculptures. There was no central hub where a crew might dwell; there was no crew. The cluster extended over several kilometers of space. Several bowl-shaped collectors glowed dully, receiving beamed energy from much larger solar collectors a hundred kilometers away. The larger collectors were arrayed like petals around a flower with the launcher at the center. The barrel of the weapon, a long series of linear-accelerator rings, was moving very slowly, changing its alignment to point toward Uduon.

The planet was now a wispy blue and brown and white ball, prominent in the unmagnified portion of the main viewspace, three times the size of Earth as seen from the Moon. Bandicut and everyone else just stared at the magnified image of that barrel, imagining it hurling killer asteroids down onto its own home-world. If anyone had wanted to make sure the Uduon were truly afraid of the Mindaru, this was definitely doing that. *The Long View* was coming in fast, but was still too far away to do any good.

In the magnified window, something emerged into view from behind one of the energy-collection bowls, gliding toward the axis of the launch system. It was the Mindaru, a shimmering blur, not quite in focus. Copernicus tried to adjust the image to give them a clear view of it, but it seemed impossible. "Either it's employing some kind of shielding field, or it still isn't quite solid,"

Copernicus said. "It does seem similar in appearance to the one in the starstream."

"Did it look that way back at Karellia?" Bandicut asked.

"We never got close enough to see," said Copernicus.

Ruall, who had been staying quiet, clanged loudly. "It is still in a waveform state. That's what Bria and Dark talked about."

Bandicut opened his hands emphatically, prompting for more.

Ruall let out a shivering-cymbal sound. "Bria and Dark noticed that it had not taken any offensive action, even back at Karellia. Other than hacking . . .everything available to be hacked. Possibly it *can't* take offensive action, not while it's in this form."

"And *our* weapons can't touch *it*? Because it's not solid?"

"Quite likely." Ruall paused. "But Bria and Dark think they know a way to kill it."

Bandicut blinked in surprise, remembering Bria's urgency upon returning to the ship, and the hasty conference. "Now's the time to tell us! How do we kill it?"

The Tintangle didn't speak for a few seconds, but just spun in frustration. Finally she stopped with a long reverberation. "It is too dangerous for Bria! She must throw herself at the Mindaru, and try to induce it to collapse out of its wave function and become solid! So that it can attack her."

Bandicut's stomach lurched. "Bria is going to take on the Mindaru? By herself? That's—"

"As soon as it's solid, Dark believes she can hold it steady long enough for us to kill it."

Li-Jared had turned to hear the last part of the conversation. He bonged softly in amazement.

Copernicus broke in to say, "I can't tell how long it will take the Mindaru to aim the launcher, or where on the planet its target will be. But if you look in this other direction, you'll see there's no lack of ammunition waiting . . ."

The viewing window split, and the right half zoomed out, pitched down, and settled on a much larger ring, some distance from the launcher. This was a collection ring; inside it, a sizable cluster of rocks was drifting around an invisible center. It was an enormous ammunition magazine, ready to supply the launcher. "As soon as they're done aiming," Copernicus said, "I don't see what's to keep them from launching."

"Can we go any faster to intercept?" Bandicut asked. He was trying to imagine how they could coordinate an attack with Bria and Dark—if Ruall was willing to take that chance with the gokat.

"We are closing rapidly, Cap'n. But the timing will be close."

Li-Jared abruptly became animated, waving his hands and shouting, "Wait—why don't we forget the Mindaru for now—and just take out the launcher instead? Can we shoot at it from this range?"

Jeaves and Ruall floated together to the center of the viewspace and studied the image. "It's a longer shot. But I think, my friend, it's a good suggestion," Jeaves said, turning. "At least it's not moving. Three quantum implosion warheads ought to destroy it, or at least disable it. Ruall?"

The Tintangle spun, considering. "It will be in range soon. It is worth trying. I authorize the use of *two* warheads. We have a limited number, and there may be many Mindaru."

The two Uduon were grimly silent, and Quin and Koro simply looked stunned.

The quantum-bolts flashed out from *The Long View*. Bandicut held his breath. The points of light snicked into the dark and vanished, and then after a heartbeat reappeared in the magnified view. The points streaked toward the accelerator rings, and then . . .

The Mindaru suddenly was between the bolts and the launcher. The bolts *winked out*, one after the other.

Ruall made a dissonant sound of distress.

"What happened?" Bandicut asked.

"I am not certain," Jeaves said.

"The damn thing isn't solid! How could it have stopped the warheads?"

"Well, the warheads are designed to cause a sudden and devastating collapse of quantum states. Maybe our friend was able to short them out, or turn them against themselves." Jeaves sounded sorrowful. "I am only guessing."

"What now?" Li-Jared demanded, with his gaze angled at the unhappy Akura and Sheeawn.

Copernicus said, "Does anyone mind if I try to reach Dark?"

"Call her!" Ruall rang. "Tell her we need her *now*. In the meantime, change course for the nearest solar collector!"

Sheeawn stirred back to life and gathered his nerve to ask, "Why? What will we do there?"

Ruall made a soft ringing sound, almost like laughter. "They can't use the launcher without power from the collectors, can they? I doubt the Mindaru can move fast enough to protect them all."

Bandicut murmured approval. "Let's do it. Now."

Ruall gonged, "Be ready to fire particle-beams at the collectors. That might even draw the thing toward us, so we can take another shot at it!"

"Dark," Copernicus said, "is asking what we want her to do."

Ruall gonged again. "Tell her to prepare to do what she planned with Bria—and *hurry!*"

The first petal of the gigantic, flower-shaped solar array began to wither under fire from *The Long View*. It was unprotected. But it was also spread out over a vast area, and this was just one petal of a dozen feeding power to the launcher. By destroying this one petal, they were whittling away at the power supply—but this was not a quick way to disable the launcher. It was, however, getting the Mindaru's attention.

Copernicus steered them along the edge of the solar array, burning metal and glass as they went. The Mindaru would catch up with them in about seven minutes.

Bandicut felt Dark approaching before he saw her. His stones tingled, exchanging long-range greetings. Bria strutted past him like a wiry cartoon character, cocking her triangular head one way and another, as though taking a good last look at everyone. Then she murmured something to Ruall that Bandicut could not understand, and blinked away.

"Dark is about three minutes from intercept," Copernicus said. As they all gathered to watch, Copernicus began to zigzag across the open swath of the solar collector, flying like an angry child, burning and slicing with *The Long View*'s particle beams.

"May I ask why you are flying that way?" Sheeawn asked.

"Distraction," Copernicus said. "If the Mindaru is focused on us, it might not notice Dark coming down on it from above. And it might not notice Bria. We hope she can startle it."

For the next minute, Ruall was exceptionally tense. Bandicut suspected she badly wanted to be out there with Bria, but could not, because she was in command here.

In the viewspace now, they could see the great curve of the solar panel, gleaming against space, huge furrows being plowed in it by the particle beams; and sliding across the face of the panel was what looked like a blurry spot of rain on a windshield. It was the Mindaru, shimmering and not quite real; except it *was* real, and it was threatening to kill uncounted Uduon down on the planet.

Ruall suddenly ordered Copernicus to fly straight and maintain distance. "Bria is getting close to it. Let her do what she can."

Jeaves reported, "The enemy is probing at the periphery of our intelligence systems. Our firewalls are holding, but it is learning fast."

Ruall muttered a low gong, and instructed Copernicus: "Calculate best firing range. If Bria can jolt it into taking solid form, be ready to spike it."

Sheeawn was pleading in his silence. *Kill it*, his eyes said. *Kill it!*

Bandicut opened his mouth to say something encouraging, but never got the chance. Ruall clanged wordlessly, and out in space near the Mindaru, there was a flash, and then Bria was visible—tiny in the distance, but coruscating with white and crimson light.

"It's noticed her," Copernicus said. "I think she must be drawing strength from Dark somehow."

And then Bandicut felt in his stones, connecting to Dark's stones, that the cloudlike singularity was on the move. Dark became visible in the viewspace also, a shadow-shape rippling across the sky, three times larger than the Mindaru. Pulsations of fire appeared in the murk within her. Bandicut felt Dark's presence through his wrist-stones, felt her hard determination to protect her friends. She moved quickly. She dropped onto the Mindaru. At the same time, Bria strobed brighter still.

With an abrupt convulsion, the Mindaru was transformed from a blur to an angular shape with crystalline spines sticking in a dozen directions. It was shockingly beautiful, like a mineral specimen—so beautiful that for an instant, Bandicut almost felt it would be wrong to destroy it.

And then, inside the Mindaru, something came alight.

Ruall let out a twang, a cry of warning to Bria.

"I believe it's energizing weapons," Copernicus said. "It had to become solid to do that."

Bria darted left, and Dark veered right. Now it was Dark that changed abruptly, stretching wide, and in an eye-blink transforming into a bubble around the Mindaru. Bandicut felt a sharp tingle in his stones, and Copernicus cried, "She wants us to take the shot. She's *holding* it!"

Ruall's head was spinning, *whick whick whick.* "Shoot!"

There was a buzzing in the deck, and a *snap,* and the beam of a high-energy pulse lanced out into space, followed half an instant later by a quantum warhead. Both vanished into the bubble of Dark.

Nothing else happened.

The Mindaru sparkled visibly inside Dark, perhaps trying to escape. Then *all* the light was extinguished, and the bubble of Dark was dark, indeed. Nothing moved.

"Yes?" Bandicut whispered. Was Dark holding both of them in some kind of stasis, a time-freeze?

Bria suddenly popped into the air on the bridge, making a trilling sound as she landed forepaws first.

The shadow of Dark's bubble abruptly softened, and an intense violet light welled where the Mindaru had been. In that fireball,

Bandicut imagined, quantum forces were breaking down, atomic structure collapsing, the Mindaru dying. After three heartbeats, the starburst faded.

And his translator-stones spoke. *Dark says this Mindaru is gone.*

Dark's bubble vanished, and the shadowy singularity glided to take up a position on *The Long View*'s left flank. Copernicus was drowned out by cries of joy and relief when he reported the same thing Bandicut had just heard.

Bandicut could not keep from grinning. But he also thought: *We're not out of this yet.* He shouted through the commotion, "We need to go see if it left any launch commands ticking!" He hooked a thumb back toward the launcher complex. "*Now*, Ruall."

CHAPTER 16

Protecting Karellia

AS THE ASTEROID launcher grew again in the viewspace, Jeaves announced, "The accelerator rings are powered up! And it's pointed at Uduon. I can't determine the exact target yet, but somewhere on the planet."

"That can't be right!" cried Sheeawn, with Akura speaking in a distraught voice beside him.

Bandicut felt his head spinning. *Mother of . . .* He strode to the front of the viewspace. "It must have programmed the shot before we got it. Can you take out the launcher, Coppy?"

"Without the Mindaru protecting it, I think so," said Copernicus.

"Particle beam on the main ring," Ruall ordered. "Then work your way back."

Moving the ship into position and setting up the shot took a few minutes, during which power levels steadily mounted in the launcher. Then Copernicus fired. The first burst exploded on the left-hand side of the main ring. A minute later, the control section was vapor and dust and slag, drifting apart in a cloud. There would be no more asteroids fired from here.

"We need to check the other launchers," Ruall said to Akura. "Unless you can assure me that you have control over them?"

That sent Akura back to the comm system to speak to the defense chief. Ruall hovered impatiently. Bria appeared at her feet with a *pop*, and the Tintangle and the gokat engaged in a raspy, metallic-sounding conversation. Ruall seemed to become less impatient as she talked to Bria. Finally Akura turned from the console and said, "The other launchers are all shut down, and there is no indication of Mindaru interference."

"All right," said Ruall. "Bria confirms."

"Huh?" said Bandicut.

"She just went and checked for us."

"Um, *how?*"

"She—no, that discussion can wait until later. Our next immediate concern is back at Karellia. There may be more Mindaru coming. We must return at once."

"Wait," said Akura. "Can we stay long enough for me to go down to the surface and meet with the Circle? There is so much they need to know."

Ruall's head spun around, and she seemed to give the request serious thought. "We cannot afford the time," she said finally. "The temporal field is still in place around Karellia, which means more Mindaru may be on their way. You may use the communication equipment as long as you need to."

"But—"

"Copernicus, let's visit the other main launcher and make sure it can never be used again. Then we must set course for Karellia. Best speed."

"Excuse me," Sheeawn said. "But if Watcher Akura needs to confer with her Circle—"

Ruall made a sharp ringing sound. "I have given my reasons and allowed her use of the comm. Do you want to risk more such attacks?"

"No, but—"

"Then we must see at once to shutting down the Karellian shield." Ruall buzzed, which produced an unpleasant vibration in the air. "So kindly refrain from interfering."

For about ten seconds, there was no sound on the bridge. But Bandicut saw the two Uduon and the two Karellians exchange long, silent looks. He wondered what was being communicated in those wordless gazes. The silence was broken when Akura stepped forward. "Would you think it . . . interfering . . . if we were to share with you information about any asteroids still in flight? So that they could be deflected before they arrive at Karellia?"

"I would welcome such information," Ruall said. "I would not consider it interfering."

Akura bowed. Bandicut imagined her thinking, *This Tintangle has no sense of irony at all.* All she said was, "Then I will seek that information." She returned to the comm unit.

Ocellet Quin stepped forward and spoke quietly to Sheeawn, words that Bandicut couldn't hear, but was pretty sure translated as *Thank you.*

While Akura made her call, Ruall approached Quin and Koro. The two Karellians had spoken little since the ship's arrival at Uduon. Ruall made a muted steel-drum sound. "You've now seen firsthand what's at stake. Will you order the shield around your planet to be shut down?" She paused a beat, then continued, "*Can* you do that? Or will we need to take that action ourselves?"

Given all that they had just seen, Quin seemed remarkably composed as she said, "Yes, I can and will order it. *Provided* we can be assured that any asteroids currently in flight are deflected or destroyed beforehand. There may be those in my government who disagree. But I hope we will not have too many problems on that account." She looked squarely at Koro, who nodded reluctantly. He clearly had been shocked by what he'd seen, but just as clearly, he did not find it easy to acknowledge that shutting down their main planetary defense was the right thing to do. "Thank you, Commander," Quin said. Her tone seemed to say, *Yes, we can talk more later. But I have decided.*

The Ocellet flicked her right hand open toward Ruall. "I believe when our people have seen the images of what just happened—you did take images, didn't you—?"

"Of course."

"Then I believe they will see the wisdom." She bowed to Ruall. "Please—get us back to Karellia as quickly as you can."

It took several hours to maneuver to the other main launcher, on the opposite side of the planet, and two minutes to destroy it. After that, *The Long View* set course for Karellia. Dark flanked them, more or less, though from time to time she ranged off through the nebula, searching for Mindaru, or maybe just scouting the territory. Akura spent considerable time communicating with the Uduon leadership, and she reported that there were no asteroids in flight. Ruall accepted that statement, though it was clear she intended to scan continuously on the flight back, to verify.

Li-Jared was starting to feel like a veteran of the back-and-forth trip. He spent much of the time talking with Quin. If they were related, even distantly across multiple generations, he wanted to get to know her at least a little during this enforced waiting period, and maybe learn something of his own family lore. Quin wanted to talk, too, but her reasons were more urgent. That evening, after everyone else had left the commons, she fixed him with a penetrating, blue-green gaze.

"Li-Jared, I need to know that the people of Karellia can trust you." She raised a hand to stop his protest before he could even draw a breath. "I'm not talking about myself. I *do* trust you. But there are others, powerful people, whom I must persuade to trust you. This is not just about our personal relationship; it is about ending a war; it is about lowering our defenses. This is no easy thing to contemplate."

"I know," Li-Jared began. "But you have seen—"

"Yes, I have seen the Mindaru, and I fear them. But my council has not. They must trust *me* when I vouch for *you*. We may be cousins, but there is a gulf of time and experience between us."

Li-Jared gazed at her evenly for a long minute. Finally he flicked his fingertips outward to her, and laid his hands palm-up on the table. "Ask me what you want to know."

———

What she wanted to know was pretty much everything that had happened to him since his mysterious disappearance from Karellia, hundreds of years before she was born. Rubbing his chest unconsciously, he told her: of his abduction to the astounding place called Shipworld, and his subsequent meeting and partnering with Ik, and later Bandicut and his robots, and Antares. "I think they are the most loyal and trustworthy companions I have ever had," Li-Jared declared, thinking, *I have never said that to anyone, not even to them.*

Quin wanted to know about their missions together, and why, if they were so trustworthy, Ik and Antares were not here with him. He told her, and it took a pot and a half of jorrel tea between them to get through his condensed account. He lingered on the details of the Starmaker mission, because that was where they had first encountered the Mindaru, at least by that name. He did wonder, sometimes, if they were in any way connected to the boojum that had nearly crippled Shipworld, or the adversary that had threatened the sea world of the Neri. Quin's eyes were bright as she listened to him. She seemed genuinely moved by the risks Li-Jared and his friends had taken on behalf of people they didn't even know, and he found himself thinking, *Did we really do all that?* Retelling it to her now, it all seemed hard to believe. Was this a point of connection, or pride, that she might use in "vouching for" him? *Karellian scientist becomes galactic hero . . .*

She did not say anything like that to him directly, but her body language softened as he spoke, and he gradually acquired the distinct feeling that he was talking to kin once more, rather than to an interrogator.

Finally he had to ask *her*: "What happened after I left Karellia? Did anyone miss me? Did my work come to anything? How did you come to be leader of the planet?"

Quin hissed a quiet laugh, in spite of the gravity of their situation. "It would take days to tell you all that. And remember, most of this was before my time."

"Tell me *something*," he pleaded.

With a hint of dry humor, Quin said, "I think your cousin Sari—or should I say my great-great-great-great-grandmother Sari?—might have missed you. And some of your colleagues who were waiting for you to finish work on your time research." He gulped and nodded, waiting for more. Quin waggled her hands in a shrug. "As I told you before, you apparently became something of a legend, so yes, I think people missed you, *and* your work was seen to be important."

"In what way?" He was trying not to tremble now, but he couldn't help it. To finally be in reach of learning what had happened in his absence . . .

Quin whispered a sigh and rested her right hand on his left for a moment. He quivered at the touch, a connection across the centuries. "I wish I could tell you everything. But Li-Jared, it is not my field. Perhaps, when this is all over, I can find a scholar to help you learn all about it."

He twitched again, hopes receding.

Quin released his hand and added, "From the records I saw very briefly, it seemed that some of your colleagues thought there was something almost magical about you and your work." She tapped the back of his hand again. "Or perhaps you just owed them money," she added wryly.

He stared at her in disbelief for several long heartbeats—and then he decided she was joking, and they both hissed in laughter.

As they talked, Li-Jared began to feel as if he might truly be *returning home.* It was a very strange feeling. He had never quite felt at home in his own life, even when he was living on Karellia. On Shipworld, with the friendship of his newfound company, he had discovered a kind of belonging that he'd never known before. He had mostly stopped thinking about any chance of returning to Karellia. But now, here he was forming a new bond, a familial and collegial bond, that felt different.

They were brewing their third pot of tea when Akura came into the commons to get something to drink. "Oh," she said, in halting Karellian. "I am . . . sorry to intrude."

"No, it is all right," Quin said gently. "Would you please join us? And call Sheeawn? I think perhaps we all have a lot to talk about."

When *The Long View* exited the Clouds of Fire once more, with Karellia approaching fast, everyone gathered on the bridge to decide how to handle the next step. Ruall's view was that Quin's word ought to be sufficient to change Karellia's policy regarding the temporal shield—and if it wasn't, well, the Karellians had been warned. But Li-Jared doubted that gaining the Karellian government's full cooperation would happen that seamlessly, a view confirmed by the Ocellet. They had Quin's word, yes, and she was already using the comm to talk to Aylen and other trusted counselors. But Quin was not an absolute ruler. She had Koro's backing, and his supporters were to some degree a different group from her own base; but that was still no guarantee that shutting down the defensive shield wouldn't spark a movement to topple her leadership.

"We need to go back down to the planet with her," Li-Jared said to Bandicut. "Quin's seriously worried about opposition to her decision, and that's not something we can really deal with from up here in orbit."

Bandicut raised his hands. "Your world, your people. Whatever you think."

Li-Jared rubbed his chest, considering the question. "Actually," he said, "I think maybe you should stay here with Akura and Sheeawn. We might need to bring them down later. But right now, I'm afraid they'd just be caught in the middle of a political hurricane. I don't think bringing them down into the middle of it will help."

Ruall floated up alongside them, reverberating softly. "At the risk of agreeing with my Karellian colleague, I agree. Li-Jared should handle that while you, John Bandicut, serve as liaison here. The less we confuse the issue the better, I think. Besides, we might not be done with the Mindaru."

"That's just what I was saying," Li-Jared began, nonplussed by the idea of Ruall actually agreeing with him.

"Are you ready to board the landing craft?" Ruall asked.

"Uhh . . ." They were still well outside the range of the Karellian space forces and the temporal shield. "Aren't you going to get us closer first?"

"You should be on your way as soon as possible. We'll take you inside the defensive screen. But then we must be off in the other direction. We must be positioned to intercept any other Mindaru coming out of the starstream."

Li-Jared didn't like the idea of leaving his friends to face more Mindaru without him. But it seemed the best option. He glanced at Akura, wondering if it would be better after all to take the Uduon down and spare them the danger of another firefight. But no—they had been through it and made the decision, and Akura looked satisfied. "All right," he said.

Jeaves broke in from the console near Copernicus. "Sorry, but this just in: One of our remotes has detected another object in the direction of the starstream, heading this way—probably another Mindaru. We've asked Dark to go take a look."

Li-Jared swore. "Moon and stars! Quin? Koro? Are you ready for a ride down to the surface?"

Ocellet Quin responded at once. "We will get our things now. Yes, Commander Koro?" She gazed out the viewspace, perhaps to enjoy one last time the stunning view of the slowly grow-ing ball that was her homeworld. The luminous energy clouds curved around behind the planet, as though enfolding it in a blanket.

Koro coughed sharply, once, getting her attention. "Shall we communicate our intentions to the defense forces before we fly in across their protection zone?"

"A good idea," said Quin. "A *very* good idea,"

———

By the time she'd alerted the planetary defenses to their approach, and issued a call for a meeting of the defense board immediately upon her return, the planet had grown visibly in the viewspace. They'd passed through the time-shield with barely a ripple, thanks to Copernicus's increasing mastery of the interface. Li-Jared beck-oned to her and to Koro, and with a bow to the Uduon, Ruall, and the robots, they left the bridge and made their way back to the docking bay.

Bandicut walked with them. "Can you fly this crate, if you need to?" he asked, as Li-Jared paused at the craft's hatch.

Li-Jared rubbed his jaw, waiting for Quin and Koro to get aboard. "I think so," he said quietly. "But I won't need to, will I? If I had to, wouldn't that mean we were about to die anyway?"

Bandicut looked thoughtful. "Probably true," he conceded. "But don't worry, the autopilot on this thing is rock solid. And if it goes out—well, maybe *Bria* can fly it."

Li-Jared shivered, wondering if the gokat had slipped aboard. She seemed capable of just about everything else. With a hissing sigh, he reached out and clasped Bandicut's hands. "Don't you worry, Bandie. We'll get this straightened out down there, and be back up to help you with the Mindaru. All right?"

"I'll be looking for you," Bandicut said. He tightened his grip on Li-Jared's hands. "I promised Ik I'd look out for you."

"Me too," said Li-Jared. Then he turned and ducked through the door of the little spacecraft.

The little vessel dropped away and streaked across their field of view and twinkled out of sight in the direction of Karellia. Bandicut sighed and said to no one in particular, "What's the word from out by the starstream?"

Jeaves answered immediately, "The word is, we must make another intercept. Dark has just confirmed the second Mindaru. This one is solid already, probably preparing to fight. But that means we have something to shoot at."

Bandicut felt a sourness in his stomach. "Ah, man. So soon? Is Dark going to be here to give us an assist?"

"She's begun a wide sweep, to reconnoiter the area around the starstream and see if there are others. She'll be back soon."

Bandicut sighed, suddenly deeply missing Charli. /Where are you, my friend?/ There was, alas, no answer. With Li-Jared gone, he had no one to talk to but two robots and a Tintangle. Well, also the Uduon, who were resting now in their quarters. He regretted the need to have them here, if their immediate future was to face repeated, deadly confrontations. It was one thing to make them viscerally aware of the danger. But he hadn't really meant to expose them to the enemy again and again.

He noticed that Copernicus had already put them on a fast course in the direction of the starstream and the incoming Mindaru. "Battle plan?" he asked.

Ruall made a rumbling sound. "I am open to suggestions. Our previous plans did not seem overly effective."

"Except when Bria took charge."

Gong. Her voice sounded distressed; she wasn't happy about the reminder of the danger to the gokat. "I do not plan for that to happen again."

"Agreed." Bandicut had no immediate suggestion, but he bent his thoughts to the question. They probably couldn't expect Dark to grab every Mindaru and hold them for shooting practice. He wondered how many would be coming. Somehow, he didn't think it would be just one more.

There was little to see in the viewspace, just Karellia shrinking to a little ball behind them, and empty-looking space ahead. Somewhere out there was the second Mindaru. It had taken on solid form, so it was ready for a fight. Had it received reports from the first one? Or did they *always* expect an attack? Perhaps that was part of their makeup.

Bandicut recalled what Jeaves had told them about the origins of the Mindaru. They were believed to have been born from the ashes of the most terrible war in galactic history—the survivors of deadly fighting machines that had been pounded to radioactive dust. They were the unexpected remnant that had come back for revenge. Or more precisely, as Jeaves had suggested, to eradicate organic life, set off as many supernovas as possible, and wait for the universe to become more completely seeded with heavy elements and thus hospitable to machine life. They seemed to be nothing if not single-minded.

Did that help him better understand how to defeat them?

Not really.

"John Bandicut, you look thoughtful. Do you have thoughts?" Ruall called.

He realized he'd been standing defiantly with his arms crossed over his chest, lips puckered as though he were working out the final details of a plan to destroy the enemy. If only it were so. Bandicut cleared his throat, unfolded his arms. "We have to nail it before it knows what hit it."

"And? How might we do that?"

He turned his palms up. "That's all I have so far."

Ruall made a thrumming sound that he imagined was disgust. Finally she spun away and returned to her conversation with Copernicus. Bandicut shrugged and went to fortify himself with some strong coffee.

A long-range probe confirmed tracking on the Mindaru moving through n-space, and precisely aimed for an intercept of the planet Karellia. Ruall set them back on battle alert status and put the weapons on standby. She called Bandicut back to the bridge and asked for his newly considered thoughts on dealing with the adversary.

"I was hoping you had it figured out," Bandicut said, meaning every word. "Any more word from Dark? Will she join us for the fight?"

Copernicus replied, "She believes there are more Mindaru—but to find them, she must keep searching around the possible starstream exit points."

"That could take a while. So she's not coming unless we scream for help?"

"For now, no."

Bandicut scratched his side, thinking. "What do we have that we can use at long range?"

Ruall answered. "We have intelligent missiles. But the Mindaru would likely detect their power trace. Unless . . . we approach at speed, and drop them . . ."

Bandicut's eyes widened. "And let them just coast in, silent and dark. And then, boom." He smiled. "I like that. I like it a lot."

"High praise," said Ruall, making Bandicut wonder if she was actually learning to use humor. "That is what we shall do, then. Copernicus, prepare for a high-speed pass."

"Sir, yes sir," said the robot.

———————

Several hours later, two dark objects dropped from the spacecraft and fell away through the strange void that was n-space. They would take better than an hour to reach their target. When Jeaves reported the missile tracks satisfactory, Ruall called for a course change for *The Long View*—enough to ease them well clear of the Mindaru, but keeping them between it and Karellia.

Now they could only wait.

Bandicut felt exceptionally twitchy, sitting by himself in the commons with a huge mug of coffee, and not just because he was nervous about yet another fight with a Mindaru. There was something about this leg of the mission: he had too much time to think. Damn, but he already missed Li-Jared, his nervous, jumpy, brilliant friend. And Charli, of course, always Charli. Was she really dead for good? Or alive, lost somewhere in space without a host? What an end to a lifetime that spanned millions of years!

And Antares, Ik, and Napoleon. Oh, how he missed Antares! For most of this trip, he had managed to keep her mostly out of his thoughts. But now, his heart aching, he could not stop thinking about her. What he wouldn't give right now to hold her in his arms, to feel her gaze, and her empathic touch warming his spirits and his soul. He felt more alone, and lonely, than he had since that first, nerve-wracking journey with the quarx, the journey that started at Neptune and ended at the terribly strange Shipworld, alien and immense. The memory gave him a shiver.

He yearned for a way to contact Shipworld and discover what Antares was doing, and whether she had ever found Ik. He longed to tell them about his and Li-Jared's struggles and their progress so far, and about the loss of Charli. More than anything, he longed to share his heartache with Antares! And even—but no, Julie Stone was far in the past, hundreds of years gone, with everyone else he had known.

Except Dakota. What had happened to her and her ship? Had they survived the encounter?

"Excuse me, John Bandicut—but could you—?" Sheeawn was standing in the doorway to the commons. Bandicut blinked and waved him in. "I'm sorry to bother you," Sheeawn said. "We just wanted to ask you—well, I mean, what we should *expect to be happening?*"

"I'm sorry, please sit." Bandicut gestured to the table before him. "I should have filled you in earlier. Is the Watcher coming to join us?"

Sheeawn looked troubled as he sat. "No, she is very quiet. I believe she fears that she made a mistake in remaining on this ship."

"Is she afraid of this new Mindaru?" Bandicut asked softly.

"Of course. Aren't we all afraid?" Sheeawn's expression was cast down, his eyes barely visible, glinting under his brows.

Bandicut nodded, acknowledging the point. "You're right. But consider this. At least you're showing the Karellians that you're willing to put your lives on the line against the Mindaru—and that's not nothing."

Sheeawn considered that, and seemed to accept it. "But," he continued, "her fear is not for her life, so much. I think it is that if we die, are destroyed—and cannot get back to Uduon—" Sheeawn paused to gulp a breath, and to run his fingers through his hair in agitation "—all that we have to tell our people—"

"—about the Mindaru?" Bandicut asked.

"Yes, but also about you, and about Karellia. All that would be lost."

Bandicut sighed and took another sip of his coffee, now cold. He grimaced. "We will just have to do our best not to be destroyed, eh?"

He was interrupted by a sharp tone, and Ruall's voice: "John Bandicut to the bridge! All hands to the bridge at once!"

Bandicut stood, leaving his coffee. "Fair enough? Let's go see what's about to happen."

Ruall clanged as they strode onto the bridge. Akura was already there. "Intercept in five minutes!" Ruall barked. "Copernicus, can you let us see what the missiles are doing?"

The view ahead zoomed in rapidly, and two seconds later Bandicut saw two gray shadows that were probably artificial representations of the missiles. Four and three-quarter minutes passed. "They are going to have to make course corrections," Copernicus reported. "At the last possible moment."

Two faint halos of light appeared, nudging the missiles into slightly altered paths. The Mindaru came into view. Like the first one, it looked like a mineral specimen with spines, but it was darker and uglier. The missiles glowed again—and veered. They shot past the Mindaru in a clean miss, and the Mindaru continued undisturbed on its course.

Ruall rumbled with displeasure as Copernicus reported, "The enemy seized the missiles' steering control at the last instant. Now it's powering up weapons."

Bandicut gulped.

"Change to defensive profile!" Ruall clanged. "Protect all data inputs. Copernicus, bring us around!"

"You intend to engage directly?" Bandicut asked. He glanced at Sheeawn and Akura, who were trying to disguise their alarm behind stoic expressions.

"Better here than wait until we're back at Karellia," Ruall said. "Copernicus, particle beam ready?"

"Ready, skipper. How well do you want me to aim?"

Ruall spun. "Explain the question."

"For best aim, I would integrate all available sensors. For best protection against enemy penetration, I would shut down all sensors." Copernicus paused. "I must strike a balance. Do you want me to use my own best judgment?"

Bandicut felt a cold claw of fear as he remembered how the enemy had penetrated *The Long View*'s systems on the Starmaker mission, and how close they had come to losing the ship—because that Mindaru had gotten in through a sensor port. They'd escaped because Copernicus had taken the place of the ship's AI, fused with the ship, and shut down its compromised systems. "I think," Bandicut managed, "you should use your own judgment."

"Agreed," said Ruall.

The image in the viewspace went black-and-white and grainy. A blocky object in the view grew in size. "That's the enemy," Copernicus said. "I've cut the sensor input to the bare minimum. The enemy is trying to penetrate our grid, but shield protocols are holding. Twenty seconds to firing range."

Bandicut held his breath.

At twenty seconds, Copernicus loosed a particle-beam burst. A splash of light came back at once from the Mindaru. It struck *The Long View*'s protective shields and blazed, lighting up the bridge like an atomic blast. The ship veered away from the Mindaru, but the blaze left Bandicut reeling. "*Christ!*" he muttered. "What was *that?*"

"Our own burst, reflected and amplified," Jeaves reported.

"Jesus! What did it do to us?" Bandicut cried. He knew he wasn't reassuring Akura and Sheeawn, but he couldn't help it. That blast looked powerful enough to fry them.

"No damage to us, or to them," Jeaves said.

"No damage from *that?*"

"Remember, this craft is made of n-space fields," Jeaves said. "If they ever fail, we won't last long enough to feel it."

"I recommend—" Copernicus began, but he never finished.

A jarring blow hit them, shaking the deck. Bandicut grabbed for a seat to hold onto. Akura and Sheeawn were sprawled on the floor, gasping. Bandicut staggered over to help them up. "What was *that*, Jeaves?"

Jeaves had fallen down, too, and was getting back up with the rest of them. "It did not take them long to learn to manipulate n-space," he muttered, sounding as disgruntled as a robot could sound. "It may have used the energy in our beam—" and he paused as a fresh rumble shook them "—to send shock waves in our direction, directly through n-space."

"Well, what the f—?"

Another splash of light burst over them, and then another. Each was accompanied by a reverberation in n-space. Ruall clanged to

Copernicus to get them out of there. But before Copernicus could complete the ship's turn, the firing stopped, and the enemy went dark.

"Wait," Ruall said. "Jeaves? What just happened?"

"I don't know."

"Copernicus, prepare a quantum pulse. Are we still close enough for a solid shot?"

"Aye." Then, "Firing in four seconds. Three."

"*Wait!*" Ruall went spinning out to the front of the viewspace, then spun back, reverberating. "Don't shoot! Do not shoot! Where is Bria?"

Bandicut looked around and said, "I don't—"

"She is not on this ship," said Jeaves.

"Then where—?" Ruall spun faster, and a ringing cymbal sound turned into a high-pitched keening. "She is not . . . she is not here . . ."

Bandicut was holding his ears. "What, Ruall?"

Ruall spun out of three-space and vanished. For two seconds, Bandicut stood with his mouth open.

Then Ruall reappeared, ringing madly. "Do not fire, Copernicus! *Do not fire!*"

"Why not?" Bandicut demanded. He pointed to the enemy in the viewspace. It appeared dead, but three of its spines had curled into gleaming spirals. It could be alive and gathering power to fire again.

Ruall's ringing crescendoed, then abruptly cut off. "Bria is there! She is *aboard the Mindaru!* She has disabled it! But she is hurt!"

Bandicut stared at her, dumbfounded. "She *what?* She went after a Mindaru by herself?"

Ruall, with her shiny blank face, seemed to glare at him. "Yes," she rang softly. "Apparently she did. And now I must find a way to save her."

Bandicut was still speechless. He looked around at the others—Copernicus, the wide-eyed Uduon, Jeaves—to see if they were hearing what he was hearing. He reached into his thoughts, instinctively searching for the missing Charli.

When he looked back, Ruall was gone.

CHAPTER 17

Getting a Message Off

ANTARES HAD HAD no success at all trying to get through to the yaantel, to see if a warning could be transmitted to Bandie and Li-Jared. While the mission team had granted her permission—and told her that communication to Shipworld was possible via the star-spanner connection—the actual comm options out here half a light-year from Shipworld seemed severely limited. There was a channel that purported to permit messaging through the Shipworld iceline, but neither the yaantel nor Amaduse nor the shadow-people were responding. Napoleon had tried to reproduce his success from the Scalapoorie Sector, to no avail. They might as well have been using a megaphone.

A request to the mission leaders for help hadn't gotten her very far, either—raising the question of whether they were actively interfering, or just blindly indifferent. Did they *see* the potential for danger, with two missions, uncoordinated, both trying to effect change to the timestream? Or was there some unspoken antagonism between the leaders of the two teams, some bone of contention so serious that they would risk the safety of mission personnel over it?

And where was Rings? He had disappeared shortly after their arrival here.

Tapping her fingers moodily on the console she'd been assigned near the back of the control center, Antares decided to check on Ik and Julie's progress. She got up and walked over to the data-pedestal where Napoleon was plugged in. Around them, the control center was quiet, though a great many team members were watching their holo-displays closely.

"I am sorry, milady," the norg said before she could speak. "I have requested a more robust channel to Shipworld, but so far no response. Until that is granted, I am focusing on our mission here." *Our mission. Ik and Julie's.*

"That's what I'm here to ask you. What's the latest, metal-friend?" she asked, laying a hand affectionately on the robot's head.

"They are still in the stream with the Mindaru and the Ancestors. I know little more than the last time we spoke. The slow speed of transmission is problematic, and their being on the move seems to make it worse."

She had watched the slowly compiling low-res images of the alien world, of the early Mindaru, of the flight of the pre-translators, which the stones were now calling the Ancestors. It didn't give them much to act on. But it was enough to give her a rush of anxiety every time she came back to it. She knew her friends must be frantically compiling data. But most of it would stay locked up in their heads, or their knowing-stones, until they were back and the entanglement broken. "*Any* indication of what they're going to do?"

"Just that they are going to try—may be trying now, as we speak—to block the Mindaru from attacking the Ancestors." The norg twitched his mechanical hands together, in what seemed to be emerging as a nervous tic.

"Did they say how?" she asked, surprised by how tight her voice felt.

"No, milady. They spoke of surprise, and blocking."

The anxiety in her chest was squeezing out her breath. She *hated* not knowing what her friends were doing—even if knowing might have made her feel worse. After all this, she found it hard to accept that her friends *here*, in the launch-pod, could die if anything bad happened to their projections *there*, a billion years in the past. She would never really understand it; she just had to take the word of the mission leaders.

She wondered, though, if one reason for the team's rush in launching this second mission of Ik and Julie's wasn't the same thing that had her so worried—the risk of unintentional interference at the Karellia end. Maybe they were in a hurry to get this mission finished before anything could happen at Karellia.

Or maybe they were in a hurry to take credit themselves for stopping the Mindaru.

Surely not.

"Tell me when you hear more," she sighed, turning away.

She had not taken four steps before she saw Cromus shuffling toward her from the rear of the control center. She greeted him, and he clicked his pincers together and rasped, "Rings! Rings-at-Need-d-d w-wishes to speak-k to you!"

Rings! "Where?"

Cromus pointed an eyestalk back the way he had come. "In the lobby."

Antares strode that way and at once spotted Rings-at-Need through the glass partition at the back of the control center. He was bobbing in the air, flexing his thin arms with their paddle-hands. What was he doing out there instead of coming in to find her? "Rings!" she called, pushing through the door.

"Ah, Miss Antares!" the Tintangle twanged. "I have been looking for you!" He made a beckoning motion with his right paddle. "Please come."

"I've been looking for *you*," she said, following him to a corner of the lobby. "Where have you been? Where are we going?"

"We must speak privately," Rings said, as they stopped, a little out of the traffic area, although there was no one else here at the moment. "I have been with the yaantel."

"The translator! Do you have news? I've been hoping you can help me."

"That is what I heard, and why I came," Rings gonged, waving his paddle-hands. "I have no news, I am afraid, but the yaantel is worried. How can I help you?"

"*Worried* doesn't begin to describe it. I need to find a way to get a message to John Bandicut. Do you know if that can be done? Could the yaantel help?"

Rings spun thoughtfully. "Have you tried contacting Amaduse?"

"*Uhhl!*" Antares blew out a long sigh of exasperation. "People like you and Amaduse don't seem to have addresses on what passes for the iceline out here!"

Rings bonged softly. "I will try. But I am not certain how the mission team will respond."

"No?" She was surprised.

"We work together. We do not find agreement on all things. However, they did make you a promise," Rings said, with a metallic riff. "I believe they must keep it. I am certain a way can be found. Do you have a place to connect from?"

Antares puffed air through her lips. "Just my console. But it's in the main control room."

Rings rang softly. "Let us see what we can do."

Even after she watched Rings put the call through, she still wasn't entirely sure how he did it. Maybe Napoleon was following—something about comm shunts through borrowed packets on the mission team's reporting lines. Antares wondered if the mission leaders would approve. Rings made a soft humming sound, which seemed to have an oddly soothing effect on everyone in the immediate vicinity.

The hooded face of Amaduse appeared in her console, eyes sparkling in the darkness of his hood. "I've been hoping to hear from you," the librarian whispered.

Antares sighed with relief and joy. "I have been *trying.* I didn't know how to reach you, until Rings-at-Need came and helped me."

"My apologies-sss. Here, keep this code and use it to call me whenever you have need." The Logothian's serpentine visage weaved from side to side in the monitor. "Are you well? Are your friends still engaged in the mission down-ssstream in time?"

Antares filed the code and said, "I am well, and yes, they are. But I have serious concerns about the mission, and that is why I am reaching out to you. Is there some way to send a message to *The Long View?*"

"Ssss." The librarian's eyes glittered and blinked in the shadow of his hood. "I wondered if that might come up. Discord among factions-s-s of the Round Table, and s-so on. I have already been, sss, exploring the influences and permissions-s that might be needed to get a, sss, transmission approved."

Influences? Permissions? "Uhhl," Antares said carefully, "so it's not easy, but it can be done?"

"Not easy, no. And *verrrry* cos-s-s-tly. Pulsar time is perhaps the most expen-s-sive communication time there is. But since this entire mission plan, if you can, sss, call it a plan, is about s-saving all of us from a galactic calamity, sss . . . I think I can jus-s-s-tify the cost to those who will care."

Antares felt the tension in her body ease a fraction. "Good. How do we do it?"

The Logothian stretched and did something to one side, out of the view of the monitor. "We can send text only, and it mus-s-t be brief. Please tell me the message as concis-s-s-ely as you can."

"Do you want me to dictate it now?" Antares focused her thoughts. "How about this: *'Ik and Julie Stone on mission in timestream. Danger! Ancestors of translator—no, just say,* translator—*at risk! Do nothing to disrupt timestream until we send word it is safe. Please advise your progress. Antares.'* Can you send that?"

Amaduse fussed for a few moments and then said, showing her the screen so she could read, "Shortened to this-s-s:

> *Amds/Antrs to LV. Danger! Ik/JulieS in timestrm. No*
> *disrpt untl AllSafe frm us. Rsk harm trnsltr. [REPEAT]*

"Does that suffice-s-s? It will be compressed by standard algorithm for transmission."

Antares squinted, interpreting the message. "Must it be that cryptic?"

"Sending messages through n-space is a tricky business-ss," Amaduse said. "The transmission will be at one character per ssecond, repeated many times for redundancy. They could be in circumstances where reception is-s-s difficult or nonexistent. They might catch only fragments-s-s. Briefer is better."

Antares bobbed her head. She glanced at Napoleon. "Does that seem understandable to you, Nappy?" If Napoleon could understand it, then there was some chance Bandie—or perhaps Jeaves, if they were still together—could, as well.

Napoleon ticked and read the message back in expanded form. "It is good," he said.

She was aware of Rings just out of her peripheral vision, and she glanced at him, too. "Rings? Can you think of anything else?"

Rings twirled. "I suggest you send it-t."

Amaduse made a sinuous movement with his head and neck. "I cannot guarantee. But if logic and reasonableness-s prevail among higher authorities-s-s, it will be s-s-sent."

"Uhl," Antares said, twitching a little at the *if*. "Will you call me if there is a reply?"

"I am afraid, Miss Antares-s-s, that this-s-s communication can be only one way."

Amaduse let a shrug travel down his sinuous body. Getting a message to *The Long View* was iffier than he had made it sound. There was no need to trouble Antares about something she couldn't influence. But now he had his work cut out for him: to get the Council to release the communications pulsar to him long enough to get the message out. Fortunately, he didn't require pulsar time to listen for a reply. There would *be* no reply, not from a small ship that had no access to the power of a harnessed pulsar—unless they stumbled across similar technology at the other end.

"Gonjee, I need you."

There was a scuffling sound, before the hairy face of Gonjee popped up beside him. "More research?"

"Not this time, Gonjee. I need to contact the Interstellar Communications Subgroup of the Shipworld Council, on a matter of utmost critical importance."

Gonjee cocked his head. "Excuse me, Master Amaduse, but shouldn't such an urgent request come directly from you? I am merely your representative."

"No, you make the contacts, Gonjee. If they ask, you may imply that I am too busy managing the emergency to make the call personally. Here is what I want you to say . . ."

"Amaduse," said the councilor's aide, a tall, sticklike biped who looked severely agitated. "I have had a difficult time getting through to you. Your assistant, Gonjee, was adamant that you were too busy to speak personally. But as I am sure you must know, for a request of this magnitude we *must* be briefed more thoroughly. Can you attend the next subcouncil meeting, and present a peer-reviewed statement of intent—?"

"Ssss, forgive me," Amaduse interrupted, trying to remember this aide's name. He couldn't. Perhaps just as well. "Ssurely you know that time is *far* too short for that. Thisss is a critical matter potentially affecting the ssafety of worlds throughout the galaxy. No, Councilor" —he knew this was an aide, not a councilor, but flattery rarely hurt— "I must have access to the pulsar—tonight, if possible. There is nothing else on the transmission schedule of this urgency. If you mussst have a reviewed statement, use the mission orders-s for *The Long View*, and the Galactic Core team."

"But," said the aide, "those missions were authorized by two different Council entities, and they—"

"I *know* they were authorized by different, sss, entities, and they do not talk. That is *precissssely* why I need to sssend the message, and sssend it now."

"But—"

"Councilor, time grows sshort, sss, and why are we wasting it, you and I?" Amaduse said briskly. "If you need more information, why don't you asssk those entities why they sssent out two high-risk missions with conflicting orderss." Amaduse peered into the monitor, hoping it wouldn't occur to the aide to ask why a *librarian*, even such a highly placed one as Amaduse, was involved in an operational matter.

The aide made odd little snicking sounds and clenching gestures with its upper limbs. It leaned forward. "But *you* know that those factions are feuding," it said in a muted voice. "We're constantly dancing around the two, trying to avoid a fight. They haven't worked together without quarreling in, oh—"

"A long time. Yesss, I know."

"Anyway—" The aide reared its head back slightly and flared its eyes wider. "What is *your* interest in this matter? Isn't mission operations somewhat outside the realm of . . . information storage and retrieval? I intend no offense."

"And I take no offense," Amaduse said, bobbing his head and weaving side to side in a way that he hoped would convey just the opposite. The aide was sharper than he had hoped. "Information management isss in my view one of the most crucial jobs in the running of Shipworld. How could I take offenssse?"

"I am sorry, I meant no—"

"But in this case, sss, Counselor, mission operations *on both sidesss* omitted the crucial detail of *information flow to the operativess!* Both missions, in case you were unaware, are at risk, sss, of making *massively harmful mistakesss* unless appropriate information is provided to them."

"Oh, I—"

"In the case of *The Long View*, all the information I can provide must be compresssssed into a fearsomely short message. But . . . it is *crucial* that they get that message soon-esssst." Amaduse drew himself up to his full serpentine height. The aide's eyes tracked his upward movement in the monitor. "And sso . . . I ask you . . . once again. Will you secure me the pul-s-sar time I need for the transmission?"

The aide was bobbing his own head now. "I will speak to the group leader. Perhaps we can find a way. Can I reach you at this node for the next few hours?"

"You may," Amaduse said. "Thank you." He nodded to Gonjee to end the call. Amaduse the librarian was too pressed for time to terminate his own iceline calls. Or so he hoped it would appear.

Two more calls from other Subgroup members went more or less the same way. The final obstacle was cost. Was Amaduse going to pay for it? It was a government responsibility, he argued. But here he met stronger resistance. In the end, to get the thing done, he agreed to meet the cost himself—which he managed by plundering discretionary funds from several of his other ongoing projects. By dinner time, Amaduse had his clearance to commandeer the pulsar-transmitter for the night. He was also cleared to send a similar message to the Shipworld naval vessels somewhere en route to Karellia. That was a longer shot, since transmissions to ships in n-space were notoriously difficult to complete. But when it came to that, they didn't even know if *The Long View* itself had yet come out of n-space.

By the time he actually sat to dinner, the message to *The Long View* was on its third repeat cycle of transmission. He'd closely watched the first cycle, not that there was terribly much to see. In visible light, a slight haze of violet light grew on one side of the pulsar's accretion disk, where the transmission modulators applied their leverage to the natural *whup-whup-whup* rhythm of the neutron star. That glow built for a few seconds, while—as he understood it—the bursts of energy from the spinning neutron star were given some kind of phase shift, converted to tachyons, and dropped into the deeper dimensions of n-space.

Riding the intensely powerful beats of the pulsar, the tachyons flashed out at translight-speed, carrying the message inward into the galaxy, toward the vicinity of a world called Karellia. Perhaps *The Long View* would detect the fluctuations and recognize them for what they were. Perhaps they would not. The hard part was not knowing. In all likelihood, the next message they received from *The Long View* would be its approach contact upon their return. *If* they returned.

Amaduse watched until he was satisfied that the messages had gone out, and would repeat through the night. Then he turned away. He had done all he could do.

———————

Antares was left anxious and at loose ends in the control center. The matter was in Amaduse's hands now. But even if he got the message sent, would John and Li-Jared be able to receive it? Would they understand it—if they were even at Karellia—if they were still alive?

All Antares could do was wait with Napoleon and pray for Ik and Julie's safe return. The robot rested nearby as she sat at her console. He hadn't had a lot to say today, and she was a little worried that he might be running down, or losing interest—or worse, heart. She gazed at him with affection. His camera eyes were focused straight ahead at the monitor consoles at the front of the control room. From time to time, his eyes flicked to one side, then the other, then back to center. At first he didn't seem to notice Antares watching him; then his eyes rotated suddenly to look at her. "Is everything all right, Lady Antares?" he asked.

"I don't know," she answered truthfully. "I just don't know. Sometimes I think it's worse to be just waiting than to be on a mission and in danger." At that moment, she noticed that the norg was plugged in, recharging. So running down wasn't the problem. "How about you?"

"I don't know, either," Napoleon said, turning his eyes forward again. He didn't say anything else for a few moments, and she wondered if that was all he had to say. Suddenly he blurted—it sounded like a blurt: "Sometimes I worry whether we're doing the right thing."

"Napoleon, you surprise me! What exactly do you worry about?"

"What's *not* to worry about?" the norg said, breaking his forward stare to look back at her. "Whether Ik and Julie will return unharmed. Whether they will change all of history by accident. Whether going back in time is just a terrible mistake. Whether John Bandicut and Li-Jared are safe and will return." He jerked suddenly, shifting the position of his arms and back as though to relieve cramped muscles. His eyes suddenly flicked back to the consoles. "Whether we, you and I, have been left in the backwater doing nothing while our friends go out to die."

Antares sighed. "I worry about all that, too, my friend. Also, whether we really can stop the Mindaru from overrunning the galaxy. I'm trying to just hold on to my hope that Amaduse sent the message, and that they'll get it. And that they'll all be safe. Because if I can't hope for that, then I'll go crazy."

Napoleon's mechanical hands were slowly opening and closing.

Antares had a sudden piercing thought, and she wondered why she hadn't asked before. "Do you especially miss Copernicus?"

Napoleon tapped and clicked for a few seconds before saying, "I am uncertain how to answer, milady. If I say no, I may seem cold and . . . robotic." He turned his head to gaze straight at her, and his metal face seemed somehow stranger to her than it had in a long time. "If I say yes, Lady Antares, you may think I am only saying what you want to hear—or worry that I have been influenced by romance novels again." He lowered his head slightly, his eyes downcast. "I think perhaps it is best if I don't answer."

Antares cocked her own head to one side, studying the robot. They had been through a lot together in their crazy company, and she had grown quite fond of him. She hardly thought of him as "inorganic" anymore. "I won't think any of those things," she said quietly. "I really want to know what you think."

Napoleon raised his eyes to her again. "Then I will tell you. Yes. I miss Copernicus terribly, like the sibling I never had. Or perhaps like a parent misses the son who has run off and left no word."

Antares felt her heart break. "Napoleon, that makes me sad, as well!"

The robot cocked his head to one side, as though mimicking her. "I know it sounds like one of those novels, but it is the truth. I hope I will one day see Copernicus again. But it feels increasingly like a forlorn hope."

"Don't say that. Don't *ever* say that! They are very resourceful, all of them. I have faith they'll be back." *Because to think anything else would be to give in to despair, and I will not do that.*

Napoleon said nothing to that, but turned to look back at the monitors. "At least we can be here for Ik and Julie. And I must be ready to gather all the data possible—whatever happens."

Because what we do here could determine the future for the whole galaxy, she thought. *Funny how hard it is to keep our eyes on that prize when our friends' lives are at stake.*

The console in front of her lit, and a text communication appeared. It said simply,

The message has been sent. Keep your hope alive.

—Amaduse.

Antares slowly relaxed back into her seat and hissed a smile of gratitude and relief.

CHAPTER 18

Blowback

PERHAPS THE STRANGEST thing about the starstream, from Charli's point of view, was the presence of other living, sentient minds inside it. In a way, it felt surprisingly quarxlike to her, all of these minds with no body. The others were at once almost intimately close, while remaining distant and impossible to connect with. She *had* managed to glean a little, from listening to their thoughts and words, however indistinct. She thought one of them might actually have once been *human*. There was also the robotic one, who might have been an earlier form of Jeaves. Yes, *their* Jeaves, the Jeaves she knew. There were others, with names like Ganz, Dax, Ali'Maksam. A hrisi, a construct, a Logothian. There was the mind of a great, red star, which had died in the fire of the starstream's creation, and other minds as well, reaching up from the far end.

In a way, it was like coming home, living among quarx. While at the same time, it was hopelessly alien.

Except for that touch of familiarity that came every so often. Could it be—?

Ik? And Julie Stone?

The connection was so tenuous, it was like hearing a voice from your distant past, so faint over the rustle of other sounds, you couldn't be sure what you were hearing. But something else curious about this starstream: Every point seemed connected somehow to every other point, so that distance just didn't matter in the way it had in what, through John Bandicut, she had come to think of as the normal world. And so she strained to focus on that familiar connection, on the voice of Ik, and Julie Stone, John Bandicut's friend and lover from Triton.

Charli *felt* their presence; when she listened just so, she *heard* them; but though she tried, she could not *see* them. But she felt something else, though: Mindaru near. That was why there was tension, and fear, in the whispers of her friends. They were in danger.

Now Charli knew why Ik was in the timestream. He was here to stop the Mindaru.

And Julie? What had brought her here to help? Surely the translator was involved.

If so, then she, quarx, must become involved as well. She wasn't sure how to do this, but she tried calling out into the stream.

/// Ik? Julie?
Can you hear me?
Can I help? ///

Over and over she tried, determined not to stop until her friends had heard.

———

In the instant before the blowback hit, Julie imagined a voice she did not recognize, across the eons and light-years: *Can I help . . . ?*

The blowback came with a blast of snow and hail and thunder, obliterating everything. She was carried like a leaf on the wind; and the wind careened and shifted violently, and she spun now like a snowflake on a gale. She was tossed toward the galactic origins, toward the Mindaru rushing up the timestream; and she was tossed toward the future. Was Ik still here? It was impossible to know.

Her direction changed, and changed again. She caught glimpses of stars . . . and then of whiteout, and movement . . . and then abrupt nothingness, void, not even darkness, just nothing . . .

And then light cracked across the void, and the wind roared, and she could only shake with fear. /Ik, are you *here?*/ she cried against the fear and roar, suddenly utterly terrified of being left alone here. No place, no time . . .

Another crack of light, color with no name.

/Stones . . . ?/

And heartbreakingly distant, and answering /Hrah . . . /

Dwindling . . .

And the faintest echo of, *Can I help . . . ?*

She wanted to hold onto Ik, but there was nothing physical to hold onto, no Ik, no stones, nothing but void. And pounding wind. And light, flickering in and out, like a faulty image . . .

The blizzard swirled and tore at Ik. There had been a series of violent shifts in his own momentum through time, which felt like physical movements in space. The storm overwhelmed it all; it bit at him and cut, and tore at his soul. He was afraid. Wild animals stalked through the swirl. A wrong move could bring them into the open, where they would see him and attack. But what of the Mindaru? What of them? Ik clutched at his breast. Were *they* the wild animals? Where was Julie? Did he hear her cry out? He tried to answer, but his voice was lost on the rushing wind.

Can I help?

What was that voice? Could *who* help? It did not sound like his voice-stones, or Julie, or anyone else he knew. But he clung to those words while he quaked in fear, as the blizzard blinked away, and darkness struck.

Darkness. But in the distance, shards of light.

What was that? What were those jagged shards?

Why were they suddenly turning, as though on an enormous wheel, everything in all of creation turning around him?

The wind was dying away.

The wheel beneath him turned awhile, and then slowly coasted to a stop. The darkness faded into purplish light. He was standing at the edge of some great ice field, a weird landscape of jutting crystalline splinters and spikes. It did not seem natural; it reminded him of the Caverns of Ice back on Shipworld, where the deadly boojum had lurked. He shivered, but did not actually feel cold. He heard only silence.

But echoing in his mind, the memory of words, *Can I help?*

"Hrah," he murmured, just to hear his own voice. It sounded far, far away. He called to his stones, /What is this?/ He called to his companion, /Julie? Are you here?/ He heard no answer, and felt afraid to call again, lest he break whatever spell held this strange and fragile place together. He feared that she would not answer, would never answer.

The silence returned.

He could not stand it. He called out again to his stones. Had he lost them, too? Had he once more lost his voice-stones? He shivered again, more afraid of that than anything else he could imagine, even death.

Finally he heard them speak—sounding more shaken than he had ever heard the stones sound.

Uncertain . . . of our status. We may have lost entanglement . . . with home base.

Lost entanglement? That would be bad, he thought. Catastrophic. He asked, /What then is keeping me alive? Aren't I nothing but a quantum-entangled ghost?/

We are uncertain.

Ik drew slow, steady breaths through his ears. He felt his heart pounding. /Are we stranded? Have I lost my connection to Julie Stone?/ He paused. /Please do not say you are uncertain./

The stones took a moment, before saying, *We do not know.*

/Well, that, hrrm, is not acceptable./ To be so utterly helpless here? Wherever *here* was? He growled softly. /Not acceptable at all./

The pounding wind died down, and with it the snowstorm. In perhaps the oddest change to the world since it had exploded around Julie, sunlight suddenly broke through. Golden and blissfully warm.

Sunlight? Warmth?

She was no longer a ghostly entity. She was solid. But she was alone, standing by herself in a meadow.

Meadow? Sunlight?

The meadow was gently sloped and speckled with delicate white wildflowers. She stood near the upper edge of the sward, facing downslope. The flowers went briefly out of focus, as though a lens were being adjusted; then they came into sharp focus and began opening wide, one by one, to reveal delicate petals, pearl white with pale blue interiors. They released a fragrance that took her instantly back to a mountain glade she had once visited in the Rocky Mountains of North America, on Earth.

Earth. The memory of her homeworld suddenly overwhelmed her, making her so nostalgic and homesick that her knees buckled, and she staggered to keep from going down. There was no chance of her ever seeing that blue-and-white planet again, or any of the people that she loved. The thought made her weep. But what about her friend right here in *this* place? Where was Ik? What had happened to Ik? She called out to him, and called again.

What was this place? Was she dead, waiting to be ushered into an afterlife?

She could think of nothing else to do. So she knelt in the meadow and wept.

CHAPTER 19

Inside the Mindaru

COPERNICUS CLICKED AND made fussing sounds. Jeaves said to Bandicut, "Ruall has left you in command. She said she was crossing over to the Mindaru to retrieve Bria. And then she disappeared."

Bandicut was stunned. "You mean, she actually left the ship and crossed over? Through the dimensions? Like Bria?"

"John, I can't see across the dimensions any better than you can. I've told you what I know." Jeaves floated out to the center of the bridge and seemed to regard the view pensively.

Bandicut was startled to realize that they had drifted closer to the Mindaru. "Coppy? Are you doing that on purpose? Did Ruall ask you to maneuver in closer? I'm not sure this is safe."

"Probably not," said Copernicus. "But it appears to be dead. And Ruall did ask me to get closer. Just in case—"

"We have to pull Bria back somehow? Or both of them?"

"Yes. Do you want me to back off?"

Bandicut grimaced. "I guess not. But no closer for now." He sighed deeply and stood, hands on hips, gazing out at the tactical situation. The dead Mindaru was, in the unmagnified view, still rather small and indistinct. In the close-up window, it looked like the corpse of a particularly nasty, spiny sea creature.

"Can you explain, please, what is happening?"

Sheeawn's question, so exquisitely polite, made Bandicut wonder if Sheeawn thought he was in actual control of their situation. "I'll try," he said. "Ruall and Bria have used another . . . dimension . . . to board that Mindaru. And we can only wait for them."

It had been hours now, without word from Ruall. *What was she doing? What were they doing?* The Uduon were getting restless and worried, and Bandicut didn't blame them a bit. "Hang on," he said, and turned and called to Jeaves, who was in his usual spot in the corner of the viewspace, near Copernicus. "Anything at all?"

The robot just rotated his head back and forth.

Bandicut sighed. Despite the company of the Uduon, he felt acutely alone in this situation. No Li-Jared, no Ruall, no Bria. No Antares, no Ik. And no Charli, who might actually have been able to detect something in the mysterious hyperdimensional realm into which Ruall had vanished. Even the stars seemed unusually cold, lonely, and distant. Where was the starstream that was causing so much trouble, anyway? It was completely invisible from here. "Copernicus," he called, "are the probes detecting any additional movements out in the direction of the starstream?"

Copernicus made a rasping noise that he guessed was supposed to be a clearing-of-the-throat sound. "Actually, Cap'n, we're not getting any signals at all anymore from the probes."

He tensed. "Why not?"

"Speculation: It may be that the Mindaru knocked them all out on its way here."

"But you didn't say anything about them dropping out earlier."

"No," Copernicus conceded. "But their routine reports are only transmitted twice a day, so I didn't notice."

"Why only twice a day?"

"To conserve power, and to reduce the risk of being detected, and eliminated or corrupted."

"But you're saying that other Mindaru may have followed, quietly eliminating them anyway?"

"It is possible, Cap'n."

Bandicut rubbed his knuckles. "What about Dark?"

Copernicus made a ticking sound. "At last report, still sweeping the space around the starstream. She was concerned that these might be the first two Mindaru of many."

"Right. But it still leaves our flanks wide open, doesn't it?"

"It does, Cap'n. Recommend we be prepared for action on short notice."

"Most definitely," Bandicut said softly. "Full alert status. All weapons ready."

"Of course, Cap'n. Do you have a firing sequence in mind—if we have to fire? Or shall I use my own judgment?"

"If immediate action is called for, I trust you to choose the best weapon. But—I want you and Jeaves to analyze our results so far. Figure out what works and what doesn't."

"Aye, Cap'n."

"But Coppy, listen—we're not going to fly off and leave Ruall and Bria, if there's any way we can avoid it."

"Of course not, Cap'n."

Bandicut finally turned back to Sheeawn and Akura, wondering how much of the conversation they'd followed. "The plan," he said, "is to continue to wait here for Ruall and Bria, unless circumstances—and by that I mean an imminent threat—force us to move."

Sheeawn nodded, but Akura kept her head cocked at an odd angle, looking not at them, but somewhere out into space. Was she wondering if she had made a terrible mistake in coming on board this ship?

———

The continuum squirreled around Ruall as she slipped through splinter-space toward the Mindaru. That much was easy, as far as it went, but the path over to and then *into* the Mindaru was tricky to pick out. The Mindaru had distorted the space-time surrounding it, and Ruall had to poke and prod before she found her way in. Bria, she believed, was in here somewhere.

The enemy vessel was a compact object in round-space, mostly a mass of solid-state circuitry; but in the other dimensional frames, it was a very different thing. Ruall rotated through thread-space, flat-space, round-space, diamond-space, spindle-space . . . and found the Mindaru configured differently in each space: a tesser-figure in one, a tight solid in another, and a wild series of trusses and spikes in still another. Ruall encountered no active opposition. She felt she was being watched, but the watcher seemed helpless to act. It felt as though there were pieces missing from the enemy—as though Bria had *removed* parts of the Mindaru, much as she had removed the weapons from soldiers in another setting.

That was probably how she had disabled it—but at what cost? Bria was in here somewhere, wounded. But with every dimensional view of this place looking different, it was distinctly possible that she could only be seen in exactly the one right view. */Bria?/* Ruall called. */Bria!/* And again. And again.

Perhaps Ruall was taking the wrong approach. Maybe *looking* wasn't the answer. Ruall tried shifting to other senses. For a time, she did not move at all. She thought she sensed *pain*, somewhere in the distance; she also thought she sensed happiness. Bria's? Ruall called out again, this time focusing on the tightly wound interdimension she called *chaiee*, which offered neither sight nor sound, but did give rise to other senses. Sometimes, the *chaiee* provided a channel for the bond she shared with Bria.

Not now, though.

Still, as Ruall rotated through the diamond-space view of the Mindaru, she thought she sensed a fold in its structure, and within the fold an opening. She followed her instinct and moved deeper into the enemy's body. Space here was strange, a multi-dimensional maze echoing with a brooding intelligence. In the background was a faint rumble, as of systems trying to work, but failing, because they were too broken.

Again, Ruall called. This time she heard a cry—a thin, reedy, cry—Bria in pain. Ruall rotated quickly through splinter-space to get to where the sound had originated. She came to a chamber, deep in the truss-work of the Mindaru structure. Some of the truss-supports ended abruptly, as though cut. Had this chamber been carved somehow out of the fabric of the continuum? */Bria?/*

And then Ruall saw her. The gokat was huddled on the far side of the chamber—shivering, as though cold, frightened, and exhausted. She peered at Ruall, but there was no recognition in her gaze. Ruall streaked across the space to her, ringing over and over: /*I am here. I am here. I am here to help you!*/

Bria whimpered.

That was not like her. She must be badly hurt. /*I have come to get you out of here,*/ Ruall said, but Bria seemed not to understand. Was she physically injured, or in shock? Ruall could not tend to her here; they truly needed to get out. But how?

Ruall began to spin. First she rotated around her own axis; then she started swinging wide, encircling Bria, like a moon around a planet. She was tracing out a space, creating a bubble of protection around the gokat, in diamond-space. Bria raised her head a little. Then the rest of her body began to lift, levitated by the localized distortion of space that Ruall was creating. Once Ruall had the gokat inside her sphere of control, she began to ease her out, back the way she had come. Ruall found a thin slipstream through splinter-space that took them most of the way. They were almost out now.

Almost.

A tendril of *something* reached across splinter-space and hooked them. Ruall felt it, and Bria flinched. It was not a physical restraint, but something hooked into her mind—something telling her to stop, telling her to turn back, telling her to open her thoughts and reveal all that she knew. *It's safe*, she felt. *You must come back.* The feeling was so compelling that for an instant she was tempted to comply; but then she realized it was an instruction from *outside*—and she immediately resisted, twisted, slipped, struggling to escape the thing's touch. But it was not a physical thing to be evaded; it was a thought tangled up with her own thoughts. *Come back. It's safe. Help us rebuild.*

The Mindaru was not dead.

The gokat flexed her body, straining to obey.

Ruall tightened around her, but Ruall herself felt the temptation powerfully pulling her, entwining itself in her mind, as though it was *her own* thought, her own will coaxing her on. Could they, should they move closer to this intelligence, join with it and make something even stronger, something indomitable and indestructible? Wasn't that why she was here? Wasn't that why they were all here?

Why did they keep fighting it? Surely this was the better way. Not just better, but so much easier . . .

She squeezed Bria a little tighter. The gokat shrieked in pain, jolting her. Something in Ruall broke loose, and she caught a sudden vision of Bria giving in to the darkness, to the predatory mind of the thing that would rule them. Devour them.

No! /Bria, we must not!/

Join. It is better.

It was a serpent wrapped around her neck, choking and twisting and pulling. Ruall fought angrily, but she could not simply expel the voice from her thoughts; it was entangled with her own knowing and being, and it was tenacious.

Help us rebuild.

Bria shrieked in pain again. Ruall suddenly realized Bria had shown her what to do when she'd attacked the Mindaru. Ruall might have this predator's thoughts in hers, but she had her own strength and speed, and she knew how to rotate matter into other dimensions.

Before the enemy could block her thought, she spun herself up and became Ruall, dimensional chopping machine. She sliced viciously across the trusses that held together what was left of the Mindaru, flinging the pieces into opposite ends of spindle-space. She sliced back, up, across, down, chopping and spinning pieces of the Mindaru into unconnected dimensions. The voice in her head screeched, losing its hold. The Mindaru was weakening.

Bria squeaked and whistled. Joy? Or pain from having the Mindaru ripped away? It didn't matter; it had to be done.

Ruall was possessed by her fury. This thing had hurt Bria, and threatened them all. She would destroy it; she knew how to do that now. She would not stop until it was destroyed. She slashed, and carved, and shouted to Bria that *she* deserved the credit for leading the way. The Mindaru was in tiny pieces now, scattered through all the higher dimensions. The voice was gone. Its hold on them was gone. Ruall did not stop. She would continue the demolition until there was nothing whatsoever left to hold a thought, or even to feel the pain.

Bandicut waited anxiously, feeling useless. He'd been over everything he could think of to do to help Ruall (nothing), and rehearsed possible intervention schemes (none that made any sense), and was starting to wonder under what extreme circumstances he might need to abandon Ruall and Bria and continue the mission. If more Mindaru showed up, he might have no choice. He hated the idea. He had no idea whether Ruall was in trouble, or just taking a long time. He didn't know whether this Mindaru was still a threat or not, and he didn't feel he could risk the ship by taking her in closer—not with passengers on board, and the mission unfinished.

"Coppy, are you still signaling Ruall?"

"Yes, Cap'n. No reply."

Bandicut felt the eyes of the two Uduon boring into him as he walked past them, pacing. He almost turned to speak to them, but then turned away again. What would he say?

"John Bandicut," Jeaves said, interrupting his thoughts. "Word from Dark. She has detected other objects moving from the starstream toward the Karellian system—nature unidentified."

Bandicut cursed under his breath. But he sensed that there was more. "What else?"

"I am not sure what to make of this, but we are detecting a strange signal, *possibly* a signal. Possibly tachyonic. Embedded in n-space layers. I am uncertain, but think it could be a transmission from home."

"You mean *Shipworld*?"

"Yes, sorry. I am trying to process the signal. We don't have a proper antenna for such a thing. I don't even know what such an antenna would look like. The n-space generators that form our hull and move us through n-space are detecting the vibrations, and the patterns suggest a deliberate signal. The direction of origin is right for Shipworld."

"I'll be damned," Bandicut breathed.

"It might take a while to make any sense of it. I suggest Copernicus and I work on it in the background while we deal with the rest of the mission. Speaking of which, shall we send an update to Li-Jared?"

"Definitely. And find out if he's made any progress with the Karellians!"

"Initiating contact now," Jeaves said.

It took the better part of an hour to reach Li-Jared, because he was in conference with the Karellians. When Jeaves finally got him on the line, he sounded tired. *"It's been a difficult proposition to convince the council, but I think they may be coming around,"* he said, his voice thin but clear. *"The members who agree with us actually had a good idea . . ."*

"That's encouraging. What's their idea?"

Li-Jared seemed to have turned away to speak to someone else for a moment. When he came back, he said, *"Aylen rallied the physicists, who say they could configure the time-shield to send a disruptive temporal shock pulse into the timestream. They think it might destroy any more Mindaru on their way up, before they can reach the present."* Li-Jared paused. *"What do you think?"*

Bandicut thought about it. "I don't know. What about innocent people traveling in the starstream?"

"They say they can tune it, so that only things entrained in the time distortion would be affected. Presumably that would be just the Mindaru."

"Probably true," Bandicut said slowly. "But we don't know."

"No, but we do know letting the Mindaru continue to come through is bad," Li-Jared said.

"Definitely true. But I'd like to talk with Jeaves and Ruall first."

"Ruall! How is the little dictator? And did you get rid of that second Mindaru?"

Bandicut explained what had happened so far.

Li-Jared was silent for a time. *"Moon and stars!"* he said finally. *"That's tough. Still, you can't wait forever for Ruall. You've got to protect the ship and the mission."*

"I'm open to suggestions."

Li-Jared made a puffing sound. *"I don't know. But if any more of those things show up, beat it out of there and go back for Ruall later."*

"More or less my plan."

"Good." Bong. *"Well, there are lots of people here wanting to talk to me. I'll try to be ready with that pulse thing, whenever you want to call for it."*

"Okay. Let me know."

The connection went silent. Bandicut stared into space. He realized he was lightheaded; he hadn't eaten in hours. "Jeaves," he said. "I'm going to the commons for some food. Come chat with me."

CHAPTER 20

Diving into Junk-Space

TALKING THE KARELLIAN proposal over with Jeaves only left Bandicut with even more questions: If sending a destructive temporal shock pulse down the starstream might stop (or kill) the Mindaru, who else might it stop (or kill)? The chances might be slight, but did they know enough to justify the risk? What about innocent ships in the stream? What about Dakota and her ship? What about the quarx? *Charli could still be alive out there in the starstream.*

He gloomily ripped off another hunk of his cheddar-ish and something on something-like-pumpernickel sandwich. "We have a little time yet before they'll even be ready. What about that tachyon signal? Any progress deciphering it?" He shoved the oversized hunk into his mouth.

"It is difficult," said Jeaves, speaking from the bridge via holo.

He answered around a full mouth. "So you've said."

"But I'm pretty sure it *is* a modulated signal."

"For us?"

"Pretty sure. It is no doubt compressed. I have several decoding methods."

Bandicut swallowed, lifted a mug of coffee to wash it down. "And?"

"By all but one, we get a pretty hashed up signal."

"So what about the one?"

"By that one, we get a phrase that includes something close to the name *Amaduse.*"

Bandicut frowned, taking a moment to absorb that.

"And . . . something that *could* be rendered as *danger.*"

"*Jesu,*" Bandicut whispered. Had that Logothian found a way to send a message across those thousands of light-years? How? And more importantly, why? A warning? About what? Bandicut spoke slowly. "If it is Amaduse, then he must have something pretty important to tell us. We should make damn sure we know what it is."

"Agreed," Jeaves said. "I am continuing to work on it."

"Every available resource?"

"Of course. Was there anything else you wanted to talk about right now? Because I'd like to give it my full attention."

Bandicut shook his head, and the holo of the robot blinked out.

He rubbed his eyes. He was very tired, and if he didn't get some rest, he was going to start making stupid mistakes. It would be smart to rest before he was needed again.

He was buzzed awake from a fitful nap by Jeaves summoning him to the bridge. When he arrived, massaging a stiff neck, he was greeted by Copernicus with:

"The two new incoming? It's three now, and they seem to have gone solid—ready for action."

Bandicut swore. He looked around to see if the Uduon were paying attention, but they had left the bridge. Just as well.

"And something's happening to the one here," Copernicus continued. "The one Ruall went into. It seems to be coming apart."

Now he was wide awake. "Let me see!"

"I don't have a good image—the visuals are degrading to hash, as if they're being jammed somehow—but the multi-radar echoes are coming back as if the target is literally in pieces."

"That's good, right?"

"Depends on Ruall and Bria's status, doesn't it?"

Bandicut found it hard to take a breath. "If the Mindaru is coming apart, wouldn't that mean they're free?"

Copernicus seemed to ponder the question. "One can hope. It depends on the manner in which it broke up, I think."

Jeaves spoke suddenly. "We're picking up some fragments of signal. I'm pretty sure it's from Ruall. I think she's trapped somehow in junk-space and needs help getting back."

Bandicut jerked his head back and forth between the two robots, trying to parse all this. *Junk-space?* "What kind of help?" he asked finally.

"The kind you're not going to like hearing about," said Jeaves.

"And what kind is that?"

"I'm not certain, but I think before it died, the Mindaru managed to wrap Ruall and Bria into some weird kind of folded-over, knotted-up n-space."

"Junk space?"

"The kind of space that's really hard to move around in, or do anything in," Jeaves explained.

Mokin' A! Bandicut thought. He knew little about n-space except what Jeaves and Copernicus had told him, notwithstanding the fact that he had flown thousands of light-years through the stuff. He certainly didn't know how to rescue someone from "junk-space."

"I believe," Jeaves said, "that what Ruall might be stuck in is a "twist" in n-space where the structure curves in on itself in all relevant dimensions, blocking any path out."

Like my life in these missions? Bandicut thought. "Okay. Then what can we do about it? Is Bria still with her?"

"Unknown," Jeaves said. "But as for *what* we can do, that's what I have been discussing with Copernicus."

Bandicut swung back toward Copernicus, thinking, *It's just me and two robots—and we're going to rescue a pair of sheet-metal creatures who do things in dimensions I can't even imagine?* He felt a twinge in his wrists, a reminder from the stones that he was not quite *that* alone; he had them, as well.

"We cannot be certain what she needs," Copernicus said. "Based on what I can map of the Mindaru wreckage, I believe our best approach is to move in close, and then try to match the approximate level of n-space that they're in, and see if we can unravel the blocking layers to get them out."

"Which you will do by—?"

The robot tapped. "I'm working this out as we go, Cap'n. If I can't find a way to pull them free, I hope they will be able to cross over into our n-space field once we have removed enough of the barriers. Then we should be able to bring them back aboard, I think."

"And you can do all that by modulating our own n-space field?"

"That is my thought." Copernicus tapped again. "But—"

"What?"

"While we're busy doing that, we could be vulnerable to attack from those incoming Mindaru if they decide to investigate."

That thought gave Bandicut the shivers. "How far away are they? And how long do you think this rescue will take?"

"Threading our way through pieces of crumbling Mindaru—and finding Ruall and Bria—and hauling them out of n-space? I have no idea. It's not exactly a standard procedure."

"No. No, I don't suppose it is. And the incoming Mindaru?"

"Based on information from Dark," said Copernicus, "they might be here in a couple of hours. That's if they come this way. They might fly right on to Karellia and threaten them instead."

"Or just head out to conquer the galaxy," Bandicut muttered. "All right, Coppy. Get us in there as fast as you can."

"Yes, Cap'n."

"And, uh—make sure you have the best firewall protections in place. Because I haven't forgotten what it's like to have Mindaru in your AI."

"Nor have I," Copernicus said.

"Then let's do it."

It was like descending into the sea, except that what changed as they penetrated through the layers wasn't just the light, color, and visibility, but the shapes of the objects before them, or at least the way the shapes were revealed in the viewspace. The Mindaru hulk changed from what looked like a cloud of jumbled pieces to a distorted view of an intact solid. Copernicus steered them through a particularly gnarled folding of n-space and slowly brought them alongside the wreckage.

It took Bandicut a minute to parse what his eyes were telling him, what Bria and Ruall had done to the enemy. Its body, which had once resembled a cross between a burned meteorite and a sea urchin, now looked like something that had gone through a food slicer. Its sliced-up parts had drifted apart to open up the space between them; but there was more to it than that. Every slice seemed offset from the next slice, and weirdly distorted, as though each had been translated into a different dimension.

"What's holding it together?" Bandicut asked in amazement.

"It could be inertia, if the dissection happened cleanly enough," Jeaves said. "But I suspect it has to do with the n-space layers folded around it."

"Is it *dead*? Did they kill it?"

"We're doing every kind of scan we know," Copernicus said. "I haven't found any sign of activity."

"Move with caution, anyway," Bandicut said. "Don't take unnecessary risks."

Copernicus clicked three times. "What risks would you like me not to take?"

Bandicut winced. "Sorry. Use your best judgment."

It soon became clear, though, that Copernicus was relying more on guesswork than anything else. Apparently, when Ruall and Bria had killed the Mindaru, the dimensional maze inside the Mindaru had collapsed around them like a vehicle crushed in a crash. They would need to peel back the layers like bent sheet metal. If they could not do that, Ruall and Bria could wind up as dead as the Mindaru.

"Coppy, would it be better to just grab the whole thing and haul it up out of n-space?"

"Cap'n, I am hesitant to bring even a dead Mindaru object that far inside our protective n-space fields. With your permission, I'd like to try to unfold the wreckage right here."

"Go ahead, then."

There was a flicker, and a glow of purplish blue light in the viewspace. The glow expanded, enveloping the wreckage of the Mindaru. "I'm enlarging the outermost field that surrounds us in n-space, and hoping to use that as a containment field for the wreckage. The question is, will we be able to unwrap the layers of n-space around it?"

"Don't forget there are more of them coming. Shall we get started?"

"Yes," Copernicus said. "Let me see if I can cinch it in a bit tighter. Maybe twist it slightly in the outgoing manifold . . ."

As Bandicut watched, the image in the viewspace morphed, becoming luminous and soft. It looked more like interlaced clouds in a sunset. "Huh?" he said.

"Bear with me," said Copernicus. "I think what we're seeing is the folding of space, rather than the object itself."

Bandicut looked at Jeaves. "Anything from Ruall or Bria?"

"Everything I'm picking up is so distorted . . . I just don't know."

Bandicut chafed at the time. "Coppy?"

The robot ticked patiently. "This may take a little while, Captain Bandicut. May I suggest you sit down?"

"You can suggest." Bandicut turned away from Coppy and paced in front of the viewspace.

A *long* half hour later, Copernicus said, "It's harder than it looks to tease these n-space sections apart. I beg everyone's patience. Especially the captain's."

Bandicut hadn't even realized he'd circled back to stand staring down at Copernicus. "Yah," he said, and turned away again.

"John, I think you should see this," Jeaves said, snapping a tracking window up into the viewspace.

Bandicut craned his neck to see what Jeaves was showing him. The robot floated forward in the viewspace until it looked as though he might sail right out of the ship. He stopped, and green pointer beams popped into space, indicating three objects dwindling in the distance. "Those are the three incoming Mindaru. The good news is, they're passing us by. The bad news is, they're accelerating toward Karellia."

Bandicut's throat tightened. Before he could think of anything to say, he heard Sheeawn's and Akura's voices behind him, and turned to see them coming onto the bridge. They both picked up at once on the tension in the air, and stopped talking as they tried to size up the view Jeaves was showing.

"John, what is happening?" Sheeawn asked, trying unsuccessfully to keep his voice steady.

Bandicut's own voice was a tight rasp as he explained.

Sheeawn and Akura spoke for a moment, as they took in the seriousness of the moment. "Are we going to go after those Mindaru?" Sheeawn asked.

Bandicut's voice got even tighter. "Just as soon as we get Ruall and Bria out."

"But it sounds like that could take time," Sheeawn said. "Aren't you taking a risk—?"

"Yes!" Bandicut swung back toward Copernicus. "Coppy! *I really need to know!* How are you coming? How soon?"

Copernicus made a sound like sheet metal bending. "Another layer of n-space folded back."

"Good. *How long?*" With every passing minute, the three Mindaru were closer to Karellia . . . "Jeaves, how long before those Mindaru will be too close to Karellia to intercept?"

"Perhaps an hour," Jeaves said. "Maybe a little less."

"Give me a countdown. And have a plan for releasing this thing and laying rubber to intercept the others." Bandicut swallowed. "Coppy?"

"If I knew . . ." Copernicus began. "Ah, there's another layer blocking our way. You can see it up there." In the viewspace, bright line drawings indicated the stretched and creased space-time fabric stretched across their path. "I just heard something! I think it was Ruall!"

"Is she free?"

"No, but I've cleared away enough junk-space for her signal to leak out. That's—"

"A hopeful sign?"

"Yes. I'm calling back to her. I don't know if she can hear."

Bandicut managed to keep silent, as he breathed, *Hurry.*

In the viewspace, several of the n-space lines quivered, and a soft-edged shadow passed over them. After some work by Copernicus, two of the lines snapped away, revealing . . . "Another layer gone. Wait, I think—*yes, she's definitely in there!*" But a new, tangled web of lines appeared, blocking the way.

"Thirty-five minutes," said Jeaves.

Bandicut could feel his pulse throbbing in his temples. "Jesus, Coppy, how many more layers are there?"

For a few seconds Copernicus didn't answer. Then: "Remember, we're just looking at a depiction based on readings. This isn't a true image . . . But I think if I can slip aside this one strand here . . ."

Bandicut balled his hands into white-knuckled fists, watching the depiction as Copernicus did something that caused a loop to squirm and detach itself from the fragmented mess. Behind him, Sheeawn was breathlessly whispering, "*The Mindaru . . . what about the Mindaru?*"

Not now, Sheeawn! Bandicut's gaze flicked over to the window where Jeaves kept the tracking of the Mindaru visible. They were moving with frightening speed toward Karellia.

"Twenty-five minutes."

Copernicus ticked again and muttered something. Another loop snapped. Something in the image flexed, and suddenly the entire tangled wreckage let go and exploded soundlessly. Bandicut braced for a shock wave, but there was none. Instead of exploding outward, the pieces of the wreckage burst apart and vanished instantly into a hundred different layers of n-space. He blinked in shock and fear. Had they just blown up their friends, as well? Then he saw two silvery threads floating in darkness, right where they must have been contained in an inner core of the tangled thread-lines.

The two fluttered forward, as though carried on invisible magnetic lines that swept them in an arc that carried them off to the far left, and then in a smooth curve brought them directly alongside *The Long View.*

"Coppy, is that them?" Bandicut whispered. "It is, isn't it? How will you get them aboard?"

"I believe—" began the robot. He began ticking so rapidly, the ticks turned into a buzz . . .

And with a *pop!* Ruall and Bria suddenly appeared in midair on the bridge.

"—they will come through the walls," Copernicus said.

Bandicut stood speechless, gazing at them. He was too overwhelmed with joy to say a word, or even take a step toward them. Ruall hummed weakly, spinning in short bursts. Bria drifted in the air beside, not moving. Was she alive?

"We got you!" Bandicut finally managed to exclaim in a husky voice. "You're back!"

Ruall made a soft, continuous cymbal sound.

Bandicut wanted to hug her, two-dimensional blade or not. He suppressed the urge, and instead knelt to look at the gokat. "Is Bria all right? She looks—"

The gokat let out a sudden, keening sound. *Pain.* But she was alive.

Gong. "She is hurt," Ruall said, speaking for the first time. "The Mindaru hurt her. She needs rest. So do I."

"Take as long as you need," Bandicut said. "I am so glad to have you both back." He let out a heartfelt sigh of relief. "And you did one hell of a job slicing that Mindaru to pieces. How did you do that?"

Ruall bobbed, and then bent down toward the gokat. "You led the way, yes, Bria. I was merely following your example." Bria made a buzzing sound, and vanished. Ruall raised her head to the others again, but she seemed to have trouble holding it up. "We will speak—later. And I—she . . ." Ruall seemed to have trouble finding the right words. "She—cannot speak—yet. And I—"

Bandicut waited.

Ruall's disk-head turned from side to side, as though she were taking in the whole of the bridge. "I . . ." She struggled. "Captain . . . Bandicut?"

He nodded, surprised by the form of address. "Is there something we can do to help? Either of you?"

The Tintangle rang once. "Haven't you already? Thank you." And with that, she rotated once and vanished.

Bandicut stared at the empty space, briefly wondering if he had dreamed all this.

He heard a rasping cough, and Sheeawn was suddenly standing beside him.

"This is good news, yes? But now, are we not running out of time to stop the other Mindaru?"

"I estimate we are eleven minutes from last chance to launch intercept course," Jeaves said.

Bandicut forced himself to stand straighter. "Yes. Yes, indeed." He swung toward Copernicus. "Hit it, Coppy! Best possible speed! And ready all weapons."

"Sir, yes sir!" said the robot with a bright-sounding tick. "Cap'n."

The deck quivered as the power kicked in.

CHAPTER 21

Intercept

THE TENSION OF the pursuit was interrupted by a call from Li-Jared.

"It wasn't easy, but we're close to a consensus at the leadership Council," Li-Jared said, sounding breathless over the com. Bandicut wished he could see the Karellian's face. He imagined Li-Jared pacing in front of the com. *"There was a lot of suspicion, of course—but the fact that we destroyed those Uduon launchers went a long way toward convincing the Council that we mean to protect Karellia. Give credit to Koro—his people are not all backers of Quin, but he spoke up and supported her, and that made a huge difference."*

Bandicut felt a breath of hope. With *The Long View* speeding toward a confrontation with *three* Mindaru, he needed all the encouragement he could get. "Where do things stand now?"

"We're heading back to emergency session very shortly. They'll be voting on whether to shut down the temporal shield."

"Okay, that's good."

"And on whether to approve the temporal pulse to blast the Mindaru in the timestream."

Bandicut hummed. "We're still not sure on that one. Let's move cautiously."

Li-Jared murmured acknowledgment, but continued as though he hadn't heard. *"And then there are the defensive forces . . ."*

"Good. We need to talk about that. We are *right now* in hot pursuit of three Mindaru on their way to Karellia. If we can't stop them, it really could be up to the Karellian defenses. Do you think they're up to it?"

"Moon and stars, Bandie, I don't know. Can they stop Mindaru? They'll try. But did I tell you? They've got a big arsenal of long-range missiles already in orbit, armed with fusion warheads."

"Fusion warheads! Really? Your people really are full of surprises, Li-Jared."

"I was surprised, too."

Fusion-tipped missiles could definitely be helpful, if they could be targeted properly. Of course, the Mindaru were awfully hard to kill, and something as primitive as a fusion blast might not do it. If they saw missiles coming, they could probably evade them easily enough. But perhaps . . .

As he pondered, Bandicut saw Sheeawn and Akura staring at him, eyes wide. Had they understood the conversation? Did they know what fusion warheads were, and what their original intent likely had been? Bandicut cleared his throat and explained carefully. "We're going over the planetary defense options, for anything that might be useful if any Mindaru get past us."

Sheeawn nodded a wary acknowledgment. Bandicut thought he probably guessed *exactly* what the missiles had been intended for. But if they were to be put to a more fruitful purpose, he and Akura would support that.

"Li-Jared," Bandicut said, turning back to the console and dropping his voice. "Are those missiles at our disposal, if we need them?"

"I think so," said the scratchy voice of his friend. *"I'll be checking."*

"Do that. And Li-Jared—"

Bong. "Yah?"

"If we—or you—need to use the missiles, can you work on a way to keep the Mindaru from seeing them coming? Our own missiles didn't do too well." He told Li-Jared what had happened earlier. "See if you can find some way to block the damned Mindaru from taking control."

"I understand. We'll work on it right away." Li-Jared hesitated. *"Bandie, maybe we shouldn't say more. How secure are these transmissions?"*

"Good point." The Mindaru were excellent listeners. Copernicus had his best firewalls up against intrusion, but the Mindaru were bound to detect and listen in on their comm signals sooner or later. Bandicut hoped it would be later.

"All right—those incoming will be our focus right now," Li-Jared said. *"We'll need tracking data from Copernicus or Jeaves. But I think we should consider sending that blast down the timestream. Before it's too late and a lot more arrive."*

You might be right, Bandicut thought. *You might very well be right.*

The Long View was now in close pursuit. The three Mindaru were approaching Karellia along the inner boundary of the Heart of Fire—using the clouds as cover for their approach, most likely. Dark had just informed Copernicus that three additional objects had been sighted farther out—not an immediate threat, but definitely a concern for later.

The Long View was at a state of battle readiness, but they still had to endure waiting while they overtook the enemy. Bandicut had briefed the Uduon as well as he could, though there was little for them to do except take it all in. Copernicus estimated first possible engagement in a few hours, if the Mindaru kept their present course. They would catch up with the enemy not far outside the temporal shield, assuming the Mindaru followed the curvature of their path into a turn toward the planet. Right now the intruders were close enough to the clouds that Copernicus was concerned they might easily escape *into* the clouds if pursued. He therefore kept *The Long View* even closer to the boundary, in hopes of being able to cut off any escape attempt that way, while still setting *The Long View* up to dive and intercept.

"Let's call Li-Jared again," Bandicut said, after wolfing a sandwich from the commons.

While Copernicus was making the call, Bandicut checked with Jeaves. The robot didn't want to talk yet. He felt he was on the verge of a full translation of the tachyon signal.

Li-Jared came on the com to report, *"All defenses are committed. And the pulse, if you want it, has been approved."*

Bandicut felt his mouth grow dry.

"They're actually almost ready to release it," Li-Jared said. *"Some coils or other are nearly at full power. Are you safely out of the line of fire—just in case? Shall we go ahead?"*

"No!" Jeaves barked suddenly. *"Do not release the pulse!"* He shot out to the center of the bridge, metal arms out wide, as though prepared to stop an oncoming bus.

"Why?" Bandicut asked. "What is it?"

"Don't fire the pulse! Li-Jared, shut it down!"

Bandicut was too startled to speak, and so it seemed was Li-Jared. Jeaves continued rapidly, "I've got the translation of the tachyon message—ninety-five percent probability of accuracy. Do not—*repeat, do not!*—send any kind of pulse down the timestream!"

Bandicut raised his own hands in bewilderment. "Why not?"

"Here's the message, in expanded form: *'Amaduse/Antares to Long View. Danger! Ik and JulieS in timestream. Do not disrupt timestream until you receive All Safe from us. Risk of harm to the translator.'* That's it—and then the message repeats."

"But that's—what do you mean you expanded it? Are you sure you—"

"The expansion seemed pretty clear. Look." Jeaves displayed the text against the viewspace, in its original form:

to LV. Danger!

Ik/JulieS n timstrm.

No disrpt ntl AllSafe frm us.

Rsk harm trnsltr.

[repeats]

Bandicut stared at the message in disbelief, Jeaves' expansion echoing in his ears. "Ik and . . . *Julie S?* In the timestream? What does that—who is—? Is that *Julie Stone?* In the timestream?" Bandicut staggered, mind reeling, groping for something to hold onto. "Julie Stone?" he repeated. /Julie Stone?/ he cried in his thoughts, to the Charli who was no longer there.

"The message says JulieS," Jeaves said. "I cannot be sure of anything further. But I know of no other JulieS. And I do not know what to make of 'risk to translator.' Do you?"

Bandicut shook his head. He was suddenly aware of Li-Jared's voice, calling, *"What are you saying? Talk to me, Bandie! You got a message from Antares?"*

"Yes! Yes, from Antares and Amaduse."

"Moon, stars, wind, and hail," Li-Jared breathed. *"And she's telling us not to do anything to the timestream?"*

"That's right! Don't!"

"Then what are we going to do instead?"

Bandicut rubbed his forehead. "I don't know. Fight the Mindaru until we get an All Clear."

"And what was that about the translator?"

"*Risk* to the translator."

"Meaning what?"

"I don't *know*. There's more. The message says Ik is *in* the timestream now. And . . . Julie S. My, I mean . . . I *think* it means, Julie Stone from my world."

"Moon, stars, hail, and thunder!"

Bandicut shut his eyes and massaged his temples. Starbursts flashed behind his closed eyelids.

Copernicus broke in. "I know one thing. We're about to intercept three Mindaru. What is our plan?"

"Hold that thought, Coppy." Bandicut blinked back to the Karellian. "Li-Jared, you've got to stop the pulse. Stop it cold. And *we've* got to stop these Mindaru. Can you get your people to target those—" *Don't use the word; they might be listening!* "—flying things, if we ask for it?"

"*I will do my best,*" Li-Jared said.

They brought *The Long View* in an extended arc to intercept the lead Mindaru about fifty thousand kilometers outside the Karellian temporal shield. Bandicut's plan was to come down on it out of the background noise of the energy clouds, and hit it as hard as they could. He wished he had something better, considering their experience so far. "Coppy, any word from Ruall?"

"Can't reach her, Cap'n. I think we're on our own for this one."

"Power up the weapons, then. Your recommendation?"

"Cap'n, the first Mindaru was tough because it hadn't fully materialized. These have. I am hopeful we can land some shots on them. I recommend the n-space disrupter beams, a fast barrage, and then immediately quantum pulses."

"All right. Give us a count when we're in range. Jeaves, any other suggestions?"

The robot glided around to hover beside Copernicus. "Don't miss."

"That's it?"

"Mainly."

"How is it we never thought of that?" Bandicut murmured. Still, it was always good to get back to fundamentals. "Coppy, let's shoot to kill."

The robot ticked.

"How soon?" Bandicut asked.

"Half hour. Less, if you want me to accelerate the run. But if I do that, targeting will be more difficult. Do you want me to?"

Bandicut shook his head. "No, this is a good speed. Have you tried again to contact Ruall? Or Bria? Any luck?"

"No luck. Captain, you and our guests should prepare for combat maneuvering."

Bandicut looked around. "Are Akura and Sheeawn in the commons?"

"Yes," Jeaves said. "I'll let them know."

Bandicut nodded. He was tired. Tired of thinking about the Mindaru, tired of thinking of battle plans when he knew nothing of battle plans. He was practically in a fugue state—not silence-fugue, but a weariness that bordered on indifference. If Charli were here, she would have found a way to jog him out of it . . .

His dazed state lasted for several more minutes—until Copernicus began his maneuvers, and the ship slewed violently as incoming fire from the Mindaru lanced past, just beyond the viewspace. "Cripes!" Bandicut shouted, grabbing for a handhold as the deck swayed. "That was fast! Have we even gotten a shot off yet? Coppy, can you get us into a better firing position, without being hit?"

"It's difficult, Cap'n," said the robot. "I am doing my best." With that, the deck tilted sharply to the right, and the view spun.

Copernicus brought them through a steep horizontal turn and also a sharp vertical climb, out of easy firing range and up toward the glowing energy clouds. With a loop-over at the top, he brought them back down like a diving fighter plane. "Broad spread," he murmured, and loosed a volley of n-space disrupter pulses. The points of light streaked out. They missed the lead Mindaru, which changed course with astonishing quickness. Without slowing, the Mindaru rotated, almost lazily, and sparkled.

Another shot flashed toward *The Long View*.

Copernicus rolled them sharply to the left, slamming Bandicut to the right against a column in the instant before the inertial damping caught up. "That was a neutron beam," the robot reported. "Evaded successfully. Our layering probably would have stopped it—but if not, you'd all have been cooked. I'm trying to avoid that."

Bandicut gasped. "Yes, let's. Avoid that. Are those other two moving to box us in?"

"Looks like," Copernicus said, accelerating them away from the area. "With your permission—"

"Yah, get us out of here!" Bandicut's heart thumped as he watched the ship gain distance from the Mindaru. The first continued accelerating toward Karellia. The other two turned to follow *The Long View*. *Ruall, where are you? I'm out of my league here!* He dragged a breath. "Jeaves, can you get Li-Jared back on the line?"

A blast of static. *"I'm here, Bandy! What do you need?"*

Missiles. Lot of missiles. Bandicut took a deep breath and focused. "We're outnumbered, and you've got a Mindaru fast inbound. We missed our shot on it, and we've got two others on us. Can you send a wide spread of . . . what we talked about? Smartly?" *Can you hit it before it knows it's under attack?*

Li-Jared's voice sounded distant but reassuring. *"We've been working on an idea about that. I'm sure they'll see it, so not to worry."*

You're sure they'll . . . "Don't tell me—"

"I'm not. But trust us."

The light surrounding Ruall was softened by being broken into thousands of rays of ultra-green and sub-blue. Fortunately, the sensation of noise was subsiding at last. She was still reeling from the wrenching assault on her mind from the Mindaru, and her imprisonment in dimensional folds by the dying entity. Her own fear, and Bria's pain, had brought her a kind of terror she'd never experienced before; and the peeling back of the dimensional prison by her friends, in saving her, had nearly taken her own physical integrity with it.

Ruall had never expected such tenacity from a tri-space enemy. It had been remarkably reluctant to die, and had not done so until Ruall and Bria had sliced and shredded it and scattered its pieces through a hundred dimensions. It was a victory, but one that left her shaken to her Tintangle core.

And what if the pieces came back to life in those places? In all of those places?

She was nearly sure that such a thing was impossible, but the doubt kept ringing through her with all the reverberation of a gong.

And Bria, poor Bria, pressed flat against her, shaking like a slip of paper pressed by wind onto steel . . .

The others were going to have to do without them a little longer. She and Bria needed longer recovery time, here in petal-space where the gently shifting dimensions of space soothed, and brought healing.

Nothing about this made Bandicut happy. The number one Mindaru was accelerating in shallow n-space toward Karellia, beyond their power to stop. Numbers two and three Mindaru were coming after them in n-space, and he had no real strategy, except to run like hell until they could regroup with Dark, or find some other tactical advantage. But run where? They needed safety, while staying close to striking range. There was a small moon not too far away, but that didn't seem too promising.

A raspy cough made him suddenly aware of Sheeawn standing beside him. Both of the Uduon had returned to the bridge, but had been quiet and staying out of his way. "Sorry," Bandicut said. "I know I haven't been keeping you up to date."

"The Watcher asked me to convey a suggestion," Sheeawn said.

Bandicut opened his hands. "I need all the help I can get. What's the suggestion?"

"Retreat into the Clouds of Fire," Sheeawn said. "The most energetic part, where tracking is difficult. Perhaps the enemy won't be able to follow us there."

"Good idea. But we wouldn't be able to track them from in there, either."

Akura, listening, said something to Sheeawn. He added, "We can help with that."

Bandicut looked at him for a moment, but didn't take time to question the assertion, because he had no better idea and he needed to give Coppy a course five minutes ago. "Into the Clouds, Coppy. Go dense. Go where tracking is hardest."

"Setting course now, Cap'n. Flank speed."

The emerald- and ruby-glowing clouds grew in the viewspace. Bandicut practiced his deep breathing—and then they were in, arrowing toward the region of greatest energy density. At first it was just a haze, like being surrounded by green auroras, and then suddenly they were being chased by sapphire heat lightning. The density of the plasma flux in the zone ahead was far greater than what they had traversed in their flight between the planets.

Soon, bolts of fire were rippling around them, and hammering in thunderous patterns around the ship's hull. He felt both audible and visceral booms, as the bolts of electricity and quantum flux pelted the n-space fields that enfolded the ship, and fed back through the systems generating those fields. And this was just the outskirts of the fiery region.

Karellia: World of beautiful, perilous skies.

Bandicut had thought he'd understood why they called it that. But he hadn't, not really. In their previous passages through the clouds, they had steered clear of such intense activity. Now, Copernicus was deliberately plowing into them, to discourage the Mindaru from following. The space-time fabric rippled around them with waves of magnetic and quantum turbulence. Winds of charged particles sleeted against them, and the ship was shaking like a seagoing ship in a storm. There was a keening sound of cosmic wind, like a speaker verging on overload.

"Coppy, is this safe?" he yelled, over the noise. "Seems like we're taking a hell of a pounding. Don't you think we'd better stay to the edge of it?"

Copernicus was busy piloting them through the discharges, and Jeaves answered for him. "This *is* the edge. We can take it. But you're right—it's putting stress on the n-space systems. We shouldn't go through this if we don't have to."

Bandicut caught the eye of Sheeawn, who somehow managed to look terrified and happy at the same time. "You folks okay?" he called.

Akura leaned into Sheeawn and said something, and Sheeawn called back, "We're fine. But the Watcher can't sense the Mindaru following. She thought she would be able to sense them, but there's nothing."

Puzzled, Bandicut answered, "Why would she—? But no, I don't know if they've followed us in. Jeaves?"

"They are no longer in ordinary sensor range," the robot answered, "but with all this interference, I can't say they're not in here with us. Let me see what we can pick up on acoustic."

"*Acoustic!* There's no *sound* here."

"Actually, there are various acoustic indicators, Captain. Shock waves moving through the plasma. Or vibrations in the quantum foam."

"Quantum foam!"

"You know, down at the level where virtual particles are fizzing in and out of existence. That's finicky to measure—but if we had time maybe we could—"

"Maybe we could get the hell clear of this." Bandicut chafed with worry about them saving their own necks while the Mindaru descended on Karellia. "Coppy—seriously, keep us outside of the really bad stuff, all right? Maybe we've already shaken them. But I want to know where they are!"

"My thinking exactly, Cap'n," said Copernicus.

Music filled the space now, but it was a dissonant, clamoring, metallic music, ringing around Ruall like something whirring around and around inside a steel drum. It was a powerful annoyance, and she couldn't seem to get away from it, even by escaping deeper into petal-space, with Bria under her arm. Right now she was having trouble staying focused in *any* dimension. How long was this going to keep on?

And perhaps more important: *What was happening on the ship?*
/Bria, I think our rest is over. We'll just have to manage./

Before Copernicus could act on Bandicut's instructions, there was a flash and a *bang* in the middle of the bridge. Bandicut nearly jumped out of his skin, and Sheeawn yelped. Out of the afterimage in his vision, Ruall reappeared, followed an instant later by Bria. They rose and bounced from the ceiling, and then sank and bounced up from the deck. Ruall stuck out a paddle-shaped hand to steady them both, and they came to a bobbing rest in midair. Ruall didn't speak at once, but she seemed a redder, more coppery color than usual, as though she were made of heated metal.

Before anyone could greet her, Ruall let out a ringing cry: *"Are we under attack? What is happening?"*

"We're all right so far!" Bandicut said reassuringly. "We're in the Clouds of Fire, *evading* attack."

Ruall spun, perhaps trying to take it all in by sight. "Evading? *Why?* Explain! *Quickly!* Why are we in this danger?"

Bandicut did his best to explain.

"After our victory, you *fled*?" Ruall gonged. "How long?"

Bandicut raised his hands to slow her down, quelling an impulse to be defensive. An electric crackle made him pause, before he said, "We can't fight three of them at once. We had to get clear while we looked for a tactical advantage. But I was just telling Copernicus to get us out of here so we can see what's happening."

Ruall bobbed slightly.

"Copernicus! Edge of the cloud. Let's find those Mindaru. And find out how far away Dark is!"

"Roger, Cap'n," said the robot, and instantly performed a flip-over maneuver that took them directly away from the electrical fire.

The shaking subsided quickly, along with the mind-numbing hum and the electrical charge in the air. Within minutes, the glowing clouds began to thin to transparency. The black of space emerged around them. They were back in normal-space.

Bandicut strode out to the center of the viewspace, searching for signs of the enemy.

"There they are," Copernicus said, putting bright circles around one point of light moving toward Karellia—and, some distance off to the right, two more, also just emerging from the clouds. Apparently numbers two and three *had* pursued them into the clouds, but lost them. All three of the Mindaru were now between them and Karellia. "Those circles are my markers," Copernicus said. "You cannot see the actual Mindaru."

"What's that?" Sheeawn asked, pointing to the left of the Mindaru.

Bandicut started at Sheeawn's presence beside him again. "What?" he said, blinking. Then he saw it: a cluster of dim lights moving from the planet toward the first Mindaru. "Coppy?"

Copernicus highlighted those, as well. "Those are the Karellian missiles, under power in normal-space. They're still inside the temporal shield. The Mindaru are still outside. It is possible that the Mindaru are not able to track them from n-space." The lights dimmed, and were replaced by Copernicus's markers. "The missiles have gone dark, and are in coasting phase."

"Let's hope this works better than when we tried it," Bandicut muttered.

"But Cap'n, by my calculations, they are aimed wrong. Their course does not take into account passing through the temporal shield. After the displacement, they will miss their target."

"*Explain*, please!" Ruall cried harshly. "What missiles?"

Bandicut did, briefly. As he did so, he thought furiously. If Li-Jared was involved in plotting this course, it did not seem likely they would miss. "Let's get the shield up there on the display, please."

A shimmering boundary appeared, between the first Mindaru and the rapidly closing missiles, now blinking to represent their presumed trajectories.

Bandicut squinted, trying to visualize what was going to happen. The missiles were going to reach the time-shield just before the enemy. They were going to shift sideways . . . and miss . . .

Which the Mindaru would be able to anticipate, if they came out of n-space to cross the shield boundary. Which they should do, because it would make for a more predictable crossing. So, if they tracked the missiles, they would see a clean miss coming.

"Cap'n, Mindaru numbers two and three have turned this way."

Spotted us. Damn. "Okay, let's—" He hesitated. "Ruall, were you—planning to resume battle command?"

Ruall reverberated. "Not at this time. I do not wish to disrupt in mid-battle. But I suggest we prepare to evade two and three, in favor of targeting the lead enemy, after the missile strike fails."

"Agreed," Bandicut said. "Coppy, be ready for smart maneuvering."

"Heads up, everyone!" Jeaves called.

In the viewspace display, the markers for the missiles and for the lead Mindaru were approaching the temporal shield from opposite sides. A computer projection of the missiles' course showed a jog at the shield, resulting in a clean miss. The marker for the Mindaru changed color, and Jeaves announced, "Mindaru has dropped into normal-space."

They were vulnerable. If by a miracle something was there to hit them. If they weren't impervious to fusion blasts.

Without warning, the pale boundary of the temporal shield winked off. "What?" Bandicut shouted. "Coppy, did you do that?"

"No," Jeaves answered. "The shield has shut down!"

"Shut down?"

The missiles blazed to life, and in the blink of an eye their track *shifted to the right,* squarely into the path of the Mindaru. Suddenly Bandicut understood. The missiles had been aimed at the Mindaru all along, but only the Karellians knew that the time-shift would abruptly vanish.

Jeaves said, "The Mindaru is—"

Too late. In a rapid cascade, the missiles mushroomed into blinding light. The viewspace compensated quickly, and then magnified. "Fusion explosions, all missiles," Jeaves reported. "I am trying to analyze the result . . ."

Bandicut waited anxiously.

"Cap'n, Li-Jared on comm," said Copernicus.

"Bandie, did it work? All we can see is a debris cloud."

"We're not sure yet, either!" Bandicut answered. "We're trying—"

Jeaves interrupted. "The debris cloud matches the spectrum and mass of the Mindaru. No indication of a remaining solid body. We need to keep some scopes on it, but I believe the enemy is destroyed."

Bandicut's shout of satisfaction was matched by Ruall's clang, the Uduon's cheers, and Li-Jared's whoop. "Li-Jared!" Bandicut called when he could be heard. "Brilliant job with the time-shield!"

"Thanks," Li-Jared said. *"I don't think they would have turned off the shield, if it hadn't seemed the only way to stop that Mindaru."*

"I am trying to understand why it worked," Jeaves said. "Not the feint, but their vulnerability to simple fusion blasts."

Simple? Bandicut thought. Compared to quantum implosion, maybe.

"I think we overwhelmed them with something they were not expecting," Li-Jared said.

"Yes," Jeaves said, "but your cascade of extreme temperature and pressure may also have created an interdimensional *pinch*, which could have destructively—"

"Wait—" Li-Jared interrupted. *"Are you saying we just independently discovered n-space?"*

"Possibly . . ."

"I don't suppose we can use it a second time," Bandicut said, suddenly remembering numbers two and three bearing down on them. "These other two will be wise to it." Time for a different plan.

Li-Jared answered, *"We can't, anyway. We have more missiles, but the fast shutdown damaged the field generators. It's off, maybe for good."*

Bandicut winced. That was exactly what they had wanted, but now it felt like an arrow gone from their quiver.

"Something you need to know," Jeaves said. "There's a whiplash effect from the dropping of the shield. It's moving along the path of the distortion and will be hitting the starstream, and timestream, shortly. Not as powerful as the pulse we talked about earlier, but maybe bad enough."

That shook Bandicut a little. Had they just destroyed one Mindaru, at a risk to Ik and Julie, Dakota, and who knew how many thousands of others in the starstream?

He didn't get a chance to think about it. Ruall gonged a reminder. "Mindaru two and three are closing. Do you have a plan?"

"Copernicus! Let's see if they care enough about killing us to follow us away from the planet."

"Aye, Cap'n."

"Toward Dark. Can we lead them toward Dark?"

"I will lead and hope they follow."

CHAPTER 22

Mindaru Attack

GETTING THE MINDARU to follow them wasn't the problem. Figuring out how to fight them was. They had no strategic advantage against two Mindaru combined, and the enemy had already closed some of the distance between them. It was clear they could not rejoin Dark before the enemy caught them; the Heart of Fire was closer. Should they go back there and dive all the way in this time? Would the enemy be mad enough to follow?

"Is there *any* chance Dark could make it to us, if she poured on the coal?" Bandicut asked.

"Unlikely. Dark appears to be engaged with numbers four, five, and—is it six? Yes, six," Jeaves said. "Wait—number six does *not* appear to be Mindaru. At least not the kind we know."

Bandicut scowled. Were they going to have to deal with yet another kind of Mindaru? "What is it, then?"

"Difficult to tell. Another kind of ship."

"Different kind of *Mindaru?*"

"Stand by; I am trying to correlate some readings. John Bandicut, number six matches many of the characteristics of your niece's ship. It may be *Plato.*"

"*What?*" Bandicut felt as if he'd been hit in the chest with cold water. Whatever he'd been thinking about was gone. "*Dakota's ship? Are you sure?*"

"I cannot be certain at this distance. But here, look," Jeaves said, putting an image up for them to inspect. It was blurry with distance and movement, but it sure looked like *Plato*.

"Well, that's . . . I don't know what it is! Great news? And *terrible* news?" His thoughts raced. "They're alive! They survived the blowup in the starstream! That's wonderful!"

"And they seem to have detoured—perhaps to help us?" Jeaves offered.

Bandicut gulped hard. "And that's . . . terrible! If they're chasing the Mindaru for us, they're in awful danger! My God!" He blanched at the thought.

"They are definitely in danger from the Mindaru," Jeaves said. "But they are too far away for us to intercede."

If Bandicut and his shipmates had put Dakota and her shipmates in mortal peril . . . if his mission killed his niece, after she had survived to come so far forward in time? And the rest of the *Plato* crew? He would never forgive himself.

Ruall gonged loudly. "This is all very interesting, but have you forgotten that *we* are in imminent danger?" The Tintangle flew far into the viewspace and waved a paddle-hand at the view astern, where two Mindaru were in hard pursuit of *The Long View*. They would be in firing range soon.

There was nothing they could do for *Plato* now. "Coppy, get us back up into the clouds—fast!" Bandicut said.

"Roger, Cap'n." The ship vibrated as Copernicus made the course change he had obviously been waiting for.

And then Bandicut had a sudden thought. "Coppy—?"

Copernicus turned his camera eyes, as though wondering if he should take his foot off the throttle. "Cap'n?"

"Go fast. But not *too* fast," Bandicut said. "Can you make it look like we're limping a little?"

"Because—?" Copernicus said. "And I'm not sure how to go fast and make the ship limp."

Bandicut waved in exasperation. "Make them think we're wounded. Can you make our drive sputter a little? Like we're losing power? I want them to hope they can come finish us off. Maybe we can get them fried by the cloud itself, or at the very least, even up the playing field."

The deck trembled again. "That's the drive sputtering," Copernicus said. "They're following. Still gaining."

"A little faster, please. Give them hope, but don't let them catch us."

He turned to look at the others. Sheeawn and Akura were silent, but fear was written in their eyes.

———————

The first of the luminous plasma clouds already enveloped *The Long View* like curtains of emerald and ruby aurora. Soon they hit brighter and more turbulent layers, and then a region of rampant electrical discharge. Perhaps emboldened by their recent foray, Copernicus steered them directly toward the heart of the nearest active zone. As they plunged deeper, it began to feel more personally threatening. Branches of lightning danced toward the ship, as though guided by some magnetic attraction, arcing and crackling with dazzling flashes. The view was so bright it had to be cut with filters. A rising and falling hum came from the deck, like the cry of a chained monster in the basement. The air began to tingle with ionization and hints of ozone.

This was much worse than last time—and the true maelstrom still lay ahead, glittering and dancing like nuclear fire.

Bandicut tried to hide his worry—they had flown into a star once, after all—but the gnawing in his gut was real, and growing. This was the belt of energy that was so dangerous it kept Karellia's space fleet bound to its homeworld. "We're taking a beating here, guys," he said to the robots. "Are you sure we can handle it?"

"We can for a while," Jeaves said. "N-space fields are holding well. But we're taking some fire from the enemy."

"Are they still gaining on us?"

"I am afraid so," Jeaves said.

"But that's what we want, isn't it?" Ruall boomed. "We're hoping it will be worse on them than on us?"

"That's the idea," Bandicut said. "But if they're shooting at us, it can't be *that* much worse on them. Do we still have clear tracking?"

"Not really," said Copernicus. "Cap'n, visible and radio-spectrum scans are all washed out. I'm relying more on acoustic now." As Copernicus spoke, the speakers came alive with groans and staccato chirps and rumblings like the amplified sounds of animals on a coral reef.

Bandicut pressed two fingers to his forehead, trying to interpret that. It was hopeless. "Can you do something to make that visual?"

"I'll try," Jeaves said.

The viewspace was suddenly painted with blotches and streaks, and shimmering representations of sound. For a mind-jarring instant, he felt as if he were in an old war movie, a submarine sonarman watching his display and hoping to pick out the enemy, or possibly the sound of his own torpedoes. "Are you making sense of this—either of you?"

"It is difficult," both robots said.

"Ruall, how about you? Can you make anything out?"

The Tintangle hummed, waving her paddles. "I cannot."

Hell's bells.

"Cap'n, I can pick out their weapons fire," Copernicus said.

The left half of the display changed to some kind of refined rendering of the visualized acoustics. The two Mindaru weren't visible, but their weapons fire took the form of lurid-red blobs that extruded themselves like jets of dye in the clouds behind the ship and squirted toward *The Long View*—where they diminished to yellowish droplets that mostly vanished in flares of green when they grazed *The Long View*'s n-space shields. But then two of the droplets connected. There was a slam through the deck as if pile-drivers had hit the ship. Everyone on the bridge crashed to the deck.

As he scrambled to get up, Bandicut yelled, "Can't you do something to evade that?"

"Trying, Cap'n!"

Bandicut hauled himself onto one of the bench seats and gripped its edge, waiting for the next blow. He gradually became aware of a voice beside him. "John Bandicut! Captain!" It was

Sheeawn. He looked agitated, and again Bandicut realized he had been leaving them out of the loop.

"I'm sorry—look—it's not as bad as—"

Sheeawn cut him off. "*Please!* Watcher Akura says she can help!" Sheeawn pointed. The Watcher was sitting on the floor against the back wall with her eyes closed. Her hood was drawn forward, obscuring much of her face. Her hands held the front of her cloak in a death grip.

"She is *watching*," Sheeawn said. "She can sense the positions of the enemy."

Startled, Bandicut said, "You mean like what she tried before—?"

"Yes, but now we're farther into the clouds. All the energy here is creating a sort of—" Sheeawn paused, wringing his hands together. "I don't know how to describe it! But it's like what happens in the earth at home—the thing that lets the Watchers connect. She is *seeing* things she cannot see with her eyes. The enemy ships. The layout of the cloud structure."

Bandicut stared at him. "Are you certain? Because that would be—"

The viewspace flared as another Mindaru shot caught the ship, a glancing strike on the protective fields. Bandicut steadied himself, and then lurched toward Akura. "What do you see, Akura? Sheeawn tells me—"

Akura burst into words, interrupting him.

"She says the enemy is following us easily," Sheeawn said. "We have to get to where the energy flux is higher."

Bandicut stared. "Higher? Can she really see the layout of the cloud? Can she guide us?"

Ruall suddenly zoomed in close to Akura, and made several pinging sounds. Akura opened her eyes wide and said something. Ruall pinged again, and said to Sheeawn, "I think I am following. Please check my understanding." Ruall rattled off a series of directional descriptions. Sheeawn bobbed his head and muttered a single correction. Ruall clanged and then spoke to Copernicus in some kind of fast machine language.

"Cap'n," Copernicus said, "I have a course laid in to where it really gets bad, if you want me to take it."

Bandicut raised his hands, trying to think clearly. *Should I trust Ruall and Akura on this?* If he took time to ask for clarification... "Yes," he said. "Go!"

The ship banked sharply left, and slipped precipitously downward for several seconds, before coiling back into a spiraling ascent, relative to some dimly perceived structure. In the viewspace, the clouds grew momentarily darker, and then burst back to life with popping lightning bolts. It didn't seem that much different to Bandicut, but Copernicus called, "We're now flying between two cloud banks with extreme energy potential building up. Frankly, Cap'n, it's a dangerous place to be."

Akura spoke, and Sheeawn translated, his voice quavering a little, "If the Mindaru follow us here, we may be able to lead them into a discharge that will disable or destroy them."

Bandicut felt his hands clenching; he opened them and pressed them flat together, his index fingers against his lips. "That sounds good. Can you guide us *out* of it?"

"Pretty sure," said Sheeawn.

Bandicut nodded. "Go ahead, then. Give directional updates directly to Copernicus."

The Uduon agreed, and called out to the robot.

Bandicut watched with amazement and terror. As Ruall drifted near, he murmured, "When did you start understanding Uduon?"

"I have been working on it," Ruall hummed. "It's no worse than learning your language."

Sheeawn said, "The Mindaru are following us in."

Outside, the clouds whistled and shrieked like maddened whales.

Under the pilotage of Copernicus and the Uduon, *The Long View* threaded its way through what to Bandicut was an incomprehensible channel in the fiery maze. It felt as though they were navigating through synapses in a gigantic gaseous brain. "Can you tell when this thing is going to let go?" he asked, wondering if his own heart would burst before the discharge of energy blew them all to kingdom come. "And are you sure *we* can avoid it?"

"We hope so, and we hope so," Jeaves said.

"Uh-huh," Bandicut said, and turned to Akura. "What are you seeing now?"

The Watcher's face was still mostly obscured by her hood, and Sheeawn was pacing in front of her, but Bandicut could see that her features were tight with concentration. At first she seemed not to hear his question, but after a minute she murmured something, and Sheeawn barked, "Our course is good. She can feel it, a massive discharge building, like a great pressure under the ground. It is coming. Powerful enough to destroy anything solid, she thinks."

Bandicut's hands had closed into a fist-clench again; this time he didn't try to stop. "How soon?"

"Very," Sheeawn said, and then Akura launched into a stream of pathway descriptions and upcoming turns and accelerations, which Sheeawn passed at once to Copernicus.

A keening sound came out of nowhere in the acoustic tracking, and a moment later came the twin thuds of two more shots from the Mindaru, weakened by their passage around the bends of the gaseous channels. Copernicus fired back a burst of his own, to goad them on; the kill, if it happened, would not come from their shots in here, but from the power of the Heart of Fire.

The keening grew shriller, louder, nearly unbearable. The clouds that flanked them roiled and began to come together.

Akura barked a command, and before Sheeawn could translate, Copernicus wrenched the ship up into a steep climb. Were the Mindaru following? The place where *The Long View* had been a moment ago erupted in a dazzling frenzy of light and lightning and what felt like exploding stars. The acoustic tracking screeched off the scale. Bandicut instinctively yelled, *"Get us out of here!"* even though they already were on their way.

Everything behind them was lost in whiteout and supersaturation. *The Long View* was away, shuddering, heaving ominously but clear of ground zero. Copernicus had them twisting and turning through angry turbulence, plunging through some escape route that only he—or perhaps only Akura—could see. In the firestorm behind them, a faint shadow seemed to be following them. But another shadow was swallowed by the storm.

Ruall gonged furiously. "Did we get them? Did they die?"

Bandicut craned his neck to see Akura. She was holding her head. She cried out, her eyes blinking open. She said something that probably only Sheeawn could hear. He listened a moment and then shouted to the others, *"We got one of them! She felt it die!"*

Ruall rang in uncertainty, and Sheeawn bent down, listening to more. Then he sprang upright and waved his hands wildly, shouting, "The other is damaged, but it's coming after us. She thinks we can get it coming out!"

Bandicut clapped his hands in anticipation. "Coppy, can you get us out of the clouds, and turn and hit it before it can get a sensor lock on us?"

"Aye, Cap'n." The ship dropped through the thinning clouds like a brick out of the sky. The acoustic signals fell to a low hiss. "We'll be in the clear in about twenty seconds . . . fifteen . . . ten . . ."

"Akura?" Bandicut asked.

"It's coming behind us, but her ability to sense is fading as we leave the energy flux," Sheeawn said.

The glowing gases whipped away from the viewspace, and they were out. "Coming around," Copernicus said, maneuvering sharply back up into the edge of the cloud. They would take the Mindaru from behind when it came out. "There it is."

The enemy came out of the clouds sparkling with light like Saint Elmo's fire. Copernicus calmly said, "Firing once, twice, thrice," as a lance of light, a ball of fire, and a missile streaked out from *The Long View.*

The Mindaru looked afire with electricity dancing along its spines. It was clearly damaged, and it was rotating—no, tumbling—perhaps trying to locate its foe.

The three-spread from *The Long View* hit it: *one two three.* There was a flower of violet, and then a dazzling flare of diamond fire. The Mindaru turned into an expanding spot of brightness against space, became transparent, and faded.

"It is destroyed," Copernicus said.

"Well done!" Bandicut shouted.

"Who shall we go after now?"

It took a few minutes to scan the area extending out to where the two remaining Mindaru had last been seen, pursued by Dark and *Plato*. One of the Mindaru had gotten out ahead of the other and was speeding toward Karellia. Dark was in pursuit. The second Mindaru had apparently turned to challenge *Plato*, and the two were engaged in a long-distance dogfight. Weapons fire flashed from time to time, but if any harm was being inflicted, it wasn't visible to Copernicus or Jeaves.

Ruall floated forward, perhaps restored by the recent victory. "John Bandicut?"

Bandicut didn't answer at once. He was concerned that Dakota's ship might be out of its depth in that fight, but also worried that even that single Mindaru streaking toward the planet could pose an unacceptable risk to Karellia. "Yes, Ruall."

"Your leadership of that encounter was exemplary; and I am not yet ready to resume battle command. But I suggest we assist Dark in attacking the lead Mindaru first. Once it has been neutralized, we can go assist the human ship."

Bandicut couldn't argue with the logical priority, but Ruall didn't have a niece in danger out there in *Plato*. "Coppy, can you establish contact with Dark?"

"Trying now, Cap'n."

Akura came forward and inclined her head in Bandicut's direction. He was a little startled, and said the first thing that came to him, which was, "Great job back there. Thank you."

As Sheeawn repeated his words, in Uduon, Akura tilted her head and nodded. But she spoke again, and Sheeawn said, "You seem worried. Do we understand correctly that there is a ship out there with people you know, and care about?"

Bandicut let out a sigh. "Yes. Humans like me. Including . . . my niece. My brother's daughter." It took a moment for Sheeawn to translate. When he finished, Akura put a hand on Bandicut's arm, and bobbed her head several times. That small gesture touched Bandicut with surprising power. With all of their concerns about the two planets, this was perhaps the first time anyone here besides the robots had ever expressed any concern about *his* feelings.

Before he could think of anything more to say, Copernicus reported on his conversation with Dark.

"Cap'n, she says this Mindaru is a slippery one. The damn things are all different. She's having trouble closing and holding it. If we can get to her, she wants to try something involving the foam we were talking about earlier."

"The quantum foam?"

"Yes, Cap'n. All that energy popping in and out of existence from the vacuum. She wants to know if we can move in just close enough to box it in for a few moments. If we can, Dark will take it from there." As Copernicus spoke, *The Long View* was accelerating to intercept.

That left him a little puzzled, but the stones spoke up in his thoughts. *Dark is saying, frame the enemy with weapons fire. Restrict its maneuvering. That will give Dark a chance to do something clever—*

/With the quantum vacuum—?/

I think we'll see in a few minutes.

Looking around, it seemed to him that Ruall and Copernicus already got it. Akura and Sheeawn looked mystified. He would explain later, if there *was* a later. "If you understand, Coppy, can you follow Dark's lead?"

"Affirmative, Cap'n. In about two minutes, we'll be close enough to get off some bracketing shots."

"At your discretion."

Copernicus acknowledged, but before he was able to do anything, a series of flashes erupted from the Mindaru. It was not waiting passively for them. The first two hit *The Long View*'s shielding and shook the ship. The next two missed, as Copernicus maneuvered. A stream of fire came from the Mindaru, until they were corkscrewing wildly to keep from absorbing too much energy. Bandicut began cursing quietly, then not so quietly. The Mindaru was keeping them too far away to get in any shots of their own.

This is good. This is good, the stones said.

"How is this good?" Bandicut shouted, startling the others on the bridge.

It's keeping the Mindaru occupied. It's flying a straight line. Dark is slipping in ...

Even as the stones spoke, Bandicut thought he caught a glimpse of a shadow moving across the field—maybe it was the stones that gave him the vision—and a moment later, something seemed to glitch in the display, and the Mindaru appeared to freeze, abruptly halting fire.

Dark is manipulating all those trillions of particle-pairs appearing spontaneously from the vacuum—matter and antimatter.

/And—/

And when the pairs come back together and mutually annihilate—

At that instant there was a flash of actinic light where the Mindaru was, not a point, but a *patch* of light that left Bandicut's eyes strobing with afterimages. When it faded, he saw nothing where the Mindaru had been. /Is that what happens when a trillion particle pairs recombine and mutually annihilate?/ he asked, awestruck.

Apparently so, murmured his stones.

"It is destroyed," Copernicus announced. "Reported by Dark, confirmed by our own scans."

"Damn. *Hot damn!*" Bandicut yelled. "*Way to go, Dark!*" He paused for breath and gazed hopefully at the beachball-sized planet of Karellia floating in the viewspace. They had protected it one more time. Behind him, Akura and Sheeawn were gesturing and chattering excitedly.

Bandicut shook a fist in triumph. "All right, then, let's go help *Plato!*"

Dark wheeled in space and sped off ahead of them.

CHAPTER 23

Long Shot

FOR DAKOTA BANDICUT, the pursuit of ghosts across the interstellar void was both stressful and tedious in the extreme, maybe more so than for her shipmates. They all were worried about getting back alive from this crazy pursuit, but Dakota had the added worry that if something more went wrong, it would be her fault. She had urged going after her uncle's ship, and Captain Brody had agreed to it.

But none of them had counted on more of those hostile things, the Mindaru, popping out of the starstream and streaking right past *Plato* (at a safe distance, fortunately) in the same direction. If that hadn't been alarming enough, the targets were observed, on the long-range scanners, to have gone through some kind of transformation from a ghostly echo into solid spacecraft. *Plato*'s sensors couldn't get much of a read on them, except that they seemed like solid-state objects with no internal air space, and therefore presumably crewless, and very powerful. They appeared to be heading in exactly the same direction as *Plato*—on the faint trail of her uncle's ship, *The Long View*.

The crew of Plato were a solid and loyal team, and no one openly complained about their off-the-books pursuit of something this dangerous, but it was obvious that few of them liked the idea. Captain Brody clearly didn't like it, either, but turning back was not a great option. They had no way to get back into the starstream without a years-long journey; and if they couldn't reach an entry node, their journey home would be measured in many more years. Their k-space drive was many times better than lightspeed, but that was still a lot slower than the n-space of the starstream. And so, they flew headlong into the unknown, and a possible fight, aiming for a mysterious star system two and a half light-years away. Whatever the star system was, there seemed to be a lot of interest in it.

———

Alone, off shift, in her cabin, Dakota gazed up at the ceiling, pondering the state of affairs she had helped bring about. Could things possibly have gone any more differently from her expectations when she'd stepped aboard, back at High Concept? Her mind was churning, and writing to Harrad seemed the best way to corral her thoughts. She shook her head, rocked forward in her chair, and started typing:

> Harrad, Luv,
>
> What is this, feels like the tenth time I've written you since we were thrown out of the starstream. It always feels foolish, and probably is, knowing how unlikely it is that you'll see any of these messages before you see me—assuming I get back in one piece. But still I want to put my thoughts down. Since we may be heading into conflict, there's always the chance that *Plato* will survive but I won't. That's pretty unlikely, and I don't say it to be morbid—but if it happens, I hope you'll at least get these little snippets of my thought. I've recorded some holo for you, too, but sometimes I seem to think more clearly when I'm writing.
>
> Every day, I ask myself why we are doing this—why *I*, of all people, urged us to do this. I so want to get back to you, more than I can tell you! But we have our responsibility to protect the

starstream, and human space. I don't necessarily think it will come to that. But my translator-stones consider it that important. My human head has to agree. And my human heart can't abide standing by while my uncle flees before these things, whatever they are. We have to help, if we can.

We are now just a few days out from the star system we've labeled "Geronimo A." The things we presume to be Mindaru are still ahead of us, but we don't know exactly how far, and won't until we drop out of k-space. We were tracking a blip that we thought was *The Long View*, but it barely paused at Geronimo A and went right on through the energetic nebula that envelops the whole binary system, toward Geronimo B, the other star in the system. No idea what it did there, but it or something like it came back a few days later. Is it even my uncle's ship? I think it is, but at this distance we can't be sure.

If so, I'm worried for it, because the first of the Mindaru we tracked arrived at A right around the same time. We picked up some energy discharges, and then both of them flew off toward B! It's got us all mystified. Tracking through k-space is tricky at best, so there's a lot of guesswork in our analysis.

Well, I do want to have some of this transcribed—just in case—but that's not the real reason I'm writing. I'm writing to let you know I love you, and I can't wait to get back to you. (Although I hope you hear it from my lips before there's any reason for you to be sifting through my stack of messages!) How are you, and how is your sis? How's the alt'spatial vision study coming? Found a way yet for us to mimic the eyesight

of those Parasian doves? Seeing in five dimensions
could really be handy for *us* right about now.
  Drat. Don't you know, it's almost time for me
to go back on shift. More later. Love you.
  DB

Two days later, tracking indicated that the two Mindaru ahead of
Plato had slowed and dropped into normal-space as they entered
the outer region of the Geronimo A star system. Taking stock of
the situation, probably. Whatever the reason, it gave *Plato* a chance
to catch up, if they were quick about it. *Plato*'s crew were now
preparing as best they could for various first-contact scenarios,
and also for battle.

Not everyone was convinced that what they were doing made
any sense. At Dakota's request, Captain Brody called the officers
and department heads together for a briefing. "I'm going to let
Commander Bandicut run this meeting," he said, once they were
all gathered around the briefing room table. "She has something
she wants to share with you." He extended a hand. "Exo?"

Dakota took a minute to look over the roomful of officers, and
give them a chance to absorb her serious intent. Then she began:
"Some of you are wondering why we are, to put it baldly, sticking
our necks out so far on the long shot of pursuing these targets
that we know so little about. Especially since the first one that we
met, back in the starstream, displayed alarming hostility and
striking power." That brought nods. "You already know that one
reason is concern for the safety of the friendly contact we made
in the stream—and yes, one of the people on that ship is my uncle—but our reasoning goes way beyond that. His ship also represents an important first-contact with an extremely advanced
culture. Another reason for pursuit, obviously, is concern for the
inhabitants of that planet ahead of us. But I want to share a third
reason with you. And in order to do that, I must first share something else."

That got everyone stirring. She suppressed a rush of nerves; she had never before tried anything like what she was about to do. But the stones had agreed to try it. She cleared her throat. "Most of you know by now that I carry with me—" she rubbed her wrists as she spoke "—communication devices of alien origin. They are called translator-stones, and I've had them since I lived back in Earth space. They are offspring of the very first alien artifact discovered by humanity, in the home system, pre-starflight. They are old, or their progenitor is, and by old I mean in the millions of years. And they communicate with others of their kind."

"Begging your pardon, Commander, but how does this—?"

Dakota silenced the question from the power-deck chief with a raised finger. "Bear with me, please." She held up her hands, showing the glowing gem embedded in each of her wrists. "These stones shared a lot of information with a sister pair that my uncle, in that ship we're following, carries. The stones are very private in their communication with me, but they have consented to attempt to speak with all of you, to share some of what they learned." Dakota made a small adjustment to a communications unit on the table in front of her, and closed her eyes. /Are you ready?/

Her wrists vibrated, tickling her, and a soft, alto voice came out of the box. "Greetings. Thank you for your attention. We are not used to this. Forgive us if we stumble."

Navigator Tanaki's eyes went wide. "Is that really the stones speaking?"

"Yes, we are the daughter-stones. It is an unusual mode of communication for us, but we are trying. We thought it important that you know what you face."

"You mean the Mindaru?" Dakota said. She rested her forearms on the table, keeping the stones close to the comm box.

"Yes, the Mindaru." The voice quavered slightly, then steadied. "We learned much about them from contact with John Bandicut. Also from stones of Daarooaack, the cloud you saw in the starstream. They have both faced Mindaru. They know the terrible danger Mindaru pose. And that is why they fought it in the stream, protecting us. We believe they continue to fight. Mindaru are ancient, and seek death."

At Dakota's prompting, the stones related a condensed account of the Mindaru history, and threat.

There were many questions, which the stones tried to answer. The most difficult came from Kamya, the weapons chief. "If these things are as dangerous as you say, wouldn't it be better to get this ship back home at top speed, and warn the Patrol and the rest of humanity? I'm willing to die in the right cause, but if we die out here without getting word back, what good will that do? We need to warn people!"

Dakota did her best to conceal her own distress at that question, because it was one she'd wrestled with ever since they'd set out in pursuit. She waited for the stones to answer.

"We share that concern. But from here, there is no apparent way back to where you can report in a reasonable time."

"Even so," said the weapons officer, "and please don't judge me for saying this, but I think we're all thinking it. This planet ahead is just one world, and the Habitat of Humanity is many. What if we let the Mindaru have this one—"

"Throw them to the wolves?" asked Gordon-Wu, the systems chief.

"To put it crassly, yes. And buy us time to get back and get the rest of humanity ready for them. If they're as dangerous as you say—"

"Indeed they are. And even if we disregard the ethics of sacrificing an innocent world—"

"I don't think it would be right to just leave that world helpless," Tanaki interrupted.

"We agree. And there is this: They will only grow stronger if we give them victory here. Instead of a few, they will have the power of a world."

"We need to kill them now. And kill them good," said the first pilot. "It would be crazy to let them get stronger."

"Our point, precisely. Yes."

"So," said Captain Brody, turning from a wall comm, where he'd been having a muted conversation. "I've just been given the latest from long-range tracking. The signature of *The Long View* has been picked up again in the Geronimo A system, and there have been multiple indications of high-energy discharges. Tactical believes there may be a battle underway right now near the inhabited planet."

Dakota let out a sigh. "Let's wrap this up, then. Thank you, stones." She turned off the comm box and flexed her fingers. "I wanted you to know what we're facing, and *why* we're facing it head-on. I have the utmost confidence in all of you." She caught the captain's eye.

Brody stepped forward. "Let's get ready, then. Nav, prepare a course for interception of the closest of the Mindaru. Everyone else, be prepared for battle stations." He nodded to Dakota.

She rose. "Thank you. Meeting dismissed."

The Mindaru had stayed in normal-space, and *Plato*'s pursuit was bringing the rearmost one very close to engagement range. Long-range sensors were producing a much clearer picture now of the situation in the Geronimo A system. The planet had identifiable signatures of technological civilization, and some spacefaring capability. But the fighting, largely, was between the contact they believed to be *The Long View* and the Mindaru. There had been some fusion blasts of considerable power. *The Long View* was still active and moving, but appeared outnumbered and under attack.

An hour ago, Captain Brody had announced his intention to engage the nearest Mindaru, tagged as target India, as soon as *Plato* had closed the range sufficiently. "The least we can do is try to improve the odds for *The Long View*," he'd said. It escaped no one's attention that there were *two* Mindaru in their area. The first one, target Hotel, was speeding ahead toward the planet, but there was no reason to think it couldn't turn back on them. Whether it did or not, *Plato* had its hands full with target India, lagging behind.

The bridge was very quiet, just the occasional murmur between nav and piloting, or the low voice of Captain Brody or Dakota herself. The concentration of the bridge officers was ferocious, each absorbed with a holo-display, analyzing data as it came in. Dakota felt the pressure mounting, as they pursued the enemy toward the planet.

"Fifteen minutes to firing range," reported Tanaki.

Dakota breathed a silent prayer.

"Laser range in one minute," said the tactical officer. "Particle beam in two."

Brody rubbed his chin. "Exo, any last-minute advice from your stones?"

Dakota shook her head. "Afraid they can't tell us anything more about the best weapons to use."

Brody grunted. "All right. Weapons, give me a one-two punch of laser and particle-beam. See if we can land a shot and evaluate the effects. Ten seconds each, no gap, on my order."

Kamya on weapons control acknowledged both beams powered up. Dakota tried to remain relaxed. *Plato* had none of the fancy weapons such as they'd seen *The Long View* use. No quantum devices or n-space disrupters. Besides the two beams, they had a total of six missiles with EMP warheads, and four more with fusion warheads. And finally, more or less a last resort in this case, they had a kinetic-kill railgun, basically a hyper-powered electric slingshot. For any of the projectile weapons, they would need to partially drop the protective force screens for an instant. Better to get their longest-distance shots in early, before they got too close to the target.

"Skipper, it's rotating; it may be reacting to our approach," Kamya said.

Brody didn't reply. He waited until he heard tactical report that they were in range for both, before saying, *"Fire weapons."*

The laser flashed out, in pulses barely visible against the rarefied dust in the interplanetary medium. Ten seconds later, it winked out and a faintly glowing thread of particle-beam destruction lanced in its place. Kamya reported in a subdued tone, "Both beams at least fifty percent on target. No measurable effect."

"Not no effect," said Tanaki. "It's cut velocity. It's turning on us."

Dakota swore under her breath.

"Prepare for high-gee maneuvering," Brody ordered. "Weapons, have two fusion missiles ready to launch on my command."

The bridge was shockingly quiet as Kamya acknowledged, and they watched the now-rapid approach of the enemy. Dakota had to remind herself to breathe.

The Mindaru, jittering slightly in the view from the image magnification, looked like a pitted metal asteroid with menacing spines.

Tanaki's voice was muted, but audible to everyone on the bridge: "One thousand klicks . . . eight hundred . . . six hundred . . ."

Brody raised a hand with pointed finger. At four hundred klicks, he snapped the finger toward Kamya and said, *"Launch missiles."*

The deck shuddered slightly, and two glowing objects shot out of the front of the ship. At the same instant, something bright flashed on the surface of the enemy. Dakota felt a jolt, and the viewer went white. Half a dozen alarms flashed red, blaring their alerts, and a smell of ozone filled the air. The bridge lights went dark, and the alarms fell silent. Something groaned deep in the ship, and Dakota felt a vibration beneath her feet. Chemical emergency light flickered on, ghostly red, and steadied. "Report!" she shouted, and in rapid sequence the bridge officers replied. There had been a beam strike from the enemy in the instant their force screen was down, hitting them with an electromagnetic pulse. Propulsion was down; comms were down; life support was compromised, holding at minimum. Respirators were out. Dakota put hers on and turned to Brody. "Your orders, Captain?"

"I need eyes, Exo. Get me vision outside the ship."

Dakota strode to Gordon-Wu at the systems console. "Kyle, first priority, screens and sensors."

"Yes, sir. Nanos are rebooting. Okay, they're back, in safe mode. Starting repairs now."

"Good." Dakota adjusted her air mask and made a scan of the bridge crew to see that all were wearing theirs. She sent another crewman down to gather reports from sections of the ship cut off by the comm failure.

By the time she'd completed a round of bridge stations, the viewscreen area was flickering. A small window appeared in the center, providing a lo-res view forward of the ship. The Mindaru was not visible, but sensors indicated a patch of residual radiation where the fusion warheads might have exploded. Brody stood staring at it for a moment, then said, "I don't see any debris. Can you get me a sweep tracking the target's path?"

"Trying, Captain," Gordon-Wu said, working at a console that was a lot more cumbersome to work manually than a holo, and in very dim light. The window of view began to move to the side.

"Wrong way!" Dakota yelled.

"Damn. How's this?"

The view drifted to the left, and then began a steady sweep. Black, black, black, and then a twinkling object. "Hold it right there!" Brody called. "Can you bring it in? Magnify?"

"Half a second." A few seconds passed, and suddenly the full viewer sprang back to life. "Okay—magnifying." The view zoomed. The object was the Mindaru, rotating slowly. It appeared completely intact. "Bugger!"

"Tactical?" Brody snapped.

"It's still moving away at high velocity."

"Does it look like it's going to come back after us?"

"Can't tell. Wait. Yes, it's deflecting its course, and slowing. Intent unclear. But it must have taken some damage, or it would have hit us again."

"Keep monitoring it. Exo, do you have an update on our condition?"

Dakota was making another round of her people. Without holos, it was impossible to take everything in at a glance. Her voice was muffled behind the air mask. "Not yet. Kyle, what's the state of comm and weapons?"

"I've got a repair crew of nanos on both," Gordon-Wu said. "Comm cables are intact; I'm waiting for the self-repair bots to bring the head units back up. Should be—there we go! Commander, you can talk to power deck." As he said that, half the bridge lighting returned.

Dakota stepped to the comm and said, "Power, this is the Exo. Talk to me."

She heard some crackling; then the voice of the power assistant answered. *"We're piecing it back together, Commander. I can give you power to essential systems, but propulsion is going to take—well—"*

"Is going to take what, Smits?"

"Longer, sir . . ."

For the next hour and a half, *Plato* coasted, unable to maneuver from her last trajectory. Life-support and communications were back, but propulsion, force-screens, and most of weapons were down. The Mindaru appeared to be having difficulty maneuvering, also. Perhaps it really had been damaged by the two missiles, but it was slowly altering course to make another pass. Apparently it thought it had a better chance with its weapons than *Plato*. Dakota thought that likely, too. The captain wasn't saying what he thought, but he had every human and nano resource working on restoring firepower to the ship.

Tactical reported the Mindaru almost within range of the beam weapons; likely that meant *Plato* was also in range of the Mindaru's beam weapon. Dakota stepped quickly to check the weapons status. They had railgun capability, nothing else. The railgun was the simplest weapon on the ship, and also the least likely to be effective against the Mindaru, given their ability to dodge. *Damn*, she whispered and turned to the captain.

Before she could speak, her stones buzzed. **Dark is here to help.**

Brody spoke with a sharp edge in his voice. "Tell me once more what your friend wants us to do."

Dakota answered quickly. "Be ready to fire the railgun."

"What I thought you said. Might as well throw rocks at it. This had better be good." He gave the order to rotate the ship to face straight into the oncoming Mindaru, and to bring the railgun into firing alignment.

"It's what Dark is asking for. David and Goliath, maybe. She's going to make a grab for the thing and try to hold it still." It had better be good, indeed.

In the viewer, a tracking tag showed the tiny smudge that was Dark speeding across the star-field, past *Plato*, aiming straight for the Mindaru and interposing itself between the Mindaru and *Plato*. Something flashed behind it, and Dark glowed momentarily. Had Dark just absorbed a shot intended for *Plato*? Or maybe for itself? /Is Dark okay?/ she asked her stones.

Yes. Be ready to fire on command.

Dakota asked, "Is the railgun ready? Spread of three?"

"Charged and ready," Kamya called.

Brody nodded, fist raised. "Firing approved. You call the shot, Exo."

Dark intercepted the twinkling Mindaru. On full magnification, they could all see the hazy cloud-being envelop the enemy. The Mindaru jerked one way and then another. Amazingly, Dark appeared to be holding the enemy immobile. Dark glowed twice, briefly, as the Mindaru tried to shoot.

Fire now.

"Fire!" Dakota called.

There was an audible *thumpthumpthump* through the deck as the electric gun shot its projectiles with machine-gun rapidity. Three sparks, hot and bright from the acceleration, flew toward Dark. Toward the Mindaru. The bridge was silent; nobody breathed.

Another second passed.

Light blazed where the Mindaru was, and then was swallowed by Dark. A secondary flash was partially obscured, and a third. All three projectiles had hit their target, their considerable kinetic energy converted to heat and light.

Brody stared at the screen. "Is it dead? Is the damn thing dead?" He could have been asking anyone, but he was talking to Dakota.

She didn't have to ask the stones.

Waiting to be certain. Yes. It is destroyed. Dark will convert its remaining matter to energy.

Another blaze of violet-white, much brighter and larger. An instant later it was swallowed into the blackness of Dark.

The Mindaru is no more. Dark wonders if we require further assistance.

Dakota whooped. "It's gone! We killed it!"

Brody jerked two thumbs up and smiled. But before he could speak, the comm came to life. "Bridge, power deck. If it's not too late, would you like propulsion now?"

Dakota grinned back at her captain.

The Long View was about halfway across the distance to the last Mindaru when Bandicut saw the Mindaru and Plato exchange fire. It was impossible to tell what was happening, except that the Mindaru flew on past Plato, and no further shots were fired for the moment. But a little later, the Mindaru turned back for another run on Plato.

Copernicus reported, "Dark is reaching them." They could see it in the viewspace, under magnification. Dark flew *fast*, and grabbed the Mindaru.

A needle of light against space seemed to split Plato in two. It exploded into fine rays that reminded Bandicut of splintering glass. His heart stopped.

An instant later, there was a starburst, from *inside Dark*. Suddenly he realized that the needle of light had not hit Plato, but had come *from* it.

He stared into the viewspace, fixed on the distant point that was Plato, and on the fading fire now being released into space by Dark. "What just happened?" he demanded.

Jeaves spoke. "A most unusual technique . . ."

"What happened, damn it?"

"Sorry," Jeaves said. "I believe your niece's ship has just destroyed the last of the Mindaru in this system."

PART TWO

Worlds and Time Together

"Time is an illusion."
—Albert Einstein

"For the present is the point at which time
touches eternity."
—C.S. Lewis

CHAPTER 24

Searching the Timestream

AN INSISTENT PINGING woke Antares from a fitful sleep. Though she was weary from anxiety, her restlessness had kept her awake for the first half of the night. She had finally gotten to sleep—not long ago, she realized, peering at the clock to the right of her head. But what was this damn *pinging*?

"Uuhll," she gurgled softly and called, in the general direction of the comm, "Who is it?" The pinging stopped and she heard Napoleon's voice: *"Lady Antares!"*

"I'm here, Napoleon," she said huskily, trying to make her voice sound as if she were wide awake. "What is it?"

"Lady Antares, I am sorry to disturb your rest, but I think you had better come here at once."

"What is it, Napoleon?"

"Trouble, I'm afraid."

It took her less than a minute to get to Napoleon's side. She ran right past Cromus, who was pacing up and down the control center, muttering to himself and clicking his pincers. He started to speak to her, but she ignored him. Braking her run with a hand on Napoleon's console, she leaned close to the norg. "What is it, Napoleon? What's happening?" Glancing around, she saw that the rest of the control team appeared agitated. *What the hell?*

Napoleon was clicking disapprovingly and fussing with the screen in front of him. He rotated his right eye-camera to look at her. "There was a disentanglement pulse sent from here, and they didn't alert either you or me about it."

"What's that mean? What's a disentanglement pulse?"

Napoleon buzzed in frustration. "It's a wave sent down the ghoststream to try to sweep the Mindaru out of the temporal channel leading up to the present, and to close the entry point down at the other end."

Antares recoiled. "Isn't that—?"

"Yes, it is!" Napoleon barked. "They did it before, and for them to do it again without consulting us—!"

"That's not acceptable." Antares straightened and called out to Cromus, "What have you done, and why did you not tell us?"

Cromus came over, hissing and stuttering clicks. "The crew—your friends—called for the puls-se. The Mindaru pursuit-t—"

"Isn't that what killed the last crew?" Antares demanded.

Cromus's head jerked, and he snapped one claw, loudly. "S-superficially, yes-s. But that-t pulse went wrong, badly t-timed and badly calculated-d. They've learned from that-t and are better at it now. The people here, I mean. They modulated this one so it was less dangerous-s to our crew."

Napoleon's eyes glowed a darker and more troubled hue of red. He rotated his head and said to Cromus, "Modulated or not, it weakened the entanglement that's at the heart of the ghoststream, did it not?"

"Weakened, yes-s," Cromus admitted.

"Weakened?" Napoleon said. "Or broke?"

Antares felt a chill in her spine. Is that why the controllers up there were conferring so animatedly? Every minute or so, one of them glanced in their direction and hurriedly looked away.

Cromus hissed unhappily and waved his pincers in the direction of the controllers. "Broken-n? We do not think so. We do not hope so. But—"

"But what?" Antares demanded.

"But their connection back to us is compromised-d."

Antares stared at him, trying to parse how bad that was. "But . . . you have a plan to reestablish connection, don't you?" *Don't you?*

"Hk-k-k . . . they are working on it-t." Cromus looked miserable. "They believe the crew are still alive, but having trouble linking back-k," he said finally.

Can't the launch crew just pull them out? The question boomed in her mind, but she already knew the answer, made clear from the beginning. The answer was no. Their minds and souls were too entwined in that fragile thread of entanglement. If that was compromised . . .

Napoleon was watching her with gleaming camera eyes. He flexed his neck, as though in sympathy, and said, "I suggest *we* focus on what we might do to help bring them back. Don't you think, Lady Antares?"

Antares felt her breath go out in a sigh. "Napoleon, do you have something in mind?"

What the robot had in mind would require the approval and assistance of the ghoststream crew, and even Antares was skeptical at first. Sending Napoleon into the ghoststream after Ik and Julie made sense on the surface, but Antares wasn't sure this was a job that an inorg could do. Still, she let him propose it to Cromus. To soften him up for her own proposal.

Cromus rejected the idea out of hand. "The situation-n is delicate enough already. Introducing an inorg into the stream could generate new failure modes that we can't predict-t."

"But," Napoleon pointed out, "you have lost them at this point. I could look for them."

"No, our systems are not optimized for—"

Antares waited as they went back and forth a couple of times. Finally she interrupted to say, "Or . . . you could send *me* into the stream. I am org, and close enough to what your systems are optimized for. I have yaantel stones similar to theirs, and I can search using an empathic reach that I believe may exceed any of your technical capabilities here."

Cromus bent one eyestalk to glance at the spindly controller named Watts, who had come up alongside in time to hear most of the conversation. Without speaking to Watts, he continued, "No, the risk is too great—"

"For a chance at their safe return?" Antares asked, with an edge of sarcasm. "If I voluntarily take the risk?"

Cromus rumbled with displeasure, and clicked appendages she couldn't even see. "Clearly, I do not object to our crew's safe return-n. I do, however, object to the possibility of losing them-m *and* losing you, *and* at the same time affecting the ghoststream in ways unpredicted-d."

"Uhhl, Cromus," Antares said, with a low growl deep in her voice, "this entire mission has carried such risks."

Cromus rumbled. "Yes. Yes, it has. But that does not mean I wish to multiply the risk-k."

She felt her anger harden. "No. Perhaps you'd rather make the situation seem impossible. So that if you can't get them back, you can cut them loose and say there was never any hope of saving them. Is that it?"

Cromus stared at her in silence.

Then Watts leaned in and spoke to him, too softly for Antares to hear.

Cromus snapped his pincers several times as Watts spoke. Antares wondered if he was threatening to snap Watts's thin neck. She could not read his emotions, though it was obvious she had offended him.

"Please tell me what you are saying," she said finally.

Cromus peered at her with one eyestalk. "Wait here," he said abruptly. He turned with creaking joints and strode with surprising speed down to the front of the control center. Watts bowed to Antares and hurried after him. Antares followed.

Cromus rotated this way and that, speaking to the individual controllers. Finally he turned to beckon to Antares, and was startled to see her already there. Cromus gestured with a claw to indicate that she should face the control crew. He clicked loudly for attention. "*Hk-k-k-k, team!* We are going to try something new . . ."

The technical preparation took a couple of hours. Antares would be strapped into a small cockpit alongside the one Julie and Ik were in, and her consciousness would be projected down the same ghoststream. While this was being set up, Antares was briefed by the controllers—but only after the controllers debated the best approach among themselves: whether to ease her in slowly and not stress the system; or act quickly to reach the crew before the thread weakened any further; or to not travel down the stream at all, but to try to lead them back home by voice alone. Antares shook her head as they debated. They obviously had no more idea than she did; she was going to follow her own instincts and do what seemed best.

She was, in practical terms, reaching out to *ghosts* in the stream. Physically, Ik and Julie would be right next to her, sometimes still and sometimes twitching and straining, trying to recall their own spirits. She was there to help them, even if it felt strange beyond belief.

She considered looking in on the faces of her friends before she was launched, to freshen the memory and the connection. In the end, she could not bear to, could not stand the thought of seeing her friends' faces when their souls were somewhere else. She thought it would feel too empty.

"Lady Antares," said Enwin, at the entrance to the launch pod. "This way, please."

The launch was terrifying. Antares held her breath as the world around her darkened, and the walls of the pod melted away into the ghoststream. In a silent transition, she was suddenly flying in space, as though in a star-spanner, but without the protective bubble. Vertigo threatened to overwhelm her, and for several minutes she could do nothing except try to keep her thoughts focused on her goals, and by concentrating, keep from being ill.

We are here. We can help you.

As the knowing-stones stabilized her body against vertigo, she felt a rush of gratitude. She caught her breath and risked another look. She was floating gently pastward through time. She remembered the last words from Enwin, before launch: *Proceed slowly. Control your movement. Try to sense them from this end, if you can. If you must stretch down the ghoststream into deep time, do so with caution.* That was the approach that had sounded so arbitrarily conservative when she'd heard the controllers discussing it. But now that she was here, it made perfect sense.

She started by testing her control. Enlisting the help of her stones, she found she could make adjustments to the view. She could regulate her movement away from the launch point, and she could pull herself back. With a slight hand gesture and a low murmur, she caused the ghoststream itself to become visible: a hollow, misty channel of extremely pale light, extending to infinity—blue nearby, and shifting toward crimson in the distance. More than a channel, it was a delicate thread—or perhaps a tattered yarn—stretching down through time and far across space.

Somewhere down that strand were Ik and Julie. Somewhere a long way down. She could see nothing down the stream. Would they be able to hear a call? How would a call even work, in this strange reality? She'd been told to try using her voice, and the ghoststream technology would handle the rest. She should listen for an answer the same way, by pretending that time and distance did not exist here.

She cupped her hands and shouted, *"Ik! I-i-i-k-k-k! Juu-leeee!"* Her voice vanished in the distance, no better than a sigh into the wind. She tried again, giving it more force. This time she imagined a tiny echo. But there was no answer.

She wondered how far her empathic reach could extend down the ghoststream, and backward in time. Only one way to find out. Carefully, deliberately, she stilled her thoughts and listened. Or rather, *felt*. For any sign of her friends.

What she felt was a ringing emptiness.

She kept trying.

But there was no answer.

CHAPTER 25

Reunion with Dakota

As *THE LONG VIEW* closed the distance to *Plato*, Bandicut sat in the commons, his thoughts spinning in a hundred directions. Where did they stand with their mission now? *Plato* was damaged but recovering, and making headway toward Karellia. They had eliminated all of the Mindaru in detection range, and the temporal shield was off. Had they really stopped the influx of Mindaru? For good? What about Ik? And . . . *Julie Stone?* (That still seemed impossible; surely Jeaves had misinterpreted the message. But what if it was true?) Were they okay, if they were somewhere in the timestream? Had *The Long View*'s victory here cost them somehow, stranded them somewhere deep in the past? The thought made him shudder.

But of more immediate concern—so astounding he could hardly believe it—he was about to see Dakota again! His *niece*, his last living relative—not through some scratchy comm connection in weird-space, but in person, flesh and blood! He would have to be careful not to overwhelm her in his enthusiasm. Despite their ship-to-ship conversations, the Dakota he saw in his mind was still the twelve-year-old daughter of his brother. Or really, the nine-year-old, because that's how old she had been when he'd said good-bye to go to Neptune. A child. Now she was the XO on a starship, five hundred years removed!

And what about *Plato*'s crew? If Dakota was going to be the first human he'd laid eyes on since Neptune, her shipmates were going to be next. What would it be like to be among *humans* again? He wasn't actually sure he was ready for it. What a strange thought. They would be close enough for docking in a few hours. He should try to get some sleep.

When Copernicus woke him on the intercom, he felt as if he'd just dozed off. He groped to look at the time; it had been closer to three hours. Not long enough. "What is it, Coppy?"

"Cap'n, we're approaching rendezvous. What arrangements would you prefer for docking? Shall I extend a tube? Or would you rather cross over in the number two shuttle?"

Bandicut heaved himself to a sitting position. "Coppy, you just piloted us to victory against killer Mindaru. I think you've earned the right to dock us however you want."

"If you say so, Cap'n, but you are the captain."

"Yeaaah, but I'm delegating the authority on this one. Look, do I have time to take a shower? And can you put some coffee on?"

"Affirmative to both."

Ten minutes later, when Bandicut stepped onto the bridge, steaming cup in his hand, he was greeted in person by Copernicus. "Cap'n, I thought you and Ruall might want to discuss security protocols—since the last time we met *Plato*, there were concerns about getting too close."

Bandicut remembered. "But that was before *Plato* came all this way to help us knock back the enemy. I think they've earned our trust."

"I concur," said the robot. "Ruall, do you concur? Do you have any special concerns?"

Ruall rang softly. "Your pardon? No—go ahead and set it up however seems best for human contact."

Bandicut was surprised by her easy acquiescence. "Ruall, is something wrong?"

For a few moments, Ruall didn't answer. Then she said, "I don't know where Bria has gone."

Bandicut thought. He hadn't seen her in a while, either. "She didn't wander out into the middle of the fight, I hope."

"No, she was here when we started on our current course. She was feeling stronger. Restless, I think. She said something about speaking to Dark, and then she slipped off, as she sometimes does. But that was hours ago, and I don't know where Dark has gone."

"Do you think they might be in trouble?"

Ruall spun out of sight, spun back. "I don't know."

"Do you want to go looking for her?"

Ruall made a *tsk*ing sound. "Where would we look? This ship's mastery of n-space is quite primitive compared to Bria's. Or Dark's." She stopped the sound. "No, do what is needed to reunite with your kin."

Bandicut accepted that in silence. It didn't sound like Ruall. Was her concern for Bria mellowing her?

Jeaves spoke up. "If I may interrupt. We've just received a signal from Li-Jared. He and Ocellet Quin will be departing shortly in the landing craft to meet us. Quin wishes to pursue talks with the Uduon, to see if they can negotiate peace. They will likely join us in about one half day's time."

"How close are we to rendezvous with *Plato*?" Bandicut asked.

"Perhaps an hour, Cap'n," said Copernicus.

"Plenty of time for you to meet with your people," said Jeaves.

The two ships came together in normal-space, Copernicus handling the approach with his usual aplomb. Bandicut pondered how best to introduce his alien companions to the crew of *Plato*. Maybe *they* had protocols for meeting new galactic species. Well, he would go over alone for this first visit, anyway.

Thinking about that, he looked down at what he was wearing. His jumpsuit was looking pretty ratty. That was no way to meet his niece and her shipmates. He returned to his quarters to have a new jumpsuit made by the ship's fabricator.

Now, better dressed, he floated weightless in the outer door of *The Long View*'s airlock. He gazed down the connecting tunnel, waiting for word to proceed. His heart was pounding. *"They're ready for you,"* Jeaves said in his ear.

Bandicut pushed out of the airlock and down the tunnel. It was empty; it could be leading anywhere, he thought. He was two-thirds of the way across when *Plato*'s airlock slid open. He grabbed for a handhold to slow down, and paused to see who was coming to greet him.

There was no mistaking Dakota. Commander Dakota Bandicut. She wore a dark blue uniform, closely fitted, with silver trim on the collar and shoulders. She looked slender and athletic, maybe twenty-eight or thirty, and startlingly attractive, with a bright and engaging face, filled with poise and confidence. Her golden-brown hair was cut shorter than he remembered, but the sparkle in her green Bandicut eyes was just the same, and so was the slightly off-center grin.

"My God!" he murmured, the exclamation never quite leaving his throat.

"Uncle John!" His niece launched herself from the airlock and caught him in a bear-hug that set them spinning in the zero-g. He felt his stones tingling in his wrists, reacting to the proximity to hers. He had forgotten she had stones! With a laughing, "Whoa!" she grabbed a handhold to steady them both. "Jeez, it's so damn good to see you!" she cried, holding him at arm's length. She tugged him toward the far airlock. "I have so many things to ask you! Come, see my ship!"

"Lead on! Permission to come aboard?"

She laughed gaily. "We don't say that anymore, in the service."

"You don't?" He caught the edge of the *Plato* airlock and swung himself to the open hatch. Large arrows inside the airlock were accompanied by the words, *This side up.* "What do you say instead?" He clunked down feet-first in the local gravity field.

Dakota laughed again. "We say *Hello.* The scanner IDs us. If we don't belong here, it doesn't let us in. Unless, of course, we've told it to expect you." The airlock door slid closed behind them.

The inner hatch opened, and they stepped together into a small ready room. It wasn't the racks of gear he saw first, but the greeting party—a man and a woman, both dressed like Dakota. The man had more silver trimming on his tunic. The captain?

His guess was confirmed a moment later when Dakota introduced them. "Uncle John, this is Captain Brody, commander of *Plato*. Captain, John Bandicut . . . of Earth, originally. I hope we'll learn more about where he's from now." Bandicut shook hands with the man, who appeared about his own age, sharp-nosed, with salt-and-pepper hair, hazel eyes, and a serious, almost nervous, expression.

"John Bandicut—Captain, is it?—welcome aboard *Plato*," he said, with a quick, energetic handshake. "This is my second officer and navigator, Tanaki Frank." Bandicut turned to greet a wiry woman with Asian features. Were they Asian? Who knew what those eyes with a hint of an epicanthic fold would be called today?

"I imagine you have quite a story to tell us, Captain," Brody said.

"Well, yes, I suppose I do." Bandicut decided to forego explaining that he wasn't actually a captain, even if his robots treated him like one. To these people, he was a long-lost human from another century, commanding a starship. "I've had some amazing experiences. But I'm so glad circumstances brought us together! I'm extremely fond of my niece, here, and I haven't seen her in five centuries." He caught Dakota's forearm with a grin.

Brody nodded in acknowledgment, but seemed to have other things on his mind. "I do hope you'll explain what some of these *circumstances* were that brought us together, Captain. I don't mind saying, I'm more than a little confused about everything that's happened."

Bandicut reached into his breast pocket and produced a small chip. "I had our robot Jeaves put together a report on the Mindaru for you. It's something you—and by *you*, I mean humanity—need to know about."

"Thank you," Brody said, slipping it into his own breast pocket. "We'll look at it right away."

Bandicut had a thought. "I hope you can read it okay. Jeaves said he put it into a format that was common back when the star-stream was created. How long ago was that?"

"A hundred years or so, depending on where you are when you're reading the calendar," Brody said. "But we've had stable file formats for a while—we had to, or communication would have turned to chaos across the galaxy." Brody gestured down the corridor. "I'll let you know if we have any trouble. Now, why don't we go where we can talk." He touched a fingertip to his right temple. "Senior staff, to the wardroom, please."

"Does that include you?" Bandicut asked Dakota.

Brody answered for her. "You'd better believe it. Commander Bandicut is not only my exec, I don't think we'd *be* here without her foresight and leadership." He lowered his voice to a murmur. "She's also got these alien things from back in Earth System. Translator-stones, she calls them." Brody tapped his wrists meaningfully, as Dakota looked self-conscious.

Bandicut allowed a smile to flicker. He held up his own wrists. "I guess we all have stories to tell," he said wryly, and followed the captain into the passageway.

––––––––––––

He tried to keep his part of the story short, but how could he? After an hour in the wardroom, over real coffee and pastries, Bandicut had given the *Plato* officers a condensed version of how he had gotten to Shipworld, and thence onto other worlds. After that, he gave them the gist of the Mindaru problem, the Karellia/Uduon problem, the temporal distortion problem, and how *Plato* might have helped avert a calamity by providing *The Long View* with backup against the Mindaru here in this system. "So you see," he said, nodding *yes* to more coffee, "we're happy in many ways that we encountered you. I certainly was not expecting to meet humans of any kind on this mission—much less my niece!"

Around the table, he saw faces that were dazed with amazement, if not incredulity. "I guess it does sound pretty incredible, when I say it all at once like that," he admitted.

"No argument," Brody said, with a glance at Dakota, who looked perhaps the most amazed of all. The *Plato* captain steepled his fingers. "I do believe you. But . . . well, it's a lot." Dakota nodded at that, a Bandicut glint in her eye.

Bandicut shifted around in his chair. "Maybe it will all seem more real to you when you meet my companions over on my ship—who, by the way, represent—let's see—two—no, three different worlds. Plus, my robot Copernicus, who comes from Earth system of my own era—and Jeaves, a robot of human manufacture, but from another time and place altogether."

Brody sat forward, his hands flat on the table. "We would very much like to meet them. We do have protocols about making first contact with a new species, but I'm sure we can make those work."

"If it helps, it's not really first contact with the human race." Bandicut chuckled. "I've already blundered into that for you. So maybe that puts less pressure on you to do it strictly by the book."

"Hm." Captain Brody sat back, working that over in his mind.

"And I assume you'll want to go down to Karellia to establish contact there. I can give you a good reference."

"Well—yes, if there's time."

"Why, do you have someplace to be?"

"In a manner of speaking. We have significant concerns about getting back into the starstream, to complete our mission and return home. It seems likely that the longer we stay here, the farther we'll be from achieving that."

Bandicut held up a hand to interrupt the thought. "I'm pretty sure we can help you with that. The starstream isn't going anywhere. But may I ask a personal favor? May I have a little private family time to catch up with my niece and the last five hundred years?"

Brody cracked a strained smile, nodded, and rose from his seat. "I think you've both earned that," he said, and shooed the other officers ahead of him out of the wardroom.

He hugged her again, long and hard. Bandicut tried once more to picture the twelve-year-old girl he had last seen in a holo. Now she was all grown up, just like him. He took a long, appraising look at her, his heart bursting with joy, relief, pride. After all this time . . .

He finally realized he was staring, and he barked a self-conscious laugh. "I must say, Dakota, you've grown up into a—" he gestured awkwardly "—*stunning* young woman. If your parents could only see you now! I'm pleased to see those good Bandicut genes holding strong." He thought of his brother Joe, and Joe's wife Megan, with wistful affection and a twinge of guilt. When had he last even thought of his Earthly family, all of whom had died before he'd gone to space? *Joe? Mom and Dad?*

Dakota's eyes gleamed with pleasure. "I am very pleased to see *you*, Uncle John."

"Uncle—damn, you make me feel old. You probably barely *remember* me. I think you were nine when I left."

"I remember you just fine. And now I finally get a chance to say thank you!"

"Thank you?" He frowned. "For what?"

She smacked him on the arm. "Don't tell me you've forgotten!"

"Forgotten what? *Oh*—you mean—?"

"*Of course* I mean the trust! Uncle John—or John, if you prefer not to feel old—that money was what got me into space! That and your example to follow. Without both of those, I don't know how I would have gone anywhere. I sure as hell wouldn't be *here* now." She grabbed his right hand and squeezed it, hard. "So, yes—thank you. I can never repay you for that."

He hmm'd softly. "I think maybe you already did, coming along and smoking that Mindaru just when we needed you."

"Hah—thank the translator-stones for that! And that black cloud friend of yours that showed up and brought us along. It seemed to think you needed some help."

"Putting it mildly." He remembered something and chuckled. "I think in my last letter to you I told you to come visit me in space. This is not what I was imagining!" He pointed to her wrists. "How did you get those, anyway?"

Dakota grinned wryly. "Same way you did, I imagine. I visited Triton, where you discovered the translator—they were giving tours of the cavern!—and the little devils were lying in wait for me."

Bandicut was stunned. Tours of Triton, and the stones were waiting? What, were they keeping it in the family?

"Which reminds me," Dakota continued. "Did Julie Stone ever catch up with you?"

"Jul—!" His voice caught, and he couldn't get past the first syllable.

"Julie, yes. She had stones, too! Did I tell you that before?" Dakota nodded briskly to herself. "She got in touch with me by holo, and we exchanged a few messages." An old sadness seemed to fall across Dakota's face. "She was last seen on long-range scanner, falling into the sun with the big translator . . ." Bandicut was stunned when she told him the more complete story of Julie's interplanetary pursuit. "*She* was convinced *you* were still alive. Later, after my stones gave me some background, I figured something similar might have happened to both of you."

Bandicut reached for a glass of water and gulped, choking. He shook his head finally. "I have no idea. Except . . ." Except for that message they had received from Amaduse, mentioning *JulieS.* "Except maybe . . ." he murmured, his voice trailing off. *Maybe there's news waiting for me back on Shipworld?*

Dakota looked worried that she might have touched a raw nerve.

He waved off the subject before it could swallow him. "So tell me—" he said, his voice cracking a little, "how *did* a nice girl like you wind up in a century like this? And here in the starstream, of all places?"

Dakota snorted, and for a moment he recognized the young girl he had once known. She sat back and ran her fingers through her hair. "It's almost as crazy as your story. I was living in the Earth 3 colony when a call went out for volunteers to settle Alpha Centauri!"

"Incredible," he murmured. "Was it a relativistic ship? Is that why you didn't age much?"

"Barely. Mainly it was the cold sleep that let me keep my youth." Dakota hesitated, and then told him of their discovery on arrival that other ships had leapfrogged past them. "I didn't want to join a well-established colony, so I moved on . . ."

Bandicut listened in fascination.

"Barnard's Star next, and then a star called Don't Stop Thinking . . . a hundred years into the future, give or take. Then I was on a planet called No Pain . . ."

"Does that planet circle a sun called No Gain?"

She grinned. "Yah. You know it?"

"Lucky guess."

Dakota nodded. "By now, we were doing FTL, in k-space, which is pretty fast, though nowhere near as fast as the starstream. I was in the Space Patrol out of No Pain, when we learned of the creation of the starstream."

"And you wound up on a patrol ship, in the starstream?"

She grinned again. "Did I do okay with the nest egg you left me, Uncle John?"

He nodded dizzily.

"It was a dream come true! Join the Space Patrol and see the stars!" She stopped and looked thoughtful. "You and I both wound up seeing the stars, didn't we?" They sat facing each other with that thought hanging between them for a moment. Then she reached forward. "Tell me more about what happened after you chased that comet that was threatening Earth!"

He searched for words, but his stones spoke first.

Why don't you let us join with her stones? She'll see so much more.

He cleared his throat. "I don't know why I didn't think of this before. There might be a way to show you that's *lots* better than my trying to explain it all to you. Have you ever joined your translator-stones to exchange with another pair?"

"Huh?" Her eyes widened in surprise, and maybe a little alarm. Then she put a finger to her forehead, as if listening to an inner voice. "I have *not* done that. Never had the chance. But I guess I'm willing to try."

"You might find it pretty intense. Hell, it *is* intense—you'll be absorbing a lot in a short time."

"Okay—"

"But the stones will do all the work. You don't have to really do anything except go along for the ride."

"Uh-huh." She nodded slowly. "What do I do?"

He tugged back his sleeves to expose his wrists, where his gems, white on the right and black on the left, now gleamed visibly. He rested his forearms on the table, palms up. "Are yours in your wrists, like mine?"

She pushed her uniform sleeves up, revealing a similar pair. "Yah." There was a touch of quaver in her voice.

He offered a reassuring smile. "It won't hurt. Now, just put your wrists on top of mine. The stones don't have to touch perfectly, but being close speeds up the connection."

Taking a deep breath, Dakota placed her wrists against his. He felt a little shiver at the contact. This was the little girl he'd carried around on his shoulders. No more. Though he'd joined stones on several occasions, this was the first with another human, much less a female relative. He hoped the intimacy wouldn't feel too awkward . . .

Joining . . .

The connection occurred effortlessly, and a warm rush carried away his concerns . . . .

The flow of information was astonishingly fast, though not so fast that he couldn't perceive many of the details . . . his own life and hers, streamed out for both of them to see . . .

First time in space, bound for Earth 3.

Embarrassment and insecurity at first, feeling incompetent to do the jobs asked of her. She'd get over it. But it was a feeling that returned, over and over again, as she moved out into the galaxy in one time and then another . . .

Arriving alone, but for an alien in his head, at a staggeringly vast place called Shipworld, out at the edge of the galaxy . . . fighting invisible adversaries . . .

Uncle John—dear God—!

Watching humanity leap like a crazed frog from a habitat circling the Earth to a galactic civilization, joined by k-space, and then by the starstream . . . but for the longest time, never quite belonging in any of those places . . .

Ik and Li-Jared and Charlie and the robots, and then Antares . . . somehow triumphing over something called the boojum, only to be flung back into the galaxy to an ocean world . . .

Antares? Forbidden alien love . . . dizzying . . .

For Dakota, one world following another, and only intermittent and fleeting romantic attachments, or even friendships. Until during one of her layovers in the Patrol, on what she now considered her home world of High Concept, Harrad came into her life.

Harrad? Say more?

A flush of pleasure, and a picture of a dark-haired, brown-eyed young man with wry intelligence and a sparkling sense of humor.

Eager to get back to him?

Oh yes—!

And on to the undersea world of the Neri . . . deep-space journey to Starmaker . . . Orion Nebula? First battle with the Mindaru? Detachment and separation from his old life, the nearest human five hundred years in the past . . . new love found, with Antares . . .

Aliens of so many worlds . . . Hraachee'ans and Karellians and Imkek and Ffff'tink and noliHuman and Logothian . . .

Charli, torn away in the battle in the starstream . . . gone . . . dead? . . . gone . . .

Finding family again, after all these light-years and time-years . . .

The connection dissolved.

"Holy—" Dakota whispered.

"Yah," he said, drawing a rasping breath. "Wow." It had been like drinking from a waterfall, taking in her memories along with the replay of his own. The painful echo at the end of losing Charli had kicked him in the stomach, and it was taking him a moment to bring his thoughts—and his eyes—back into focus.

Dakota lifted her arms from the wrist contact with his. She looked dazed, probably feeling similarly overwhelmed. "Jesus," she said, rubbing her wrists. "Uncle John, that's—" She held her hands open, shaking them nervously, as she searched for words.

"I know."

For half a minute, neither of them spoke, as they tried to sort out the rush of images.

Finally he chuckled, and they both began laughing helplessly.

"Did you really have an *alien being* living in your head? Named Charlie?" A variety of expressions flickered across Dakota's face as she reviewed the downloaded images in her mind.

The question brought a fresh wave of pain. He pressed at the bridge of his nose for a moment, waiting for it to subside. "Oh yeah," he said. "I sure did." He snorted. "Hated the little bugger at first, too. But then . . ." His voice fell away. It had been so *sudden*, the way Charli had been taken from him.

Dakota's eyes filled with sympathy. "You really miss him. Or her. Don't you?"

He couldn't speak. He simply nodded.

She closed her eyes again, clearly processing more knowledge about him, as her stones released it to her. "Jesus, you've lost a *lot*. Your world, and all the people you cared about."

"Except you. Now."

She grinned briefly. "But Julie. And . . ." She pressed a finger to her cheek. "Oh! Tell me about Antares! The stones showed me a picture of her. Is she as beautiful as your memory says? Is she important to you—?"

"Oh, yes. And who is this Harrad fellow? Tell me all about him."

For the next hour, they talked intently, and without interruption.

One of the officers burst into the wardroom with a message for Bandicut. "A friend of yours—Lee Jarrod?—is on his way here from the planet ahead of us, Karellia, and will be arriving soon. Your other officers thought you might want to return to your ship to meet them."

"That was fast," Bandicut said. To Dakota he added, "Li-Jared is *from* Karellia, and has been away from his home as long as I have. Until we came here, on this mission. Do you want to meet him? And the others?"

"Now, what do you think?" Dakota said with a laugh. "But Captain Brody will want to record it, at least. You know, first contact and all."

"Would it help if I formally invited you and your staff to visit *The Long View?*"

"I think it might," Dakota said. "And as XO, I accept!" Her eyes were ablaze at the prospect. "It is *so good* to see you again! And also, I don't mind saying . . . to see someone who knew the world I grew up in."

"I feel the same way," he said, wondering, *Should I invite her to come back to Shipworld with me? She'd love it! But she has a life, and Harrad, to go back to.* His head swam a little at the overwhelming reminder of his loss and reconnection with humanity. "I guess I'd better get back to my flock. Let me know when you're all ready to come over. Sooner the better."

Dakota rose. "It'll *have* to be soon, I think. The skipper didn't want to come right out and say it, I don't think, but he and the navigator are a lot more worried than they let on about getting back to the starstream. Seriously, we don't know *how* to get back *into* it from here. If we can't solve that problem, we could be here for a very long time!" Her voice caught with fear. Was she thinking about Harrad?

Bandicut followed her to the door. "Let's talk about it with your people and mine. Dinner at my place?" *Ruall? Dark? You do know how to solve their problem, right?*

CHAPTER 26

Lost Friends

ANTARES MOVED DOWNSTREAM.

Gliding along the ghoststream felt easy to do, and yet it was like stepping out onto a long, narrow beam, bridging some unfathomable gulf high in the sky. There was no visible safety net. It was her mind, everything that was truly *her*, stretching out toward infinity, seeking to find her lost friends. The absurdity of the hope tugged at her, and she began to tremble with anxiety.

Slowly. Take it slowly.

The stones calmed her. Good thing. She needed a Thespi of her own, someone to connect with her just closely enough to ease her fears.

She imagined star clouds whirling around her, and then that happened for real, as she glided forward in space and down the slippery slopes of time, following the luminous thread.

Eventually that thread was joined by another, somehow stretching diagonally across space. It grew to become a glowing, transparent tube like a star-spanner frozen in motion. Antares and the ghoststream merged right into it and suddenly slowed to a crawl. Antares asked her stones what was happening.

We have intersected with the starstream. We thought this might be a good place to pause and try again.

Antares did so. She called out to Ik, and to Julie. She called again.

As before she felt, heard, saw nothing.

At least, she felt nothing that seemed anything like Ik and Julie. It did seem to her that there were things moving *somewhere* in the starstream. She sensed them at a great distance, but she could make nothing more of the feeling.

/What now? Do I just keep calling out? That seems futile./

Before the stones could reply, she heard, from far up the ghost-stream, a controller team member attempting communication. The distortion was considerable. /Readings here . . . -ry unsteady. Procee- . . . discretion . . . -reat care./

She called back: /You're breaking up./

And then she heard Napoleon's voice. /Lady . . . believe you must . . . closer to them . . . -haps . . . -illions . . . in time . . . light-years . . . /

She answered slowly and meticulously, through the stones, /I will proceed as advised. If you hear anything from them . . . /

The controller again: /-ill tell you. Keep . . . /

The stones interrupted to say, *Suggest you let us monitor the connection backward. You focus on listening, and watching.*

And with that, she felt herself slipping farther down the ghost-stream . . . faster, faster. With each backward spin of the invisible calendar surrounding her, her heart grew heavier.

The meadow in which Julie was kneeling already seemed other-worldly; but when holes started to yawn open in the ground all around her, it was too much. Julie cried out and grabbed at fistfuls of grass, clutching at the ground cover as if she might physically hold the meadow together. Maybe a sheer effort of will would make a difference. "What's happening?" she wailed, but there was no one to hear.

The meadow was turning into grass-covered Swiss cheese. Through the larger holes, she saw stars. The meadow would soon be a fisherman's net suspended in the stars. And after that? Would she fall through into the sky?

"Ik! Ik!" /Ik, where are you? I need you!/

This can't be real.

She closed her eyes and called silently to her stones, but all she felt was the world vibrating like a plucked string. Even with her eyes closed, she felt the meadow fade away. She felt suspended in time, vibrating like a violin string between the deep past and the far future. She felt wetness on her cheek—tears leaking from her closed eyes. What sort of existence *was* this?

She blinked her eyes open. Now there was only space, spanned by a narrow, diaphanous ribbon, pale blue with golden overtones, stretching from low and behind her on the left, and then up out of sight to her right. *The starstream.* Probably the timestream, too, entwined with it. She thought with a surge of panic that she was no longer in that stream, that she had been thrown clear of it by the blowback of the disentanglement pulse. The meadow had vanished altogether. Was this her mind imposing some kind of meaning on something that made no sense? Despair clawed at her. *I will never get home again. Not even to Shipworld. Ik . . . Ik, I hope you make it.* Except that she really didn't want Ik to make it without her. *I don't want to be stranded here alone! Please, God!*

She heard a faint whisper from her stones—they were alive!— saying, *We are working. We are trying.*

Staring through her tears at that ribbon, she felt a rapid vibration, pastfuturepastpresentfuturepastpresent . . . and she began to choke as she wept.

Ik could not understand what he was looking at, or why. *A landscape of shattered ice.* Or why he was out of contact with Julie Stone, who was encapsulated in this ghoststream with him. Surely the ghoststream could not split into separate streams. Could it?

His voice-stones remained silent. Perhaps they didn't know, either.

The frozen landscape was moving now, great ice shards rising and falling and shifting, as though the entire landscape were floating on top of a rolling ocean. "Hrah," he murmured to himself. "Why are you doing that?" He sighed through his ears, once, then barked, /*Julie Stone!* Are you here? Can you hear me?/ As before, he heard no reply.

He turned around slowly, and as he rotated, he saw that the emptiness of space was filled in as he turned, filled in with more of the churning ice pack. *Moon and stars, it's an illusion. It has to be. Is it the work of the enemy? Or my own mind?*

Something sang in the sky over him, and he looked up to see a narrow band of light stretched across the sky, diagonally from where he was facing, almost like a rainbow but far brighter and more substantial. The singing was like a high-tension line in an electrical storm, rather than a voice. It wailed and warbled, as though trying and failing to hold a steady pitch. As he focused on the strange band, he was aware that the landscape was gradually turning transparent. He stood on a single outcropping of ice and rock, but that outcropping was now adrift in space.

/Stones, I don't care if you don't understand this any better than I do. I need your help!/ He tried to make his inner voice sound commanding. /I believe we are at risk of detaching from the ghoststream. We need a plan./

There was no response.

He tried a different tack. /If you are afraid of a bad plan, it is still better than no plan at all./

At last the stones stirred.

/Do you have a plan?/

We must first try to locate Julie Stone and her translator-stones.

/Hrah, my thoughts precisely. Do you know how?/ He paused a moment, and then said, /I withdraw the question./ And then he added, /We must be rejoined. Not just to each other, but to that band out there./ He pointed. /To the ghoststream./

We agree. But we are uncertain how. The stones sounded sad, almost resigned. That, more than anything else, frightened Ik.

Charli felt the sudden change in a strangely tangible way, as though she were solid like Bandicut. It felt like all the air being sucked out of a habitat. The quarx flashed on a memory from long ago, when the Rohengen moon died in that terrible war—millions of years and many lifetimes ago. An entire world had vented to vacuum, and Charli's host had died. It was a sickening memory, and she had to force her thoughts away from it.

I am in the starstream. Air is not a question in the starstream; there is no air. So what did I just feel?

The next sensation was a perceptible chill.

There is no warmth or cold in the starstream. What is happening?

Did this involve Ik and Julie Stone? Or the Mindaru? Charli still felt their distant presence, felt the rustle of their whispers, but could not see or locate them. She felt distress, and instability. Her friends were in danger. *What danger? Should they not be moving?*

The starstream itself felt stable enough, but a significant change had just rippled through it.

She no longer sensed the timestream—the movement emanating from the disturbance at Karellia.

Had it just gone away?

If the timestream was gone, how long could her friends survive? She was suddenly afraid she was about to relive the deaths of her Rohengen friends, but this time with Ik and Julie.

Calmly, now. She focused carefully, using all of the tricks of perception that this n-dimensional existence provided. The timestream hadn't quite vanished completely, but it was a fraying ribbon of light. Its vibration had gone out of sync with the starstream's. All the power was leaving it.

Suddenly Charli realized what must have happened.

They've turned it off. John and Li-Jared and the others. They've turned off the temporal disturbance at Karellia, and the shutdown is rippling down the whole length of the starstream!

Her breath of fear sharpened, but was leavened by a bubble of hope. Would this stop the Mindaru? If that was true, it was good; it was what they had set out to do; it signaled the success of their mission. But what of Julie and Ik?

She must look harder.

She stretched her senses. She could see where the timestream had separated into strands and threads, unraveling all the way down into time and space. *Farther down, way down,* she could see other entities—Mindaru, foundering and drifting, unable to continue their movement toward the future. That was definitely good. But now she could finally make out where Ik and Julie were: in a ghostly strand that had detached from the main body of the timestream, and—worse than that—had split into two fragile threads, parted from each other. Charli did not understand all of this, but she knew that her friends were in peril.

They were tiny flecks on spidery threads of light, and both threads appeared to be in the process of disintegrating. If that happened, would Julie and Ik simply vanish into the void? Were they even physically there, or were they as noncorporeal as she was?

Charli struggled to think of a way to help. *Can I do nothing for them, except watch them die?*

Once that last battle with the plague from out of time was done and Dark was sure that her friends were safe, she'd slipped away quietly, letting them come together and join forces without interruption. There was something she wanted to check on—something she had sensed on her last survey back at the starstream. She thought about speaking of it to her friends, but decided to examine it more closely before raising any hopes. The gokat seemed to be the only one watching her leave, and Dark murmured to her, *"Not now, dancing one. I may call for you later, but this time you should stay. Stay and grow strong again. Then, if I have need, you will be able to help."* Bria stayed—but Dark felt the gokat's gaze following as she slipped away into the folds of n-space.

Dark was thinking ahead. She needed not just to approach the starstream again, but to reenter it. She needed to see if what she *thought* she'd felt was really true: that *Charli was still there.* Dark had had no communication with the quarx since the battle that knocked them all out of the starstream—and knocked Charli out of the mind of John Bandicut. But if Charli was still alive, Dark hoped to find her.

Traveling back to the starstream did not take long. Dark could move fast when she didn't have to limit her mode of travel for the sake of her companions. She circled around the ghostly ribbon of light, trying to decide on the best place to enter. She didn't know that much about the starstream, beyond the obvious, that it was a channel of stressed n-space layered along a fine fracture in the fabric of three-dimensional space, and that it provided a river down which many ships sailed. The last time she had entered it with her friends, the result had been a battle with the plague, the Mindaru. While she doubted that would happen every time someone entered the stream, it did give her pause. The starstream was beautiful; it was not harmless.

No matter; she was searching for any echo of Charli. When she had sensed the quarx before, it had been during a busy emergence from the starstream of the Mindaru they had just dispatched. She'd been too focused on the Mindaru to take a closer look. Now, she sensed no indication of the quarx from the outside, though perhaps that was because there was no active opening. After circling twice, she gave up on looking for a *best* place to enter, and simply found a small vibrational point and went in.

The starstream wall passed over her like a gentle magnetic wave, in a rainbow of dimensions. It flared nicely, and sang softly in a rising and falling tone as she settled into the flowing current. Soon she heard a variety of other sounds: cries, murmurs, sighs, warbles, stutters. Some sounded like natural processes and some like living things.

It took a little while. But then she heard it: Charli's voice, as distinct to her as the voice of a star. Charli was calling out to someone, or something. It seemed to Dark that she sounded worried. Dark wasn't sure how things worked in this place, or exactly how to communicate with Charli. She couldn't pick out Charli's location in the starstream, and she wasn't sure if "location" meant anything here. She had a strange feeling that the quarx might be everywhere and nowhere, and that perhaps she, Dark, should simply call out and see if Charli could hear her. So she did.

"Charli, can you hear me?"

"Charli, can you hear me?
"Charli, can you hear me?"
For a little time, she heard nothing in response. Until:

/// Dark?
Dark, is that you? ///

Charli's voice seemed faint at first. Then she seemed to find the right range, and her voice became stronger:

/// Dark, have you come back? ///

"Charli, you are alive!"

/// I am alive!
It is so good to hear a familiar voice!
And you? Are you well? ///

"I am well. Our friends are well. We have destroyed many of the enemy." Dark felt a surprising surge of satisfaction and pride as she reported that.

/// That delights me beyond measure!
And John Bandicut? Is he well? ///

"He seems so."

/// I miss him terribly!
Do you know if he thinks of me?///

A sadness whispered through Dark. Charli seemed to be every-where in this place, and where Charli was, there was the grief of losing Bandicut. *"I do not know his thoughts. I am sorry."*

/// Of course not. How could you?
Dark, I am grateful to hear your voice. ///

For a moment Charli paused, as though gathering important thoughts. Then she blurted,

/// Dark, you have come just in time.
I need your help! ///

That got Dark's attention. *"My help? What help can I give you?"*

/// There are other friends—Ik and Julie.
Do you remember them? ///

Dark was surprised by the sudden mention of friends from another time, not of this mission. Ik she remembered, clearly. But hard as she tried, she could not recall a "Julie." She said as much to Charli.

/// No, of course not.
Julie is from John Bandicut's world,
a fellow human.
She must have come to Shipworld and met Ik.
I do not believe John knows she is here. ///

"Here? In the starstream? Or—?"

/// In Shipworld.
But also here, in the starstream.
She and Ik are ... ///

The quarx was clearly struggling to find words.

/// They are here, but in danger! Grave danger!
If we do not help them, they may drown and be lost! ///

"Drown? Lost? I do not understand."

/// Their hold in the stream is tenuous,
and I fear it is coming apart. ///

Dark puzzled over that. She extended her own senses again, scanning upstream and downstream, seeking a sign of the one she knew as Ik. If she could find Ik, she should also find Julie. *"Can you show me?"*

/// Quiet your thoughts and search the stream. ///

"I will try."

Dark shifted her focus and shifted again, exploring wavelengths and amplitudes, inhabited dimensions, sifting the starstream through her awareness like a stellar wind whispering through the singularity at her core. The starstream was a surprisingly noisy place—stray voices and thoughts, which were puzzling, but mostly just noises of the cosmos, the drumming of black holes at either end of the stream, the strumming of the cosmic hyperstring that ran through its heart, the dying echoes of the time-tide that had brought them all here, fading away now because it had been turned off at its source at Karellia.

And it was in those echoes that she caught the first hint of what she was looking for: a kind of thread—fainter, but more structured, more *intentional.*

This thread ran down the dimensions of time and space, inter-twining with the path of the Karellian disturbance. But rather than being limited to the starstream, it seemed to come from a place *beyond* the starstream, beyond the edge of the galaxy itself—from the place, Dark thought in wonder, that her friends called Shipworld.

And now she thought that she felt within this thread the faint imprint of her ephemeral friend Ik. How odd, she thought. How *very* odd. How had Ik become a part of something like this? She might have doubted her own impressions, except that her ephem-eral-stones, the gift from her friends, were prickling within her. They detected something, also. What they detected seemed to be others of their own kind. Ik's? Dark wondered.

"I think I see. I must get closer."

Dark tried to push inward. But the ghostly thread proved dif-ficult to approach. Her movement toward it seemed to nudge it away and distort it; perhaps her mass and energy were too great to be near. She felt a clear pang of danger. *Don't force!* Whatever this thread was, the boundary was too delicate; it was endangered by her proximity.

She heard, or felt, Charli speaking to her.

/// You have found them, yes? ///

"Ik, yes, I believe." About the one called Julie, she was not certain. But now her stones spoke softly and reported that *they* sensed more than one pair of stones in that place. The quarx said,

/// *They need our help to*
get back to Shipworld. ///

Dark did not know how to answer that. She had many abilities, but it seemed something more was needed. ***"What is wrong with them?"***

/// *The thread that anchors them to their home*
has become weakened, and they have nearly
slipped out of its grasp. ///

Dark pondered. Ik had been an important friend in their battle at Starmaker. And Julie a friend of John Bandicut's? Surely there had to be a way.

She spoke carefully. ***"I want to help. But I cannot approach without disrupting the thing they are a part of."***

/// *I see that.*
I cannot touch them directly, either.
I can try to speak to them.
But I cannot bring them back into the stream
or to safety. ///

Dark suddenly had an idea. *Perhaps*, she thought. *If she will come help. If she is strong enough.*

Bria had the sneaky pleasure of surprising Dark, when Dark started back to the ship to look for her. Bria had followed Dark, right up to the point at which the cloud had vanished into the starstream. There the gokat had stopped, feeling not quite sure enough of where she was going to follow Dark inside.

They were a long way from the ship where Ruall and her friends huddled, but only in a certain light. Really, it wasn't that far at all—just a matter of slipping out of four-space down the quarto fractal slide, tesserating one-and-three-quarters times around to catch an offshoot of spindle-space—and then, when she was close, simply hopping across the gap to the outside of the starstream. She could see Dark through the starstream wall, and it seemed that she was talking to someone.

After a time, Dark slipped back out. She sang a surprised greeting when she saw Bria. At first, there was a hint of remonstration in her greeting—and it was true, she had instructed Bria to stay with the ship, which Bria had not done. But there was no harm done, and soon Dark welcomed Bria into her protective presence. Bria felt relief and warmth there. She was more tired from her trip here than she'd expected.

But the question that bubbled up was, Why had Dark been looking for her?

The explanation followed, and to Bria the problem Dark outlined came as a welcome challenge. True, Bria was still healing from the battle with the malevolent Mindaru. But she was also restless, and a chance to *do something* appealed to her, especially if it involved an adventure with Dark. Bria sometimes wondered if the others—including Ruall—truly appreciated Dark's gokat-like abilities, or her contributions to their cause.

Dark's request made Bria feel *needed*. She was sure she could do it.

"Bria!" Dark began abruptly, even though she was deeply gladdened to see the gokat. *"We need your help! Two ephemerals are in danger in the starstream. They are friends of our friend John Bandicut. Do you know which is John Bandicut?"*

Bria said she did. He was the one who hopped around a lot, and sometimes became overly excited.

"No," said Dark, *"that is Li-Jared. John Bandicut is his friend. And his friend Charli is the one who sometimes spoke from out of nowhere, and became separated when we flew out of the starstream."*

/Charli/, Bria repeated back to her, and indicated that she had been aware of Charli, but had never seen her, separate or apart from John Bandicut.

"Charli is here, now, in the starstream. You may be able to talk to her. You may have to, if we are to save our friends from dying."

Bria did not seem to understand. Dark tried to explain, but they did not have enough language in common to make it clear. Finally Dark said, *"Our friends are in a place where I cannot reach them. But perhaps you can. Will you try? And lead them back here, if you can?"*

The gokat made a low yowl of willingness. Dark opened a window and tried to show her the dimensional folds that would take her to where Ik and the other were located. Bria bobbed and twisted her head. Before Dark could judge whether it was clear enough, and whether Bria was strong enough, the gokat was gone, vanished through a pocket of n-space.

CHAPTER 27

Gokat Rescue

THE QUARX'S HEART was heavy with worry as she watched Dark bring the gokat into this space, and then send her on again through the confusing geometry of the starstream and the two other streams entwined with it. Charli felt certain that the danger to Ik and Julie was growing with the fading strength of the Karellian timestream. Those two had come here through their own Shipworld stream. But that thread had become so intertwined with the starstream and the Karellian time tide that it was difficult to distinguish one from another. It seemed as if it was all coming unraveled.

What could the gokat do? Would she put herself at risk, as Julie and Ik had? Would she understand the risk she was taking?

Charli resisted an impulse to stop her. If the gokat could work her way through the folds of space and time all the way to the two, perhaps she really could do some good.

And so Charli watched, her nerves on fire with worry. Bria was in a labyrinth with multiple dimensions; the possibilities were endless. It wasn't long, in fact, before Bria took a turn into a channel that Charli could see would lead only to a cul-de-sac in the manifolds of space-time. She called across the dimensions to the gokat:

/// Bria, that is the wrong way! ///

Bria jumped at her voice like a tiny fish startled by a shadow. Charli spoke again, more softly this time, and the gokat seemed to relax a little. But when Charli suggested backtracking, Bria grew agitated and darted around with increasing urgency.

> */// Bria, let me try to tell you*
> *what you're looking for.*
> *It's like a thread with a vibration.*
> *And that vibration is moving . . . ///*

But as Charli tried to explain, it became apparent that none of this was *explainable* to the gokat, who had a remarkable talent for *moving* through such things, but without any abstract understanding of what it all meant. If Charli could just *show* her . . . then perhaps Bria could get to Julie and Ik—and perhaps lead them back from the edge of the abyss, to where the temporal strands were stronger.

Was there some way to *illuminate* the path, or maybe give her simpler, more progressive instructions?

> */// Bria. Can you understand if I say go UP? ///*

Off in the maze, the small, distant figure of the gokat veered sideways.

> */// No, that's LEFT.*
> *Can you raise your head and tip it back? ///*

Bria bobbed uncertainly. Charli wondered if there was some other way to say it . . . Suddenly Bria raised her nose and went up.

> */// Yes—that's UP! ///*

And when the gokat bobbed down again, Charli called:

> */// That's DOWN! ///*

Soon they had a working language of basic directions. It was time to get moving in a better direction.

> */// Good! Good!*
> *Let's move for real now.*
> *Go up—yes!—and now left! ///*

Bria soon turned down a channel between two folded layers of n-space; then, when a passageway opened to her right, she turned into it. This should take her toward Ik. But for Charli, the view was becoming cloudier, the correct path harder to pick out. A moment later, Bria crossed a subtle boundary within the ghostly time-travel streams, and Charli's view began to break up.

/// Bria, wait!
I'm losing my connection to you!
Look around for Julie and Ik!
Do you see them?
Watch carefully where you go, so you can
find your way back. ///

Bria stopped abruptly, suddenly afraid to go on alone.

This was going to be nearly impossible. Charli hesitated, considering her options. Then she reached out in a way she had not done in a long time. Perhaps, she thought, she could join minds with Bria long enough to carry out this rescue . . .

/// Bria, can you back up a little?
Do you mind if I try something?
It won't hurt, but it might feel strange. ///

Bria remained still, waiting. When Charli slipped across the intervening space and time, and into her mind, she felt the go-kat's sudden surprise. Bria hadn't expected her right here in her mind. To Charli, too, there was an element of the unexpected. *This is not John Bandicut. Do not expect the same reactions.* It should have been obvious, but it wasn't, and her landing in the gokat's mind was rather graceless.

/// I am sorry.
Be patient. ///

The creature was quick of mind and fleet of movement, and she adapted readily. Where Bandicut had a deep reservoir of thought and opinion and questioning, Bria was all zippy input and output, reaction and quick-thought. She lived at a different pace. There were layers in the gokat's mind, for sure; but her inner world was a fast-moving place, full of shifting planes and dazzling flashes of light. Charli sensed Bria's intense desire to pursue her mission, to save these people, to bring them safely back to their other friends. But it had to be done soon, because the world was a roiling and dangerous place.

Charli felt some hope. But she also felt herself stretched dangerously thin. There *was* one thing she could do. Did she dare? What choice did she have? Without giving herself time to think any more about it, she cut this part of her consciousness loose from her main self. It felt risky, but she had to; she could not stretch to where Bria was going. It was jarring to divide herself like that—too much like the first time she had gone from Bandicut to Deep, during the Starmaker flight, a jump that had nearly killed her for good. She tried to hide her unease from Bria, but the gokat picked up on it right away and became agitated.

Charli tried to speak soothingly.

> /// *Hello, Bria.*
> *Where we're going,*
> *I think we have to go together.* ///

Bria quivered. But she did not object.

Something changed for Julie—a tangible sensation, like a prickling under her skin, strong enough to interrupt the dizzying endless vibration between past and future. But what exactly had changed? /Stones? Do you know?/

The stones were silent. They seemed scarily gloomy, as if they had hit a wall and run out of ideas. That was unthinkable. /Are you still there?/ With the starry space swallowing her, it was easy to imagine that the stones had vanished, or never existed in the first place.

The answer was a sharp poke. What was that supposed to mean? Was she being told to pay attention? To what? She focused on her surroundings. A semblance of the meadow was back, enough to provide a shadowy ground in the night. /*I see movement!* Is that what you mean?/

Was it a *thing* moving, against what little remained of the terrain?

There it is again! It was a tiny triangle poking up from behind a vague mound-shape. The flat base of the triangle was on top, with the point at the bottom, like a chin. A head? It was shiny in the starlight. There were two cartoon eyes up near the top. The head rotated one way and then the other, and when it did, it almost vanished into two dimensions, the way Rings-at-Need did. /Hello!/ Julie called. At once she felt foolish. There could hardly be a living creature here, surely. It had to be some kind of illusion, created by her mind.

No, the stones said. *We think it is real.*

Julie was shocked. *Real?* What was it, then? And why was it here?

The creature that Charli had asked Bria to find was at the end of a long maze, in a kind of place that looked to Bria like "between dimensions." Was she trapped? Why didn't she move? Bria couldn't quite make out her body, but there was something about her that reminded Bria of John Bandicut.

Charli, sharing the gokat's vision and even her thoughts, was so filled with relief and joy at seeing Julie that for a moment she almost forgot why she was here. But Bria was moving quickly, no time for sentimentality, and that prompted the quarx to speak. She did so quickly, hoping that between their seeming proximity and their stones, her words would reach Julie.

/// *Can you see us, Julie?*
Can you hear us? ///

An answer came haltingly, /Who are you? I see . . . something. Someone? How is this possible?/

/// We are a gokat named Bria.
But we are also a quarx named Charli,
and friend of John Bandicut.
We have come to help you. ///

All the while, another part of Charli was thinking, *I hope I'm right about what you need—and that I can make you understand.*

From Julie, there came waves of confusion and disbelief.

When the thing that looked like a creature spoke to Julie, she heard it through her stones, just the way she heard the translator. That alone was enough to make her shiver. But when it said . . . *quarx named Charli* . . . she was so stunned she hardly knew how to react.

John Bandicut had mentioned a "quarx," way back when he left Neptune.

She tried to remember: a lifetime ago, in a message he'd left when he stole the spaceship from Triton, John had spoken of an alien called a quarx. Hadn't he said it was a noncorporeal being, speaking to him in his head, possibly through his translator-stones? *This is insane. Am I slipping away, dreaming before death?*

Before her, the meadow was dissolving again, pitching up and down like flotsam on a choppy sea. But perched there, riding up and down on the waves, was that small, triangular-headed creature that said it was Bria, a gokat. And also Charli, a quarx. John's quarx?

/Stones,/ Julie whispered, reeling. /Help me! This is unreal! Am I dying?/

Strange and unexpected . . .

/Just tell me—am I dreaming? Dreaming or dying/

No . . . no . . . not dying, no. The stones stirred with hope and said, *We lived with the quarx even before John Bandicut.*

/You what? Well, then . . . / She strained to think clearly. Could it really be the quarx John had known? Or was it something pretending to be the quarx? She thought quickly and asked, /If you are really the quarx, who is Dakota?/

The voice that answered seemed to cry out with delight.

/// Dakota! John's niece!
We met her in the starstream! ///

Julie was stunned all over again. *Met her in the starstream?* That was too weird. But weirder than *this?* She took a long, deep breath. /Please—are you nearby? Or are you calling from a long way away? From home base? From Shipworld?/

/// Not Shipworld, no.
I am in the starstream with Bria,
whom you see here.
I was with John a long time,
until we got separated . . . ///

Julie's mind flailed. Too much, too much . . . /I don't understand!/ she cried. /You said you came to *help?* Can you find Ik? Can you get us back to Shipworld?/

For a few seconds, she was so excited, she could hardly hear what the quarx was saying. But finally words came through.

/// Your stones. Do you have translator-stones? ///

/Yes. Yes!/

/// Can they hear what I'm telling you? ///

The stones themselves answered, and she could have sworn she heard joy in their voice, as if they were just now believing what they heard. *We hear the quarx. We know the quarx.*

Julie felt a rush of joy herself at that, followed by confusion. In front of her, the gokat was dancing and shuffling, as though eager to get going somewhere. Was she supposed to follow it? How?

/// Listen closely.
You must follow Bria. Follow the gokat.
We will guide, but you must follow.
Your stones can do this. ///

Follow a gokat across space-time? She didn't even know what a gokat was! It was preposterous.

But it was all she had. /Can you do this?/ she asked her stones.

We will do that.

She took a deep breath and forced the doubts out of her mind. She listened as the quarx gave her instructions. Then the gokat turned, stretched upward to her left, and jumped. And she jumped after it.

As far as Ik could tell, he was wobbling back and forth on a shifting piece of ice in a hostile sea. High above the ice floes, the sky was luminous with nebulas and star clusters, shifting and flaring. Under other circumstances, he might have appreciated the view, but right now it terrified him.

There was a constant buzz . . . pastfuturepresentfuturepast-presentfuturepast . . . and it was getting worse.

But a moment came when that droning fell silent before something new: a voice calling out to him, calling him by name. It wasn't Julie, and he didn't think it was his voice-stones. But he was feeling lightheaded and unsure. How much longer before he simply faded and ceased to be? But this voice was insistent, calling out:

/// *Ik! Can you hear me, Ik?* ///

He started to answer, but then he held back, because he was afraid it was all in his imagination.

And then it said something that jolted him:

/// *I am Charli!*
John Bandicut's quarx.
Can you hear me? ///

Ik gasped through his ears in disbelief. At last he replied, /From Shipworld? Are you calling from Shipworld? Is John Bandicut there? Where is Julie? Can you help me?/

The ice underfoot suddenly steadied, and something shiny knifed up through the ice, landed on top of it, and then twisted around to look at him. It looked like a tiny creature of some kind—a strange thing, with four feet and a triangular head.

/// Wait! ///

it cried in the same voice that had just claimed to be Charli.

Ik puffed air from his cheeks, to steady himself. But then *Julie Stone* rose through the ice after the little creature—and he lost his careful reserve. He cried out for joy; and then he cried out again, for fear that it was an illusion.

But it wasn't. Julie reached out and took his hand, squeezing it. It was a tingly contact, more electrical or magical than solid. She tugged him forward. /It's really me,/ she said. /No time to explain. Link your stones to mine. Now./

Ik needed no convincing. The landscape was starting to melt again. It was now or never. He squeezed Julie's hand, and felt the voice-stones in his temples pulse with renewed strength; and he stumbled after Julie, as she and the little creature ran across the ice. He held on, as they jumped out over a chasm in the ice, and fell through into a starry abyss, fell silently . . .

Joined to the two travelers, on the brink of nothingness, Charli/Bria guided their way toward a fold they could just make out in the maze of spatial dimensions. The tattered thread stretching all the way back to Shipworld was fluttering in the whispers of deep space and time. It felt as though a breath might tear it apart. They could only hope it would hold. They were still in the starstream, which could help, but at a fuzzy boundary layer where any kind of stability was more a matter of probability than of certainty.

To the Charli half, it seemed as though they were flying on an infinitely frayed fishing line sparkling with fire. They had to zip along that fine line until it merged into something else, or somehow became stronger.

The gokat part of Charli/Bria thought not at all about these things; she simply sensed, saw, felt the changing layers of space-time,

and slipped forward by instinct, away from the brink of nothingness, to a place where pathways still led through n-space back toward the future.

Those pathways twisted and wound through space-time like
a roller coaster, turning and dipping and offering false choices left
and right.

/// Do you remember the way? ///

the Charli-part asked the Bria-part.

/Brrrrrrrr-yes,/ came a purring reply. In fact the gokat seemed
positively to delight in the slaloming motions that took them
through the dimensional maze. Still, something didn't feel right
to Charli, and she kept looking around to see what it might be. It
felt to her as if they were carrying some extra weight, a *drag* of
some kind. Was something following them? Or hanging on? Were
they perhaps dragging a bit of the space-time fabric along with
them?

At last they popped into the clear field of the starstream. And
then she saw what was holding them back.

Something had hitched a ride, all right. Something dark and
asymmetrical.

Something like a Mindaru.

CHAPTER 28

Dinner with Plato

LI-JARED RADIATED GOOD spirits as he and Ocellet Quin stepped out of the lander. Bandicut greeted them eagerly. He'd lost track of how long they'd been gone—not that long, really, but so much had happened it *felt* like weeks.

"How are things down on the surface? Still in an uproar?" Bandicut asked, walking them back to the bridge.

"I should say so!" Li-Jared said, whistling a sharp laugh. "I don't think they were sorry to see *me* go."

"I'd say their feelings were mixed," Quin said. "Definitely mixed. Things went better than they might have. But we still have to try to broker a permanent peace with the Uduon."

"But you got them to lower the temporal defense! Was there much resistance?"

Li-Jared stopped in the passageway and laughed again, not quite a snort.

"Oh yes," said Quin ruefully. "Strong resistance. When the council saw how dangerous the Mindaru were, they wanted to *strengthen* the shield, not turn it off—even after I showed them how ineffective it was. But a lot of minds changed when they realized the Mindaru were coming from another direction altogether, and not from Uduon. And they were coming *because of* the shield."

Bandicut breathed a sigh of relief. "I'm glad they saw that."

Quin stared at him, the emerald bands across the vertical gold almonds of her eyes seeming particularly electric. "They saw something else, too. They saw that you put yourselves in danger to defend our world. That made a definite impression."

Bandicut smiled just a little at that, and murmured his appreciation that they had noticed. Then he added, "We *were* defending your world. But we were also defending the whole galaxy, including the Uduon. It's important that your people remember that, too."

The Ocellet held his gaze, as though appraising him anew. "That message . . . came through a little more slowly. But it came through." As they resumed walking, she asked, "Where *are* Akura and Sheeawn? We have a lot to talk about with them."

"On the bridge, waiting. We were just discussing when we might take them home."

A look of alarm came over Quin. "Not too soon, please. We hoped to bring them planetside again, to meet with the Council."

Bandicut inclined his head. "Let's put the question to them."

Akura hesitated only a moment before replying. "I truly appreciate the offer, and we do want to meet with your representatives. But we must report home as soon as possible. My people are almost entirely in the dark about all that has happened. Remember, they witnessed a battle in their skies between us and the Mindaru, with no one to explain what was going on. They know very little about the Mindaru or the danger they pose. I was authorized to visit and learn, not to negotiate a peace. We need to take back what we have learned."

"But a peace agreement is surely what we both want, as quickly as possible," Quin said. She made a small gesture with her fingers that was probably only for herself; it reminded Bandicut of someone making the sign of the cross. "The members of my council are probably more open to the idea now than they ever will be. I do not want them to have time to forget, and start remembering the old days, of the unseen . . ." She hesitated, breathed into a closed fist, and gave a small sigh. "Ignorance and fear have long memories."

"No doubt," said Akura, with a bob of her head. "I understand, and my people will likely be much the same. But such an agreement *must* come from the will of my own circle of Watchers, and indeed all the people, not just from me. That is the only way it will be accepted by Uduon."

"I wonder," Bandicut said, "if we could arrange a *brief* visit planetside for you—or perhaps a holo-conference. That might be a first step toward setting up a permanent communications link between Uduon and Karellia. Jeaves, what do you think?"

The robot floated over to join the conversation. "An excellent idea. Let me work with Copernicus and see what we can come up with for communications equipment."

Quin bowed. "That would be extremely helpful." She put a finger to her lips. "Is it possible that Sheeawn could stay as our guest, while you go home?"

Sheeawn's eyes widened, but he translated dutifully.

Akura regarded both of them. She and Sheeawn spoke back and forth for a minute. Sheeawn finally addressed Quin, speaking for himself. "Thank you. I, uh . . . I am not a diplomat, or official of any kind. I am—" and his translator-stones had to work for a moment "—a simple fisherman back home."

The Ocellet cocked her head and studied him. "A fisherman? Perhaps. But simple? I do not think so. I think you already know more about the matters affecting our two worlds than most of the members of my own council. I think you would be an excellent representative."

"But I could not negotiate, or . . . do anything like that."

"No. We would not ask that of you. But you could learn something of what we Karellians are like, and we could learn from you of the Uduon."

Sheeawn glanced nervously at Akura, whose expression was neutral. Perhaps she was waiting to see what he really wanted to do. "Well, I . . ."

Ocellet flicked her fingers outward to him. "You do not need to decide now. But consider it. Please?"

Sheeawn bowed his head and touched his chest in assent.

Bandicut cleared his throat and changed the subject. "Folks, what would you all say to meeting some of *my* people? The other ship, called *Plato*—which helped us in the fight against the Mindaru—comes from much closer to my own home world. It is an explorer craft, and its crew are humans, like me. They will be coming aboard in a short time, to meet all of you and to share a meal."

That, they all agreed, was a fine idea.

The dinner with Dakota and her shipmates proved lively. Copernicus resized the commons to a dining room large enough to seat a dozen, and Jeaves assumed the role of butler, seating everyone and bringing out the food that the synthesizer worked overtime to produce. Besides dishes intended to please the Uduon and Karellians, there was something resembling roast beef, with mashed potatoes and gravy, fresh-baked bread that actually tasted freshly baked, four different kinds of vegetables that in their way were reminiscent of carrots and green beans and spinach and broccoli, something purple and lumpy that Bandicut could not identify, and red and white wine. Jeaves showed remarkable grace in moving about, setting down platters and glasses. When Bandicut complimented him on his skills, Jeaves bowed diffidently and said, "It was my first job, Captain. One never really forgets how to do it."

Conversation around the table quickly shifted from the food to the wonder and uncertainty that everyone felt in meeting new sapient beings. Amazingly, they were all able to communicate with each other. Those with translator-stones were kept busy interpreting, but this was so much better than anything the *Plato* crew expected that they transitioned quickly into meaningful conversation. The human crew were eager to learn about both the Karellians and the Uduon, although when Ruall appeared in the room, she immediately became the center of attention for a little while. That wasn't a position she necessarily seemed to enjoy, and before long, she found a reason to excuse herself to the bridge.

Li-Jared appeared interested in meeting all of the *Plato* crew, but after a while, he maneuvered himself to sit and talk with Dakota. Any family of Bandie John Bandicut's was family of his, he told her solemnly, and promptly launched into a tale about his experiences with her Uncle John. Dakota listened with a big smile. Her link with the stones had probably given her a starting point in understanding Li-Jared, Bandicut thought, but she clearly was enjoying meeting the effervescent Karellian in person.

"Bandie," Li-Jared said, raising a glass of Karellian wine as though to make a toast, "your niece is a thoroughly delightful individual. Much more civilized than any humans I have previously known."

That brought a laugh from Dakota. "You have keen powers of observation," Bandicut said.

"I think you should invite her to come back with us to Shipworld. She would be excellent company for everyone," Li-Jared said. "And maybe you'd stop moping so much about *Earth*."

That brought another laugh, but it also gave Bandicut a pang. He had, in fact, been wrestling with that same thought. He glanced around at the other guests, before turning to Dakota. "Not to put you on the spot or anything, but what *would* you think about coming to Shipworld with us?"

"Wha—?"

"Sure. Wouldn't you like to see the galaxy from the outside? You could be an ambassador from present-day human-space—not an old fossil from another era like me—and there could be lots of travel. You like travel, don't you?"

Dakota sat with her mouth hanging open. She looked stricken—intrigued, appalled, torn, all in a single moment. She let out a half-muted cry that was not at all what one expected from the XO of a starship. She blinked and tugged self-consciously at her uniform cuffs. "Jeez, Unc—John—you shouldn't tempt me like that!"

He felt a buzzing in his wrists, but chose to ignore it. This wasn't the stones' business. "I'm sorry—I didn't mean to make you feel uncomfortable. But really, if you wanted to—we'd love to have you join us. We Bandicuts—" and for a second, his voice caught "—we—need to stick together. There are only two of us left, that I know of." And as he said that, he felt a pang of sadness.

She blushed and cleared her throat, obviously feeling some strong emotion herself. "I know. Don't think it isn't a tempting offer, really! But—"

"You have a job and a life." He sighed. "I know. Still."

"Well, *yeah*. I'm an officer on a ship. Not to mention I have someone waiting for me at home." She exhaled sharply and forced a smile. "Remember?"

"Harrad. I remember." Bandicut barked a laugh—at himself, for, in fact, forgetting that important point. He squinted at her. "Is this Harrad good enough for you?"

"Ha. Isn't that always the question?" A series of expressions crossed her face, ending in a soft smile. "Yes, I think he is."

"You're sure?"

She smiled wryly. "Is Antares good enough for you? Or Julie?"

"Touché." Just hearing the names made his heart ache. "I think . . . isn't the real question whether I'm good enough for either of them?"

Dakota laughed. "Probably. But I'll bet they think so. Of course, if they ever get together," she teased, "they might change their minds about that."

A smile twitched on his lips, but he couldn't bear to follow that line of thought any further. Looking down the table, he saw Captain Brody watching him with a serious expression. Had he overheard Bandicut trying to steal Dakota away from him?

Dakota, perhaps reading his glance, smoothed her napkin on the table and reached for her glass of wine. Sipping, she said, "You could always come back with *us*. Wouldn't you like to join up with humanity again? You could be Shipworld's ambassador. Plus, you could meet Harrad and tell me yourself if you think he's worthy."

He pressed his lips together in a not-quite-grimace. He wasn't sure why, but he was suddenly finding it hard to take a breath. Return to humanity? Would he even want to? Of course, he wouldn't want to leave Antares and—Julie?—but apart from that, he was starting to feel as if he had a place, maybe, in Shipworld, more than he ever had back home. Plus, there was no way he could go without learning whether Ik and—Julie?—were okay. Was it so hard to just say that?

Dakota lowered her nose slightly, studying his reaction. "Is that a no?" she asked finally.

Now it was his turn to laugh. He shook his head, nodded. Yes, it was a no. "I, uh—I don't think I could do that," he managed.

He saw pain flicker in her eyes, as the mutual acknowledgment passed between them that they were going to go their separate ways again soon. He sighed and lifted his wine, and they clinked their glasses softly together.

———

Captain Brody cornered Bandicut and Dakota a few minutes later, and waved Tanaki over. If he'd overheard the earlier conversation, he didn't mention it. "Captain Bandicut, we have a serious concern to discuss."

Bandicut glanced around at the fascinating mixed group of aliens, thinking, this had to be a space explorer's dream. And yet: "Is it about getting back into the starstream?"

Brody's face darkened. Tanaki answered, "We simply are out of our range of knowledge and experience. We don't know quite how we got thrown out of the starstream in the first place, and we don't know how to reverse the process."

"And," Brody continued, "we are already overdue reporting back to our home base. Of course, right here we have an astounding opportunity to establish lasting contact with—" he gestured around the room "—well, with every civilization represented in this room. But we're a patrol ship. We need to see that a properly outfitted ship is sent here to oversee that. This is fabulous, but it's not really our job. We don't even carry a proper landing shuttle."

"You aren't going to let that stop you, are you?" Bandicut asked. "A chance to be the first humans to visit Karellia?" *Besides me?* "Listen, what if you used our lander to fly a few of your people down for a short visit? It's got practically unlimited fuel, as far as I can tell. And about the starstream, I did promise to put our people with that expertise at your disposal. But besides that—may I suggest you wait and fly back to the starstream with us? We'd be in a better position to help you, if you have difficulty."

Brody furrowed his brow at the unexpected suggestions.

Bandicut said, "Let's go to the bridge and talk to Jeaves and Copernicus and Ruall. I'm sure they'll have some ideas."

Ideas they had, but the two robots and Ruall were in agreement that the one to help with this was Dark. But Dark was off checking on something—having to do, come to think of it, with the starstream. Also, though this was not of direct concern to the *Plato* crew, Ruall was increasingly worried that Bria had gone with Dark.

"Captain, I'm sure Dark will be back before too much longer," Bandicut said to Brody. "In the meantime, it's late, at least by our time zone. Will you sleep on what I suggested? Wait until tomorrow before you decide?" He glanced imploringly at Dakota. She nudged Brody's arm to request a private moment with him. After they'd talked, Brody said, "All right. We will wait. Maybe by tomorrow, your friend Dark will have returned. I'm sure I'd have no trouble finding volunteers to ride your lander down to the planet."

"Good, then. We'll talk again in the morning," Bandicut said.

"Good night, Captain," Brody said.

"Good night." Bandicut nodded as Brody turned away to go to the airlock and the tunnel connector. Gazing wearily at Dakota, Bandicut realized how happy he was, despite the fatigue. "Talk more tomorrow, okay? Can you stop over for breakfast?"

"Sure will. We'll talk about the future." She leaned in and kissed him on the cheek, and then turned to follow Brody off the ship. Bandicut watched her leave, a growing sadness in his heart.

When Bandicut woke from what seemed like much too short a night's sleep, he came out of his cabin to find Ruall waiting for him. She was bobbing urgently. "I have searched everywhere I can from here," she said. "Bria is not in this area—and Dark has not returned. I am concerned."

Bandicut winced. Bad way to start the day. "What do you want to do?"

"I am not certain. I will ask Copernicus to try once more to reach Dark."

Copernicus greeted them on the bridge with a completely un-related announcement: Several new ships had been detected ap-proaching the Karellian system.

"Ships!" Bandicut cried. *"Mindaru?"*

"No, Cap'n. I think they may be ours."

"Huh? You mean from Shipworld? How?"

"There's a communication coming in now. Yes, they *are* from Shipworld. It's the naval squadron we were told would follow."

Bandicut had to focus on that for a moment. He had completely forgotten: When they left Shipworld, they had been promised a backup fleet, as soon as it could be made ready. He'd put it out of his mind, because he hadn't really believed it. For one thing, it had sounded as though they had to *build* the fleet first. But now they had arrived? In time to help write the report? "They really sent ships to help us?"

"Apparently so. Cap'n, here's the transmission coming via wide-band. I don't think they know exactly where we are now. They're calling to see if we're here. Shall I put the essentials of what happened into a report for them?"

"You're sure it's really them?"

"Pretty sure, sir."

"Pretty sure?"

Copernicus ticked. "Of course I'm sure, Cap'n."

"In that case—hell, yes. Tell them we can use their help."

The prospect of new arrivals from Shipworld excited everyone on *The Long View.* It was a chance to establish some continuity of contact with this new outside world. From the viewpoint of the

Karellians and Uduon, however, there was also a certain caution. What if this signaled the start of an invasion—or at least unwelcome meddling? Bandicut tried to reassure them; but in truth, what did he know about the fleet's orders?

Maybe he should ask, he thought. The next time he talked to Copernicus, he posed a question for the robot to pass on to the fleet commander: *What are your intentions regarding these two worlds? We have established a fragile peace between them, and believe we have eliminated the Mindaru threat for now. We welcome your assistance, but wish to reassure the local leaders.*

The reply, when it came, expressed pleasure at the success of the mission, et cetera, and asked where they should rendezvous and how they might help. They were here to provide assistance, and no more.

Bandicut started making a list.

CHAPTER 29

To the Death

SPEEDING DOWN THE ghoststream, Antares was aware of a certain . . . she didn't know what exactly . . . a faint scent on the air? Or was it more like a sound, an almost imperceptible rumble? Echoes of her friends' passage, perhaps? Or of other living beings in the stream? Now *there* was a disturbing thought. More and more, she was feeling the absurdity of trying to find her friends in all this infinity of space—and perhaps worse, the cosmic eons of time. She was looking for a pin in eternity. What were the chances?

Her stones spoke at once to arrest that downward spiral. *Do not think it is hopeless. It is true we are exploring a long, thin thread between launch and end points. You might be thinking: If they have moved off the thread, it will be impossible to find them. But how could they? They can only exist on the thread of the ghoststream. Therefore, we will eventually find them.*

Antares refocused, and for the moment chose to accept the stones' reassurance, which at least sounded logical. *Concentrate on the line in front of you, and not the vistas on all sides. Reach out. Concentrate. Call out.*

/Ik! Ik, can you hear me? Julie? *This is Antares! If you can hear me, please answer!*/

She imagined her words flying down the thread like a train on a track, a track of almost infinite length. Eventually the words had to reach their target.

Julie heard Charli cry *Mindaru!* and fought back a rush of panic. *Mindaru?* She'd thought Charli and the gokat had pulled them *free* of the damned things! But one was here now? She cried out to anyone who could hear, /What can we do?/

It was Ik who answered. /You and I, hrah, should still be nothing but ghosts to it. I do not think we can do anything, except try to get *home* so they can turn off this moon-cursed *ghoststream*./

Julie hoped he was right. But Charli/Bria could not just run away. The Mindaru had somehow attached itself to Bria, and the gokat was twisting and turning, trying to shake it. Charli/Bria shouted,

> /// Let us handle this!
> If we can get you hooked into your thread of time,
> let go of us and take it.
> Get yourselves home! ///

/We can't just—/ Julie began. But Charli interrupted with,

> /// Yes, you can! And must!
> Ik was right.
> The one thing you must do
> is get the ghoststream turned off.
> We'll manage here. ///

That was hard for her to accept. But it made sense. She and Ik could do nothing to help here.

Right now they were holding tight to Bria/Charli. They could let go and try to re-center themselves in the ghoststream. But they would have to time it just right, or they'd knock themselves back into free-fall.

The river that was the starstream shimmered around them. Somewhere in here, a frayed thread of light sparkled down its length: the ghoststream from Shipworld. Julie and Ik were still a part of it; they had to be, or they would be dead; but they had slipped to its tattered edges, where probability was thin, and they needed to be squarely in its heart if they were to ride it home.

Bria was whipping violently back and forth, trying to shake the Mindaru. It clung to her like a monstrous sucker-fish. Charli's voice cried out over the gyrations,

/// You're coming up on it!
Be ready! ///

Something sparkled that might have been the heart of the stream. /Is that it?/ Julie cried.

/// Go! ///

She and Ik released, and they spun around in the stream . . . almost, *almost* reaching what they were after.

––––––––––––

Dark had watched Bria's progress through the various dimensional threads of the starstream. Peering down through time—which to Dark appeared compressed and magnified, as if by a tremendous lens—she had watched Charli join with Bria as she wove her way down the timestream to reach the imperiled travelers. Dark felt responsible for Bria's safety, but there was little she could do, except watch as Bria ventured out into the frayed extremities of the timestream, to connect with Ik and Julie.

Now, as those two, joined to the little gokat, moved back toward the center, Dark's spirits welled up with relief and pride. Bria was succeeding, where Dark herself and even Charli alone could not.

And then she saw it: the glistening shadow, creeping after them, another of the silent, ghastly, Mindaru waveforms.

Dark tried to call out a warning, but they were too far away. She hovered where she was, trying to think of a way to help. If Bria could just bring them all a little farther back *up* the timestream, Dark might be able to intercede. If she had enough room to work, she could slice the accursed thing away, and let them all get to safety. *If* Bria could bring them close enough.

The shadows feinted and split and circled and merged. Bria knew that things had gone wrong, without exactly understanding what was happening. *It was the enemy.* It was like the things she had fought before. It *looked* quite different, but she could smell the same malice. It had somehow broken right into her space. It was preparing an attack.

When Bria had fought these things before, there was form and substance to attack. But this was all shadow and smoke, *here* now and *there* now. She wasn't sure what to do. *Get our people home. Get them home.* But to do that, she had to *fight this thing.* But how? She just knew she'd fought them before, and won.

The Charli-part of her was spinning through memory even faster, remembering previous mind-battles with the enemy, battles they had nearly lost. She couldn't let that happen again. But this thing was just a complicated wave. How could they kill a wave form? They needed to collapse it somehow. But how?

Bria-part didn't understand the Charli-part's thoughts, but she knew she had come here to get these friends of Dark to safety, and she needed to hang on long enough to do that. Frantically she pulled them onward, shadows or no shadows, through the fault-lines of splinter-space, and on to a place where she felt a glow come over her, almost a feeling of warmth—and she sensed the gaze of Dark nearby. She also saw channels opening up into flower-space that seemed to say *home.* With a sudden rush of hope, she released Julie and Ik into what she hoped was their ghost-stream, tingling with a cry of satisfaction from the Charli-part.

Bria yelped and yowled a farewell—and then she slid side-ways out of that place, and turned and attacked the shadows, wave or not, with all of the fury of someone who had one last chance to destroy a mortal enemy.

Ik felt the gokat release them, and saw her suddenly move away, enveloped by the dark, dancing silhouette of the Mindaru.

It was hard to keep Bria in sight. He wasn't sure where he and Julie were at this point, but he understood their job was to get clear. Unfortunately, he had no control over his movements; they were spinning and corkscrewing, barely holding together, in a turbulent current that only vaguely felt like the ghoststream.

Now he caught sight of the gokat again, moving with astonishing speed, raining violence down on what truly appeared to be shadows, projections on a distant screen. It was a scene of unbridled fury; but was it doing any good? Bria seemed to spin in and out of existence. *What was she doing?* She appeared to be slicing at the Mindaru like a chopping knife, but her target swirled and bobbed like a chip of wood in a pounding surf.

It was out of his hands. /Julie!/ he called. /*Julie Stone*, we must move away! This is beyond us!/

He felt Julie's voice-stones respond even before she did. The two pairs of stones joined forces, and with their help, Julie and Ik fought to bring their own movement under control.

Bria had started the attack the same way she'd gone after the other Mindaru, slicing and hoping to scatter the pieces to the many dimensions. But this thing wasn't solid, it was just waves, and her attack had no effect.

The Charli-part was starting to interrupt, to tell her it was no use, when Bria suddenly realized the Mindaru was struggling as much as she was, struggling just to hold itself together. It was in trouble—dying, maybe.

/// You're right, it's losing strength!
The Karellian time-tides have been turned off!
I think the effects are just now reaching us
this far down the timeline. ///

To Bria, those words carried only the sketchiest meaning. But she did know that the rip-current of time that had come from way back near that planet was now losing its strength. Maybe this nasty thing needed that current to live. If so, that was fine with her, though she'd rather have torn it apart herself.

/// Bria, I think that's exactly right.
It can't live without that current,
because it's nothing but a wave in the current.
Just keep a safe distance from it
and let it die. ///

So it was as good as dead already?

Dark saw it, too, from her position up-time; the strength of the thing was ebbing away. She was relieved to see Bria break off her futile attack. Let it die alone. It was a problem they hadn't expected and didn't need. Dark tried to call down to her: *"Bria, can you pull back from it? You're losing energy. Save it for helping the others!"*

Dark could see that the continuum of space and time were all twisted up into channels and mazes in this area, probably because of the fading away of the time-tides from Karellia. Changes were still rippling down the main starstream and causing things to kink and twist in that special thread stretching all the long way down from Shipworld. Ik and Julie were not yet out of the dimensional eddies that impeded them from reconnecting to that thread. They were not out of danger.

And then Dark heard something in the far, far distance, something that seemed startlingly familiar and wholly unexpected.

Space-time was growing more agitated around Bria—openings to shard-space here, spindle-space there, rays shooting toward infinity, and others curling into infinitesimal hidden dimensions. Through the confusion, Bria caught sight of long, long connections. One reached deep into the past, to the beginning and the core of this great, spiraling swirl of stars. Another arrowed in a different direction, back toward something that looked like the home they had all left. Was that Shipworld she sensed through the haze of the travelers' ghoststream?

"Bria, listen! Do you hear that?"

Hear what? She heard Dark. But Dark seemed to want her to hear something else. She listened, and as she did so, she heard something like a voice, calling down. Whose? It didn't sound like Ruall, and couldn't be her, anyway. Bria suddenly, intensely, missed Ruall. Why couldn't she be here? Had she even said good-bye to Ruall before she left? She couldn't remember.

"Listen—do you hear it?"

Yes, she did. She couldn't quite make it out. But there was something familiar in it, something that reminded Bria of her friends from the ship. It seemed to be calling down through a fragile kind of splinter-space, from very far away, and saying, *"Can you hear me, Ik? Can you hear me, Julie? This is Antares."* Calling and calling.

Now, that was strange, Bria thought.

The Charli-part in her was electrified. *Antares?* That wasn't just strange, it was astonishing!

Urged by Charli, Bria tried to reach out and catch the sound.

———

Charli saw it, but too late. The Mindaru, drifting away in the starstream, had not died and dispersed, but instead had collapsed from its tortured wave function and transformed in a twinkling into a solid thing in the starstream. It had crystalline sides and splintered thorns. It was almost beautiful in a terrible way—but it had *weapons*, and an inner light flickered as it powered them up.

/// Bria, danger! ///

The Mindaru spun toward them.

———

Bria had already forgotten the Mindaru—and she barely even saw the fountain of purple light that burst upon her from behind. Only as the light—and all of the higher radiations that came with it—coruscated through her did she register Charli's warning cry. The radiation flashed all of her thoughts and her world white, and she felt something shatter inside.

———————

Dark was nearly upon the Mindaru, to make sure it was dead, when she saw it transform in an instant into something quite different, a small but solid vessel in the starstream. Before Dark could react, it had belched a gout of radiation directly into Bria.

Dark did not need to hear any words from Bria to know that this was bad.

"Bria, no!"

But the cry was in vain. Bria probably never saw the blow coming.

The gokat tumbled backward up the starstream. It seemed to Dark that she was on fire.

———————

/Do you hear that voice?/ Ik asked. /Am I dreaming it?/

But Julie was having so much trouble orienting herself in the stream, she couldn't listen for voices in the ghoststream. Everything seemed to be wobbling and swaying.

/Ik! Ik!/ she cried. /Can you tell which way we should be going?/ She looked frantically for a direction that would connect them with home. When they'd let go of Bria, she'd hoped it would be a straight shot right back up the ghoststream to Shipworld and the launch point. But she couldn't find the way. Did they still need Bria? Where was she?

Something flashed, lighting up the starstream like a bomb.

Julie forgot about finding her way and scanned everywhere, trying to understand what was happening. Some distance behind them in the stream, she saw something tumbling out of control, and ablaze with light. /Bria?/ she whispered.

Ik snarled with wordless fury.

There was another shape against the pale light of the starstream; it was weirdly crystalline and spiky, and shimmered with inner fire—and it seemed to be turning in flight. Turning toward Julie and Ik.

The Mindaru? They knew the things had the ability to change form. But so quickly?

/Ik, we need to do something! *Stones—help!*/

Now the thing was accelerating toward them.

We have no way to fight it. We can only try to shield our thoughts from attack.

/That's not—/

She didn't get to finish her protest, because from out of nowhere a shockingly dark shadow stretched suddenly across the stream, directly in the path of the oncoming Mindaru.

Dark's first instinct was to go to Bria. But Bria and the travelers were still downtime from her and hard to get to. Dark knew she could disrupt things dangerously if she got too near the ghost-stream. But if she didn't, she would be abandoning not just Bria, but Ik and the human, to the Mindaru. She *had* to eliminate the threat. And if that thing had harmed Bria, Dark would see it dead.

Dark let out a cry and arrowed down the luminous river, skimming the embedded thread of the ghoststream, the displacer of time. Her friend Deep could have done this easily, but for her it was difficult. The time dimension compressed like a collapsing tube, and then she was reaching into the part of the stream where the travelers were, and Bria, and . . . the thing of malice, the Mindaru.

Bria was the farthest away, and would have to be last. Dark put herself between the Mindaru and the two travelers. She allowed herself a moment to evaluate the foe. It was newly solid; it was comparatively weak; it had caught Bria only through the element of surprise.

Dark slammed into it like a falling comet, crushing it with a sudden wrench of gravity. In an instant, she engulfed what was left of it and *squeezed* and *twisted*, and compressed all of the energy that was in it, ignoring its dying shrieks of dismay, squeezed it white hot. Then she drained all of that energy out of it and spat out the dead, frozen remnants, spat each piece into a separate, curled up dimension of space.

With that, she was sure, the thing was gone.

If only she had done it sooner!

The starstream boomed and reverberated from the wrenching she had imposed on local space-time. But the fragile ghoststream still seemed intact. Go, travelers! No time for caution! She needed to get to Bria!

Bria felt that she was dying; but she was not dead yet. She was tumbling, spasming, flying away from everyone she cared about. She felt Charli still with her, and together their hearts were filled with pain and terror. She didn't even really know what had happened. But she could feel herself coming apart into the many dimensions she inhabited, and no one could survive that.

But she still had her mind and her hope, for a few moments more, at least.

And of all things, she still heard that voice, the one Dark had wanted her to listen to. It was important somehow. It was coming from way up the ghostly stream. It seemed to be calling to *them*. It said its name was *Antares*, and it was calling down the stream to *Ik* and *Julie*—the beings Bria had come to help!

From within herself, she barely heard Charli's voice:

*/// I don't think they can reach Antares
or hear her.
Can we bring them together—somehow? ///*

Would that save them? Would that accomplish what she had come here to do? Would it save Dark's friends?

Yes, Bria thought. *If we can do that one thing . . .*

Dark was stretched downtime, and it was torturous for her, but she caught Bria and cradled the gokat there in the twisted, half-wrecked emptiness of the merged streams. She spoke softly to the little one. *"I have destroyed the one who did this to you. If I knew how to save you, I would. But I will try to help you now. Hold tight, little one."*

The gokat responded weakly. She still had enough life to bristle at being called "little one." It seemed to Dark she was clinging to the time thread, to the thing they called the ghoststream. She heard that voice at the far end now, the voice calling itself Antares, whom Dark could barely hear at this point.

Dark wasn't really sure what to do, but perhaps she could add some energy to strengthen that thread, to keep it straight and open. She'd done something like that in a star once, to help Deep. That had ended in success but terrible sadness, and she feared this might end the same. But it was too soon to grieve. Bria was still here, trying to finish the job. Dark had to help her bring Ik and Julie and Antares together again, if she could.

With extreme care, she bent her thought toward boosting the signal strength in the ghoststream.

"Antares, if you can hear me, keep trying!"

"Bria, and traveling friends, join yourself to Antares' voice. Put everything you have into it."

Dark felt her speaking stones sparking with life and connection, not quite able to do it themselves, but able to touch Bria and boost her along.

/Hrah! Dark, is that you?/ Ik asked in astonishment. He felt his voice-stones make a connection, and he knew it was. *How could Dark be here?* It was impossible, and yet she was, nonetheless— telling him to join himself to . . .

Antares?

That was astonishing. But he sensed Julie having a similar reaction. And there was Bria—no longer providing a strong, steady light of guidance, but sputtering like a failing torch, just bright enough to open up the ghoststream. And . . . there was someone else, just a voice . . .

It is Antares, truly. A long distance away. We feel her voice-stones.

/Is she in the ghoststream? Is she coming this way?/

And he heard Julie gasping to her own stones, /If she is, we have to warn her back! It's too dangerous!/

She is far up the stream. She is rescuing us.

Ik wasn't even sure whose stones had just spoken. But the next voice he heard was Dark's, and she spoke with terrible urgency. *"Bria has reached her! She has reached up the stream for Antares! We must join you to her before she—"*

Dark's voice cut off, and energy seemed to flow out of her like glowing matter out of a white hole, strengthening the connection. It felt to Ik as if he were being flung by an enormous blast of static. Then the signal steadied, and he heard a thin voice: /Ik? Julie? Can you hear me?/

/Yes!/ Ik and Julie cried in unison.

In that instant, he felt Antares, or her stones, reach out from somewhere beyond infinity to hook a line around him, and around Julie. And an instant later he felt, rather than heard, a soft cry that sounded like a small creature sighing, and he felt a spark of life go out of the ghoststream.

The end for Bria came gently, even through the haze of pain. The Charli part of her held on to the very end, and was an intimate witness to the gokat's death, the spirit slipping out of the tiny, torn body—but not before she'd accomplished her final act and flashed a glimmer of satisfaction to her semi-quarx partner. The Charli-part lingered long enough to pay her own tribute to the gokat.

/// *You have done well,*
my two-dimensional friend.
Rest, now. Rest. ///

And with that, the Charli-part, too, evaporated and passed into the busy emptiness of n-space.

Dark watched her friend die, and she wept inwardly, remembering, as she grieved for Bria, all of the friends she had lost before this, especially Deep, but also stars whom she had known and shared with. They all concatenated into a daisy-chain of grief, and became one single cry of pain. In the weight of that grief, this little gokat was no less than the greatest of the talking suns. *Bria. Little Bria.*

Then Dark poured all of her concentration into making absolutely certain that the ghoststream held, while Ik and Julie flowed back into it and were pulled with dizzying speed back toward Shipworld, toward their present time and the waiting Antares.

CHAPTER 30

Aftershocks

CHARLI HAD WATCHED helplessly as the Mindaru struck Bria. It was a terrible blow, the death of the gokat, and a part of Charli herself. She'd known going in how dangerous the Mindaru were—but even so, she was unprepared for the shock. It was not that she had known the gokat so well. Prior to Charli's separation from Bandicut, she had seen Bria only through John's eyes. But when she joined thoughts with the gokat, that all changed. Their time together was brief, but long enough for the lonely quarx to receive a glimpse into the creature's soul, to gain a sense of her sly sense of play, and her fierce loyalty to her tribe. Stealing weapons from soldiers on Uduon and sending them into alter-space (so satisfying)! And after that, defeating not just one Mindaru, but several!

After *all* that, Bria had come here, in an act of loyalty to Dark, to save people she didn't even know. And now she was gone.

If anyone was responsible for Bria's death, besides the Mindaru, it was Charli. *She* had called on Dark and Bria to help her save *her* friends. She'd put them both in harm's way—and Bria had died for it. So had the piece of Charli that was riding with her; and the death of that part of herself was another ripping wound.

Others would feel the loss as well, she knew. Ruall, of course, but also John and Li-Jared. Was there any way she could get word to them of what had happened—that their small friend had died well, fighting the enemy? That her loss was not in vain? Bria had helped Ik and Julie escape from the Mindaru, and that was a triumph not just for her, but for the mission they all served.

The mission. Why was it that so often her missions took the lives of the people she most cared for?

Charli became aware of Dark circling. She called out to the shadowy being.

/// How much did you see? ///

Dark moved in a somber arc, from one side to the other, and up and down, as though hunting for any remnant sign of the gokat. Her voice filled the space surrounding Charli.

"I felt her spirit go. I grieve."

/// I grieve, too.
But not for what she's done.
It was a remarkable rescue. ///

"It was. It seemed to me that some part of you was with her. What does that part say?"

/// That part of me died with her, ///

Charli answered, a crushing weight coming over her as she spoke. Was some bit of them still adrift out there in the starstream? Who could say? The starstream was a nearly limitless place, but she had no heart right now to think about it.

"I am sorry. I hope we succeeded. I can no longer see Ik and the human."

No. Ik and Julie were gone from Charli's field of view, also. She hoped they had made a clean return to Shipworld, and to their present. There was nothing more she could do for them.

As for her, she did not much like this starstream. It carried pain down its river. Too much pain.

Antares had no idea what just happened, far down the ghost-stream, but she had felt the unmistakable presence of Dark, who seemed to recognize her even at such a distance. *Dark!* How could that be? Wasn't Dark off in the galaxy somewhere? And then . . . she had felt, or imagined she felt, the touch of *Charli*, John's quarx! *Charli!* But without John. Surely that *was* impossible. Was she hallucinating?

It had all been so disorienting; she felt reality spinning around her. But Dark had tried to speak, and her knowing-stones buzzed with a connection that seemed to release a powerful wave of *something* that caught her and spun her into a higher state of energy and reach. And suddenly there they were, far down the stream: Ik, and Julie, billowing up the ghoststream toward her.

Antares wondered dizzily if this was what a tornado felt like.

Ik was stunned to realize it *was* Antares he felt at the end of the connection. How was that possible, unless she had entered the ghoststream herself? Had she come to find them?

He strained to call out to her. But then she was gone in a rush of static and a pounding beat—as though the passing eons were beating time. /Julie, did you hear that?/ he cried. He had to look to confirm that Julie was, thank the stars, right beside him. Everyone else had vanished behind them.

/Whatever they did back there . . . / Julie managed, struggling to speak. /Are we on our way home?/

Whatever they did, Ik thought. Charli and Dark and some tiny creature he'd never gotten a good look at . . . together, had freed Ik and Julie from where they were stuck, and had somehow protected them from a threatening Mindaru. But at what cost? Ik was certain he had felt a *death*, and not just the Mindaru's. He thought maybe that someone was the smallest of them.

The pulsing rhythm grew more and more frantic around them. It was in the ghoststream walls, like an underground train rumbling in the dark at breakneck speed. It felt as though they were being reeled in by a tremendous winch, the light-years and time-years flying past by the millions, Antares somehow there with them, too . . .

———————

Antares poured all of her own strength into the connection, trying to pull them close. She was not going to lose them now! /Hold on to me! Don't let go!/

There was so much noise and confusion in the whirlwind, she could not hear their answer, if there was any. No matter; she had her feet rooted in the present and her arms stretched down into the deep past, and she simply pulled, and pulled.

And somewhere in that effort, something slipped . . .

For an instant, she was terrified that she'd lost them, back in deep time. But that wasn't it. She *had* lost her grip on them—and Ik and Julie sailed *past* her like a cracked whip. Antares fought like crazy to catch them again, to break their speed through time, but she couldn't get a grip on them. Pain flashed through her as the connection sizzled and parted. Ik and Julie flew by into the future, and were gone.

And Antares crashed home in a sheet of white light.

CHAPTER 31

Shipworld Fleet

THE NAVAL SQUADRON from Shipworld was six vessels strong. They closed into a matching orbit, and one, slightly larger than the others, dispatched a shuttle to *The Long View*.

Bandicut and Ruall met the fleet commander in the meeting room where they had entertained the *Plato* crew, just two days earlier. *The Long View* was feeling rather empty, as Li-Jared and Ocellet Quin had gone back planetside with the two Uduon for a brief visit, and a team from *Plato*, led by Dakota Bandicut, had done likewise. The Shipworld fleet commander, Torno, was a Skakolloan, a terrier-faced biped with eyes that bulged slightly, giving him an alarmingly agitated appearance. His support staff consisted of one other of his own species, and two tripedal Madharrassi, who stayed quietly in the background. Introductions were a little confusing at first, due to translation difficulties—none of them had translator-stones—until the new arrivals managed to get their own translation devices properly calibrated to speak with Bandicut and Ruall.

Once they had actual conversation going, Bandicut discovered that Commander Torno had a sense of humor and reasonable communication skills, which was a relief after their early experiences with Ruall. Torno had reviewed Jeaves' summary report on their mission, but he wanted to go over the whole thing and hear it in Bandicut's and Ruall's words, from beginning to end.

He listened intently, stopping them occasionally to let the translator catch up, or to ask for clarification. *The Long View*'s story was a long one, with multiple first contacts and battles— but what most provoked tooth-baring interest on Torno's face was the appearance of Dark, and the surprise meeting with the human ship *Plato*. Torno's own fleet had not entered the star-stream, but had humped it all the way here through ordinary n-space. When the report was finished, Commander Torno asked what help *The Long View* crew needed. "You've won the peace— hah! How can we help you hold it?"

"Well," Bandicut said, "if you're going to stick around, you can help safeguard the system by making sure no more Mindaru wander in. We're in a very fragile state between Karellia and Uduon."

"Hah! You want to make sure they don't start shooting at each other again!"

"Well, yes. But more than that. Right now, there is no means of transportation or even communication between their planets. I am hoping you can help with that. We need a means for the worlds to talk to one another, and for representatives to travel back and forth. Our Uduon guests must return home soon, to tell their people what has been happening. We were planning to take them. But perhaps with the ships you have available . . ."

Torno made a whuffing sound. "We can do that, of course. I think that would be better. We can detach a ship or two for courier duty, and we are prepared to send study teams to both worlds."

Ruall rang softly at the first part of that, causing Bandicut to say, "Is there a particular reason why you say it would be better for you to take them?"

Torno scratched behind his floppy ears. "Wh-ell, yes. Perhaps we should tell you now? Our orders include orders for you. You are requested to return to Shipworld as soon as possible after the immediate crisis is resolved."

"Why's that? Is there a rush?"

"Yes and no," Torno answered. "There is some urgency." He scratched behind his ears again. "You are aware there was a parallel mission to yours, directly down the timestream? All the way back to where the Mindaru came from?"

Bandicut started to nod slowly—was this to be his first formal briefing on it?—and then the full meaning of Torno's words struck home. "Wait—what are you saying? Back in time to where they started? That's millions of years! *Billions*, I think!" He glanced at Ruall, who appeared to be vibrating with contained emotion. "Are you serious?"

Torno shook his head with vigor, his ears flapping. "I don't really know the details." He seemed perturbed. "That mission was not well coordinated with your mission, I am afraid."

"Not coordinated at all, as far as I know!" Bandicut muttered.

"Yes. Politics, I suppose. Nothing to be proud of."

"But why? What was the other mission sent to do?"

"Well, I know pretty damn little about it myself," said Torno. "But the Peloi who sent us made clear their urgency to reconcile the two missions, you see? Great concern about avoiding accidental time effects." He made another whuffling sound. "Something like that. The Peloi said they were made aware of the other mission only after your departure. They indicated you may be familiar with some members of the other team. Someone named Ik? And someone named . . . Stone?"

Bandicut closed his eyes. He felt a boa constrictor coiling around his throat. Ik—and somehow Julie—had been *sent back in deep time? Billions of years?* Why? He could barely wrap his mind around the idea. To stop the Mindaru? To make an end-run around *The Long View*'s mission—in case they failed? Why would anyone in Shipworld do such a thing without coordinating the two efforts? He tried to keep from flinching, but the dog-faced Torno grunted softly and cocked his head. "You do know them, then? I'm sorry that I cannot tell you their status. I have no information about that."

The boa constrictor tightened a little more.

Torno cocked his head the other way. "We must hope for the best. I imagine the fastest way to learn more is to make haste back to Shipworld. May I ask when you plan to depart? Do you have any unfinished business in this star system?"

"Well, yes," said Bandicut with difficulty. "Several things—"

Before he could finish speaking, Ruall spun and clanged. "We have a missing crew member. I fear we may be forced to undertake a search."

Bandicut winced. He felt Ruall's raw pain, but he was at a loss as to how to search for Bria. Space was terribly large, and they didn't know where to start.

"I believe," Ruall rang, "she may have gone back toward the starstream with Dark."

That made Bandicut take a sharp breath. *Toward the starstream* was a huge space to search. "Are you sure? Have you found a trail?"

Ruall spun once and bobbed. "No physical evidence. But before Dark disappeared, she spoke of Mindaru in the starstream, of trying to block any further—"

"Yes, but why would that include Bria?"

Ruall was starting her low cymbal sound of uneasy thought. "Bria had become quite interested in working with Dark. I believe she may have followed her."

"That's not a lot to go on."

The cymbal rang, taut with pain. "Maybe not. But it's the best I have." Ruall spun in place. "I intend to try to reach Dark. But that might not be possible from here. We might have to go ourselves."

Bandicut puffed his cheeks and exhaled. "Well, we can't leave until we're sure Akura and Sheeawn are being taken care of. We also have to escort *Plato*, once they bring their team back up from the planet, and help them reenter the starstream. *That* involves meeting up with Dark. But yeah, sure, once we have things under control here."

Torno looked from one to the other, and waggled his hands in a shrug.

Jeaves appeared then with a serving cart and offered refreshments. Holding small plates, Torno and his aides wandered over to gaze out the observation bubble Copernicus had given them on the outboard side of the room. Karellia floated fat and serene against the backdrop of the Heart of Fire clouds. Jeaves stood with them, and as he began pointing out some of the surface features of the planet, Bandicut sat down at the table, holding a mug of coffee and his own thoughts.

His thoughts were somewhere in the starstream, wondering where Ik and Julie were—and Antares and Napoleon!—when Copernicus's voice rattled the air through the intercom speaker. "Can you come to the bridge, Cap'n? And Ruall? I've just heard from Dark."

Bandicut's gaze latched onto Ruall—and then she was gone in a blink, and Bandicut called an apology to Torno and the others. Hurrying onto the bridge, he found Ruall bobbing at the front of the viewspace, as though peering into the distance. Copernicus was rolling back and forth with impatience, until he saw Bandicut. "Ah, Cap'n! Dark is coming alongside. She says she needs to speak to us urgently. Shall I call our guests to the bridge, as well?"

Bandicut shook his head. "No, let's find out what it is first." He hurried up alongside Ruall. He felt an irrational urge to put an arm around the fretting Tintangle. But Ruall was blinking in and out of view, perhaps jaunting in and out of the ship, searching for Bria. Bandicut wanted to say he knew how she felt, but how could he convey that to the Tintangle? Were her feelings the same as what he felt about Charli? He had no idea.

Minutes later, a shadow that was just a little darker than space hove into view and floated, barely visible except for two twinkling translator-stones in its heart. For a moment, no one spoke—and then Ruall and Bandicut spoke at once. "Dark—" began Bandicut, while Ruall clanged, "Do you know the whereabouts of Bria?"

Bandicut felt an immediate twinge in his wrist-stones, as they communicated with Dark's. Something was wrong, something terrible. But also something was good.

Dark spoke. *"I met Charli in the starstream."*

Charli! Bandicut's heart leaped. *Charli's alive!*

"Also your friend Ik. And another, named Julie."

Bandicut reeled, not even knowing how to react. Dark continued without pausing:

"Also Mindaru. There was a great battle. Bria came to help."

Beside Bandicut, Ruall started to shake. Dark continued, in terse phrases. The fight had been a bad one. Bria made contact with the friends, helped them get away. A terrifyingly near thing. The Mindaru was broken. But . . .

And Dark paused, while Bandicut's heart cried out with joy that his friends had escaped. But . . .

Bandicut's joy shut down. *"What?* What happened?"

Dark's words became a moan. *"Bria died. Struck down by the Mindaru. I could not stop it. Too far away. She saved the others — with her life . . ."*

A metallic, dissonant wail filled the bridge. It was Ruall, vibrating uncontrollably, the pitch of her cry rising and falling in her distress. She blurred in the viewspace, spinning and fading in and out of the continuum, neither fully present nor absent. Three times he saw her outside the ship, near Dark, and then she was back on the bridge.

"BRIAAAA!! BRIAAA-A-A-A!!" Ruall's cry filled the bridge, and echoed back from the light-years and the eons.

Dark continued speaking, perhaps unaware of Ruall's outpouring of grief. Copernicus finally stopped her, and they all waited in mournful silence until Ruall's last wail faded away. Her voice rang dully. "Are you certain . . . she died? And did not just . . . disappear?"

"I am sorry. I felt her die. I also felt . . . a part of Charli die."

Bandicut felt the blood drain from his face, and nearly staggered. "Charli?" he whispered. He forced his voice to work. "I didn't know Charli was alive. But now you say she's died?"

"She lives, in the stream. But a part of her died. The part that was with Bria."

Bandicut shook his head, trying to absorb it all. Charli in the starstream, in Bria, part of her dying. How much loss and grief could one quarx survive? Even before coming to Bandicut, she had suffered terrible losses. Then with Bandicut, multiple deaths of her own, and the splitting of herself on the Starmaker mission; a part of her had gone with Deep when Deep was lost to this universe. Then, being ripped from Bandicut in their battle in the starstream. Now this.

Bandicut felt every muscle in his body tighten. "Dark, did you say that the others, that Julie and Ik, got away?"

"We believe so. Antares reached them. Pulled them back toward that place where you live."

Antares! Now he did stagger. "Toward Shipworld?" he managed.

"Toward Shipworld. Toward your present. Toward your now."

Bandicut's heart thundered. *Saved! By Antares! On their way back to Shipworld!* He wondered what their mission had been, and whether they had succeeded. He felt a sudden, overpowering need to return to Shipworld. To see them all again. His work here was done. It was time to go home.

And then he looked at Ruall, and her grief stabbed his heart. What could they possibly do for Ruall? How could they help her in her grief?

"Ruall," he whispered. *"I'm so sorry—"*

But the Tintangle was already speaking. "We must finalize our arrangements, then, and leave for home as soon as possible."

"Wait, Ruall." She seemed about to sweep away, and he moved to stop her. "Listen, do you need some time to . . . I don't know . . . go to the scene, maybe, and see what you can learn?"

Ruall seemed to brush off the suggestion. "We must move quickly," she bonged, in as expressionless a tone as Bandicut had ever heard from her. "They need us back at Shipworld. Let's arrange for the Uduon, finish up with Quin and Karellia, and be on our way." With that, she spun in place and then winked out.

Bandicut was left staring at empty space, stunned by how quickly victory had turned to ashes.

CHAPTER 32

Disagreements Among Friends

TWO DAYS LATER, the lander rose from the planet twice, with Jeaves in control. First it brought the *Plato* ground team back to their own ship from a "first contact" meeting with Karellian officials. The second flight brought Li-Jared, Ocellet Quin, and the two Uduon back from their own meetings with the Council. Bandicut asked, somewhat distractedly, how it had gone this time. He was still shaken up by the news from Dark, and Ruall's hard-edged intensity since learning of Bria's death hadn't helped.

Quin seemed to sense that something had changed, and she tilted her head a little as she answered his question. "It went better than it might have, but it wasn't easy." Introducing the Council to their former sworn enemies, the Uduon, plus the sudden visit from the humans, and the news that *more* ships had arrived from Shipworld, had left most of the Council reeling. Nevertheless, they were willing to undertake diplomacy with Uduon.

Bandicut accepted that without comment, and glanced at Li-Jared, who was watching him in silence. He opened his hands slightly, inviting Li-Jared to speak.

Li-Jared exhibited none of Quin's reserve. "What's—" *bong* "—going on here, Bandie? You look like you've stared into the abyss and didn't like what you saw. What's the problem? Is something wrong with the Shipworld fleet?"

Bandicut told them everything Dark had reported. Li-Jared's face brightened when he heard that Charli was still alive, and that

Ik and Julie were apparently on their way home—but upon learning of Bria's death, he sagged in shock. He bonged mournfully, and did not move a muscle until Quin said, softly, "I am sorry, Li-Jared. And John Bandicut." She extended her left hand, and Li-Jared took it and squeezed it, and then he turned away to gaze out the observation dome.

Finally he spoke to the distant stars. "There's always a price, isn't there? Always a price."

A short time later, Ruall entered the meeting room and asked them to gather around. Her voice was low but metal-hard. "We must make our plans for departure."

Li-Jared started visibly, but it was Quin who said, "So soon?"

Ruall responded by moving off a little way, as if to leave it to Bandicut to explain. With some reluctance, he did. "We're being called back to Shipworld. But the new Shipworld squadron will stay on to help out, especially if any more Mindaru show up. I'll introduce you to their commander. I hope you'll let them make more permanent contact with both of your worlds."

Quin looked unsettled by those words. The people she had come to trust were leaving, and strangers taking their place? Bandicut felt that he could read her thoughts, but he had no answer. He shifted his gaze to the Uduon. "Watcher Akura, would it be agreeable for you and Sheeawn to fly back home aboard one of our sister ships? Commander Torno, of the lead ship, has offered to place two vessels at your disposal—to transport you back and forth between Uduon and Karellia, and to set up long-range communications. Also, to establish their own contact with your people, if you are willing."

Akura gazed at him gravely before answering, with an inclination of her head toward her right shoulder. "We accept, of course," she murmured. "But—" and she and Sheeawn went back and forth for a moment, before Sheeawn continued the translation, "—we would feel more . . . secure . . . if we were to continue this journey with you."

Bandicut nodded, and felt a constriction in his throat as it hit home—he was getting ready to say good-bye to these people. "I am truly sorry. I would have liked to spend more time with you, also. Will Sheeawn—I mean—" he turned to speak directly to the younger Uduon "—Sheeawn, will you return with Akura, or stay here?"

Sheeawn bowed his own head slightly. "I will go with Watcher Akura. But I will return, later, if permitted."

"I tried to persuade him to stay," Quin said. "But—" She flicked her fingers in the air.

"I think just now I am needed more by the Watchers," Sheeawn said—a little shyly, Bandicut thought.

Ruall floated silently back toward them. "That is settled, then," she said, with a trace of her old officiousness. "We will set up a meeting with Commander Torno and his staff as soon as you are ready. Do you wish to rest first? Ocellet Quin and Watcher Akura, what are your needs from us before we leave?"

For a moment, there was no answer. There was so much, no doubt, that both would have liked to say. So much happening, so little time to take stock. It was Li-Jared who spoke. "There is something I need—or want." He looked quickly at Quin, at Bandicut, and at Ruall. "Everyone? Look—" *bong* "—this isn't easy, but I have to say it."

"Say what, Li-Jared?"

"I want to stay here. On Karellia. With my people."

Bandicut stared at him, stunned. *"What?"* he said, feeling stupid. "What do you mean? Why would you—?"

Li-Jared spread his arms wide. "Well—" *bwang* "—why do you think? It's my *home.*"

"Of course it is, I'm sorry. But I thought—" *What—that you would want to leave your home all over again?*

"Bandie, I—no. I mean, thank you. You and Ik and Antares— you're my *friends* and I love you. But Bandie—I belong here, with my people." Li-Jared's eyes had narrowed to thin, vertical slits crossed in the middle by small, dark bands of blue. "I know this isn't what we planned, but think about it. This is *my homeworld.*

I may never get another chance. To return, to get to know it again, in the now. To get to know Quin, to learn what happened to my family, and my friends here." He shut his eyes for a second, and when they reopened, they were wider, with the usual bright blue band across the center. He rubbed his fingertips on his chest. He added, softly, "I could live a normal life again, Bandie John."

"Well, I—" Bandicut started, but he stopped, not knowing how to reply. *Of course he wants to go back home. And why didn't you see it coming? But damn!*

"I know what you're thinking. What about Ik, and you, and Antares? And the robots?"

"Yes—"

"Well, I . . . just hope you'll all understand." Li-Jared gazed at him fiercely. "You'll explain for me, won't you? Won't you, Bandie John?"

"I—"

"Will you do that for me? Tell them all I think the world of them, and explain why I didn't come back?"

Bandicut stared at him, thinking, *Our group . . .*

Li-Jared must have read his mind. "Our group is coming apart, Bandie. Ik breaking away like that—and your losing Charli. I hope you can find Antares again, and your Julie—I do. But for me, it's time to leave. Tell me you wouldn't go back to Earth, if you could!"

Bandicut could only think, *My family is all in space now. At Shipworld. Or in the starstream.* Finally he choked, "Maybe you could take some time for a long visit here, and then return with the fleet, when they come back to Shipworld. Hell, maybe they'll set up regular commerce between Karellia and Shipworld." *Right—just like they did with Earth? Not impossible, but . . .*

"I am sorry, Band . . . Bandie John Bandicut," Li-Jared said, and his voice had gone a little thick. "I truly am. I will miss you, and it will grieve me not to see Ik again, or Antares. Or your norgs. Moon and stars, I'll probably even miss this idiot Ruall."

"Still, it—" Bandicut began, and extended his hands, and then dropped them. *It sounds so final,* is what he had been about to say.

Quin made a clicking sound. "We would be glad to have Li-Jared stay with us," she murmured. Her gaze lingered on Li-Jared for a moment, and Bandicut wondered if that was a personal or professional desire.

Ruall began to make a low, ominous, ringing sound. "No, no, I am sorry, but this will not be possible."

"What do you mean?" Bandicut asked, as Li-Jared stiffened. "Why not?"

"It is simply impossible, per the mission requirements." Ruall spun once, then twice.

Li-Jared stood rooted, a flicker of fire in his eyes. "What do your mission rules have to do with my personal life?"

Ruall's voice seemed to break a little. "They are not *my* rules. They are the rules for all of us."

The Li-Jared who had shrunk at the news of Bria now seemed to grow taller again. "And *you* are the arbiter of the rules?"

Ruall's shiny disk spun. Stopped. Spun. Stopped. "Apparently so."

"Well—" *bong* "—who appointed *you* ruler over my life?"

Ruall spun, and spun again. "We all agreed to the mission when we left Shipworld. And now, we all must return."

"Why *all* of us?"

Ruall rang a brighter tone—*ding!*—as though she'd at last been asked a question she knew how to answer. "Because we all need to report what we've seen and heard and felt."

"About *what*?"

"About *everything*. Everything you have experienced and learned."

"That is stupid." *Bong.* "John can report on everything. Can't you, John?"

"Well, yeah, sure."

A low murmur, like steel drums, *wuh-wuh-wuh-wuh*, came from Ruall's lower body. "Please understand, I am not making this decision myself! Do you think the controllers have not thought of these possibilities?"

"Apparently—" *bong* "—not." Anger was growing visibly on Li-Jared's face as the muscles tightened around his eyes.

"Li-Jared, I ask you please to step back and look at the larger picture." *Wuh-wuh-wuh-wuh.*

"Okay, I'm stepping back," Li-Jared said, and took an actual step backward.

Ruall appeared not to notice the sarcasm in his movement. "Well, then. Remember the Mindaru. You know this well: They may be the greatest danger Shipworld, and probably the galaxy, have ever faced. Shipworld may be the only center of defense against them, the only place where knowledge of the threat is gathered. Any bit of information from any of us may prove crucial. The ruling councils need you as much as they need John Bandicut."

"Moon and stars," Li-Jared muttered. "I'll provide you anything I know. I'm not saying I'm not on your side! But I'd think you'd want me *here*—establishing a relationship with the people, and with the *leadership* of Karellia! And Uduon! Don't you want someone who knows Karellia, who can help make sure there's no backsliding with this temporal shield, help solidify the peace? Isn't that important in keeping the Mindaru away?"

Ruall's sound subsided to a soft *hummmmm.* Her polished face betrayed no emotion, but Bandicut imagined he saw pain in that metallic glow. "These are not bad ideas, Li-Jared, these things you suggest. Not bad at all. But the orders are explicit. All surviving members of the mission must return as soon as possible, to fully report any and all information."

"That's not the real reason, and I think you know it," Li-Jared said in a low voice. He began bouncing up and down lightly on the balls of his feet now.

Ruall's hum went to a buzz of distress. "Really, I have told you what I know. I am not hiding anything from you."

The Karellian clenched a fist. "You won't admit that I'm . . ." He paused and opened his fist and stared it as if his hand held the answer. His gaze flicked back up to Ruall's. "I'm Karellia's *payment* to Shipworld. Isn't that right? Shipworld saved Bandie's planet, and hired *him* on—forever, apparently—as some kind of galactic troubleshooter. Same with Ik and his planet. Well, I guess Ik's planet wasn't saved, but some of his people were. I don't know *what* my planet was saved from, if anything, before this. But you snatched me, for the same purpose. Same with Antares, I presume." Li-Jared flicked his fingers outward for emphasis. "Do I have it right so far?"

Ruall gave a shudder. She rotated out of sight for an instant, then returned. "Li-Jared, in truth I do not know. I only know our mission."

"Are you going to force me to stay on, then?" Li-Jared asked, rubbing his thumbs and fingers together in defiance. "Lock the doors of the landing craft?"

"I do not believe it will come to that. But I ask you to remember all that Shipworld has done for Karellia. Defense against the Mindaru, and end to a war . . ."

Li-Jared stretched his arms open. "Yes, of course, and we are deeply grateful."

A single metallic tap, *ding.* "Your homeworld, and the Uduon world—you want them under the protection of the Shipworld fleet, don't you?"

Li-Jared drew back in obvious shock. "Am I *hearing* you right? Are you threatening *attack?*"

Rapid tapping on cymbals, *ting ting ting ting.* "Of course not. But the primary mission here is complete. The time distortion has ended. The only *necessity* for the fleet to stay for is to offer protection against Mindaru stragglers, and optionally, to offer transport between the two worlds, and to facilitate better relations." Ruall paused. "Does Shipworld have an obligation to remain?"

"*Mokin' foke*—" Li-Jared whispered, using the human imprecation with more power than Bandicut ever had "—is this the kind of thing you hold over the heads of every world you help? Are you exacting some kind of *tax* for our defense? Is that it?"

Ruall rasped and muttered. Bandicut felt his stones struggling to get the translation right. "*Quid pro quo?*" he asked. "One for the other? A life of service, for the safety of a world?"

"Yes," Li-Jared answered bitterly. "That's it exactly."

"Truly, I do not know." Ruall pinged several times, spun and stopped sideways, nearly invisible. Slowly, then, she rotated back. "I know only that we all suffer losses."

Li-Jared squinted hard. "You lost Bria. I know. I'm sorry. And John lost Charli."

Soft gong. "Yes."

"And that's . . . *heartbreaking*. But it doesn't answer my question: Do you ever let *anyone* return to their homeworld, once you've—" *bwang* "—pinched them away?"

In answer, Ruall made a *wow*'ing sound that grew louder and louder until Li-Jared and Bandicut both clamped their hands over their ears. Then the Tintangle blinked out of sight, leaving them standing speechless.

The second meeting with Torno and his staff, later in the day, kept Bandicut focused on introducing Quin and Akura to the Skakolloan squadron leader and the other ship commanders. He was learning about them as he went, though he expected to have little use for any of this knowledge once they left Karellia behind. After a time, he became aware that Li-Jared was not in the meeting room, nor was Ruall. Cocking an ear toward the door, he thought he heard them arguing, out in the passageway. He felt a deep pang for Li-Jared, whose request he thought was perfectly reasonable, though he hated the idea of leaving his friend behind.

"Is something wrong?" Torno asked, turning his canine face toward Bandicut. His eyes bulged as usual.

Bandicut wasn't sure what to say.

Torno's bushy eyebrows twitched. "Is it that your crewmate Li-Jared does not want to leave?"

"How did you know that?"

The Skakolloan blew out a fishy-smelling breath through his whiskers. "He has been audible for some time now."

"Can you blame him?" Ocellet Quin asked—sounding, Bandicut thought, more than a little annoyed. "His people are here."

"Ah yes," Torno said, fluttering his whiskers again. "His original people are here. But his people *now* are at Shipworld."

"No, but don't you see—?"

"I think you misunderstand," Torno said sharply. "His people at Shipworld *need* him to come back. It is not a matter of wanting to control his life, or of exacting some—feh!—some tax for our services." He paused to pick delicately at his teeth with a hairy hand.

"Then what—?" Quin began.

"It is," Torno said, "a matter of the very livelihood and stability of Shipworld itself."

Bandicut started to protest, but Torno waved him to silence. "You see, Shipworld holds in protectorate many, many worlds throughout the galaxy. Thousands of worlds, probably. I do not know the actual number. Mostly this is at a distance, with little or no contact. But for each of these it must have a base of information, knowledge, tools with which to understand the people, insights to guide actions that might be needed in the future."

"So?" Bandicut said. "There is a wealth of knowledge to be gained right here! Li-Jared *here* could do so much!"

"That is true. But is that the greatest need of Shipworld? You see, they must think about all these worlds—not just as individuals, but all together, and . . ." Torno paused and stroked his snout. "Well. Do you know really what the purpose of Shipworld is?"

"I—" Bandicut opened his hands. "As far I can tell, it exists to rescue planets in distress—or maybe that's just a hobby. It apparently provides shelter for displaced—"

"Yes, yes!" Torno snorted. "That much anyone can see! But it's more than a protector of *worlds*. Shipworld is a lifeboat! That is how I see it."

"A lifeboat for *what?*" That came from a new voice. Li-Jared had stalked up in the middle of Torno's discourse, and now he was waving a hand under the nose of the Skakolloan. "If we're not saving worlds—"

"We *are* saving worlds—when we can. But more than that, we're saving *civilization itself!*" Torno barked. "Not just individual civilizations like yours—or yours—" he pointed to Bandicut "—or mine." He reared his head back, and his teeth showed. "Yes, my world was imperiled by a radiation storm, and most died. But my ancestors came to Shipworld, and that is where they have made themselves a part of a larger civilization."

Li-Jared stared at him.

As Bandicut too struggled to absorb that, he felt a nudge from his stones, reminding him of his own situation. He had offered his life, and then his service, in order to save Earth from annihilation from a rogue comet. It had seemed a bitter but acceptable trade at the time. Was this so different? Who could say? He had never had the option to visit his homeworld again. "So," he began cautiously, "you're trying to say that we're just being petty—"

"Not petty! You have your rightful concerns."

"Parochial, then?"

Torno appeared to struggle with the translation. "Not that, no."

"What, then?" Li-Jared cried.

Torno flung his arms wide—and they were long arms. "*Big picture!* You must think of the big picture! We are trying to protect *intelligent civilization* from possible extinction!"

Bandicut blinked at that. "Possible extinction? All of us? From what cause? I can see any particular world blowing up. Or the Mindaru or something like them killing us. But—"

"Yes, it could be that! It could be anything. Galactic core explosion. Galactic merger—and we have one of those coming up, you know, in just a few million years!"

"So, *really* big picture," Bandicut murmured, as Li-Jared made a sound somewhere between a snort and a burp.

Torno's eyes bulged even more than usual out of his terrier face. "Really big picture," he agreed. "And that is why, in the end, what they really care about is gathering and protecting knowledge and wisdom."

"Well, that's just—" Li-Jared began.

"That's just what I was trying to say but did not know how," gonged another voice, and Bandicut turned, startled to see that Ruall had also floated up to join the conversation.

Li-Jared looked startled, too, and for a moment, he seemed about to flare up. But then he let his breath out, half-closed his eyes, and said softly, as though to no one in particular, "I am not so sure how much any of them know about wisdom." And with that he walked silently from the room, not pausing even for an outstretched hand from Ocellet Quin.

CHAPTER 33

Many Departures

DAKOTA CAME OVER with the *Plato* ground team the following ship-day, to confer with everyone one last time before *Plato* departed for the starstream. Due to *Plato*'s slower cruising speed compared to *The Long View*'s, they were leaving first with a planned rendez-vous point not far from the starstream.

Dakota stayed after the rest of her crew had returned to *Plato*, and Copernicus reconfigured the meeting room into a more inti-mate den for them. Coffee steamed from a pot on the side table, which caught Dakota's eye. "I nearly gave up coffee a couple of hundred years ago, because it seemed like a lost art." She bent and inhaled the vapors. "This smells better than the stuff we drink on *Plato*—and it comes from Shipworld!"

Bandicut laughed and poured two cups. "It wasn't easy, get-ting to this from what they first served me. The first few attempts were pretty awful. But I have to tell you, I got a rush drinking the real thing over on *Plato*. You don't think yours is better? Milk?"

"Nope. This beats ours, hands down. Milk, yes." She took her cup and sat in one of the armchairs Copernicus had created for them. An *Eames* chair, the robot had called it. She was dressed in dark blue uniform slacks and blouse, and looked every bit the competent officer. Bandicut thought her eyes looked tired. It had been a hectic visit planetside to Karellia, they had all agreed, since they were trying to pack a full "first contact" visit into just a couple of days. It had been fascinating, though no one cared to guess how long it would take before a return expedition would be sent.

"I'd invite you one more time to come back to humanity with us," Dakota said, "but I hear they wouldn't let you off this boat even if you wanted to come." Her voice was joking, but in her gaze he saw worry. Was her uncle being held against his will? she seemed to be wondering.

"That got around fast," Bandicut said, surprised but not *that* surprised. "Anyway, I'd *love* to see your world, but I do have, er, two ladies waiting for me. I hope."

"Two ladies? You *sure* you want to go?" she teased.

He laughed. "Point taken. Are you sure you don't want to come see Shipworld? Lots of men there. Well, males. Some of them even bipeds. Anyway, the view is spectacular."

Dakota grinned, but there was a crease of pain across her brow. She gave a heavy sigh. He could almost see a vision of that boy-friend back home in her eyes. What was his name? *Better be worthy of her,* Bandicut thought. "Sorry, I'm giving you a hard time. But it really is a wrench to see you go, after all these centuries."

Dakota said nothing for a moment. She seemed to be swallow-ing hard. "Yes," she said finally, so softly he leaned forward to hear, after the syllable was spoken.

"Yeh." He sipped his coffee. He had trouble swallowing, too, because of the constriction in his throat. He barked a laugh. "This is just great! I invite you over for a last family visit, and I feel as if I've brought you over for a funeral instead!"

She echoed his laugh. "Uncle John, do you remember when I was little, and you used to ask me what I wanted to be if I grew up? *If* I grew up?"

He searched his memory. Had he asked her that way? He wasn't sure, but he wouldn't have put it past himself. "I guess so," he said.

She peered over the top of her cup at him, eyes twinkling. "Well, do you know how many years I fretted over that? Because I thought you meant, I might not *live to grow up!*"

He stared back at her in horror. "You mean I *traumatized* you by saying that?"

"*Yes! Yes, you did!*" She rocked back in laughter. "Oh God—for years you did! I'm glad I can laugh about it now!" She clinked her cup down and wiped tears from her eyes. Then she leaned forward and reached to take his hands. "Oh, you were a good uncle—*are* a good uncle—but man, you could be exasperating, even to a kid." She rose up, bent forward, and kissed him lightly on the cheek. "I am so going to miss you, too."

At the airlock, Dakota turned one last time to face her uncle. She put her hands on his shoulders. Her eyes shone bright. "Write me, okay? Send a message if you hear of any more missions from Shipworld to the starstream. No—don't write. Come! Okay?"

"Okay," he said huskily. He didn't know why, but he couldn't help feeling somehow that this parting was his fault. *Hold it together. Who's the strong uncle here?*

"You think there's any chance of that happening, ever?" she asked.

"Who knows?" he said, with a chuckle that turned into a shiver of sadness. "Who would have thought we'd meet up here at Karellia, of all places?"

"True." She squeezed him close for a hug, and they held each other for a long moment. When they stepped apart, their hands catching, there was a sudden ripple of connection between his stones and hers, an electric tingle that went up his arms. "Whoa!" she cried, letting go with a laugh. "Be good!" she said, and stepping back toward the connection tunnel, blew him a kiss. Then she turned and floated back to *Plato*.

Bandicut rubbed his wrists as he watched her disappear with a final wave into the other ship's airlock. So far as he knew, no images or memories had passed in that brief connection of the translator-stones. But *something* had. Maybe the stones were wrapping up their own conversation? He would have to ask them later.

Once she was back inside her ship, and both hatches closed, he whispered to Copernicus, "Release the crossover tube." And he turned and headed back for the bridge.

Forty-five minutes later, he watched in the viewspace as *Plato* started her maneuvering engines and moved slowly away from *The Long View*. When she was sufficiently clear, *Plato*'s main engines lit up, rippling violet, and she accelerated away toward the dark emptiness of interstellar space. Bandicut swelled with pride and wistfulness, watching it go. Unlike the ship that carried him, *Plato* was the work of human hands and human ingenuity. It did him good to see how far human space-faring technology had come since his departure, and that slightly softened the blow of seeing Dakota depart.

The two Uduon were the next to go. The Shipworld frigate *Stem* had sent a small craft over to fetch them. Li-Jared saw the two off, after Bandie and Quin had said their good-byes. Li-Jared wasn't especially in the mood to be nice—he was still furious at Ruall— but he had grown closer to Akura and Sheeawn than anyone else on the ship, and it only seemed right.

He knew he was being stiff and awkward, and his hearts were pounding out of sync because of all that was on his mind. Akura sensed his mood and made no attempt at conversation. But when they faced each other at the airlock door, she took his hands and said, "Li-Jared, I am sorry for your troubles. Truly. I feel honored to know you, and I thank you for helping us to end this war and avoid a terrible catastrophe. If you do chance to come this way again, it would gladden me to see you. Any time." And as he stood speechless and trembling with conflicting emotions, she drew him close and pressed her forehead to his. That contact made something surge through him. He didn't know what, but his hearts fell back into rhythm, and he immediately felt calmer.

When she stepped away and raised her hood, he was able to whistle in gladness, and even give Sheeawn a genuine nod of affection. Then they were gone, and Li-Jared was on his way back to prepare to say good-bye to the Ocellet Quin.

She was waiting in the common room, sipping tea and talking to Bandicut. She touched his arm as he slid into the seat next to her. "Bandie John and I were just discussing whether or not there might someday be regular travel, or at least communication between Karellia and Shipworld. Our discussion was inconclusive. What do you think?"

Li-Jared flicked his fingers in a shrug. "They wouldn't tell *us*, even if they were thinking of it."

"That's exactly what Bandie said."

At that, Bandicut chuckled and stood up. "I'm going to let the two of you talk. Your shuttle will be docking soon."

Quin's gaze followed Bandicut as he left the commons room. Then she shifted around the little table to face Li-Jared more directly. "He is a good friend, I think."

"That is so," Li-Jared acknowledged. *Though he could have done more to stand up for me.*

Quin's gaze was intense now. "You would do well, I think, to give weight to that friendship."

"Given the circumstances—"

"*Especially* given the circumstances," Quin said. "You need your friends more than ever."

Li-Jared gave his fingers a little flick, a shrug.

Quin eyed him. "Li-Jared, I am heartbroken that you need to leave. But please don't—"

He clapped a hand to his chest, wincing at a stab of pain.

"*Li-Jared, are you all right?*"

He grunted and lowered his hand. The pain had diminished to a burning sensation near his breastbone. *Wait, don't tell me—*

Please hold still a moment, said his knowing-stones.

He did so, thinking, *If one of my hearts is going, they can help me.*

Don't be dramatic. We've done this before.

Oh . . .

"*Li-Jared—*" Quin began, and was taking a breath, probably to call out for help, when two sparks of light flew out from Li-Jared's chest and embedded in precisely the same spot in Quin's, right over the breastbone. She yelped, started to cry out, and then sank back in her seat, looking stunned. After a moment, she put a hand over her breastbone, felt what was there, and tried to look down to see it.

Li-Jared gasped, the pain abruptly gone; and, fearfully, he looked across to see if Quin was okay.

She is fine.

Indeed she was, with two new daughter stones gleaming just below her throat. "I think—" he said, and then they both half leaned and half fell forward toward each other, their arms going around each other's necks for support; and Li-Jared felt their stones link together, sharing a final cascade of knowledge . . .

Quin's shuttle docked soon thereafter, and Li-Jared walked her to the entry, his head aswarm with the images and memories that had crossed between them. Bandicut, on saying his good-bye, had seen the new daughter-stones gleaming but said nothing to either of them. Li-Jared didn't want to speak of it just now.

"Farewell, and be well," Quin said to him, and he squeezed her hands hard, and then watched her board the Shipworld shuttle that would take her down to Karellendon and her staff and the Council, and all the Karellians who would have to make sense of what was happening to their world. On the bridge, he stood watching in the viewspace until long after the shuttle had dwindled to invisibility.

"Copernicus," he said, not turning, "do you think we did all right on this mission?"

"Co-Captain Li-Jared," answered the robot, rolling up beside him. "I think we did very well."

"I guess it will be one hell of a story to tell Ik when we get back."

"Hell of a story for sure," said Copernicus.

The Long View's own departure seemed almost anticlimactic after the others. After a final palaver over the comm with Torno and the rest of the squadron leaders, Bandicut gave a nod to Copernicus. He looked out to see that *The Long View* was gliding past and away from the Shipworld fleet like a silent train accelerating out of a station. Soon enough they were plowing through the waves of n-space, on their way to the starstream.

Bandicut spent much of the trip sitting by himself in the lounge, staring out at the nothingness of n-space, and thinking about those they had lost or left behind. The vessel felt empty without the Uduon and Karellian passengers. And without Bria. And Charli. As they came closer and closer to the starstream, he started to think more about those he hoped to see soon.

Li-Jared remained in his cabin for most of the flight out. He spoke little to Bandicut and not at all to Ruall. But when the glowing thread of the starstream became visible ahead, Bandicut asked Copernicus to call him. After some delay, the Karellian appeared on the bridge. He no longer looked angry, exactly, but his countenance was muted. Ruall wasn't on the bridge; she was out of the ship, searching for any echo of Bria. No one expected her to find any—Dark was quite clear about what she had seen—but no one, or certainly not Bandicut, begrudged her a final search. After all, no one had expected Charli to be alive still, either.

"What do you need?" Li-Jared asked, gazing forward with his hands on his hips in a humanlike fashion.

Bandicut walked up and stood beside him with his arms folded across his chest. "I thought we might need your brains, Li-Jared." He tipped his head and angled a glance at his shipmate. There was no crack in the Karellian's stolid expression. "We're beginning a search for any hint that Bria might have survived in some form. You aren't mad at Bria, are you?"

"Only for dying," Li-Jared muttered.

Bandicut nodded. Hard to argue with that. "We're also looking for *Plato*. We're close to the rendezvous point." Such as it was. It was pretty hard to specify a parking orbit out here with no close reference points. Dark should be able to find them, though, once they dropped out of n-space. She'd better.

Dark did. *Plato* arrived a little after *The Long View*, coming out of k-space far enough away that *The Long View* probably would have missed them, but well within Dark's sensitivity range. Due to their significant velocities, they did not attempt to bring the ships within visual range, but they did establish holo-communication. The starstream itself had grown to an endless, luminous tube arrowing from one end of infinity to the other. It finally looked large enough to hold their spaceships.

The holo sprang to life in the center of the viewspace. *"Greetings again, Captain Bandicut,"* said Captain Brody, his image distorting just a bit in the display. *"I trust your flight was satisfactory. Have you had any success in mapping a way back into the starstream?"*

Bandicut answered, "Dark says she can lead us both in, but one at a time. She'll take you in first." Getting into the stream was only half the challenge. Since the starstream was a highly elongated, closed loop of highly stressed space, the boundary between the inbound and outbound streams might be a tricky thing to negotiate. They were putting complete trust in Dark for this.

"Quite acceptable, and we thank you. May I pass communication over to my Executive Officer?"

"Please. Safe voyage, Captain," said Bandicut, and then Brody stepped out of view.

"Captain and Uncle, I'm glad to see you safely here," said Dakota, radiant even in the holo.

"Likewise! Are you ready for a ride?"

"More than ready. Communication lock with Copernicus looks good. But I'm not yet picking up Dark."

Copernicus spoke up to answer that. "Dark has located your daughter stones . . . she says she will be making contact in a few . . ."

"Whoa!" Dakota yelped. *"She has made contact. Wow. I might need a minute to . . . never mind, she is giving me nav instructions. Looks like we will be starting our entry run in just a minute. I did not expect it so soon. We need to make a minor course correction to set up our entry."* She leaned sideways out of the picture.

Copernicus said, "Dark has mapped their entry slot based on their flight path. She's going to slip in ahead of them and create the opening."

Dakota reappeared. *"Dark is telling us to fly straight into the wall of the starstream. We detect no entry point."*

"You are just going to have to trust her. Trust Dark," Bandicut said. A band of tension once more had a grip on his chest. They were all trusting Dark to do the impossible.

"Affirmative." Dakota stepped back, out of the field of view. Then she returned to the center and said, *"Roger and wilco, Uncle John. I think this might all happen pretty suddenly, so I'm going to say good-bye, just in case. I'm so glad I saw you. All my love, and give that Li-Jared a big hug for me, all right?"*

"All right." Bandicut glanced at Li-Jared and mouthed, *I am not giving you a hug.* "Listen, kiddo. You take care out there, and I hope to see you again someday. We Shipworlders get around, especially the Bandicuts among us." He felt the stones in his wrists tingle, and knew they were exchanging a last link.

Then he saw Dark disappear into the starstream, and an instant later reappear back on the outside. She did that twice more, and then on the final time, she pulled *Plato* inside along with her. There was a tiny flash as they passed through the wall of the starstream, and *Plato* was gone.

———

Dark remained out of sight for several minutes, long enough to make Bandicut become twitchy and nervous. But finally Jeaves called out, "Dark is returning, along the outside. She stayed with *Plato* long enough to make sure she was safely on course."

"Please tell her thank-you," Bandicut murmured.

Soon Dark was back, and then it was their turn.

Dark dipped in and out a couple of times, before advising Copernicus to skate right across the inbound stream and straight into the outbound. That, she said, would be easier than circling around to the far side and altering their trajectory and momentum to go straight into the outbound stream.

Easier for Dark, perhaps. For Copernicus, the entry was a pretty piece of flying under stress. The starstream loomed before them like a streamer of clouds lit by a setting sun, expanding fast. Dark floated sideways through the streamer, and *The Long View* followed in a silent arc, lining up with Dark's point of entry, and then slipped through like a needle into a fine fabric.

It was an elegant entry.

And then they hit the first boundary layer of moving force— and the viewspace flared and a solid *whump* went through the floor, and they started shaking. "Whoops," Copernicus said, his display lights flickering madly. "Half a moment."

The shaking intensified. "Coppy?" Bandicut asked, his voice restrained but urgent. The ship jerked sharply to his left. *"Coppy?"*

"Almost there," the robot said cheerfully. "Hang on."

Almost where? Bandicut wondered, gripping the nearest support. In the viewspace, something appeared out of the whiteout— a churning plane of flickering colors, slanting toward them and then angling away as the ship jerked the other way.

"Hold tight, please!" Copernicus called—and with a last, bone-jarring *thunk!* the shaking stopped, and the ship glided on as before. The viewspace revealed the steady flow of the starstream stretching around and before them.

"We're in!" Bandicut cried. "Are we going the right direction?"

"That's not easy to tell at a glance," Copernicus answered. "But I've just finished a scan, and yes—we are."

Ruall vibrated. "Is Dark still with us?"

"Still there," said Copernicus. "She says our course looks good. She's going to scout ahead."

Not a trace of Bria did Ruall find in or out of the starstream. Riding half in and half out of the local tri-space and the surrounding n-space, she had tested splinter-space, diamond-space, and other dimensional permutations that might conceivably give echo to Bria's presence, even in her death. It was a hopeless effort. She had expected it, and so it proved.

It was a bitter conclusion, nonetheless.

———————

Bandicut hung out in the lounge, intending to eat a long-delayed meal, and found he couldn't eat. What would it have been, anyway? Lunch? Dinner? He couldn't remember. He gave up and returned to the bridge. Five minutes later, Copernicus chimed for attention and said, "I've just heard from Dark. She's made contact with Charli."

CHAPTER 34

Charli

BANDICUT FELT AN odd hiccup in his perception of time as he absorbed the news. Contact with Charli—here in the starstream, where he had lost her? It was all coming back to him, though he still couldn't remember how it had happened—whether she had jumped or been torn away by the Mindaru, or something else entirely. Even after Dark's report, he had not dared to hope to find her on their return.

But would this really be her, or just another echo of her, like Charlene-echo, lodged in the thoughts of Deep?

Ruall voiced what Bandicut could not get out. "Does Dark say whether Charli can speak?"

How am I supposed to make contact with her? /Stones? Can you help?/

We are trying.

Copernicus said, "I am trying to establish—"

And before the robot could finish, Bandicut felt a sudden fire in his wrists. A light blossomed around him, and a voice boomed in his skull.

/// John Bandicut? ///

My God! "Charli!" Bandicut shouted out loud. Jeaves and Ruall turned toward him in surprise.

He felt an explosion of joy in his chest so powerful and incandescent surely everyone on the bridge could feel it, too. /Charli!

Charli, where are you?/ He had heard her thoughts, but she was not back in his head. Where in all the starstream—?

/// John, I'm trying to focus on you.
You are in one point, but you're moving.
Keep your thoughts still, if you can. ///

His thoughts were about as still as a barroom brawl. Questions and hopes and fears were all crowding to get out at the same time. /Charli, I can't see you./

/// Don't try to locate me.
Let me locate you.
It's hard, because I am— ///

/Far away?/

/// Not exactly.
I am . . . everywhere and nowhere.
Up and down
through the starstream.
It's strange here. ///

/Strange. Yes, I can imagine,/ he whispered, although really he couldn't. Charli didn't answer right away, and for a moment, he feared he had lost the connection to the quarx. /Charli? Still there?/

/// Yes. Sorry.
I was trying something.
But the movement of your ship . . .
It takes some readjusting on my part. ///

/We're on course back to Shipworld. Charli—listen, I know I should probably build up to this, but is there any chance you could come back and join me? In my head?/

Charli's answer sounded wistful.

/// I don't think so, John.
I wish I could,

but I don't think it's possible.
I think the starstream
may be my final home. ///

Though he could not be surprised, Bandicut felt a fresh new pang of grief.

/// John, I'm glad
you were successful in your mission.
Can you tell me about it?
What about Dakota?
What was it like to visit Li-Jared's world?
Is he still with you?
Is he all right? ///

This time Bandicut sighed. /He is here. He is not too happy./

/// Tell me everything that happened. ///

Bandicut laughed briefly and spread his hands. /Where do I start?/

/// At the beginning.
From the time I saw you leave the starstream. ///

/Do you have time for a long story?/

/// John, I've got all the time
in eternity. ///

Bandicut told her everything. Not all at once, but over several days of ship-time. He spoke little to his shipmates; when he wasn't sleeping, he was usually conversing with Charli. It felt so unutterably strange with the quarx on the outside. While he was grateful for this time together, a profound sadness dominated his feelings. Charli was out there, and in a little while, they would be separated again. He missed the friend in his head more than he would ever have imagined.

They spoke only briefly about the seeming impossibility of getting back together, and then avoided the painful subject. At first he couldn't bring himself to ask about Charli's jump into the starstream. What if it had been intentional? But finally, after he had told the quarx everything that had happened—and heard in turn everything Charli could tell him about Ik and Julie—he had to ask.

/Charli, do you *like* it here in the starstream? Have you ever been—/ he hesitated, searching for words /— I don't know—glad you jumped? Or got knocked out of my head? Or *whatever* happened?/

The wave of surprise that hit him was almost physical.

/// What?
John, I didn't jump!
Not intentionally! ///

/I'm glad. Because it felt as if you did./

/// No!
I wouldn't have done that! ///

Bandicut searched back in his memory. It had been in the middle of a firefight. Chaos and confusion . . . /Are you sure? When the Mindaru was coming at us? I thought maybe you had some idea that you could—I don't know—take it on yourself or something./

/// John—
jump out of your head during a battle?
Absolutely no!
I remember stretching out toward Dark.
I was hoping to connect with her,
to find some way to help. ///

/Oh, you helped, all right, Charli! Whatever you did in that moment, it tipped the balance, and we got away. Even if it was an accident. We were deeply grateful. But also . . . / He stopped speaking for a moment, because he was getting choked up. It took him a few moments to be able to say the words. /I thought you were probably dead, or lost forever. I grieved hard for you, Charli. I truly did./ And as he spoke, he realized he was grieving all over again.

/// Oh, John—I grieved, too.
I still grieve. ///

Suddenly, from out of Bandicut's grief came an unexpected burst of satisfaction. /But Charli, we did all right! We stopped a war—and we stopped those goddamn Mindaru when they showed up! And we stopped any more of them from coming up the time-stream! At least . . . I think we did. Did we, Charli? Could you tell from where you were?/

Charli's laugh seemed to roll down the light-years.

/// I'm pretty sure you did, all right.
With help from Ik and Julie. ///

Bandicut grimaced at that, because what Charli had been able to tell him about Julie and Ik's mission seemed so strange and un-real to him. /And *you*,/ he said pointedly to the quarx. /*You* helped them in *their* need!/ Against Mindaru in the starstream! Against getting lost.

It was all making his head spin.

————————

Some amount of time had slipped by him—he didn't know how much—when he heard Charli say,

/// I really wish I could go back to Shipworld
with you. ///

Bandicut had been staring out the viewspace at the slowly passing starstream, and he started at Charli's words. /Do you, Charli? If you *could* come back and rejoin me, would you do that?/

Charli seemed surprised by his question.

/// Would I?
Of course I would! ///

/Well, I'd want you to. But are *you* sure? You've got a pretty incredible spot here—with all of creation laid out for you!/

>/// *It is an amazing view, John,*
>*but I'd much rather be with you,*
>*and with your friends.*
>*It's lonely here, John.*
>*Infinity is a very large place.* ///

Stunned, Bandicut took a few seconds to answer. His thoughts jumped around. If it was what Charli wanted, surely there was *something* they could do. Some way to make it possible for Charli to jump back into his head, and make things as they were before? He looked to his stones, to see if they had anything to say. They seemed preoccupied, buzzing with activity in a way that usually meant they were searching for a solution to a problem. /Do you think there's any way, Charli?/

>/// *It would be an extreme long-shot.*
>*But I'd like to try anyway.* ///

He felt a pulse of hope. /What would we have to do?/

Charli was silent for the better part of a minute, thinking, and then she said,

>/// *Do you suppose Ruall would be willing*
>*to help us?* ///

Ruall surprised Bandicut by, in fact, being willing to try the quarx's idea. "As long as it doesn't endanger the ship, or you," she said. Her concern for his safety surprised him a little. "You are still required back at Shipworld," she said. "If we lose you, we lose your knowledge. Just as with Li-Jared."

"Ah," he said—though he wondered if the loss of Bria had given Ruall greater sympathy for the losses of others.

The Tintangle spun, and said, "This will be a challenge. But it seems a risk worth taking."

Li-Jared, just stepping onto the bridge, glanced at them and appeared about to ask *what challenge*—but then turned and went to talk to Copernicus instead. Bandicut watched him silently. It pained him to see his friend so subdued. He was afraid the Karellian might be more than just angry with Ruall; he might be spiraling into a deep depression. Bandicut intended to keep an eye on him, though it was unclear what he could do to help.

Swinging back to Ruall, he asked, "How much time do you need to get ready?"

Ruall turned edge-on, and then back. "I am not certain. My plan is to create new channels in splinter-space. I need to consult with Copernicus."

"While you do that, I am going to have some lunch and try to prepare myself mentally."

Ruall bobbed in acknowledgment.

Bandicut walked over to Li-Jared, "Do you want to join me for some lunch?"

The Karellian twitched his hands without turning. "Already ate," he said. *Don't want to talk,* came through clear as a bell.

———

For Charli, the preparation was all mental. She decided to take a good, long look around at everything she would leave behind, if it worked. A thousand-light-year gaze down the starstream provoked the thought, *Here to eternity.* It wasn't literally, she knew, but maybe close enough. It was a hell of a view. Was she really ready to leave it behind? There were living entities in the starstream, beings she had not yet spoken to or encountered, except to hear their voices faintly in the distance. That could be a lost opportunity. But was it enough to keep her from *this* opportunity, to rejoin with John Bandicut and continue life with her friends?

No. She was sure of what she wanted.

But she wasn't so sure she could do it.

There were definite physical limitations. Her current state was unlike any she'd lived in before—diffuse and distributed across space. Could she really pull herself together enough to make the jump back to Bandicut? She didn't know. But that was why she had asked for Ruall's help. Dark might be helpful, also—but this challenge felt like something Ruall, the crafty shifter through all the layers of n-space, might be well equipped for. Charli was asking Ruall to pave her a path, to create a channel she could pull herself together in. Would it work? They would all find out together.

Even if all that was *physically* possible, could she make the mental transition back to the life she had once known so well?

There was just one way to find out.

Bandicut felt better with some food in his stomach, and when he returned to the bridge, he found Ruall waiting for him, and Li-Jared gone. "Have you consulted, and are you ready to try?" he asked Ruall. And of Charli, he asked, /Are you ready?/ And to his stones, he said, /Are *you* ready?/

Everyone was.

"Okay, how do we start?" he asked Charli, but speaking aloud so the others could hear.

Ruall began spinning, slowly at first.

Charli said,

> /// I am drawing myself toward you,
> as well as I am able.
> I will be looking for Ruall,
> to help steer me in . . . ///

Bandicut repeated the quarx's words aloud. Ruall spun faster. Gonged once. Winked out.

Ruall moved slowly, for her. She surveyed diamond-space immediately around them, and then widened her search. Then she went deeper, into flower-space, and did the same thing. And again, in splinter-space. Each form of n-space looked different, smelled different, sounded different. There was in all of them a strum of energy, a not-quite-audible singing, a hint that there was something present but invisible, waiting to be found. It rang softly around her.

Splinter-space seemed the most likely place to find the quarx, or to be able to define a pathway back to Bandicut.

As she gradually quieted her own thoughts, she discovered what she was looking for. It wasn't so much a voice as a series of ripples in the continuum, ripples that she might have missed in the general chaos of cosmic turbulence, except for a certain familiarity that lifted them out of the background. *Charli?* she thought. She didn't expect a verbal answer and didn't get one, but she felt something in the wave motion that made her certain she had found the quarx. She set about shaping the nearby layers of splinter-space in a way that might guide the ripples of the quarx toward her, and toward John.

———————

Bandicut didn't know what to expect. He felt little at first, though he was aware of Charli's efforts to move toward him. There didn't seem to be anything *he* could do, though, except to be open to her approach. Ruall was out there, doing something he couldn't follow.

Then Charli spoke:

> /// *John, I can feel you getting nearer.*
> *I'm moving along channels*
> *Ruall has created.* ///

/Can you see the ship?/

> /// *Not exactly.*
> *Solid objects are hard to see from here.*
> *Voices and thoughts are easier.* ///

/Should I keep talking? Can you home in on my voice?/

He imagined he saw her rippling across space toward him. He was sure it was just his imagination. Charli, as he knew her, was invisible; for all the time they had been together, he knew less about what Charli was actually made of than he did Dark—or Ruall.

/// Keep talking, John. ///

He was startled, realizing he had lapsed into a reverie. /Right—sorry, Charli./ He had a panicked moment of thinking there was nothing left to talk about. But he kept talking anyway. /What's it look like out there, Charli? Tell me what you're seeing. Will you know the ship when you find it? Can you pull yourself all together before you try to join?/

/// Tricky question, John.
I'm not sure. ///

/Will it be okay if some of you gets left behind?/

/// I wish I knew, John ... ///

Charli found this much harder than she had feared. It wasn't just the difficulty of trying to regather herself into a compact form, but a challenge of mental focus. She was no longer a creature tightly bound to another, but a far more cosmic being. This was not a vain sense of grandeur, but an honest appraisal of her present state. She was stretched out across the light-years in n-space, that marvel of existence that bound the stars and the galaxies together. John had considerable comprehension of space-time by human standards, but could he hold *this* in his head? Could *she* stuff her own boundaries back into the container that had once held her?

Charli had spoken the truth when she'd said she wanted to leave this and rejoin Bandicut. But it wasn't just about what she *wanted*, but about what the Charli she was now could do.

She could hear John encouraging her; she could almost feel his heart beat, the pulse in his head. Almost. She sensed Ruall here also, spinning and darting and swooping, trying to open a path for her in the local n-space.

/// John! ///

she called.

/I'm here./

Yes, he was there, and she could see him now. She imagined him leaning out of the viewspace on the bridge like the figurehead on a ship, his hair blowing in the winds of n-space, his arms extended to welcome her. Perhaps this really would work!

As she pulled herself toward that space, she felt an unmistakable *stretching*. Part of her remained anchored in the starstream, and she sought a way to release that anchor. She could stretch *from* it to John, yes. But *move* to John? She feared it would be like the way she'd put a piece of herself into Bria—shivering off a bit of herself while most of her remained whole in the starstream. That had been a work done in haste, and at need. She wanted this to be different. She didn't want to be only a shadow of herself, in both places.

Stop second guessing. She would make the jump if she could, and whatever might happen would happen.

The layers of splinter-space began to soften, allowing her to collect herself on a level where John was open to her. She felt that part of herself approaching him, and with a sudden memory of love for the human she'd come to know so well, she called out,

/// I am about to make the jump.
Be ready. Open your thoughts . . . ///

And she launched herself across the narrowing gulf.

Bandicut could not see, but felt her coming, like a magnetic field or an electric charge. /Ready,/ he whispered, and opened his thoughts.

To the translator-stones, it seemed a long shot indeed. They wanted Charli back as deeply as Bandicut did, but they were realistic. Nothing like this had ever been tried before that they knew of.

In the moment the quarx began her jump, they saw that her setup wasn't quite right. It was like watching a spacecraft heading for a bad landing in slow motion, and being unable to do a thing about it.

Bandicut felt a warmth wash over him. He closed his eyes and tried to focus on the tactile sensations. Even with his eyes closed, he was aware of the starstream, with its glowing tunnel through space and the stars. And moving invisibly across that, the quarx.

The touch in his brain was both familiar and new. There was a hint of curiosity, a waft of affection, a rumbling of uncertainty, a shining of joy and anticipation, and more—all sighing through his head like a summer breeze. He tried to catch and retain the sensations; but they whispered right through him and out again, leaving his grasp empty. His stomach lurched; alarm rang through his head.

/Charli, I couldn't get hold of you!/

Don't try, murmured his stones. *This can only work by the quarx coming to you.*

/Okay, but . . . /

The quarx's voice sounded strained.

> /// I tried, John, but I missed!
> All the twists and turns of n-space,
> and trying to make myself small again—
> I've never done this before! ///

/But you can do it, can't you?/

> /// I am trying again . . . ///

/Yes! Keep trying!/ It was hard to stay quiet and receptive, though. It was like trying to listen to an intricate symphony when his head was full of thumping rock refrains. The quarx's thoughts circled around him, and he could feel them but couldn't read them. Open. Be open. Be receptive.

John.

He could feel the stones trying to calm him, but this was so personal, so connected to his heart and soul and not just his mind . . . he was revving up internally. *Breathe deep. Nice and slow. Calm down.* That worked for a moment, perhaps two. But then the calm skittered away.

/// John, I'm lining up again.
Imagine you're a carrier deck and
I'm a flyer coming in hot and low.
You have to stay as steady as possible,
all right? ///

/Yes,/ he whispered.

She was so close now . . . closer . . . but she was veering, or he was. He *had* to somehow reach out and grab her! /Stones, help me!/

The stones were trying, but whatever Charli was doing, they couldn't follow.

He reached out, from a tottering ladder balancing in an earthquake . . .

The ladder twisted away. Charli missed again; and Bandicut was falling . . .

Space fell apart in diamond shards of light, and now he was spinning in weightlessness, out of control . . .

He blacked out, maybe just for a second. Black, then light, then blank, then noise. Charli called in distress, from far away, and Ruall clanged in frustration, and then the bridge of the starship was spinning and flipping around him.

Charli felt the momentary connection, but it skittered away from her. It was infuriating to realize she did not know how to do this, did not know how to transport herself from where she was in the stream to where she wanted to be. On top of that, John was a *lot* shakier than she had hoped. Shakier in a way that made her afraid he was—*Oh John, no*—

The silence-fugue stole over him with a hiss and a shake and a whisper of chaos.

No . . . no . . . no . . . he hadn't fallen into silence-fugue in ages! It wasn't supposed to happen anymore! *Couldn't* be happening! He needed Charli to help him!

Charli's voice was there, coasting by like roller-skates on a ramp, moving rapidly out of reach . . . Calling to him, calling to John . . . and then gone.

Was John here? Who was home? Anyone in charge? The loss of control was terrifying.

The windows blew open onto space. He could see everything, everywhere. He was himself stretched out into n-space, embracing the cosmos. *He could stay here forever!* His grip on the deck of the starship was slipping away, and he floated out into the mesmerizing bands of flower-space and splinter-space. *So beautiful!* Heartbreaking luminous clouds of color, and shards of jewel-like radiation . . .

But he couldn't hold on. Charli was slipping away.

Charli's grip on the center could not hold. Her attachment to Bandicut could not hold. *Why was this so hard?* Because she had changed too much here in the starstream, and she could no longer make the connections? Having come so close . . . to his mind, his heart, close enough to *almost* reconnect, she couldn't hold on; she was falling away.

Failure burned in her heart. She cried out:

/// John, I haven't the strength!
Can you catch me? ///

But she already knew the answer. Even as she caromed away, she could see him falling deeper into the grip of silence-fugue. *No, John . . .* So many times she had been there to help pull him out of the fugue state—and now, when he needed it the most, she could do nothing.

Ruall, watching from the altered space outside, saw it happen as though in slow motion. She didn't understand it all, but she wondered: Was this the silence-fugue she had heard him speak of? She knew it was dangerous, and sometimes his friends had to help pull him out of it. Could Charli help? Unlikely. Ruall couldn't *see* Charli, though she had felt the movement of the quarx's consciousness nearby—but that was before and not now.

The rejoining wasn't working.

Uncertain what to do, Ruall circled the ship, and then darted back into the bridge, spinning out into four-space near Bandicut. His face seemed stretched and distended, as if he was trying to cry out, but couldn't. He was clearly in great distress. His arms were waving in front of him; he was reaching frantically toward the front of the viewspace.

"John Bandicut!" Ruall clanged. "Can you report?"

The human gave no sign of hearing. He was whispering urgently, over and over, *"Charli—Charli—!"*

Ruall spun, seriously worried now. She snapped a request to Copernicus: "Can you make contact with him?" And to Jeaves, the same question.

Copernicus rolled in front of Bandicut. "Cap'n! Cap'n, can you hear me? What is happening, John Bandicut?" In response, Bandicut shied away, shielding his eyes. He kept whispering to Charli.

Jeaves floated past Copernicus and faced Bandicut. He carefully caught Bandicut's arms in his mechanical hands. "John Bandicut, breathe deeply and listen to my voice!"

Copernicus said to Ruall, "He appears to be experiencing silence-fugue. I do not know how to help him. Li-Jared might. Can we call him to the bridge?"

"At once!" Ruall clanged.

Li-Jared heard the call through a fog of fatigue layered with resentment and self-pity. He had not been sleeping well since their departure from Karellia. He knew there was nothing to be gained from nursing a grudge, but knowing that and being able to stop it were two different things. He even resented Bandicut, who had played no role in the decision against his staying at Karellia; but again, just knowing didn't help.

When a call came from Copernicus to come to the bridge at once, he flicked his fingers and ignored it. To hell with them. If they really needed him, they could come to him.

Which, to his astonishment, they did. The door alarm sounded, and he ignored it. Then came a tapping, and Copernicus's voice saying through the door, "Li-Jared, we need you! Urgently! John Bandicut is in distress!"

Bandicut in distress? That was odd. Li-Jared got up from the end of his sleep mat, where he had been trying a meditation technique that Ik had tried to teach him. Muttering a curse, he started toward the door—just as a shadow passed through the wall and Ruall spun into view right in front of him. "Ruall! What are you doing in here? This is my private cabin."

Ruall clanged loudly—painfully—enough to make Li-Jared clap his hands over his ears. "Li-Jared, John Bandicut may be experiencing a severe form of silence-fugue. He needs our help!"

"Fugue! Ahh . . ." Li-Jared winced and began shoving on his shoes. "What can I do? I don't know how to bring him out of silence-fugue! The quarx always did that!" He stormed out past Ruall.

Ruall clanged after him. "Yes, but he was attempting to reconnect with the quarx. That may have been what caused it!"

"Moon and stars!" Li-Jared rumbled, striding onto the bridge right behind Copernicus.

What he found was John on the deck on his hands and knees, weeping. *Weeping?* Li-Jared had no idea what to do with *that.* Every few seconds, Bandicut groped with one hand toward the viewspace, crying out something largely incomprehensible, except for the name *Charli.* After a few moments of that, Bandicut would lower his shaking hand and bow his head. Then it all started up again.

Li-Jared opened his fingers to Copernicus, who was clearly waiting for him to respond. "I see it. But what do you want me to do? I don't know how to stop it!"

Jeaves floated forward. "Talk to him, Li-Jared. You are his best friend on this ship. *Talk* to him."

Talk to him? Li-Jared thought, and his gaze clouded with darkness. *Did anyone talk to* me *when I needed it? Why, sure they did. "You're needed on Shipworld, Li-Jared." "The situation is unfortunate, but it is what it is, Li-Jared." "There's nothing we can do to change it, Li-Jared."* Yes, everyone had been *so* helpful. *Bong.*

"Can't *you* talk to him?" he asked Jeaves, and then turned and gestured the same question to Copernicus.

"Yes, but we are inorganics," Copernicus said. "I don't think it is the same with norgs. You are organic, and you are his *friend.*"

At that second assertion that he was a *friend,* Li-Jared felt a sharp twinge. It was true, Bandicut was his friend and really his only friend on this ship now—organic, anyway. He sighed and crouched beside Bandicut, touching his shoulder, afraid to do anything that might send the human deeper into the fugue. "John! *Bandie, can you hear me?* It's Li-Jared! Can you talk to me?"

Raising his head, Bandicut wailed, "She's gone! Charli's gone! Gone forever on the winds of time! Eternity for Charli!"

Moon and stars, this man was in deep. Li-Jared leaned down closer to meet Bandicut's eyes. "John—I know. I know Charli's gone. She's in the starstream. I'm sorry."

"Gone forever," Bandicut sighed, giving no sign of recognizing Li-Jared's presence. Tears were streaming down his face; his eyes were glassy.

Rocking back, Li-Jared turned and stared out into space with Bandicut. He could almost feel Bandicut's pain, as an ache in his own chest. He could feel his own knowing-stones buzzing next to his breastbone, trying to stir him into some kind of action. But what? And then he thought: *Knowing-stones!* The idea dropped like a rock in his mind, and he recoiled from it. Let his stones link with John's? That could be a terrible risk—to both of them. Did he want to take that on? Let Bandie's fugue touch him that directly?

Copernicus rolled forward toward him, but the norg didn't have to speak. *Your only friend. And he needs you.*

Li-Jared swore and swung around in front of Bandicut. He put his face right up to Bandie's and grabbed Bandicut's arms, slid his hands to Bandicut's wrists. *"Bandie!"* he yelled. *"Listen to me!"* And when Bandicut didn't respond, Li-Jared gripped the human's wrists with all of this strength—and then slapped them hard against his own breastbone, where his knowing-stones burned.

The effect was electric. Bandicut jerked, and his eyes snapped shut, and then sprang open wide. He opened his mouth to speak, but all that came out was a gasp.

A sheet of white noise flashed across Bandicut's mind, cutting off whatever thought was there. His brain wheezed, grasping for the intense focus of a moment ago. But too late—those thoughts were gone now. In their place came the words of the stones: *Hold tight to us. We will not let you fall.*

His reaction came in a silent shout, because he felt more than just his own translator-stones. He felt *Li-Jared's,* as well. *What was Li-Jared doing in his thoughts?*

Before he could fully frame that question, he heard Li-Jared's words, coming maybe from this crazy Karellian face in front of him and maybe through the meeting of the stones—but either way, they had too much force behind them to ignore: *John Bandicut, do not give in to the darkness! We need you too much, my friend! Come back to us!*

The sheer force of the words rocked him back, but so did the meaning. *We need you too much, my friend . . .*

My friend? Of course Li-Jared was his friend, but he had been so angry.

But he had come to John in his need . . . in his silence-fugue. *Silence-fugue.*

Something clicked, and snapped, and ratcheted into place. *He had been in silence-fugue.* Really deep silence-fugue. He squinted and remembered what he'd seen outside the viewspace: the vastness and the emptiness and Charli somewhere in it. Just that recollection was almost enough to flip him over again, but Li-Jared had an iron grip on him, both physically on his wrists, and intangibly through his stones. Flipping back into the fugue was just not going to happen; Li-Jared was small, but right now his mass was enough to hold John firm. Silence-fugue was over.

Bandicut hissed out the breath he'd been holding and relaxed a little, and was finally able to focus his eyes on the face poised grimly in front of him. "Li-Jared!" he gasped. "You stopped it. You pulled me out. Thank you!"

"Are you all right, Bandie?" Li-Jared asked.

He had to think for a moment. He was all right, yes. But . . .

Charli was gone. Charli had failed. The quarx's presence was no longer there; it was blown away like smoke into the infinite silence and dark.

CHAPTER 35

Homecoming

AS THEIR FLIGHT up the timestream blurred to a stop, Julie felt something wrong. The connection with Antares had shredded away. It was gone. She sensed that she and Ik had *missed* something, a target maybe; she felt they had overshot, as if they were on skates, and an outstretched hand had tried to catch them, but couldn't hold on. She also sensed that some part of herself nearby, her physical body, was alive but strangely inert.

Her thoughts felt weirdly frozen in that moment.

Time stuttered . . . stopped . . . then started again.

And then something glowed around her like a halo. The unpleasant separation evaporated, replaced by a wholeness she'd almost forgotten, her own body around her, organic and breathing. But it was also struggling ferociously on the inside, jarred out of an unnatural slumber.

The powerlessness gave way, and she snapped her eyes open and rasped a searing breath. Her throat was bone dry. Her vision swam, and she fought to focus on something in front of her, cream-colored and smooth. It was the inner-eggshell of the launch-pod in which she had lain since departure. A couch pressed against her back, and a headrest behind her head. She was back. She was in the exact place where she'd begun her journey.

She forced her head to the left. Ik's pale visage gazed back at her from the other couch. He made a hoarse sound and rubbed his temples, wincing. "You okay?" she managed, her voice a sand-paper whisper.

His reply, "*Hrah*," was equally rough, but affirmative. They were home again. They had returned alive. As if in response to the thought, the pod over her head cracked open, admitting light. A shape bobbed against the opening, the silhouette of a head. She strained to recognize the shape. It was the spidery creature who'd buckled them in, a billion years ago. "Enwin!" she wheezed.

Enwin breathed a noisy sigh of relief. "You are alive, thank the One!"

Ik responded, hacking. "Hrrm, of course we are alive!"

Enwin made a buzzing sound. "We were not certain." Her face was in shadow, but she was hissing in agitation.

"What, hrahhh-h-h, do you mean?"

Enwin spoke to someone outside, then said calmly to Julie and Ik, "You have been . . . *frozen lifeless* . . . for so long."

"*What? Frozen? How long?*" Julie's voice cracked, and she dry-swallowed, then sipped water from a tube Enwin guided to her lips. She had a sudden, jarring thought. She found her voice again, though it remained husky. "Is Antares here? She came and found us! She brought us back! Is she okay?"

"She is safe," Enwin said. "She is on her way here. She has been waiting anxiously for you to emerge. As all of us have."

Julie stared at her, thoughts spinning. "You said we were frozen?"

Enwin's spidery fingers worked at Julie's harness. "More like paralyzed, I told them. Near-dead, others said."

Julie shuddered. "*How long?*"

Enwin finally got the harness loose. "It has been forty-two days since you entered the device. Thirty-seven, since your last communication from the ghoststream."

Julie raised her head to stare at the creature. The effort hurt. *Forty-two days.* She remembered the feeling of skidding, over-shooting . . .

"And thirty-four since . . . Antares emerged."

Something in Enwin's voice was troubling. "What about Antares? What aren't you telling us?"

"Just that—" and Enwin drew back "—oh, it will all be explained in the debriefing."

"What about Antares?"

Enwin sighed. "She returned safely, but before you. It will all be told. They are eager to hear your story."

That was all Enwin would say. There was a great deal of commotion around getting them out of the pod. They were hustled off for medical evaluations which, to Julie, seemed of dubious value. How many doctors on Shipworld knew anything about human physiology? All she wanted was a good, long drink of water. But she was arguing against a tide. A swarm of cyberdocs and scanners and living docs surrounded them. The examination took forever, evaluating both their physical and their mental states. Fair enough, but why were the docs so concerned about the manner of their return? Julie tried to ask, but the docs were useless as a source of information.

"We overshot, didn't we? Into the future?"

"Yes, but, well . . . Cromus is really the one to talk to . . ."

"And what happened here—while we were in the future?"

"Nearly null autonomic function . . ."

"You mean we were dead? Almost dead?"

"Difficult to say exactly. More trancelike . . ."

Voices and tempers rising. "We were in some kind of goddamn temporal stasis, weren't we? Our bodies were waiting to catch up in time with our minds. Is that it? Is that what happened?"

"That is a likely hypothesis. Are you feeling emotional distress arising from the experience?"

"I wasn't before, but I am now. What about Antares? What happened to her?"

"You will see her soon. Now, please, we need to go over one more set of parameters . . ."

"You know, I think I've given you all the parameters you're going to get. Take these goddamn monitors off me. I want to see my friend."

"Really, it would be better . . ."

Her outburst inspired Ik, whose voice was louder. Finally the docs grudgingly pronounced them fit for debriefing, and fit to travel from the launch station back to the main control center. A shuttle was waiting.

"And our friend?" Julie asked.

"She arrived with the shuttle. She is coming to join you."

Julie squinted past the crowd of alien techs and workers. "Hrah!" said Ik, raising his arm and pointing. Julie finally spotted them—first Napoleon, and then Antares. With Ik right behind, she pushed past the docs to get to them.

Antares looked tired but happy. Julie cried out, and Antares rushed to embrace them both. Antares felt thin to her, and there wasn't quite the warmth Julie expected. Clearly Antares was emotionally exhausted, probably from the ordeal of waiting to see if her friends had survived.

"You brought us home!" Julie sighed, releasing her embrace. *What did it cost you?* She said softly, "Antares, thank you. Are *you* all right? You look like you've been through—"

"Not here," Antares whispered. She was visibly subdued. "Tell me, both of you! You are well?"

Before either could speak, Napoleon surged forward, clicking loudly, and exclaimed, "Ik and Lady Julie, I am pleased beyond measure to welcome you back! Lady Antares and I were terribly concerned for you."

"Napoleon!" Julie cried. "Am I glad to see you, too, old friend." She felt an urge to hug him, too, but settled for pressing her hand to his metallic shoulder and bending close. She was genuinely moved to see the robot again. She was willing to bet he had been working in his own way to bring them home.

Antares led the way to a marginally secluded spot where they could talk for a few minutes, much as they had done the first time Ik and Julie had returned. "Did they tell you what happened when the ghoststream brought you back?" Antares asked, her voice a papery whisper.

Julie snorted. "You'd have thought we were so top-secret we weren't cleared to know our own lives. But we *think* we *overshot* the present point on our return and skidded into the future. While our bodies—"

"Hrah!" Ik rasped. "Our bodies were in the launcher and couldn't catch up. They could only wait for the *time* to catch up with where we were." He said it calmly, but Julie saw him shiver.

Antares closed her eyes, as though reliving something too painful to describe. "I'm so sorry. I brought you back too fast, and I couldn't hold onto you. I couldn't bring you in for a landing. I *tried* to slow you down, to keep you from overshooting. I just couldn't do it." She gasped for breath. "For a long time, I thought I might have killed you."

She was shaking, and Julie put out a hand to steady her. "Hey! We're okay. *You saved us!*" Julie let out a wheezing, sardonic laugh. "I guess we're lucky they didn't decide to dissect us, to see why we weren't moving."

Antares shuddered again. "I think some of them wanted to."

Napoleon raised both arms to a crossed position in front of him. "That," he said, with sharp, clear enunciation, "would not have happened. Not on my watch."

"*Bless* you, Napoleon," Julie said, and this time she really did hug his metal frame.

"No, Napoleon," Antares said. "Not on my watch, either." She glanced sideways at the mission staff who were waiting for them. "And now, we are all to board the shuttle. While we're en route, I want to hear what happened. Everything. Are you tired? Hungry?"

"Hrllll, both," Ik said fervently.

"Then let's go get aboard. There's food, and you can rest a little during the ride."

On the flight to the main station, a selection of simple food was indeed laid out for them, and they ate every crumb. There was little chance for rest, though, and no privacy to talk. Several members of the Galactic Core Mission team peppered them with questions, trying to get preliminary statements before details faded from their memories. This group was focused on what had happened at the galactic core, with the Mindaru, and Antares clearly also wanted to know these things. But Julie knew perfectly well that they were going to have to repeat all their answers once they reached the control station.

Through it all, Ik paced the length of the shuttle's passenger compartment, and Julie occasionally got up and did likewise. After the long confinement in the pod, it felt good to move, however stiffly.

It was frustrating, though, to have no chance to talk privately among themselves. Julie grew increasingly restless. Arrival at the station came none too soon.

The formal debriefing began, not with their arrival in the familiar conference space, but with the arrival of Cromus shortly thereafter. His carapace gleamed ebony with auburn highlights, as though it had just been polished. Had he dressed up for them? Julie wondered. No, it turned out, he had returned in haste from Shipworld proper, where he had been in meetings with the Ruling Circle. What was that all about? Julie wondered. But no explanation was forthcoming.

In leading the debriefing, Cromus was joined by the scientist, Watts. Besides them, Ik and Julie faced a team of perhaps two dozen mission specialists. Antares was given a seat nearby. Despite her participation at the end, Antares had had no interaction with the Mindaru, and she was asked no questions. Later they would talk about the extraction.

Cromus was all business, but he did take time to acknowledge the strain they were under. "We know you are k-k-k-tired," he rasped, clicking his claws together. "We know you need recovery time. But these first hours are—" *rasp* "k-k-critical, in gathering your reports while they are fresh in your minds." One eye stalk centered on Julie, and the other on Ik. "Your thoughts and observations must be k-k-correlated with what we were able to gather through the upstream link-k." He snapped his claws sharply. "In short-t, we need to know *what has become of the M-M-Mindaru.*"

Julie and Ik told him as much as they could—at length, over several hours, each hour dragging on more slowly than the one before. Julie slipped into a dreamy haze as they repeated answers, clarified, and repeated again. By the time the debriefing team sputtered out of questions, she was starting to wonder if she could trust her own memory. Had they really tangled with Mindaru in the deep past, and survived? If it was a dream, Ik had had the same dream. She heard a quiet assurance from her stones: *It was no dream . . .* and that lifted her like a cool breath of oxygen.

Glancing sideways at Antares, Julie was surprised to see the Thespi watching and listening with an expression of impassivity, as if she, too, had been worn down by the questioning.

Just when Julie thought she could take no more, Cromus signaled an end to the questions. "Thank-k-k you. If we are able to confirm your success in—" *rasp* "—block-k-king Mindaru passage from the source, and out of the timestream, we will rest easier. We k-k-thank-k-k you."

Julie slumped and nodded her acknowledgment.

Watts strode forward, stretching his spindly arms wide. "Tomorrow, we will look into the harrowing question of what happened on your return. I tell you honestly, it was terrifying for all of us when—as we *now* know—you overshot your return date. You were in stasis, but on the outside, you seemed as good as dead! I am pleased that we did not remove your physical bodies for scanning or autopsy."

That made Julie's eyes widen.

But Watts was already moving on. "I have some other information to pass on from our headquarters. It seems a high-priority tachyonic communication has been received from the region of the planet Krella. The fleet commander there has confirmed cessation of the temporal tide that opened the route for the Mindaru in the first place. If *this* claim holds, there may be no further need for the kind of exploration we have just concluded."

That brought chitters and rasps of approval from all the briefing team—and a question from Ik. "Are you saying, hrrm, that John Bandicut and Li-Jared's mission has succeeded?"

Watts swayed from side to side. "Possibly. *Probably.* The message was from the naval detachment that went to assist *The Long View.* There was little detail, but it seemed to indicate that the mission had already succeeded at the time of the fleet's arrival at Krella."

Ik clacked his mouth shut and sat back, his fingers twitching in obvious satisfaction.

Very good news, Julie thought.

And with that, Cromus dismissed the meeting, and told the three that they were free to retire to their quarters.

"They've given us a suite of private rooms," Antares said, leading them into the residential section. "They promised we can be undisturbed for as long as you need to rest." She made a husky sound that might have been rueful laughter. "Or at least until the next urgent meeting. Which I have a feeling will be first thing in the morning."

Julie was grateful for the privacy. But she was also thinking ahead. "Once we rest up, we'll want to talk to the translator. Not just to these people." She glanced at Ik. "And where is Rings?"

"Hrrm, yes," Ik mumbled, looking tired enough to drop.

Antares didn't answer until they were ensconced in their suite—four sleeping rooms arranged in a circle around a sitting room—and the privacy screens were turned on. Then she said to Julie, "I don't know if they will let you contact the translator. I couldn't, and I tried repeatedly."

Julie was shocked. "Why?"

"I'm not sure. But your friend Rings-at-Need has been here to see me, and I've sent messages through him. I don't think they are able to keep Rings out."

"But they're keeping you here?" Julie asked.

Antares nodded and went to sit down. "Do you see that transport window over there?" She pointed to a silver portal frame where another bedroom door might have been. "It's locked down." In response to Julie's puzzled expression, she said, "It made sense at first. I was weak—injured, really—from what happened—at the end. I probably did need people watching over me, to make sure I was okay. You should eat, by the way." A counter to the right of the portal was crowded with serving platters and decanters of drink. Napoleon whirred and parked himself near the table, apparently ready to serve if requested.

"I will. But Antares, what aren't you telling us? What *happened* to you when you returned and we did not?"

"Hrah," Ik said, gathering a plate of bread sticks, fruit, and cheeses. "My friend, what is wrong?"

Antares sat still, head bowed, moistening her lips. Finally she raised her head slightly. "When the bond broke . . . when I lost you in the ghoststream, and I felt you break into the future . . ." She looked at her trembling hands and turned them over, as if she wondered who they belonged to. "I was . . ."

"Hrrm. You were hurt, yes. But *how*, exactly?" Ik leaned forward, the yellow fruit in his hands forgotten.

"It was traumatic—the separation. I don't know what it felt like for you. But I'd linked all of my empathic senses into . . . the ghoststream." She balled her hands together into one fist. "I used my knowing-stones to amplify them. To make that long reach . . . to find you and connect with you."

Julie felt paralyzed. She wanted to say *Thank you*, and *I'm sorry*. But that would be so insufficient.

Antares rasped a sharp breath. "It is what I do—though usually not at such an extreme . . . But I was afraid that your lives might depend on it."

"Hrrm. Indeed they did." Ik reached out to touch her arm. "It is the second time you've risked yourself to save me."

Antares flinched at the touch. Ik's gaze narrowed, and he pulled his hand back.

"I'm sorry, Ik. I gladly risked . . . both times." Antares' face seemed drawn into a tight mask. "But when I lost my grip, and you *tore away into the future*, I . . ." Her voice caught, and stopped.

"What?" Ik asked softly.

Antares' eyes dilated so far they were almost totally black, just a thin sliver of her gold irises visible. "It *tore something from me.*"

Julie, moved by Antares' pain, started to reach out as Ik had. "*I lost my power, my empathic sense. I lost it all!*"

Julie drew a sharp breath. "Antares . . . I don't know what to say. If it helps, you're still the same to us." No, that was stupid. *Jesus.*

"No, I'm not. Don't you see? I can no longer reach out and touch . . . I can't search other people's feelings . . . can't share, or bring others together . . ." She looked from Julie to Ik and back, her face a mask of pain. "*Haven't you noticed? Haven't you felt it?*"

Julie's face grew hot with embarrassment, sympathy, shame. "Yes," she whispered. "Yes, I have. I'm sure Ik did, too—right, Ik? But I wasn't sure . . . well . . . I didn't know what to think."

Antares opened her hands, and they were trembling. "That is why I could not greet you properly when you returned. Oh, my friends—" her voice caught "—it is like a physical wound. It is like, I imagine, being blinded."

Yes, Julie thought, while Antares continued, "*I am a Thespi-Third female!* Who *am* I, if I cannot do those things?" She raised her hands to her temples, and after a moment, began to shake.

"Are they—?" Julie began, then stopped and shook her head. She started over, more softly. "Are your senses, your powers, gone completely? Or are they just—are they weakened, hurt somehow? I don't even know what I'm asking."

Antares shook helplessly. "Who can say? I was in shock when I came out of the launch pod." She took a deep breath and sighed it out. "They treated me medically—what else could they do?—but they didn't know enough to say if I was physically injured. I overshot the present, too, by the way. I did a lesser version of what happened to you. I got flung about a week into the future. So by the time I woke up, they were already frantic about the fact that we all looked dead, with static life signs."

"So by the time we came along . . ."

Antares shook her head. "I was useless. I'd tried a simple empathic joining, under medical supervision. I nearly passed out. They adjusted my medication. I tried again. That time I *did* pass out."

"Jesus," Julie said, aloud this time. She reached out again, and this time she rested a hand lightly on Antares' forearm. Antares tightened, but instead of pulling away, reached across with her other hand and fiercely clasped Julie's.

"I couldn't talk to anyone, really. They were still looking for a physical cause for what was wrong with me, and at the same time, increasingly convinced that they—and I—had killed you two."

"Hrah!" Ik lurched out of his seat and paced around the food table. "Why didn't they try harder to help you?"

Antares opened her hands. "They didn't know what to do, except medicate me, to help me resist the urge to even *try* to make empathic connections. To rest those senses, I suppose." Antares let her head slump in a kind of nod. "I have not tried since, except in small ways. But—" She paused and shook her head. "It is painful and draining to *suppress the effort*. It is an *affront to myself*, as a Thespi woman. Can you understand?"

Ik stopped his pacing and stood facing her. "What about your knowing-stones? Can they help, or are they damaged, too?"

"Ik, they are silent."

Ik rumbled ominously.

"They are still there. They are alive, and awake. I can sense them. But not much more."

"That," said Julie, "is something the translator ought to be able to help with."

"The yaantel—oh yes," Antares said, pressing her fingertips together. "But they have said, while I am in this condition, and until certain political matters are resolved—"

"*Political* matters?" Julie asked.

"—I have not been permitted to contact the yaantel."

"Hrah! Inexcusable nonsense!" Ik cried.

"And yet," Antares said, "there it is. It seems political matters are becoming important in this place."

"Perhaps they will find it harder to say that to all three of us," Ik said, in a more measured tone.

"Perhaps they will," Antares said, and for just a moment, there was a hint of the old spark in her eyes.

CHAPTER 36

Lockdown

FINE WAY TO come home, Julie thought, resting her head back in the uncomfortably large easy chair. Antares rested in a similar chair to her left. Ik was the only one whose frame seemed large enough to suit the furniture. Julie closed her eyes, breathing slowly. She was bone tired, but not sleepy. Bittersweet though the homecoming had been, she didn't want to leave the physical company of her friends, to go lie down. After all that time in the ghoststream, she hungered for physical companionship—broken, wounded, or otherwise.

Finally she rose and got herself some food and a glass of what she guessed was white wine, but tasted alternately astringent and sweet. After a few sips, she felt new warmth coursing through her veins. She drank a little more. Returning to her seat, she finally broke the silence. "Antares?" The Thespi turned her head. "Have you learned anything about John's and Li-Jared's mission? Beyond what Cromus told us?"

Julie could see a muscle tighten in the Thespi's throat. "Not much. But I *was* able to connect with a librarian—"

"*Librarian?*"

"Yes. A Logothian named Amaduse."

Julie shook her head in confusion.

Antares continued, "It was at the request of the yaantel. To send a warning to John—to *The Long View.* As a librarian, Amaduse seems to command an impressive array of connections. He promised to find a way to get a message sent—to warn John and the others that you were in the timestream, and they should take care what they did." Antares drummed her fingers on the arms of her chair. "I don't know how the message system works, or if they even got it. I was told not to expect a response."

Julie pondered that. "So, the thing Cromus told us . . ."

"*Might* have meant that they completed their mission, and will be coming back." Antares worked her fingers in something like a shrug. "Soon, I hope."

And not five hundred years from now, I hope, Julie thought. She hesitated, her face growing warm. "Did your message happen to mention me by name?"

"Uhhl, yes," Antares said, with a whistling sound. "*If* it got sent the way I worded it, and *if* he got it . . ."

"I imagine it would have come as quite a surprise to him to learn I was here," Julie said, a tremble in her voice.

Ik stirred. "I would guess, hrah, he was even more surprised to learn that you were not just here in his time, but *in the timestream with me.*" He paused to reflect. "Especially since they, hrrm, went out there to try to *stop* the timestream." He rubbed the side of his head with two long fingers. "I do wish we had news of them."

Julie nodded. She doubted they would get any news tonight. What was the local time, anyway? It felt late. Her gaze wandered back to Antares, whose fatigued posture reminded Julie of what the Thespi had sacrificed to bring them here.

"Perhaps," Ik said, gazing at Julie with an expression that seemed to say he knew exactly what she was thinking, "it is time we all retired."

Antares swept her gaze over both of them, and gave a twitch of agreement. Julie couldn't argue. She rose unsteadily, bade the others good night, and slipped self-consciously into her private room. Sleep did not come at once. But when it did, it was long and deep.

Though she agreed with Ik's sentiment, Antares stayed where she was after Julie and Ik retired. While she was greatly heartened by her friends' safe return, the inner quaking simply would not cease. She desperately yearned to extend and share her emotions; she could only let them circle around inside herself, slicing a trail of pain through her heart. How could she continue to live like this? /Stones, stones, can't you help me?/

From the stones, there came only silence. She was certain they were still active; she could feel them quivering from time to time. She wondered if they were as traumatized as she was. She prayed that the translator could help them . . . if she was ever permitted to go to the translator.

You should sleep. She knew perfectly well that this obsessive inward focus was helping no one, least of all herself. As a Thespi third, if she'd met someone else with this kind of self-absorption, she would have found a way to ease it—or *kick* it—off center stage. Certainly, she'd know how to keep it at bay.

You cannot let this rule you. Think of the big picture. They had beaten off a Mindaru incursion up the timestream—and John's team had miraculously shut off the timestream without killing Ik and Julie. Wasn't that worth rejoicing over? There was a cost to her, personally, but for Shipworld and the galaxy it was hardly any price at all. One Thespi woman ruined. Out of how many trillions saved, on countless worlds, who cared about one Thespi woman?

Well, *she* did. And she supposed her friends did.

Wasn't that enough?

For now, it would have to be. And with that resigned thought, she followed her friends' example and went into her room to sleep, leaving Napoleon to watch over the lounge. To her surprise, drowsiness came quickly, and after it sleep.

And dreams, vivid and troubling . . .

———

The years peeled back to her training, an arduous time, and to the cadences of the instruction, the codes of conduct . . .

"You were born to be who you are. You are no other . . ."

"I am Thespi-third. I am Autumn Aurora (Red Sun) Alexandrovens. I am bred, I am trained to facilitate joining. I will overcome all obstacles to joining."

In others. Only in others. She will have no joining. Not on Thespi, anyway . . .

The years peeled one way and another . . . the Scalapoorie sector, and so much trouble fitting in there . . . respite in the lounge in Atrium City. So many others to observe, aliens from all over the galaxy. The human and his strange companions, the norgs. The iceline, boojum, raging like a silent, killing fire.

Caught up like fate—to fight together. Her heart raced—she soared, she flew! She flew and he flew too! Yes, in that golden star-spanner bubble to the undersea world, world of drowning but not drowning, deep sea, deep deep deep . . . John inside her, in her mind and body, merging . . . No no no, she is not to do that! Not to do that! But she did, and she loved it, she fell in love with it, she fell in love with John, as well.

She became a beacon of light, flashing among worlds, flashing for all to see her love of the human, John Bandicut. Human!

Disapproval, waves of disapproval—was that Julie Stone shaking her fist?—and fell away into the darkness. She turned from the Thespi voices . . .

I am Thespi; I will be true and honest.

But her love for John Bandicut . . . ?

Life so different here.

Anger flaring . . . Who could dictate—make love for others, not for yourself?

Different now; all different.

Did John love her? He did. Did. Did he still love Julie? He did. Of course he did.

And when he returned and found her again?

Of course he would. She had sensed it in his mind always.

No!

No!

Sparks in the night. Flickering silhouette of humans, joined. She cried out in pain. How could Julie appear out of nowhere and take him?

Fight it. Fight it with your empathic senses. Fight it.

But they are gone, burned out!

A darkness came over her, and she lashed out at Julie Stone, physically driving her from John Bandicut. Striking her, striking and striking again! Uhhl, it felt good, to release the venom and pain. Striking! But with the violence rose a sickness, drowning her in remorse. This is not Thespi! This is jealousy!

Fight it with your powers—turn her emotions away!

No! Help not harm!

Are you Thespi? No! No longer!

She felt an unbearable pain, like fire, as her own powers flared back against her.

She screamed.

And screamed and screamed, until she awoke, shaking uncontrollably.

"Lady Antares." Napoleon glowed out of the darkness, clicking solicitously. "Lady Antares, what is the cause of your distress?" The doorway to her room was open. The norg must have heard her from the sitting room.

Antares gulped for air. When she could, she made a patting gesture with her hands, trying to communicate that it was okay, she was in no danger. At that moment the jealousy from the dream slipped away and she remembered the offer of friendship she had made to Julie, just before the galactic core mission. And she remembered how she had risked her life, and her sanity, to save Ik and Julie both.

She suddenly was aware of Ik's silhouette in the doorway, behind Napoleon's. He, too, must have heard her screams and come to see what was wrong. She shook her head, feeling drained and foolish.

"Antares?" Ik asked, striding past the norg into the room. He crouched beside her now, his bony face and deep-set eyes scrutinizing her. "Are you all right?"

Her breath caught, and she suddenly was shuddering with something that must have been much like John Bandicut's laughter—sharp laughter at what she had been thinking, imagining. *Attacking Julie?* After saving her life? "Oh, Ik," she whispered. "Yes. No! I don't know." She took his bony hand and held it, and imagined her flood of emotions going out to him. But that didn't happen; the rending pain was locked inside her.

I cannot make the feelings go away. But I am a Thespi-third. I can channel them, and not let them channel me. I am a Thespi-third female.

She sighed wearily. "I had a distressing night vision, in my sleep. I am all right now. Go rest. I am going to do the same."

Ik inclined his head and stroked his temple with a long finger. Finally he touched her forehead gently with his fingertip, before rising to leave.

Antares asked Napoleon if he would mind keeping watch over her in this room. Then she fell back asleep, this time with no dreams that she was aware of.

When Amaduse received word of the return of the galactic core team, the first question that arose was, *Have they changed the timeline? Is the present different? Would I even know?* He searched his own perceptions and found nothing pointing to a change. He sampled library data, hoping that if something about the present and past *had* changed, he might retain enough residual memories from before the change to notice. Here again, he found nothing. But that could also mean he simply retained no memories, because they had changed along with everything else.

He tried further afield: sending queries to members of several pandimensional races, like the yaantel, the Tintangles, and the shadow-people. Moving in and out of the continuum as they did, they had more of a birds-eye view of the universe. Perhaps they would have noticed a change.

Replies filtered in. Nobody reported seeing any changes. Perhaps time had proven its resiliency, after all—snapping back from all the small-scale changes inflicted on it in the eons past. That meant the Galactic Core Mission planning team had the right of it, at least on that particular score, at least if this information was accurate.

The Logothian pondered for a time what he might do about the information undoubtedly gained during the mission. He needed access to that information, but the GCM team was being parsimonious in sharing their data. Amaduse was not of a mind to tolerate that for long. His duty was to facilitate access to information, not just for the libraries and his own curiosity, but for all the circles of those making decisions for Shipworld. Right now that process was threatened by factions, and by a general lack of trust. There were strong partisan influences on both the GCM team's interpretation of the data and on the data's release—or non-release—to greater Shipworld. Additional reports from Rings-at-Need indicated that the GCM team was keeping the returned travelers quarantined, even from the yaantel, who had as much right as the GCM to interview them.

Amaduse saw peril in these decisions. The knowledge the travelers carried was too important to be held prisoner to politics. His duty was to ensure that that did not happen—and that meant gaining access to the travelers. If they were not permitted to travel to the yaantel, he would find another way. The GCM team did not need to like it.

Julie woke up thinking about John, and then Antares; and then, John and Antares. Her feelings were hopelessly tangled. When she remembered Antares' devastating loss on her behalf, Julie felt first a flash of guilt, and then a wrenching empathy for Antares. Was there some way she could help? *Not by lying here, helpless,* she thought. She pushed herself up from the sleeping mat and stumbled into the shower. With steam billowing around her and needles of hot water massaging her neck, she thought, *Antares could be the closest connection I'll ever have to John, especially if he doesn't come back.* She bowed her head to accept the pounding of the water on her shoulders. Finally she turned into the shower, made an adjustment to the flow, and raised her face to let the warm cascade sluice away the tears.

By the time she'd dried off, the closet had finished cleaning her clothes. She dressed and left her room to find Napoleon arranging breakfast on the table, with the help of a lithe, fine-furred creature who peered at her with enormous eyes, bowed without a word, and departed. Looking after the creature, Julie murmured to the robot, "This looks really good, Napoleon. Thanks."

Napoleon clicked.

Ik appeared from his doorway to join her. When she inquired as to whether he had rested well, he answered, "I, hrrm, found it remarkably strange to be resting in—" he gestured around with outstretched arms "—a room. A place I can stand up in, and walk around in."

Julie concurred. She had woken several times near the end of the night—disoriented, struggling to figure out where she was in the ghoststream, before remembering. And now, by the light of local day, she wondered aloud, "More debriefing today, you think?"

"I imagine so," Ik said.

"Hm." Julie poured herself a cup of coffee. She raised the cup, hands trembling.

"Hrrm?" Ik asked. She looked at him. "This may not be my business, Julie Stone . . ."

Oh God. Is it painted on my face? Can everyone read it?

"But because you are my friend, I will ask anyway . . ."

Yes, apparently it *was* painted on her face.

"Hrah. I know you are troubled. Antares was, also . . . hrrm, after you went to sleep."

Julie said nothing. She had no words.

"I am aware that there is tension between you two. Because of . . . well, *hrah.*" Ik canted his head, not finishing the sentence.

Julie strained to keep her voice neutral. "I hope it didn't keep *her* up sleepless."

Ik's head moved in a funny little pattern, side to side and forward and back. "I think, hrrm, that it might have."

Her stomach cramped.

Ik straightened. "Julie, you are my friend. And I have been Antares' companion through many difficult times."

"I know, Ik. I'm not trying to involve you."

"That's not the point. The point is, she is someone I—that is, *you*, I hope—can trust."

She barked a laugh, spilling hot coffee on her hand. "*Ow.* That's not it, Ik. Really." She sucked the coffee off the back of her hand. "I *trust* her. She brought us back, both of us. Oh God, yes, I trust her. But still, it remains . . . she loves John, and so do I. And that's not going to go away."

Ik's head bobbed as he considered. A moment later, his gaze shifted suddenly as Napoleon said, "Good morning, Lady Antares."

Julie turned to see Antares emerging from her room. The Thespi looked beautiful, of course; or actually, on second glance, a little wan, as though she really hadn't slept well. If Thespi women even slept, Julie thought. They probably just reclined there being beautiful, or maybe growing their beauty.

Antares greeted them with a throaty murmur. She selected a piece of triangular red fruit from the table and poured herself a cup of a pale green tea, then sat to one side, saying nothing. She appeared troubled.

For a minute, no one spoke. Then Julie, unable to stand the silence, cleared her throat noisily. "No word from anyone yet, that we know of."

Antares murmured, "They may give us a day to rest." She didn't sound as if she believed it, though.

"That's good, right?"

Antares shrugged and breathed a whispery sigh. "It would be easier to rest, if we could find a way to contact—"

Napoleon interrupted with, "Excuse me, but I believe we have a visitor."

Julie swung toward the entry, but Napoleon said, "No, Lady Julie—not that doorway." As he spoke, a blurred light the size of a human child appeared, floating in the center of the room. The glow subsided, and the blur resolved into Rings-at-Need.

Julie yelped in pleasure.

"I think we're all glad to see you," Napoleon said to the Tintangle. "Am I right?" he asked, swiveling his head around.

"Hrrm," said Ik. "Oh yes," said Julie, in the same instant. Antares simply looked at Rings in amazement.

"I am pleased to see you safely back," said Rings, spinning in short bursts. "But I regret that your hosts seem to want to keep you isolated. That is what Amaduse said when he asked me to look in on you. Is that true?"

Ik began to speak, but Antares interrupted to say, "Yes, true. They have prevented me from seeing the yaantel—" and her voice hardened a little "—and I have asked several times."

Julie scowled. "Doesn't the translator have influence? Can't it ask to hear what we have to say?"

Rings gonged softly. "Oh yes. It *also* asked me to come here and learn what I could from you."

At that moment, the physical door to the station slid open with a *whick*ing sound. In strode two members of the mission team. Julie groaned in annoyance. She recognized them as part of the support staff, but did not know them by name. One of them was vaguely humanoid, except for its stubby arms, and a head that looked as if an anvil had dropped on it. The other bore a passing resemblance to Cromus, but was smaller, with a tan-colored carapace. They stood just inside the doorway and stared at Rings-at-Need.

"Greetings," said Rings. "May we help you?"

"We require a conversation with the travelers, and the Thespi," answered the humanoid newcomer. "We are sorry, but we do not know how you came to be here. We must ask you to leave."

Before Rings could answer, Antares stood. "We were promised privacy and rest, for as long as we needed. Yes? We still require privacy, and that includes our invited guest."

The two beings looked at each other. The humanoid said, "The Tintangle was not invited by us, and I am afraid it represents a security risk."

"Security risk? Why?" Julie asked. When the two gazed blankly at her, she asked again, "Why is Rings a security risk? Isn't he the one who brought us to you in the first place?"

The Cromuslike creature clicked its pincers nervously. "That is true. However, circumstances have changed. At this time, the

Tintangle does not have security certification for access to this mission information."

Julie scratched her side. "That makes no sense. You trusted him before. Besides, he's our liaison with—"

"The yaantel?" asked the humanoid, with what seemed an accusing intonation. "Exactly. It has come to take information to the yaantel, has it not? When it has already been denied permission to do that?" When Julie didn't answer, it continued, "That is *why* it is a risk. The yaantel is not cleared to receive this information at this time."

At that, Julie lost what little patience she had left. "You're preventing the *translator* from knowing what happened?" she snapped. "How could you even think of doing that?"

The anvil-head said, "If it were just the yaantel, the situation might be different. But we have no way of knowing whom the yaantel might pass the information on to."

Julie threw up her hands and laughed helplessly. "Have you all taken leave of your senses? I trust the translator more than anyone on Shipworld! Let me talk to Cromus! And *then* I want to talk to the translator!"

The one like Cromus snapped its pincers in agitation. "Really! Really!" it rasped. "Cromus was the one who sent us. Cromus is busy dealing with—"

"*Busy?* Cromus is *too busy to talk to us?*"

"We did not mean—"

"Hrah," said Ik. "We are starting to wonder if you appreciate the grave risks we took for you."

"Not for you *only*," Julie said. "For the people of Shipworld, maybe. For the *galaxy*, maybe. But not for people who take our efforts and try to *own* them for I don't know what purpose!"

The humanoid emitted a soft groan. "You must not speak of the team—of the team leaders!—that way. They are only trying to prevent problems—to keep inflammatory stories and leaks from getting out and—"

"What?" Julie demanded.

"Causing problems," the creature repeated.

"Hrrm, what sort of problems?"

The humanoid shifted slightly, to speak to the Hraachee'an. "There are other circles of power in Shipworld. Surely you know that. There are those who would look at the records of your mission and say, 'It is too dangerous to do these things. They should not have been done.' And they would try to shut down our efforts to protect the future."

"I see," said Ik, though his tone indicated that he did not. "You are trying to protect your projects? Perhaps they *are* too dangerous. But as that may be, *we* have not agreed to give up our freedom for the sake of your project."

The humanoid stood a little straighter. "I believe, in fact, you have. When you agreed—"

"*No*, we have *not*," Julie interrupted. "We saved the galaxy, because you asked us to. That doesn't mean we're your slaves. We came to you through Rings-at-Need and the transl—the yaantel. We intend to share our experience with them. If your superiors don't like *that*, they can take it up with the yaantel—*after* we have our visit."

The two visitors looked shocked. They exchanged glances, before the Cromuslike one said, "This is unanticipated. We must consult our leaders. You will be restricted to this suite until we return."

Julie watched them, glaring, as they turned and left. "Well," she said, finally, "I'm starting to wonder: Rings, can you get us out of here, and to the translator?"

Rings had remained silent and motionless throughout the exchange. Now he answered, "I came to hear your story, not to break you out. I'll have to investigate. Please wait." Rings spun, blurred, and was gone.

Julie sighed deeply and spread her hands helplessly toward the others.

Rings was gone for nearly an hour. When he reappeared, he seemed to have some difficulty. He looked like a glitching holo as he spun out of his travel continuum. When at last he was solid and able to speak, he said, "*That* was interesting. There are force barriers where there weren't before. They are serious about keeping me out, and you in. I had to use some dimensional back doors to get here."

"Hrrrl," growled Ik. "They are spying on us, too, then. Watching to see what you would do. Moon and stars! I thought we could trust them!"

"Uhhl!" Antares cried. "I *hope* we can trust some of them, still!"

"Either way," said Julie, "we need to know, can you get us out of here, Rings?"

The Tintangle rotated briefly one way and then the other, as though shaking his head. "I am afraid not. At least, not immediately." He spun twitchily for another moment, and then added, "I have moderately stable communications with the yaantel right now. The yaantel is exploring options. It asks for your patience, and your story."

Julie sighed in frustration. "We've got nothing but time, right? Let's tell you our story."

CHAPTER 37

Homeward for Answers

"BANDIE JOHN BANDICUT! Are you all right?"

Bandicut stared out into space. No, he was not all right. Not even close. Charli was gone. There was nothing more to be done about it.

————————

Over the remainder of the flight home, he worked at trying to come to terms with that. He and Li-Jared began to talk again, drawn together by the commonality of loss. Li-Jared was starting to emerge from his funk, perhaps jarred out of it by the necessity of rescuing Bandicut from the silence-fugue. Li-Jared even began speaking civilly to Ruall again.

Ruall had words for Bandicut: "Charli is still out there in riverstrand-space. But search your inner thoughts carefully."

Bandicut, in fact, was constantly searching the inner vaults of his mind, just to be sure he hadn't missed anything. Was some remnant of Charli there, some connection to the Charli who lived now in the eternity of the starstream? Some Charli-echo? He imagined he heard echoes of her voice, but he was pretty sure they were only memory-echoes.

"Search again, from time to time," Ruall said.

Bandicut would, of course. He doubted he could ever stop searching, hoping for a familiar whisper across time and space.

The Long View's outbound track in the starstream was smooth and steady, like coursing down a subtly winding river whose banks were periodically interrupted by entrances to hidden harbors. *The Long View* flew past them all and hurtled single-mindedly outward, away from the galactic center.

The ship still felt eerily empty without the guests who had filled it, and without its missing members.

"I hear echoes of Bria everywhere," Ruall remarked at one point. She seemed to be inviting Bandicut to say something similar about Charli. He wished he could.

Eventually they left the starstream to head in their own direction. Dark took her leave, saying she wanted to explore the starstream further. "Thank you, and come see us again—please," Bandicut murmured. "You know where to find us." He was sorry to see her go. He strove to focus his weary thoughts on what lay ahead. He was eager to be reunited with his friends, of course—but that presumed that his friends had also made it back alive—and in the now, not a hundred years before, or after. Was that too much to hope for? Had Ik and Julie survived and returned from whatever strange mission they had been sent on? And what about Antares and Napoleon?

The questions burned in his mind.

The light-years, outside n-space, flowed past.

"Coming out of n-space," Copernicus announced, and they all gathered to watch it happen. They had reached the edge of the galaxy. Would they see anything but empty space ahead?

The viewspace shivered and swam, and then hardened once more to clarity. Ahead of them, a shadow only a little less black than the darkness stretched across their path. "One moment," said Copernicus, as he made adjustments to the image. A moment later, the shadow brightened and came into focus: It was the vast sprawl of Shipworld, stretching from the left side of the view-space to the right, a long succession of great, connected modules that seemed to go forever. Behind the immense structure, fuzzy spots of light focused to reveal the tiny shapes of faraway galaxies. Some of them were larger. Above Shipworld and to the left lay the glowing splendor of the Large and Small Magellanic Clouds, the Milky Way's largest satellite galaxies.

A quick blink to a stern view revealed the heart-wrenching majesty of the Milky Way itself behind them, a glowing splatter-painting of the starry road they'd left behind.

Ruall clanged, "Well done, Copernicus! Are you ready for me to take the con?"

"No need," said Copernicus. "Unless you really want to. I have established contact with traffic control, and I have our approach course lined up."

"Oh," Ruall said, her voice muted. She *was* mellowing. "Carry on, then."

"Aye."

The structure ballooned before them, fractal-like levels of detail crystallizing into visibility as *The Long View* closed the distance. Finally an opening yawned, and streaming lights guided them into a hangar, and then into the waiting arms of a docking cradle.

With the tactile clunk of docking, Bandicut let out an enormous sigh of relief: *Home at last. Home such as it is now.* He called out to the robots: "Can you get a time and date check? How long have we been gone?" He swung to look at Li-Jared, and thought he saw the same question in the Karellian's eyes. Was he still feeling like a prisoner? Or was the anticipation of seeing Ik and Antares winning out? "You okay?" Bandicut asked.

Li-Jared flicked his fingers. "I will be." He turned his own head. "Coppy? Jeaves? Do we know *when* we've arrived?"

Jeaves made some whirring sounds. "Sorry, it took me a minute to locate the time signal. It looks as though we were gone for about two months, Shipworld time. In days, that's about fifty—"

"Thank you, I can multiply." Li-Jared turned to Bandicut, his face alight with relief. "We're still in the present!"

Bandicut grinned. He called out, "What about our friends? Are they back, too?"

"Still trying to find that out, Cap'n," answered Copernicus.

"Keep on it! Is anyone here to meet us?"

"We *are* to be met," Jeaves said. "I'm just not sure by whom."

Their greeter and escort turned out to be a halo, a floating ring of light that reminded Bandicut of Delilah, the halo who had accompanied them on their Starmaker mission. The halo reported that she was going to take Bandicut, Li-Jared, Ruall, and Jeaves back to see the Peloi, the sea creatures who had sent them on the mission. Copernicus interrupted to request his own release from the ship. "I have done my duty here," the robot said. "Since my integration with the ship's AI has been dissolved, I believe my destiny lies with my friends and companions."

Bandicut voiced his support at once. "He is right. Copernicus is with us, and custody—if that means anything—should be returned to me. In fact, I insist on it."

The halo hung in the air for a moment, perhaps communicating with someone. Then it bobbed, brightened momentarily, and chimed, "Copernicus is released as a free agent, and may join the party to visit the Peloi. Shall we go?"

Floating luminous before them, the halo led them out of the ship into the hangar area. Bandicut turned to look back at the glowing orange lozenge that was *The Long View*. Though he was heartily sick of being cooped up in her n-space hull, he felt wistful at leaving. She was a good ship and had served them well. He wondered if they would ever fly on her again. Li-Jared was watching him, his eyes glinting; he suspected the Karellian had at least some similar feelings. Even Copernicus, tapping, had turned to look back. Ruall was spinning, stopping, spinning, stopping; it was impossible to tell what she was feeling. To the halo, Bandicut said, "Will we be coming back for our stuff?"

Chime. "It will be brought to you. Now, please come."

Copernicus punctuated the request with what sounded like a snare-drum rim shot, and they all trooped across the hangar. The halo led them to a group-sized portal, and they passed through together. And with that simple stride, Bandicut thought, they had just left their mission behind.

———————

The halo brought them to a small anteroom, which Bandicut recognized as the entry to the cave of the Peloi. A light glimmered far back in the cave, and the halo led them into the much larger cavern, where invisible ocean-tank walls held back unknown tons of water, dimly lit from within. "You will be met here," the halo said, and vanished.

Behind the invisible panes, shadowy movement could be seen in the turbid depths, just out of easy sight. Bandicut gazed into the gloom, waiting for someone to notice their presence. Finally he called, "Ho, Peloi!"

One of the shadows floated just a little nearer. "We see you," echoed a voice from somewhere. "Please be patient." And then the shape receded into the shadowy depths.

Bandicut gave it a few moments, and when the Peloi did not return, he called again. "Excuse me—but we have come a very long way! We have others we urgently wish to see, and many questions. We are tired, and our patience is in short supply!"

Apparently that was enough to get the Peloi's attention, because several shapes floated out of the shadows and resolved into the giant, colorful comb-jellies they had spoken with before their flight. Or at least they looked like the same jellies; Bandicut could not really tell. "Hello," he said, raising his voice. "We understand that you wanted to see us. I guess you'd like to hear the results of our mission?"

"We have absorbed your filed report," said one of the Peloi, surging forward, a shimmering blue shape in the water. Then, as they had done in their previous meeting, that Peloi floated back and another came forward to continue, "We wish to hear it now in your own words. Your story and personal impressions."

"I'm not sure what you mean," Bandicut said. "We reported it in our own words."

"Yes, of course," said a copper-colored giant anemone, floating forward. "What we mean is, we want to know more than the bare facts. We desire your personal impressions."

"Your emotions, if you will," said another. "The certainties and uncertainties of dealing with this foe. The Mindaru."

"Of negotiating peace with the others. Of forming the alliance."

"Why do you need all that now?" Bandicut asked, feeling a twinge of exasperation. "You know, don't you, that at the moment it's more urgent to us that we find our friends than stand here sharing all of the subtleties of our interactions with the Mindaru!"

"Yes, yes!" Still another Peloi. "We can help with all that. As soon as we have absorbed what we can of your details, while they are fresh . . ."

Ruall clanged. "They are fresh! They will remain fresh! What is it you really want?

"What we *want*," said the Peloi, and it sounded like several speaking in unison, "is to *touch* and *feel*. Would that be permitted?"

"Well, I don't know—" Bandicut began.

"What does that *mean*?" Li-Jared asked.

"Yes—" *clang* "—if it will finish this!" Ruall chimed.

"So it will be, then," said the Peloi, apparently taking Ruall's response as the final one.

Before any of them could protest, a new pulse of bioluminescence shot through the water. The chamber illumination darkened, but the light from the depths of the water grew in intensity and flashed around them in enveloping rings.

Bandicut felt suddenly lightheaded, and physically immobile. The light was doing something to his mind, penetrating like sharp vapors. He began to feel his memories bubble up in quick-moving images that billowed out of his head and flashed out to join the external light patterns. At first it felt unreal, and then he knew he was not imagining it; these really were his memories being pulled from his mind, and they included everything—not just the battles with the Mindaru, but Ik's vanishing, Antares splitting away with Napoleon, the meetings with Dakota, negotiations with the Uduon and Karellians, and the loss of Charli, and Bria. An unregulated flood of memories of the trip, fiery with fringes of emotional content, bubbled up into the halo of light and directly to the Peloi, who absorbed them silently.

Bandicut expelled his breath in a gasp. He had undergone assisted memory dumps before, but never had it felt so abrupt, so invasive—so starkly revealing. Each memory had distinct emotions attached to it, and those emotions, even the ones he would have kept private, sparkled and danced for all the Peloi to see. He doubled over, holding his head with his hands, trying to control the flow. It was impossible; all boundaries of privacy were stripped away. His fingertips burned; his thoughts were on fire. It lasted for a minute, two minutes, ten, a hundred; he couldn't tell. And as suddenly as it had started, the fire died away.

He rasped in a deep breath, and pushed against his knees to come back upright. The circles of light in the water were fading away. Beside him, Li-Jared was staggering, blinking, slapping his chest with both hands. Ruall was spinning, moaning; after a moment, her spinning started to slow down.

Li-Jared grunted, "Do that again, and I will be *very* angry."

And Bandicut, lightheaded, panted indignantly, "Who . . . gave you . . . permission to do . . . that?"

Two shapes loomed. "Ruall said—" "Did you not—?"

"*I* did not," Bandicut said tightly, though it was clear they had taken Ruall's consent as consent for all. "Why did you need all that, anyway? Why did you have to be so . . . personal?"

The Peloi drifted forward and back. "Personal . . . yes. It is important to understand the feelings around important event points. Decision markers. Mission choices . . ."

Bandicut waved wearily, trying to cut them off.

"Encounters . . ."

"Stop!" he groaned. "Are you trying to tell me you *care* how we feel? Did you *care* when you split us off from our friends, and send them on different missions?" His temper was starting to heat up again.

"We did." "We do." "But not all do."

"So you *care*, but you did it anyway?"

"Moon and stars!" Li-Jared muttered, bouncing up and down.

"No, no—*we* did not!" A new Peloi was in the fore now, and this one came closer, and lingered. "Those things were done by others! We want to know how you feel about those who would do those things. A government that would do those things."

My feelings about the government? Bandicut thought dizzily, in amazement.

"We feel pretty damn furious, that's how we feel," Li-Jared said, stepping forward in what looked like a fighter's stance, knees bent and fists clenched. "We think a government like that is pretty damn *stupid*, for one thing. Breaking up our team? Sending out two uncoordinated missions? Even if those *hadn't* been our friends on the other mission, it would have been stupid."

The Peloi crowded closer, all of them.

Something flickered inside the nearest one, all crimson and orange flame, with a hint of shuddering violet. *Anger? About Li-Jared's comments?* Bandicut wondered. He waited a heartbeat, and then said, "Li-Jared's words are strong, but—"

"We agree with them," said the Peloi. The flickering was rippling out to the others, like a wave passing into the depths. Another Peloi spoke: "We were angry, too." And another: "That is why we needed to know not just of your mission, but what you did, saw, felt, left behind."

Bong. "So you really were *not* the ones responsible?" Li-Jared asked. He was moving his hands in front of him as he spoke. Gesturing anger? Or beckoning to the Peloi to respond?

"We were shamed, shocked," said the most distant of the Peloi, a dark blue one, floating forward now into view.

"Is that really true?" Li-Jared demanded. "Then why did you allow it—?"

"Are you not aware of the limits of our power?" asked the dark Peloi. "We work for the ruling circle; we are not part of it!"

Bandicut started to speak, but had no real answer to that. He had somehow assumed they were among the mysterious masters. He was a little shocked to hear how they were speaking. They sounded almost rebellious.

"Enough!" said a Peloi who had not yet spoken. "Let Amaduse explain to them!"

"Agreed," said the closest Peloi. And to Bandicut and the others: "Thank you. We have what we need. Now, would you like to speak to Amaduse?"

Before any of them could react, a haze of purple light passed over them, and they were elsewhere.

"What now?" Bandicut murmured, turning around. He stumbled, and caught himself. They were on a rocky path, outdoors. The sky was darkening but not yet dark—early evening in this sector, he guessed. It took a moment to recognize the path as the way to Amaduse's place.

Bong. "Bandie, is this—?"

"Yes," Bandicut said. "Hey—where are Ruall and the robots?"

Ruall suddenly spun into their continuum. "Jeaves and Copernicus were kept behind for more questions," she said. "They will be sent on later to join us. If you know this Amaduse, why are we standing here? Aren't we going to go see him?"

"Right. Let's go," said Bandicut, taking the lead in following the path over a rise. On the far side of the little hill, the trail led into a forest. Nestled at the edge of the forest was Amaduse's house. The side door was cracked open, allowing a sliver of yellow light to escape into the gloom.

Amaduse greeted them in the doorway; he apparently was expecting them. The serpentine creature's white-hooded face was in shadow, but his eyes gleamed with pleasure. He backed away, hissing animatedly, to usher them into his front room—where he had welcomed them once before. The room was still dominated by a long work station along the window wall facing the woods. Small holos floated in the air over the work station. On the other side of the room, huge pillows were piled, apparently for sitting on. Once Bandicut's eyes got used to the light, he realized that the illumination was low and reddish; and he remembered that the Logothian's eyes were sensitive to light. "Thank you for seeing us," he said. "It's a relief to be back! I hope you have news for us."

Amaduse looked ready to invite them to flop on the pillows and take their rest, but once he saw their expressions, he changed his mind. "I am, sss, h-hoping," he wheezed, "that you will be able to tell me all the details-s of your journey. But I think perhapss you might prefer if I talk firsst? About your friends-s?"

"Yes, please!"

Bwang. "Yes!"

"Then—ssss—I will tell you w-what I can-n. Especially about what they have faced ssince coming back to Sh-shipworld."

"Then they *are* back! Are they safe?" Bandicut demanded. "Please just tell me that."

"They are ss-safe," said Amaduse. "They have been away, and they have returned."

Bandicut sighed deeply and with feeling. "And Antares? And . . . Julie Stone?"

"All of them—and your norg, your robot." Amaduse paused to hiss his own long breath. "As I under-ssstand, the journey wass a clossse thing. But they all returned to ssssafety."

"I am pleased. We are pleased," Ruall chimed, spinning rapidly.

Bandicut's heart thumped with pent-up fear cartwheeling into profound relief. *Julie and Antares. Ik. Napoleon.* The Logothian was gazing closely at him, perhaps finding Bandicut's emotional response easier to gauge than the others'. Amaduse gestured fluidly with white-gloved hands to a wide holo-display area with nudger controls. "I apologize for not having displays ready for you, but it has been a challenge to gather the data. Becausse . . ." He paused and hissed a long sigh, shaking his hooded head in a swaying motion. "Well. Firssst, underssstand that there was agreement among the ruling circle that the threat—"

"Wait—do you mean the ruling circle for all of Shipworld?" Li-Jared asked.

"Yess. That is what the ruling circle is! As I sssay, agreement that the Mindaru threat had to be met. But *much* disagreement on how."

"And disagreement," Ruall whirred, "spun into hostility?"

The Logothian's head bobbed again. "Unfortunately, yess. Especially animos-sity between those represented by the oness you just met with, the Peloi, and those who oversaw the mission down the timestream." He massaged the controls on his display board. "The mission team are releasssing only incomplete bits, sss, hardly enough to put together a clear picture. For me, as a manager of information, that is frussstrating. However, I do have alternate channels, and I have gained some detailss." He made an expansive gesture with his long-fingered hands.

"Such as?" Bandicut prompted impatiently.

"Sss . . . I can tell you that ssseveral major time-travel expeditionss were undertaken, two of them involving your friend Ik, and the human Julie S-stone. Antares and your robot Napoleon observed-d the last one. The risssk of the missions was considered high, and the mission team did not want knowledge of that risssk widely diss-seminated."

Bandicut felt weak in the knees, and he had to reach out to the work station to steady himself. "But they're all . . . okay?" he gulped.

"I said they were s-safe, did I not?" Amaduse's eyes glinted in the light of the work station. "Let usss get down to your perssss-onal needs, which I perceive are high. Tell me, John Bandicut, do you know this human, this Julie S-stone?"

"Oh yes! Yes. We were—" Bandicut began, and then his breath failed him. "Yes, I knew her," he whispered. "She's an—an important—friend."

Amaduse peered at him, perhaps reading his thoughts. "Then you would like to see her ssoon, if that could be arranged?"

"Yes, of course! All of them! Can we?"

Amaduse hissed cautiously and waved his hands in uncertainty. "It may not be easy. Ssss. We will have to find a—" *rasp*

"—workaround."

Li-Jared reacted to that with flailing gestures of exasperation. "Why should it be hard?"

"A good quess-tion." The Logothian nodded gravely. "And yet it is." He swung his hooded head back toward the work displays. "Becausse . . ." His fingers worked at the controls for a moment.

"Because *what?*" Li-Jared demanded.

Amaduse bobbed his head and gestured with an open hand. "The Galactic Core Mission team has-s other ideas."

Bandicut's voice rose. "What kind of—?"

"It seemss they have placed a *quarantine* re-ssstriction on your friends."

"*Quarantine?*" Bandicut cried. "*Why?* Did they bring back some alien virus? Contamination from the Mindaru?"

"Ssss. Not that kind of quarantine." Amaduse swung his serpentlike head from side to side, looking from his controls to Bandicut. "No, what they've brought back is more dangerouss, as the GCM team s-sees it. They brought *information*, and direct knowledge of the risssks of time travel—and that has frightened them."

Bandicut cocked his head, trying to follow. "So . . . they're trying to hide the risks they took?"

"Jus-sst so," said Amaduse. "Not just the risssk to their crew, but to all of Sh-shipworld. All of reality, really. Ssss. The potential for time paradoxes—" Amaduse extended his left hand "—and the threat of the Mindaru—" and he extended his right hand. "The team did very well, from what I have gleaned, sss, but that was not guaranteed."

Bong. "Time paradoxes? What time paradoxes have you detected?"

"None that *I* have ssseen." Amaduse straightened a little. "My hope is that there *are* none."

Ruall gonged, floating forward. "How can we know?"

Amaduse bowed toward the spinning Tintangle. "Your fellowss were among those I consulted, Ruall. People who could ssee outside our dimensional time flow. Tintangles and magellan-fish and shadow-people, and others. No s-sign of change in the time flow. It seemsss the theory that the past is resiss-tant to change has gained, sss, experimental support."

Thank God, Bandicut thought. But then he shook his head, as though trying to wake from a dream. He wasn't interested in time travel theory just now. "No paradox. Fine. Great. How can we get to where our friends are *now?* You said you would help us do that, right?"

Amaduse bobbed his serpentine head up and down. "I ssaid, and will try. I must enlist the aid of your friend the yaantel."

"*Yaantel?*" Bandicut asked, more perplexed than ever. "Who or what is the yaantel?" He looked to Li-Jared and Ruall, to see if either of them knew.

"The yaantel," Amaduse said, "commands great respect here. I thought you knew it perssonally. Was I wrong?" He fiddled with some controls, and read something on his screen in an unfamiliar language. "I s-see. It may be known to you by another name. Sss. Did you know ssomething called 'the transsslator'?" An image appeared on the screen: a squirming collection of black and silver spheres, exactly as Bandicut had first seen the translator in the ice caverns of Triton.

"Mokin' Jesus!" Bandicut's breath went out in a rush. This was as astounding as learning that Julie Stone was here. "The translator's *here?* On Shipworld? The same translator I left back on Earth—I mean, in my home system?"

The diamond-glitter returned to Amaduse's eyes. "The ssame. It returned to Shipworld after a long absence, sss, bringing with it the one you know as Julie S-stone."

"*I'll be . . .*" Bandicut breathed. He wished Charli could have been here for this. What about his stones? Did they know about the translator being here?

We sense something . . . just out of reach. We felt it before, but could not be certain of the source. It could be . . .

Bandicut's head was spinning now. Li-Jared was saying something to Amaduse that he didn't hear. But it brought him back to the present. "—get us to the translator? Now?"

"S-speaking to the translator may be the best next step," said Amaduse. "I am trying to make contact now." He turned and extended a long, lithe hand. "While I do that, won't you rest?"

Bandicut let out a sigh of release and took a step toward the piled cushions; then he turned back to Amaduse. "We have two more robots that will be following us. It's very important that they rejoin us."

"Ssss, I will keep watch for them," the Logothian promised, "and send them on when I can."

The librarian's assistant, Gonjee, had appeared and was scurrying around setting things up for a transport event. Something that looked like a silver door-frame was now standing at the far left end of Amaduse's work area. It resembled the transport device into which Antares had disappeared, right here—years ago, it seemed. It was different, though. More elaborate. More complex parts. Amaduse was working with great concentration at his consoles. The doorway, he informed them, required an active connection on both ends. The distance involved was considerably greater than usual within Shipworld, even between modules.

Ruall was unusually restless, spinning in and out of view as they waited. She was, she said, doing her own reconnoitering. It seemed there was another Tintangle who was close to the situation, who might be able to help open a receiving gateway near Ik and the others. That other Tintangle was busy shuttling messages. From whom to whom, Ruall didn't say.

Amaduse finally summoned them. "I believe we are nearly ready. I have spoken to the yaantel. It conveys its greetings. It is attempting to clear the way for a transport. Though it is eager to meet with you in person, it believes the greater urgency is to reunite you with your friends."

Bandicut nodded. He felt a surge of adrenaline; and the stones were stirring in his wrists. "I want to see the translator, too. But my friends first." Li-Jared, beside him, was on the balls of his feet, his fingers twitching. His eyes seemed to be alive with their own light. "When will we be ready?" He glanced at Ruall. "Do you want to come with us?"

"I wish to meet your friends," Ruall rumbled.

Bandicut responded with a hint of a smile.

Amaduse touched several switches and listened to something they could not hear. "We are ready now," he said. "There are no guarantees-s, but we have done what we can, sss, to establish the connection. Please s-stand in front of the portal. When I receive a signal from Rings-at-Need, ssss, I will tell you to s-step through."

With Li-Jared, Bandicut moved close to the doorway. He instinctively crouched, prepared to leap through, if necessary. Ruall spun in short, quick movements, behind him and over his shoulder.

"Be ready," said Amaduse. "I am receiving . . . wait . . ."

Bandicut drew a slow, deep breath. "Don't forget our robots."

"I won't. Wait . . ."

The doorway sparkled with violet-blue light. The tiny signals flared. "Now," said Amaduse.

Together, they lunged through.

CHAPTER 38

Reunion

JULIE SAT FRUSTRATED, reading on a tablet. She glanced up to find Antares gazing intently at her from near the food table. "What?" Julie asked. "Why are you staring?"

Stroking the stones embedded in her throat, Antares made that little hissing sound Julie had learned to recognize as a chuckle. "I was admiring your ability to focus on something like a book. I am too—agitated, I guess—to do that."

Julie forced a shrug. "It helps pass the time." It was a guide to the geography of Shipworld, translated in real-time by her stones. It was interesting, actually, and the knowledge might come in handy—but more to the point, it was distracting.

"I understand," Antares said. "But I think you are troubled by something today."

Julie straightened up. "Wait. Do you mean you can—?"

"*Feel* it?" Antares shook her head. "No. You just look that way—like you have something on your mind."

Julie leaned back in the easy chair and closed her eyes. "It's the damn portal," she sighed. They had tried several times now to use the local portal standing here in the room—to go see the translator, to visit the nearest shopping center, anything to get out of here. Rings had made it through a couple of times to see them, and had explained that part of the problem was they were not just quarantined; they were a considerable distance from Shipworld proper, on the ghoststream station. Linking from here was more complicated.

"Hrah, I think they have stoppered it more tightly," Ik muttered. He had been pacing the far side of the room. "Rings hasn't been here yet today."

"Exactly. I'm worried something is wrong. They may have found a way to block him."

"That would be bad," Antares agreed. "But Rings is pretty resourceful. Don't you think he'd find a way?"

Julie wanted to believe that. Until Antares pointed it out, she hadn't realized just how anxious she was feeling. "I don't know," she managed finally. "This all just feels so wrong to me. That we are kept prisoner. That we are kept from speaking to the translator."

She dropped her gaze back to the words on her tablet, but now her eyes went out of focus as she ruminated on their captivity. It hurt. After all they had done on their mission, to be treated like this . . .

It was sometime later when Ik pointed to the portal and said, "Hrrm, something is happening. I wonder if Rings has found his way past the blocks again."

Julie sat up. The window began to sparkle around the perimeter, and an almost imperceptible hum filled the air.

There was a dusting of light and no other sensation, as Bandicut's footsteps carried him forward. On the other side of the portal was a large room. As it swam into view, he discerned a table and nothing else. He was experiencing blurriness and tunnel vision. Now, to the left, he saw chairs—and three standing figures, moving toward him. He heard a cry before he could make out any faces.

"*JOHN!*" Not a cry, so much as a shriek. Pain and joy and weeping and hope, all caught up that one exclamation.

He swiveled left. *Julie? Was that Julie?* His voice couldn't form the question. His vision was blurrier still now, with sudden tears.

And then, "*Hrah, Li-Jared!*"

And "*John Bandicut!*" That was Antares, definitely. He blinked hard at the tears, trying to focus. He still couldn't see faces.

Again: "*John!*" Julie, for sure.

They all fell into focus at once. All three were running toward him and Li-Jared, arms flung wide in astonishment and joy. Their faces were alight. They looked like they might bowl him over, but he didn't care. Above his head, Ruall clanged and gonged, joined by another Tintangle spinning down from the ceiling.

"My God!" Bandicut gasped, staggering.

"*You're alive! You're really alive! And you're here!*" And with those words, Julie collided with him and crushed her face to his chest and caught him around the torso in a bear hug.

Bandicut was too stunned to do anything except hug her in return, and murmur meaningless syllables. Finally he laid his cheek against the top of her head and sighed. "*I am so . . . happy . . . to see you,*" he managed, in a whisper. Tears were running down his cheeks now. Julie, he realized, was sobbing. He squeezed her again, and kept squeezing.

Finally, he looked up and saw Ik and Li-Jared embracing heartily, gripping each other's arms. He laughed at the sight. Then he shifted right. Antares was standing a little apart, gazing at him, her black-and-gold eyes alight, her lips pressed into a crinkled expression that he recognized as a smile. "Antares," he sighed, over Julie's head.

Julie loosened her embrace at that, and he gripped her shoulders and looked into her eyes and said, "I need to greet Antares." Julie nodded and let him go without speaking. He took just one step past her and met Antares, and the Thespi fell into his arms, embracing him as tightly as Julie had. He held her for a long moment, rocking. Something felt not quite right, and it took him half a minute to realize what it was. There was no empathic wave, no rush of warmth, no inner flooding of love and welcome. Was she withholding? Was something wrong? He gently moved her to arm's length to peer into her eyes, and he found joy and pain in her gaze, but no answer.

Turning to include Julie, he caught each of their hands in his, and choked back tears. "I . . . see you two have met," he managed with a hoarse laugh, a hundred questions boiling up in his thoughts.

"We have," Julie said, and her mouth and eyes contorted, working through a range of emotions. Then she bit her lip, and the awkwardness burst somehow, and a grin broke through. Her dazzling blue eyes—oh yes, he remembered those eyes—danced, searching his. "Yes, we have met. Have we ever. I have so much to tell you!"

"Well, that's—I mean, I—"

Julie laughed and closed the short distance between them, and kissed him long and hard on the lips. "I'm glad you didn't die hitting that stupid comet," she breathed. Then she folded herself back into his arms, nestling her face into his neck. Antares pressed close, burring softly. Behind her, Napoleon—good old Napoleon!—was calling, "Cap'n! Cap'n!" And somewhere overhead, one Tintangle was saying to another, "Quarantined, yes. Un-nable to leave."

Bandicut shut all that out. He held Julie as if he would never let her go, pressing his own face once more into her hair. And he didn't let go for a long, long time. Whatever questions he had thought to ask were gone on a cosmic wind.

CODA

ACROSS THE TANGLED knot of space-time, Charli heard Bandicut's cry of distress—the long, heartrending cry of a distant train, in Bandicut's sensibility. It caused Charli's own heart to ache all over again. There was nothing she could do for John but ache for him.

Her recovery from the failed attempt had been as difficult as any she had ever experienced. Stretched across all of time and space, or so it seemed, Charli had, with tremendous effort, pulled herself back from the brink of death and despair. Pulled herself back to gaze down eternity, down the thin ribbon of space and time that had been unnaturally stressed, from the black-hole ruins of a former red-giant sun far from the galactic center, to the other black hole in the core. It was a sight of awesome grandeur—or would have been so at another time. Now it held only pain and loss.

So desperately she had tried to return to John Bandicut . . . so badly she had wanted to . . . and even with the help of that strange one, Ruall, she had failed. Or maybe it wasn't failure; maybe it just wasn't possible, in this life. Charli didn't want to believe that; she wanted to believe that maybe it would be possible one day to try again.

Yes, and maybe these tiny vessels out here moving in the starstream were the elves of galactic Christmas.

Charli mourned her loss in the only way a quarx could, by sighing her grief out into the universe, a long, slow song. She had done it before, in other lives, and she supposed she would do it again before her time was done.

It had taken a while before she'd become aware of a distant, small voice, echoing in the back of her mind. Very distant. But she knew then she was not entirely alone. How that was possible, she did not know. But as she looked inward, she realized she had *felt* his arrival back at Shipworld, without quite noticing. She felt his confusion and frustration at their reception. She sensed—oh, how far away!—his anticipation at being rejoined with his friends, and even with the long-lost Julie Stone.

Did Bandicut know she still heard rumor of his thoughts, of his doings? She felt his pain, and wished she could, somehow, let him know she was still there for him.

She thought long and thought hard.

Maybe there *was* something she could do besides ache for John. Maybe she could be his eyes and ears on the starstream, on the great river across the galaxy. Maybe she could do that for him. Maybe she could even do it for herself. Maybe one day she could have a purpose again.

Time would tell, as time always did.

The story of the company will conclude
with the final volume of THE CHAOS CHRONICLES,
The Masters of Shipworld.

Note from the Author

Thank you for reading *Crucible of Time* (and, I hope, the first half, *The Reefs of Time*). If you enjoyed the story, may I ask that you take a moment to *post a review* in your favorite store or social networking site, such as Goodreads. *And please tell your friends!* Word of mouth is the greatest appreciation you can give to an author whose work you enjoy. Every review counts, and every personal recommendation. Thanks in advance!

Acknowledgments

The Reefs of Time and *Crucible of Time* were written as a single novel. It was a long time in coming. Over the course of the writing, it grew to twice the length originally envisioned, leaving me to break it into two volumes, with the awkward questions of how to divide, title, and publish the story. You have seen the result. It outlived several generations of office computers. It survived writer's block and life gone haywire. It made it through the mire of doubt and the fire of certainty, blown deadlines and tumultuous changes in the world of book publishing. It's been through the fermenter, the extractor, refractor, distracter, distiller, and finally the kiln; and after that, it was aged in camphor-wood in the cellar. At times, I wondered if it had fallen into a black hole.

Originally it was to have been published by Tor Books, and much of the editing occurred in that framework. That didn't work out, however, and instead, I have gone one better and brought it to light under my own imprint, with the remarkable assistance of my fellow authors and colleagues at Book View Café. I cannot thank my friends there enough for their assistance, ranging from general encouragement and wisdom to solid, hands-on help. Particular thanks go out to Maya Kaathryn Bohnhoff, whose design skills have graced many of my current covers. Also, to Chaz Brenchley for his relentlessly exacting proofreading.

Speaking of covers, many thanks to Chris Howard for the beautiful artwork that served as your introduction to both *Reefs* and *Crucible*.

There are others who hung in there with me—never losing faith, or hiding it well if they did. Tom Doherty at Tor was patient and encouraging, as was my agent Richard Curtis—and my editor for much of the project, James Frenkel, whose suggestions were extremely helpful and, as always, much appreciated. Though in the end, publication took another course, I remain grateful for their support.

At home, my eagle-eyed writing group has been an ever-present source of encouragement and editorial feedback: Mary Aldridge, Richard Bowker, Craig Shaw Gardner, and the late Victoria Bolles. I could *not* have done this without you guys. (And Victoria, I wish you had lived to see the conclusion.) As well, my friends at Reservoir Church have been a continual source of inspiration, especially the incredible small groups, writing-centered and otherwise.

For total support, there is no comparison with my family. My brother, Charles S. Carver, who was so incredibly supportive throughout the process, was taken from us (and from his wonderful wife Youngmee) before he could finish reading the finished book. My sister, Nancy Carver Adams, also was taken from us (and from her husband, the other Chuck) before the book was finished. Through it all, there stood, like bedrock, my wife Allysen and my daughters Alexandra and Jayce. I love you all.

Finally, to those whose patience was tested most of all, I thank you my readers, who waited so long for this novel to arrive. I sincerely hope you found it more than worth the wait!

About the Author

JEFFREY A. CARVER was a Nebula Award finalist for his novel *Eternity's End*. He also authored *Battlestar Galactica*, a novelization of the critically acclaimed television miniseries. His novels combine thought-provoking characters with engaging storytelling, and range from the adventures of the Star Rigger universe (*Star Rigger's Way, Dragons in the Stars,* and others) to the ongoing, character-driven hard SF of *The Chaos Chronicles*—which begins with *Neptune Crossing* and continues with *Strange Attractors, The Infinite Sea, Sunborn,* and now *The Reefs of Time* and its conclusion, *Crucible of Time.*

A native of Huron, Ohio, Carver lives with his family in the Boston area. He has taught writing in a variety of settings, from educational television to conferences for young writers to MIT, as well as his own workshops. He has created a free web site for aspiring authors of all ages at *www.writesf.com.* Learn more about the author and his work, follow his blog, sign up for his occasional newsletter, and see all of his books at:

www.starrigger.net

About Starstream Publications
and Book View Café

Starstream Publications is the publishing imprint of Jeffrey A. Carver.

Book View Café Publishing Cooperative (BVC) is an author-owned cooperative of about fifty professional writers, publishing in a variety of genres, including fantasy, romance, mystery, and science fiction.

BVC authors include New York Times and USA Today bestsellers. Our authors have won and been nominated for numerous awards, including: the Agatha, Campbell, Hugo, Lambda Literary, Locus, Nebula, PEN/Malamud Award, Philip K. Dick, RITA, World Fantasy, and Writers of the Future awards, and the Academy Nicholl Fellowship.

Since its debut in 2008, BVC has gained a reputation for producing high-quality ebooks, and now brings that same quality to its print editions. Find out more and sign up for our newsletter at:

bookviewcafe.com